*Yours
Unfaithfully*

Yours Unfaithfully

Geraldine C Deer

Matador
5 Weir Road
Kibworth Beauchamp
Leicester LE8 0LQ, UK
Tel: (+44) 116 279 2299
Fax: (+44) 116 279 2277
Email: books@troubador.co.uk
Web: www.troubador.co.uk/matador

ISBN 978 1848 764 279

British Library Cataloguing in Publication Data.
A catalogue record for this book is available from the British Library.

Typeset in 11pt Sabon MT by Troubador Publishing Ltd, Leicester, UK
Printed in the UK by T J International Ltd, Padstow, Cornwall

Matador is an imprint of Troubador Publishing Ltd

CHAPTER ONE

The journey home was like a hundred nights before, heavy traffic out of the city before green fields started to replace the grey and gloomy buildings. Melanie fumed at the farm tractor heading the homeward procession. "Why," she demanded of the empty seat next to her, "is not one inch of my journey stress free? Why is my whole day a boiling cauldron of turmoil? How did I create this whirlpool of chaos that is my life?"

At thirty nine she wanted to enjoy the rewards of her twenty years of hard work, first as a trainee bank clerk, then a stay-at-home mother of three children and for the last ten years as a returnee to the regional office. "Why do I still have to cook and clean after nine hours of commuting and computing? Tim never complains about my success in the bank but does he feel frustrated and cheated at me being the prime earner?"

Ben, Tim's closest friend and their next door neighbour, never disguised *his* contempt for his wife's rapid rise to success at Osborne Melrose Law. Nina had always been the high flyer while he'd struggled to keep any job for more than a month. When Melanie and Tim had moved into their new house on the 'Willow Brook' development in Elmthorpe three years ago they struck up a close bond with their neighbours almost at once. With three children in each family it was inevitable that they'd spend time together through the long summer holiday and by the end of August Melanie and Nina had become best friends, while Tim spent most nights in the pub with Ben. For ten years Melanie had juggled her time between the needs of her three children, the ever increasing demands of the bank to shoulder more responsibility and the almost mundane desire by Tim for her to be his loving soul mate. She'd always believed that she'd satisfied them all. Tim rarely complained when she was at her laptop until midnight or when she spent entire weekends accompanying the kids on canoeing trips, music practice, or one of the streams of other activities that blacked out the kitchen calendar for months in advance. The trouble was, all this left no time for Melanie to be Melanie. She was desperate for one weekend to be different, she longed to say, "I'm staying in bed till noon then laying on my sun bed until four. Take me to a candlelit restaurant for dinner at eight then bring me home drunk on life, some time after midnight." Pondering the unfairness of her lot, she felt a tinge of anger that Tim showed no concern at simply being an also-ran in their domestic life. While she was chauffeuring three kids to six destinations on Saturday, Tim was either playing pool in the pub or fixing a car for one of his mates. She didn't know where he was most Saturdays mainly because she never found time to ask him. She just assumed his head was under a car bonnet and that he'd come home covered in grease in time to eat with them.

'Bloody Hell!' Her scream of panic shattered her thoughts as she stabbed at the Mondeo's brake pedal. The tyres squealed to a stop with inches to spare from shunting the four wheel drive in front. Her head was thumping and her hands were shaking in the knowledge that she'd just avoided a massive impact. Like every other night it was impossible to see why the traffic had stopped. Could it be to test her patience? If so she'd failed the test, her patience was stretched to breaking point. What is wrong with me for God's Sake? I'm losing the ability to stay in control, to be Supermum, Super manager, Super wife. Is it my age I wonder? Almost forty? Is that it? The change? Her hand swept across her face in a panic check for facial hair, acquired since this morning's ritual preparation for another day at the office. What Melanie hadn't seen in the dressing table mirror was the beautiful woman she really was. Light brown hair flowing softly to her shoulders, blue eyes still sparkling behind a youthful smile and perfect skin despite thirty nine years and three children. Five foot five inches and fabulously slim, not through any dedicated exercise routine but by never being still for more than five minutes, Melanie was undeniably lovely. Nina always reckoned that Mel had a lifestyle body. Melanie had read about the process of change, how to watch for it and how to deal with it in last month's *Working Wife* magazine. "Damn, I put it in the recycling bin – no I didn't – or did I?" She jumped as a horn bellowed from behind and looking up saw the four wheel drive gaining speed in the distance ahead. Ramming the gear stick forward she let out the clutch causing the car to leap two metres towards home before stalling. 'Bugger'! Frantically turning the key, she winced at the snarling noise as the engine tried to start while in gear. There was no doubt in her mind now, she'd lost it, life was closing in and those around her must be aware of her state. The rest of the journey was a fog of confusion. She slammed the car door and walked slowly up the front garden path, taking a deep breath to clear the choking sensation from her throat. She pushed open the kitchen door and fought back tears as the familiar sound of the television news confirmed to her that tonight would be just like every other night. Tim would be spread across the settee waiting to be fed. The shrieking noise upstairs would be James practicing his recorder, unless by chance it was her eldest protégé Henry squeezing the last breath from his sister Amy over their continuing dispute on territorial rights. Henry had made it clear, crystal clear, that an eleven year old girl was not welcome in a sixteen year old boy's room and he'd used force on more than one occasion to reinforce this view. Keeping the house immaculate while working full time required help from the family, but support was seldom offered. Discarded clothes, instruments and sports kit were everywhere, yet under this facade of jumble the place was clean. Melanie was proud of her home even if Tim and the kids were less than interested. She stood motionless in her kitchen desperately trying to decide what to do next. Should she creep up to the bathroom and wash her face in a futile attempt to compose herself or should she dig through the freezer to find them something to eat? With tears streaming down her cheeks she grabbed an onion and started peeling it in an effort to conceal her distress. Needing time to recover before facing questions from Tim, she hacked at the onion with no thought of what they might eat with it. A full minute passed before she realised she was still wearing her long black coat. Her sadness mounted as the truth dawned. Tim wasn't about to notice her tears or question their cause. He was too busy watching television to see that she was in desperate need of a little TLC. Wiping her hands she pushed open the lounge door hoping for words of comfort, recognition that she was home, that she was in the bosom of her family. She heard the reporter talking feverishly about a takeover bid for Manchester United Football Club and saw Tim's six foot frame laid out before the screen that was commanding his attention. Melanie had watched him reach middle age with pleasure, her arms still went round his waist without stretching and his hair was more black than grey. What did trouble her was the steady decline in his attention. In short, he took her for granted. Perhaps football was now more important to him than she was? She turned back to the kitchen and wept at the sink, openly now, no pretence of onion or hay fever. Tears of anguish, frustration, pain at being all alone in a house full of people, her people. The children she loved with every ounce of her body, the husband to whom she'd devoted nineteen years. They'd met at night school when she was studying A-level maths and he was a trainee vehicle mechanic. Where had the love gone? They were still lovers and still devoted to each other, so why did she feel so alone? Could one bad day really bring you down to this? She wasn't sure how long she'd been standing there when Tim's arm slid around her waist. Her tummy tensed with happiness until his words flattened her like she'd been hit with a brick.

"Mel, I'm starving. I'm going round to Andy's as soon as I've eaten, promised to help him with his Toyota. He bought it as a bargain but the water pump's leaking and he tops it up twice to get to work. I might be late, all depends if it turns out to be difficult or not. Wow onions! If it's steak and onions make mine a large one. Trust you to always know what I want."

"It's not steak, it's sausages and if you want chips you're out of luck. I've just looked and there're none in the freezer. Do you want to go down to the petrol station for some? If you're in a hurry I could put the sausages between bread with some fried onion."

"Mel, I don't like to moan but after a hard day at work I think a sausage sandwich is a feeble offering, don't you?"

"Yes Tim and I think a feeble offering is perfect for a feeble man, so what's your problem?"

"What the hell do you mean by that? ... Where did that come from? I'm working flat out at the yard with barely a break for lunch. I've worked the last two Saturdays but you didn't even notice because you were too busy swanning around with the kids spending money on designer trainers. You sit in your office five days a week drinking coffee and watching the profits from your precious bank growing bigger and bigger but you don't have a clue what real work is."

"Yes, you're absolutely right Tim, that's all I do. I just sit there counting the profits. But do you know what Tim? I earn twice as much as you for doing it so someone must think I'm worthwhile. I would explain what I really do but I don't suppose you'd care!"

"And I'm sure you'd love to hear about my day, changing a gearbox on a Volvo truck to go out on tonight's ferry. I've strained my back and crushed my fingers and you call me feeble. I've spent all day under a lorry. I've earned *my* money. All you care about these days is your bloody bank. Well stuff the bank and stuff you! Stick your sandwich Mel, I'll get something down at the Globe after I've done Andy's car, and don't wait up for me – after all what would you want to talk to me about?"

The door slammed leaving Melanie to wonder at what had happened. Was it her fault? It wasn't like Tim to sound off at her, in all their years together they'd only ever had three or four rows of any importance and Melanie knew she was to blame for most of those. This was different. She wasn't in control the way she'd always been, this time she'd lost it and upset the most reasonable man in the world. I could go after him, she reasoned, try to make it better? From the look he'd given her as he swept out she knew it would be better to wait for him to calm down.

The kids showed no surprise at having sausage sandwiches for their meal and the idea of spending less time than usual at the table definitely met with their approval.

As Melanie loaded the dishwasher she thought about the meal she'd offered Tim. He was right. She thought how her father would have reacted to her mother in the same situation. Her mother never failed to serve a proper evening meal, which usually meant a full roast dinner and a pudding to follow. I'm not half as good a wife as my mother. I'm a failure as a wife and as a mother. At the sound of the kitchen door she turned, hoping to see Tim but it was Nina, red faced and looking like she'd jumped the fence instead of taking the path from next door.

Every inch a professional, Nina was well respected as a quick thinking talented legal mind, someone not to mess with in matters of law. Fastidious but fair was her reputation. Her home, like her work, was pristine, thanks to Henrietta, the cleaning lady who toiled five days a week to take care of the washing, ironing, cleaning and even the preparation of the food for their evening meal. Henrietta had started the day they moved in and ran the house like it was her own. She gave orders to the children and they did as they were bid rather than incur their mother's reproach as well. Ben however, was lazy by nature and reckoned the only good thing about work was that it took him out of the house during the hours that Henrietta was there. Nina wasn't as trim as Melanie, touching on seventy five kilograms but she looked well with no sign of a sagging waistline or a double chin. Her dark hair was regularly and expensively groomed at a salon near her office, as were her nails and her make up. Nina explained that being married to Ben entitled her to be regularly and expensively pampered as this was something at which he was totally inept. He never noticed when her hair was freshly styled or her make up changed. Her expensive designer clothes turned heads whenever she made an entrance, but went completely unnoticed by her husband. Nina had poise and her polished accent was attractive to listen to, but Ben never heard. She knew exactly how to create a favourable impression on clients or on social gatherings but she couldn't enthuse Ben unless she talked about food, his food. Her statuette body was a tool, a persuasive visual asset as powerful as her arguments, which she could always use to good effect. Her finest asset however, was her wit, sharp as a sword; she could be a feisty lady with a fiery tongue. Melanie saw at once the distress in Nina's expression.

"What is it Nina? You look terrible, is something wrong?"

"I'll bloody say something's wrong, Nina exploded. Him, that's what's wrong."

"I take it we're talking about Ben?" Melanie said, trying

to calm her friend with diplomacy and sympathy at the same time.

"Can you think of anyone else who could get me in this state? Do you know what he's done now?"

Melanie racked her brain to think what Ben had done yesterday to infuriate Nina. This might give a clue to what he'd done now. Ben was hard work and she only had to cope with him second hand. Ben had lost more jobs in the last three years than anyone could remember. He'd worked in a factory, a supermarket, at the council, briefly, and for several agencies. They in turn had sent him to a factory, a supermarket and the council. At six foot two Ben was taller than Tim and larger around. Everything about Ben was large except his ability to think straight. His laugh was loud, pleasant in short bursts, like his personality, but it never helped in his search for success. At every fork in life's road Ben would head down the one marked 'Wrong Way'. He had a knack of choosing the wrong colour, the wrong size or the wrong style. He was invariably in the wrong queue on the wrong day at the wrong time. It was easy to like him, but hard to stay shackled to him for nearly twenty years, as Nina repeatedly reminded him.

"Don't tell me he's lost another job Neen?"

"He's only lost the agency job itself, I mean, did you ever know anyone who couldn't keep an agency job? Last week they found him a job with a dry cleaner in town, driving the van, delivering laundry to hotels and restaurants. How could he mess that up? He says they gave him the wrong order but the truth is he managed to give away a hundred towels. They probably think he stole them but he's given them to the wrong hotel. I can't take much more of him Mel, really I can't. I spend all day working with intelligent people and then I come home to a no brain!"

Melanie struggled for words to improve Nina's mood. It wouldn't help to agree that Ben was a total waste of space. She tried conciliation.

"Perhaps the laundry did get it wrong Neen, after all mistakes do happen, and anyway, as he was new you'd have thought they'd give him another chance, wouldn't you?"

"They did Mel, this was the second lot he lost in one week. The only mistake is Ben, he's one big mistake and mine is being married to him."

"Well if it's any consolation, Nina, I'm as fed up as you. I've had a shit day at work; a terrible drive home and now I've had a row with Tim."

"Sorry Mel, the last thing you needed was me sounding off about Big Ben. Shall I shoot back to mine for a bottle of red? We could empty it before we do anything else."

"I can't wait that long, take one off the dresser and let's get started.' Melanie managed a smile and they laughed at the prospect of an evening spent downing wine and digesting each other's news. At first they ranted on about the men they'd walked down the isle with, but once they'd exhausted that subject Nina enthused about her work, extolling the virtues of her colleagues, people who were an escape from Ben. 'We've got a new partner. He left Hoggart, Smith-Adams, a top drawer outfit to join us, which shows how well we're thought of in Chambers. He's called Rattani Naziree, specialises in contract law. He's a real class act, bounding with confidence and with the most wonderful natural tan, looks Mediterranean or maybe Asian, an absolute Adonis. I watched him today and thought I'd hate to be up against him in Court, I reckon he must work out to get a body like that, looks like a cross between Will Smith and Sylvester Stalone. Honestly if I wasn't a married woman and ten years his senior he'd have serious trouble with me. Mel, he's gorgeous, life changing, naturally tanned and seriously fanciable, He'll be hunted down by all the young things in our office poor sod. I heard today we've won a new client, Stellar Haufman plc. Their business is worth a few million pounds a year. Sam, she's our office manager, told me the papers have been signed for us to take over the building next door giving us twice the space we've got now. I'm so glad I had the sense to accept their offer three years ago when we moved in here ... that was the best career decision I ever made. Sorry Mel, you're completely pissed off and all I can do is talk about my work. What's up at the bank? I thought everything was great last time we talked?"

"It was – it's me that's wrong, I'm sliding down a slippery slope. I can't stop myself even though I know I'm doing it. Neen, I think I'm on the change! You're looking at a woman whose past her best. From here on it's all wrinkles, HRT and misery. I feel like I've got a sign on my back saying, Melonie Fisher – Menopausal – past her sell by date."

"Oh Mel, don't be daft, you probably aren't any such thing. And even if you are, which I doubt, it doesn't mean much these days. It's not going to change your life; I read the other day that women now get more out of life after than before. I'll search out the magazine and bring it home for you. If you ask me, Mel, you've just had a shitty day and by tomorrow you'll have forgotten all about it, but if not you can always talk to me about it, you know that."

"Thanks Neen, perhaps I needed that kick up the

backside from Tim. I've managed to upset him big time, and you know how calm he is. I didn't have any food in for his evening meal. Would you believe I offered him a sausage sandwich? Christ he went mad, can you blame him? You see what I mean – that proves it doesn't it? When the body begins to change the brain starts to shrink, I'm sure I read that somewhere. I've always fed him and the kids properly, you know that, but tonight I didn't even realise until it was too late that I had nothing to cook for them. Now Tim's stormed out and the kids are upstairs half fed and I'm sitting here admitting I can't cope anymore. You can't tell me that's normal, Neen, be honest with me. I've failed them haven't I? That's what I am, a failure. Soon the bank will notice and then it'll be the five o'clock briefing, 'Please clear your desk Mrs. Fisher, the bank has decided to terminate your employment. Sign here and someone will see you out. That's how it's done in the bank you know! Poor old Jenny was there for twenty two years, hardly had a day off, but we all knew she was struggling. She made so many mistakes it was embarrassing, until eventually Management sussed her out as they were bound to. She was called into the manager's office one night just before we left. When we went home she was still in there but we never saw her in the office again. She rang me the next day, in floods of tears. We met up that lunch time – she was in shock. "He just gave me this envelope, asked me to sign then took me up to my floor and gave me two minutes to pack," she said. "He stood over me while I gathered up my bits and pieces, tissues in one hand, crying so I couldn't even see what I was doing, then he escorted me down to the back entrance and let me out. That was it after twenty two years. Melanie you can't believe what they've done to me. I've cried non stop since last night, at fifty two I'm finished. No one will ever employ me now. I've been scrapped, thrown onto the heap. What am I going to do?"

"I remember that lunch time like it was yesterday. I cried with her, promised we'd meet once a week, that I'd help her find another job, told her she wasn't finished, she was just having a bad patch, it would soon pass. Do you know I think she actually believed me? When we said goodbye she smiled and said she felt a thousand times better. She said she was lucky to have a friend like me. I've only seen her once since then; we had a drink after work one night when a girl from her old office left to have a baby. Jenny looked ten years older, that was in just three months... I hugged her and said sorry I hadn't phoned her, you know how it is, I said, pressure of work, family etc. She stared at me through haunted eyes and whispered... I know Mel, I can't expect people to help me if I can't help myself. She looked like she'd given up. God I let her down and this is my just deserves, I've been punished quite rightly. Oh Jenny, I'm so sorry – I meant to keep my promise, but I'm a lousy friend, a failure at work, and a crap wife. Oh God Neen what am I going to do?"

Four hours later Nina stumbled back to her house and Melanie put three empty wine bottles in the recycling bin. When Tim returned at midnight she was in bed, deliberately still reading so as to be awake when he came in, although she'd expected him long before this.

"Did you fix Andy's car?"

"Yea, it only took an hour; I've been down the Globe with a few of the lads. We played pool... I was having a good time and I didn't realise how late it was."

"Night Tim, see you in the morning." She knew this was his way of protesting or sulking as she saw it. If he was ready to end the row he'd have come home earlier. This meant the argument was far from over.

Work was no easier the next day, and the drive home was fraught as always, but at least tonight she didn't cause a hold up. She congratulated herself on a perfect trip, which only added to her worries because she'd never doubted her driving ability until now, it was one those things you took for granted. Her low self esteem had made the journey feel like an achievement. Today had been hard. With two hours to go she was absently staring at her screen while her mind was busy exploring the evening ahead. She had his favourite, fillet steak. Thanks to a trip to Waitrose in her lunch break, Tim would have no cause to chastise her tonight, especially as she had exciting plans for this evening. After clearing the dishes she'd spend an hour upstairs with the kids so Tim could watch TV and then she'd come downstairs to him wearing something sexy. She'd curl up next to him on the settee accidentally exposing flesh well above her knees, this would arouse him and he'd soon come round. That's if he was still sulking.

Melanie carried her five feet five inches beautifully. She never worried about her looks, she only wanted to please Tim and he loved her unquestioningly, well aware that he was a lucky man. Her hair was as long as when she'd met him all those years ago and her trim figure was still cloaked with velvet smooth skin. Her legs were 'fat free' and fabulous and she knew it. Glancing to where her skirt lay just above her knee she ran her hand down the smooth skin to her ankle before pushing both palms tightly into the back of her thighs. "Not a bit of cellulite there," she boasted, totally unaware that she had announced it out loud to everyone in the office.

Joe, the Business Manager, was kind and caring and Melanie had always liked him. He looked towards her and laughed, "Am I supposed to take your word for that Mel or are you about to prove it?"

As the realisation of her utterance hit her she reddened rapidly and struggled for some sensible explanation. Her mouth went dry and knowing that nothing she could say would seem remotely reasonable she just stared at him. After a few seconds she muttered, "Sorry Joe, I was miles away."

"Are you OK Mel?"

"Why wouldn't I be?" She flared at him despite his obvious concern. Instantly guilt crept into her voice. "I'm fine Joe, what makes you think I'm not?"

"I noticed yesterday you were making hard work of everything. That's not like you. Maybe you need a holiday. Cheer up Mel, you look like you're about to kill me with your bare hands! Either you're upset or I'm losing the plot and that isn't likely because at my annual appraisal I was told I'm doing brilliantly."

"Well they won't be telling *me* that, that's for sure! More likely... Melanie you have demonstrated a complete lack of ability to do your job and we suggest you fall silently onto your sword."

"So I was right, you're having a mini-crisis. Everyone has them Mel. It's as normal as a headache or having the Monday morning feeling."

"No Joe, this isn't a mini-crisis, this is a bloody major crisis and it isn't just in the office. It stretches for twelve miles along the drive home and then into my kitchen where I am a crap cook and even to the bedroom where apparently I'm a crap wife!"

"You and Tim struggling a bit? It happens Mel but it soon turns around. Cindy and I had a massive row at the weekend. I can't even remember why, but last night she was fine, just like it had never happened. When you get home tonight Tim'll be there waiting for you, cooking a meal and raring to whisk you off to bed before you can say 'Guess what's for pudding'?"

This conversation kept coming back to her as she busied herself preparing the steak and chips that was set to win Tim over. Unusually he hadn't been in first tonight, but this sometimes happened if he had a late repair. Melanie fed the kids with burgers and chips and cleared away after them so that it would be just the two of them. She found a left over candle from Christmas and stuffed it into a glass holder before placing it in the centre of the table. When the kitchen door opened she expected it to be Tim, but to her surprise it was Nina.

"Hi Mel, I know your cooking tea but I just popped round to say Ben's out tonight and I thought we could do last night all over again, except round at my place. I want to hear all about your day and I promise I won't even mention mine, OK?"

"Oh, sorry Neen I can't. I've planned a special treat for Tim, you know ... after last night."

"Melanie Fisher," Nina said in a voice resembling a Victorian school mistress, "Do you mean what I think you mean?" She giggled ... "Mel, this treat, is it that steak or is it you that's going to be laid out on a plate for this incredibly lucky man?"

"Well, yes sort of, I'm going to give Tim bloody Fisher a night to remember. When he sees me slink down those stairs in shimmering silk he'll turn off his precious TV soap and turn on to me. I'm going to be a wicked woman tonight Nina, and the poor bugger has absolutely no idea that in two hours from now he is going to be my victim!"

"Where is he anyway?"

"Oh he's a bit late, a last minute job I expect, but don't worry, I'll soon make up for lost time!"

"Ah well never mind, I'll just empty that bottle on my own. Oh Mel, just one favour... please keep the screaming down. Have a great night and tomorrow we are definitely getting together and *you* are going to tell me every sordid detail of tonight's shenanigans, OK?"

"OK I'll see you tomorrow."

Nina closed the door and waved through the window, her huge smile underlining her approval of Mel's plan. When Melanie had everything ready she checked the clock on the cooker for the umpteenth time before deciding to ring Tim to see how much longer he was going to be. If he doesn't get here soon this steak will be *'bien cuit'* she mumbled. Tim answered his mobile but she could barely hear him for the noise going on behind him.

"How long are you going to be Tim? The tea is ready to serve, can you hurry up please! Tim, what is all that shouting I can hear, are you all right?"

"I'm fine, sorry I meant to phone you, I won't be in for a sandwich tonight. I'm having a few games of pool with the lads and then we're going into town to get a proper meal, you know steak or maybe a curry."

"You Bastard!" she yelled and slammed the phone down

so hard she feared she'd smashed it. Her eyes filled with tears as she carried the grill pan to the swing bin and tipped the two steaks into it. She went into the lounge and threw herself onto the settee letting the tears flow into the tissue she was clutching. For what seemed an age she buried her face into the cushion and wept as she hadn't done in years. From upstairs the sounds of laughter told her what she already knew. The kids were having a great time watching their TV. They didn't need her to go up and spend an hour with them. Sure they would politely let her join in their games or watch the latest DVD, but they wouldn't notice if she didn't go up. Eventually she dragged herself up and pulled on her fleece. As she closed the door she looked back into the kitchen, sadness swept over her and the tears started again. As soon as Nina answered the door she saw that Mel was in a state.

"Oh my God Mel, what's happened? Is it Tim? He hasn't had an accident has he?"

"No but he bloody will!" she cried.

Nina put her arms around her friend and guided her into her lounge. She put a glass of white wine in Mel's hand and gently waited for her to recover enough to get her story out.

"The fool, the idiot, the stupid, stupid twit!" Nina tried desperately to find words to describe Tim's treatment of this lovely lady, who only an hour ago had been willing to give everything to making Tim the happiest man on Earth.

"Why is it men have such small brains to start with, and then only use a quarter of what they've got?" she said. "That man is so lucky to have you and he doesn't see it. Right now he's with a bunch of pub losers playing pool and downing pints in order to convince himself that he is the *Man* in *His* house. I can almost hear him, 'This'll show her how important I am! This'll teach her to have a proper meal waiting for me when I get back from work!'" Nina ranted on for a few more minutes before Mel stopped her.

"It doesn't matter Neen."

"What do you mean, it doesn't matter? Of course it bloody matters. Mr Tim bloody important Fisher is down there buying his pals drinks while they all share the same brain cell to tell each other how bloody marvellous they are and how shit we are at looking after them. Well bugger him Mel, bugger him! Tomorrow night we'll go out for a nice meal together and you can leave him a note! Your sandwich is in the bread bin – make it yourself ...you stupid sod ! Christ I'm so angry at the way he's treated you tonight. I've half a mind to go down that pub and embarrass him in front of his so called mates and tell him exactly what a shit he is."

"Neen, stop a minute, have you thought that he might just be right? I am useless. I told you last night it's not just at home. People in work are beginning to notice that I can't cope. Today Joe, our Business Manager told me I need to take a holiday. It was obvious he felt sorry for me; he could see I was in a mess. I'm finished Neen. The kids don't need me any more and nor does Tim. I've never thought about life after the menopause but I am now, and there is no life after it. I'm frightened. What am I going to do Neen?"

"I don't know Mel, if I'm honest I don't know... but I don't believe you are on the change and I am as certain as I know my own name you're not finished. In fact Mel, you've never looked better, honestly, you look terrific. You know that and the kids adore you, of course they need you. OK they don't show it, but kids don't. You try not being there and you'll soon see if they need you. As for work, you're just going through a rough patch, but you'll get through. Maybe Joe is right, maybe you do need a holiday. In fact Mel, now I think about it, you haven't all gone off together in the three years you've been here, have you? No wonder you're screwed up, you've got to get something booked. Don't ask Tim, just book it and tell him afterwards, that way he won't try to put it off. And if he says he's not coming... just suppose he did... which he won't, then sod him, I'll come with you and we'll take all the kids and we'll have the best holiday we've had in years.'

Tim walked into the bar of the Globe with a heavy heart. He knew this wasn't the way to end the row but he was sure this time it was up to her. He'd kept his part of the bargain ever since they'd got married. He'd worked hard, very hard, and they'd never wanted for anything, but of course their grand lifestyle in the new house would never have been possible if Melanie hadn't gone back to work. Within months of her going back to the bank she was promoted, and she kept on getting promoted. She loved the bank, he'd never doubted that, but it was only recently that he'd felt low in her list of priorities. He couldn't recall when he'd first thought it. Was it something one of his mates had said that started him thinking it? He recalled an innuendo about Melanie being specially selected by Head Office after a recent promotion. The boys had laughed and then the subject had quickly changed, but perhaps a seed of doubt was sown in his mind.

A voice at the other end of the bar greeted him, 'Hi Tim, get the drinks in then'! Dave was always loud, and easily made himself heard over the noisy drinkers, anxious to be noticed in the way some men do when surrounded by their mates, and after being alone in his tractor all day, evenings in the pub were the highlight of his day. Ben was on a stool at the bar and joined in the melee.

"What's this Tim? It's only just gone six, has she given you permission or did you sneak out while she wasn't looking?"

Tim recoiled at this remark; it was awkwardly near the mark. He forced a smile, "She wouldn't mind if I spent five nights a week in here." As soon as he'd said it he realised it was a confession of the truth, or what he believed to be the truth. He'd just blurted to the entire pub something private that he wasn't yet ready to accept. Fortunately, as always, the subject quickly turned to something else and he escaped the embarrassment of a ribbing on the matter of his marriage. Tim stuck fifty pence on the pool table to indicate that he would play the winner of the game in progress. He was one of the best players in the pool league, which meant that he often remained on the table for hours. Tonight was no exception and as the bell sounded for last orders he was still there.

"How's the job going Ben?"

"It didn't work out Tim. I made a simple mistake over a few towels and the manager went bloody crazy. Before I could say two words he was on to the agency and that was it. I was out on my ass."

"You've had a few unlucky breaks just lately Ben. What's the problem? Is it that you don't like the agency work or what?"

"Tim, I wish I knew, honestly. Nina scolds me rotten, says I'm lazy. She throws all kinds of insults my way but she doesn't understand. She's got her high and mighty position but she's got no idea what it's like doing man's work."

"Ben, if you think Nina's hard work you should see the shit I have to put up with from Mel. Last night after a flat out day I got home to find my meal was a bloody sausage sandwich!"

"That's the trouble with us Tim, we both married intelligent women."

"I don't mind that Ben, I've always encouraged her, but she thinks my work is rubbish, not worth talking about, whereas hers is fascinating, more worthwhile, that's what pisses me off. She'll often tell me about this one or that one in the bank and how he did this or did that, as if I bloody care. I don't even know these people, how am I supposed to laugh at some guy called Roderick or whatever his bloody name is wearing a red bow tie with a yellow shirt? If I tried to tell her about the problems I had changing a gearbox and how I had to take it back out three times because the spigot shaft wouldn't go in, do you think she'd care... she wouldn't even bloody listen and before I'd got to the second try she'd cut across me with the latest exploits of Randy bloody Roderick and the rest of her circus."

"Tim, what you've got to remember is, they're not really more intelligent than us, this is just what we've let them think over the years to keep 'em happy. Ever since that women's lib crap we've had to pretend that they're just as bright as we are. So, the bank just plays the same game, see? The bank doesn't want to get sued for having more men than women 'cos that would be discrimination, so, what does it do? It employs a load of women to push bits of paper around and it gives them fancy titles, like 'This Manager' or

'That Manager' and they're happy, see? Meanwhile, the blokes in the bank are really running the show, they're the only ones who see the real figures and know how much money the bank's got in the locker. 'Course occasionally it goes a bit pear shaped like when that bloke at Bearing's Bank spent the bloody lot without telling the others and the bank went down the chute, but it just shows the women who worked there didn't have a clue what was really happening or they'd have stopped him, wouldn't they? I bet Melanie doesn't really know how much money the bank makes, but she's happy 'cos she thinks she's running the bloody show. If she was really bright she'd realise that it's blokes like Roddy who are really running it. Nina's the same; her firm has to have a few women solicitors to keep the balance fair. I expect they give her a divorce case or two and a bit of child custody stuff and she thinks she's Cherie bloody Blair. I'm clever enough to let her go on thinking that, and I let her think that I really believe she's a big cog in her firm. That way, I get a decent meal when I get home and she's as happy as a pig in shit. You gotta start playing the game like I do Tim, feed her on bullshit and she'll feed you on something better than sausages. She probably knows from your face, from the way you look at her when she's telling you all this stuff about 'good old Roddy' that you think he's a dick and she's daft for thinking he's clever in the first place. Trust me Tim, I understand women. Bloody have to ... to stay married to Neen for all these years!'

'Do you know Ben, you make it all sound so simple, but deep down I think you're right... trouble is I can't pretend the way you do. I can't sit there and laugh at Roddy's antics just so I get fed properly. If I did that I'd feel like I was a performing seal, clapping my hands and barking just to get my next mouthful of fish. No, bugger the bank and sod Roddy. I'd sooner come down here from work and eat Jim's cooking. At least that way she'll see that I'm not going to be treated like her pet puppy. More likely this dog will bite before long if she doesn't change her ways.'

'Tim, you're doing this all wrong mate, trust me. Your way can only end in trouble!'

'We'll see Ben, we'll see!'

CHAPTER TWO

As the days came ever closer to July the weather was scorching hot. But while everyone was talking about the heat wave outside, the frost inside was as thick as ever. Tim was holding out for some sign of surrender from Melanie, who was unwilling to forgive him for the way he'd treated her on the night she'd planned her surprise for him.

If he hadn't been so stupid, she reasoned, their row would be forgotten by now, but he still had no idea of the treat she'd had in store for him that evening. With neither of them prepared to make the first move to end hostilities the gulf between them widened with each passing day. Tim was still confiding in Ben, who continued to proffer advice from what he believed was his vast expanse of knowledge on the subject of relationships. Tim, experiencing the longest dispute of his married life, was unable to gauge the goodness of this advice. He listened intently to Ben's theories on marriage, sex and life in general, despite Ben's glaringly obvious failure to excel at any of them. The two took some comfort from each other's misery, convinced that eventually the women would realise how foolish they'd been. Ben kept reminding Tim that soon Melanie would be begging for forgiveness, while Tim tried to convince Ben that his career would shortly take a giant stride forward, leaving Nina to apologise for the harsh things she'd said. While Tim was talking over his problems in the Globe his wife was on the same topic at home with Nina as they emptied another bottle of Chardonnay. Melanie was indignant that someone of Ben's ilk could have the audacity to interfere in her marriage.

"Did you know that Ben has been giving Tim marriage guidance advice while they've been playing pool?"

"Oh that's brilliant! Ben couldn't give good advice on how to cross the road!"

"Well Tim seems to believe Ben has a deep understanding of women. In one of our rare moments of conversation he let on that Ben understands our marriage problems better than me! When I asked him how Ben knew about our problems he said, 'Do you think women are the only ones who can talk about these things. I bet you and Nina have talked about nothing else for the last two weeks' I couldn't really deny that could I, so I said, Well you might do better to talk to Nina than that big oaf who can't hold a job down for more than two minutes.' I'm sorry Neen, I know it wasn't my place to say that but it came out in my anger at the way Tim's treated me since the other night, you know, when I was ready to end this row."

"Don't worry Mel; you couldn't say anything about Ben that I haven't already said. Trouble is he's so thick he doesn't seem to understand that I mean all the things I say, he doesn't want to face the fact that he's a waste of space."

"How did you come to marry him Neen? You must have loved him once?"

"Yes I suppose so.... we were all hanging around together just after I'd finished my degree, he was a bit of a lad and we had a lot of fun together. He was a big lad with a big personality, which I suppose he still is. His laddish ways impressed me then and because he was always at the centre of things I felt important being with him. He always stood out from the crowd, but now it's for all the wrong reasons. At that age you don't think about spending twenty years with someone, and anyway we've both changed a lot. I've grown up and Ben, well, Ben hasn't. The thing is now what do I do? We've got three kids, he's not a bad father but I don't really love him anymore. In fact I'm not even sure if I want to be with him. You can't just find another relationship though with three kids ... so what's the choice? Life as a single parent, or carry on the way we are! Great choice isn't it?"

"I still love Tim, there's never been any doubt about that, but he's stubborn and I suppose I am as well. We can't seem to hit it off at the moment but I couldn't imagine life without him. No, I suppose sooner or later I'll have to say sorry to him because he messed up my night of dreams. No one ever said marriage was fair did they?"

"That's true, but they didn't say it would drive me to down three bottles of wine every night either. Oh! By the way Mel, I meant to tell you, I'm having a few drinks next Friday round at my place. Just a few of the people from work; most of the partners have done a drinks evening and I don't want them to think I can't manage the social side of the business. I'm hoping to get a share of this new work so I need to impress a few people."

"Leave it to Ben; he'll impress them all right. Get him to tell them about his career to date ... that should keep them riveted for a couple of hours."

"Mel, I realise you're joking but that's a good point. I can't have him buggering up my chances of moving a couple of rungs up the ladder. Can you get Tim to take him off somewhere that night, playing snooker or whatever it is they do?"

"Oh sure, Neen! Like Tim's going to do what I ask him. Aren't you forgetting that we hardly talk any more. Anyway, they always play on Fridays so if you say nothing they'll most likely go off out anyway."

"Yes, but if he knew how important this was he'd probably stay in on purpose, either trying to help, or in a bid to screw up my prospects altogether. He's bound to see me making preparations, getting the food and drink ready. Seriously Mel you must get them to go out together that night."

"I'll try, but short of challenging Tim to a game of pool in the Globe I don't know how I'm going to do it. Honestly Neen, we don't communicate with each other at the moment."

By the following evening nothing had changed. Melanie needed to talk to Tim but she couldn't bring herself to be civil to him. Sarcasm was the best she could manage.

"Are you going to see your counsellor tonight Tim?"

"Sorry ... what d'you mean?"

"Ben... he is your confident, your counsellor, your mentor isn't he? I thought you got most of your inspiration for our marital bliss from that guru of tender togetherness, Ben-No-Job!"

"Why do you have to take the piss all the time? Ben's a good friend, at least he was there, willing to treat me like another human being when all you could do was call me a bastard before slamming the phone down on me."

"Tim, you have no idea have you? That night I planned to say sorry to you and make up romantically, I'd cooked you fillet steak with all the trimmings. It could have been a wonderful night if you hadn't chosen Ben's company instead of mine!"

"How was I supposed to know all this?"

"Well let me think… you could have come home and found out what was for tea instead of heading off to the Globe with the jolly green giant."

"I didn't know that …OK, it looks as if I messed up that night, but what now?"

"You mean you want to talk, you want to end hostilities?"

"Of course I do, and anyway Jim's pasties are playing hell with my digestion."

They smiled at each other as the glimmer of a thaw appeared.

"OK Tim, here's the deal … you have your pub night with Ben next Friday and then Saturday you get home early and get scrubbed up. I'll get my Mum to have the kids, or I could ask Neen – she'll owe me a favour for getting you to keep Ben out on Friday night but it's about time they spent a night at Mum's. Oh by the way, don't take him home before midnight on Friday, Neen's got some work people coming for drinks and she doesn't want Ben ballsing it up for her. If you succeed in staying out until gone midnight with him I'll give you the best Saturday night you've had since we moved in here, so make sure you're ready and fit for action Mr. Fisher, all right?"

"Sounds good to me, and keeping Ben out late on Friday night isn't exactly difficult. I might have to let him beat me at pool a few times, but with what's on offer on Saturday I don't give a damn Mrs. Fisher."

"Both smiling broadly, they shook hands on the deal and for the first time in weeks Tim brushed his lips loosely across hers."

On Friday evening Melanie arrived next door early to help get things ready. She needn't have bothered because Nina had taken the afternoon off. The always tidy house with its abstract paintings and minimalist style was pristine. Little dishes were brimming with tasty snacks of nuts and crisps and wriggly things and Nina was a perfect picture of radiance.

"Neen you are so damned efficient, I find it irritatingly refreshing. Trouble is, it reminds me of the state I'm in."

"You're not in a state, I've told you. You're ten years at least away from all of that. You look lovelier than ever and now you've sorted things out with Tim it can only get better. I just envy you tomorrow night ... what have I got to look forward to when this lot go home tonight or tomorrow for that matter? The kids are at my Mum's and my Saturday night will either be spent on my own, or, if I'm really unlucky, I might get to spend it with Ben, which is definitely the less attractive of the two options. You sure you wouldn't like me to sort Tim out tomorrow night while you stay here and discuss job possibilities with Ben. After all I might be able to teach that husband of yours a few new tricks from my file of fantasies."

"No thanks, Neen, that's one department where he doesn't need any encouragement. I shall wake up Sunday morning with a hangover, dizzy from my sexual adventures with my lovely husband which will most likely last until breakfast. So eat your heart out Neen, I'm going to get high on life this weekend, at last."

One by one Nina's colleagues arrived. They weren't a bit like Melanie had expected. She'd imagined a load of legal eggheads in stuffy shirts and painted dolls pontificating endlessly about justice, but in fact they were quite the opposite. She found herself talking to people who were interested in her and in her work in the bank. Meeting Nina's friends was turning out to be pure pleasure, the rare enjoyment of stimulating conversation, when she spent most evenings listening to the television. Nina dragged her away from a trio that were fascinating her with stories of some eccentric clients.

"Mel, I want to introduce you to Ratty, remember I told you about him? He's joined us to work on the Stellar Haufman account. Ratty this is Mel, my neighbour and my best friend. I want you to explain to her the kind of work I really do ... she thinks I get people off parking tickets don't you Mel? While you're doing that I'll go and top you both up."

Mel's complexion jumped two shades of pink in as many seconds.

"Sorry Ratty ... is it all right to call you that? I don't mean to be rude or anything. This is typical of Nina, she throws me into conversation with people I don't know and then I'm stuck for anything to say ... well anything intelligent that is."

Mel knew she was uttering gibberish but her foot was firmly stuck in her mouth. Standing in front of this beautiful man she felt humble. Eventually she shut up and waited for Mr. Ratty to mutter his excuses before sliding away to seek more rational company.

"Mel, I would love you to call me Ratty, Rats or even Rat, it's what most of my friends call me... and I'd like us to be friends. You know, I've heard a lot about you already, from Nina? I'm sure you have lots of intelligent things to say. If not, you wouldn't have done so well in the bank. I'm just like you, believe me – although I stand up in Court and talk for hours, I'm often stuck for the right words when I meet someone I want to impress. Nina's told me so much about you I almost feel I know you, except until now I had no idea what you looked like. Nina forgot to tell me that you're beautiful."

Melanie was melting right in front of Ratty. Had she heard him right? Had he really just said he wanted to be friends? Could he seriously want to impress *her*? She felt her cheeks flush; the strength was disappearing from her legs. She was pretty sure she hadn't had that much to drink but her hands were shaking. The voice inside her head was screaming at her, 'Pull yourself together ...this guy handles the contract Nina is desperate to work on, she got rid of Ben so she wouldn't be embarrassed and now you're making a complete fool of yourself in his place.' She hammered at her brain, desperate for something sensible to say.

"Do you enjoy being a lawyer?"

She winced at her choice of words even as she uttered them. She cringed at her crass stupidity. How could she seriously ask Ratty if he enjoyed being successful in his profession? She looked into his face and begged for pity.

"Well, it's funny you should ask me that,' he said, intently studying her expression. 'Everyone assumes that because I'm doing well I must love my work. You're the only person I've admitted this to, and I'd prefer it remained our secret,

32

but sometimes I hate the job. I'd love to do something different, an action job, fly a jet fighter, drive an express train at a hundred and fifty miles an hour or maybe dive for pearls in the tropics. Some days I hang around the Court room, waiting my turn, while outside the sun is baking and I watch some wizened old Judge who hasn't seen the light of day for years, and I think... is this what the future holds for me?"

"But Ratty, you're so good at what you do, Nina's told me that clients pay extra to have you sort their problems. She's so impressed to have you in the firm; she's a great fan of yours! And anyway, you make lots of money so you can go abroad with your wife to anywhere you want, hire a boat, fly a plane... do what you want. I know you've got an Aston Martin, guess who told me that as well?"

"Nina's super to work with, she doesn't know it yet but she's going to be my assistant on the Stellar Haufman account. It's a promotion for her, one she deserves because she's very good at her job, but I will have to tell her, I don't need a fan club, especially as it only has one member. Mel, I've confessed two secrets to you in the last five minutes, please don't mention anything of what I just told you, will you? I want Nina to hear about this from me, not from her next door neighbour."

"Of course not, working for the bank I have to keep plenty of secrets, like whose going broke and whose got pots of money. Just imagine, if you banked with us I'd have three secrets of yours."

"Do you know, when Nina asked me to come here this evening I nearly refused? I was sure it would be another of those boring round of supper parties where you make small talk with people you'll never meet again while wishing you were back home with your shoes off and listening to your favourite opera. But tonight hasn't been a bit like that thanks to you, I envy Nina, having you as her best friend."

"You... you envy Nina, the woman you're about promote to be your assistant? I don't get it. Ratty I think I'm missing something here. She's your number one fan, thinks you can fly from rooftop to rooftop, arms outstretched under your cape and yet *you* envy *her*. This must be a solicitor thing because in the bank it's much more simple. Basically everyone envies the next person up the ladder. In fact that's exactly what a career in the bank is, a game of snakes and ladders. Every time you do well you go up the ladder until one day you balls up, sorry Rattani, I think I've had too much wine, until one day you make one mistake too many and then whoosh, you slide right the way down a big snake and land in the snake pit."

Melanie swung her arm around in an exaggerated demonstration just as a woman in brown tweeds was passing. She stopped her arm in mid swing but inertia ensured that the entire contents of the glass continued their flight, landing roughly amidships of the generous bust belonging to tweed lady. With white wine disappearing down her cleavage she stood motionless, in total shock. Her face slowly turned red with anger until it resembled scorched sandpaper.

Ratty and Melanie stared at her, silence had gripped the little group as each waited for another to say something, but no one wanted to speak first. After several seconds the lady, who Melanie later discovered was Miss Highnam, a partner in Nina's firm, exclaimed angrily, "Women who cannot hold their drink should not be permitted in decent company." She then turned and marched off, presumably to the bathroom. Melanie recoiled at her own stupidity. She obviously worked in Ratty's firm so he would be embarrassed by her carelessness. Before she could make an escape from this self-made mess Ratty took her by the arm and gently guided her to an alcove, which was slightly set back and a lot less prominent.

"If you will insist on throwing drinks over my esteemed colleagues," he said, "can we at least move somewhere less conspicuous." He looked straight into her eyes and smiled.

Melanie was in a trance, her muscles ceased to obey her commands. She was staring into the kindest eyes she had ever seen. From this distance they excited her like none before, of that she was certain. The warmth generated by Ratty's perpetual smile was the equal of a nuclear power station. It was evident he wasn't cross with her. They reflected on the unfortunate downfall of Miss Highnam, and, as if ignited by the same spark they were overcome by spontaneous laughter. With tears streaming down her face Melanie put her hands across her stomach to ease the pain. Ratty spoke first, "I recall you describing her bosom as a snake pit before dumping the contents of your glass into it. Brilliant," he exclaimed, 'absolutely brilliant. How am I ever going to take that woman seriously again?'

"I'm so sorry Ratty; I just got a bit carried away telling you about the bank. I was going to tell you what they did to my friend Jenny. I didn't look and... well you know what happened next, sorry."

"Don't be sorry Mel, I haven't enjoyed myself so much in years. I'm never going to miss a party you're at. I'll put a clause in Nina's contract that forbids her having a party unless we're both invited. In fact ... I'd like to invite you to a function of my own next week, if you wouldn't think me too forward. Please let me explain before you say no."

Mel wasn't about to say no, but something told her she should.

"Next Wednesday I have to address around a hundred business leaders at the Hilton Hotel in town. Our firm will have to do more of these seminars if they want to hold on to the big corporate accounts like Stellar Haufman. I've been asked to talk for an hour on contract law. Now here's the problem, I could talk to them for an hour on the origin of contract and equity. I could bleat on about tortuous liability and the classic test for establishing a duty of care, the famous formulae of Lord Atkin in Donoghue v Stevenson in the Appeal Court in 1932 but I'd have them all asleep within ten minutes. The trick is to be factual but interesting, topical and yet amusing. How will I know if I was any of these things if I'm not sitting out there listening to my speech?" He was silent, waiting for her to answer.

"I suppose you could record the whole thing and then listen to it the next day?" Melanie offered.

"Not the same as having an independent assessment ... which is why I have a huge favour to ask ... would you be my guest, sit near the front so you don't miss any of it, and afterwards tell me how I did? I'd want you to be honest of course. By the look on your face I can see you don't want to do it. Now it's my turn to say sorry. I've put you in an embarrassing position which is quite unforgivable. Melanie, I'm sorry."

"I wasn't looking like anything and I do want to come, it's just that I can't get time off work."

"Melanie, I can easily fix that, I will request that the bank send you. I'll tell them I've heard about your business skills and that I require you to assess my seminar. They'll be pleased to assist our firm; you know how much they'd love to handle our account. My firm can pay the bank for your time if that's what it takes. I was told when I joined that I could hire any resources I needed and I've decided I need you there."

"Is that what I am, a resource?" Melanie gulped at her wine, displeased at that label after his previous compliments. The room was still reverberating with chatter but a sudden silence separated them. Ratty was furious with himself. He'd unwittingly insulted her. He had to think quickly. That was what lawyers did all the time so why was it proving so hard at this moment?

"You're a lovely resource. I'm almost afraid that your presence will divert my mind from contract law so I stutter over my words and end up clasping my hands together in frustration at my verbal impotence."

"You know I would do no such thing. More likely you'll have forgotten you invited me and I'll sit silently between two fat businessmen who are wondering why I'm there."

"Melanie, that's not remotely possible ... will you do it for me?"

"Well, seeing as I tried to drown one of your staff in white wine and disgraced you by falling about laughing at her misfortune ...OK then ...yes, I'll do it."

"Thank you Melanie, and afterwards, it finishes at noon, will you join me in the Hilton restaurant for lunch. That way I can debrief you while it's still fresh in your mind."

Melanie's inhibitions were fast disappearing along with

her wine. She looked at him with a wide smile, "Sorry Ratty, You can't debrief me, I'm a married woman!"

She was making fun of him, and that was good. He quickly mustered his words to find an equally witty response, "Please don't apologise, some other time perhaps ...can we still have lunch?"

The beam on her face told him she was happy with his reply, joking together like old friends. Ratty figured his conversation with Mel would get more intimate as she put back more wine. Only the fact that she lived next door stopped him insisting they quit drinking. Getting her drunk wasn't his plan, but Mel would be safe with Nina so she couldn't come to any harm. She was enjoying herself and he wasn't about to spoil that for her. How often, he wondered was she this happy? Mel gripped his sleeve and he gently took her weight, he could see she was finding it difficult to stand unaided.

'Perhaps we ought to sit down, let's bag that sofa while we can.'

They collapsed on Nina's luxurious white leather three seater. As the cushions swallowed her up Mel relaxed and slid sideways into Ratty. He put his arm around her to avoid it digging into her side. He would have liked to caress her but it was too soon. Instinctively he pulled her closer until they were a warm mass. His arm tightened around her and he was acutely aware that she was offering no resistance. Nothing needed to be said so he let the moment take care of itself, hoping that she wouldn't make a sudden move away from him. Silence really was golden, he mused. All around them people continued to drone on, while the music kept up a steady thump, but they were unaware of it. They were enjoying these precious moments, each believing that they alone were relishing the intimacy of their encounter.

Quite by accident, Ratty reasoned, he'd ended the evening in the arms of a beautiful woman while all around people were dancing and carrying on conversations that had little or no point. He surveyed the crowded sitting room and realised that no one was taking any notice of them. It was as if they were invisible. In the midst of so many people they were quite alone. A tingling sensation was developing deep inside his chest, one he hadn't experienced in years, and still he knew exactly what it was. The last time had been fifteen years ago when he'd met Sharon, his wife, on a skiing holiday. Then he hadn't been afraid to say it, 'Love at first sight', but was it only for teenagers? Love was a silly word anyway, only in English he reasoned, could you use the same word to describe the passion you felt for your lover as for your need for a glass of beer.

The mood was surreal. He'd only come here tonight to gain his colleagues' approval. He'd never expected this. But that followed 'Ratty's Rule' to the letter, a rule he had believed ever since he was at school. 'Things never turn out the way you expect them to.' Was Melanie asleep? Was she even aware that she was ensconced in his arms? If so she must be happy with the situation? He blocked that line of thought, reminding himself that she'd consumed too much wine. In a moment she would wake up, compose herself and disappear next door, and into the arms of her loving husband. Pangs of jealousy stabbed Ratty where two minutes ago he'd felt a very different emotion. Battling with his feelings he questioned himself, should I wake her? She might be horrified to find she's been asleep in my lap in front of so many people. Go on... wake her... I will, in a minute, she looks so peaceful, so... so lovely, and she's in my arms. God this isn't meant to be ...but I'm loving every second of it. Melanie stirred and looked up at him, she took a few seconds to locate herself, and when she did she tried to remember how she had come to end up in Ratty's embrace. Despite the awareness that she was deep in the arms of a man she hardly knew, a man she'd only met two hours ago, she made no attempt to move. A sense of belonging invaded her. Her limbs refused to take orders. She was powerless to move away from him, or even to sit up straight. Her mind was translating pulses from every inch of her body, subliminal messages of contentment. She wasn't moving because she was happy where she was. Common sense was telling her that she should get up, end this interlude now before people noticed, before people pointed at her, but her heart was overruling her head. She wanted to stay fast in his arms, she wanted more! As she slowly rejoined the real world thoughts of her problems at work came flooding back. She remembered how useless she felt at work, how undervalued she was at home, that word 'failure' came charging back at her. Why then, was this lovely human being showering her with kindness? She thought about the things she'd told Nina. Nina, oh my God, where was Nina? I'm in her house laying on her new boss in a drunken stupor, and next door my children are playing, and my husband is due home at any moment. I've taken leave of my senses. With great difficulty she pushed herself away from Ratty and slowly stood up, a little wobbly at first. She looked down at the man with whom she'd spent the last two hours, two wonderful hours. She smiled tenderly.

"I must go, I had too much wine. I hope I haven't spoilt your evening!"

He looked at her longingly. "It's been the best evening I've had in a very long time. I hope we can do it again, soon."

"Maybe" she said and, offering him a parting smile, she set off gingerly to the kitchen in search of Nina. She had some apologising to do before she left. She found Nina laughing with a small group of her friends. They looked incredibly happy, joking loudly, another story about something that had happened in the office. When Nina noticed Melanie standing behind her she turned and hugged her warmly.

Melanie smiled at her, "I'd better go, Tim'll be back soon."

"Tim came back ages ago Mel, they came into the kitchen but I thought it best they went no further, so I sent them round to yours for half an hour, told her we had to clear up. They'd had a few ... never even argued. They're probably asleep in front of your TV now so if you don't want Ben for a lodger you'd better send him back, or leave him there, I don't care either way"

"You're a real friend Nina. I love you."

Melanie staggered back to her house. The short walk in the crisp night air sobered her in seconds. She packed Ben off to his own house and went up with Tim to get ready for bed.

"Did Neen tell you, we came round earlier, just as you were clearing up, a real good evening by the sound of it?" She knew Tim was probing.

"It was OK. You know what it's like with people from

work. You just talk about all the same things you've already talked about before."

"Was Roddy there in his bow tie and red braces?"

"No, it was Nina's work people not mine."

"So you didn't know any of them?"

"No not at the start, but by the end I'd got to know one or two."

One actually, she thought to herself. She realised that far from feeling guilty she was already missing Ratty. Tim climbed into bed and turned towards her back. He put his arms around her and she recognised his amorous intentions.

"Sorry Tim, I'm too tired. See you in the morning."

He let out an exaggerated sigh before turning to his side of the bed. She knew full well he was miffed but there was nothing she could do about it with her head in this state, anyway she'd made promises of great things for Saturday night. She couldn't think about that now, rather she was grateful that sleep came quickly.

As usual Saturday passed in a haze of activity and all too soon it was evening. Standing in the kitchen, cooking what was meant to be a special meal for the two of them she reflected on last night's party. The encounter with Nina's 'boss to be' had affected her deeply. Barely a minute had passed today without her mind returning to the time they'd spent together, the things he'd said, the meeting they had planned for next week. She shouldn't be thinking about him at all ... her husband was getting himself tarted up for a night of ... of what? What had she promised when she was anxious to end their feud! Whatever it was she would soon have to deliver ... trouble was she wasn't feeling that way inclined and it was all because of last night and someone called Ratty! A pet rat perhaps? The voice inside her head wouldn't stop talking; 'I wish Tim was off out tonight, fixing someone's car or playing pool with Ben. If only I could see Ratty again for five minutes I know I'd feel better.' Time was ticking away. Before long they would finish the meal, drink the wine and make small talk on the settee. It was the next bit she wasn't looking forward to. What the hell is wrong with me? She quizzed herself for answers, but none came. Two weeks ago I was willing him to take me to bed and do with me whatever he wanted. I just needed him to hold me and tell me that things were like before ...before the row. Now I can't face going upstairs, there's no way I can go through with this, not with my thoughts so full of last night and Ratty.

Melanie stood in front of the cooker with one hand on the grill handle, the other hand stirring onions in the pan. Spitting noises from under the grill told her the fillet was done. She put it on the plates and carried it into the dining room where Tim was sitting, beaming with anticipation for what was to follow.

"Don't look so nervous," he joked. "You're the best cook in Elmthorpe!"

She forced a weak smile in response to his stupid grin. She was happy to let him believe that her cooking was what was bothering her. Tim had never understood her, not even at the simplest level. When she was pregnant, when she had morning sickness he would ask, 'What's wrong?' Not once, but morning after morning. Tim didn't understand women, so it was no surprise that after eighteen years of marriage he still couldn't read her moods. Perhaps that's just as well she thought ...as her mind went over last night for the tenth time in as many minutes. Ratty understood her perfectly. He'd looked straight through her smile and got inside her head. He'd made her feel good about herself; in his arms everything had seemed so natural, so sensible, so achievable. He valued her opinion enough to want her to judge if his speech was good enough. He cared what she thought about his work. Did Tim care what she thought about anything? Although he'd always been proud of her success, Tim had never appreciated her skill, attained during her career at the bank. For him her success was something to boast about to his friends, as if it was more his than hers, but despite this he wouldn't acknowledge that it was real work. She sank into a dream as she compared Tim with Ratty. One of them needed charm to win over a jury while the other used his hands to fix broken trucks. Tim was physically strong, his work was dirty, greasy and at the end of the day he wiped his hands in his oily rag like it was a victory salute, a mark of honour to another job completed. Tim believed that his work was important. Mel didn't.

"He fixes bloody engines." she screamed.

"Who does, who fixes engines? What the hell are you going on about?" Tim sat up, startled at her sudden outburst.

"Sorry... sorry I was dreaming out loud. You know how sometimes a thought comes into your mind when you're least expecting it, and you say the words out loud?"

"No, not really. D'you mean like talking in your sleep?"

"Yes, I suppose that's what I mean." Mel stuttered.

"So who fixes engines?" Tim repeated. This meal wasn't going a bit the way he'd expected.

She could hardly say, 'You do' ... "Oh, one of Nina's friends who was at last night's party."

"Party? I didn't realise it was a party. We usually go together if it's a party. You should've said. I'd much rather have come with you than spend the night playing pool with Ben. I know you probably thought I'd be bored with a bunch of Nina's hooray-henry friends but I'd have put up with it rather than have you sit there bored stiff while they cracked on about law and stuff all night, just to help Nina out. I bet you were bored out of your mind? I'm right, aren't I?"

"Yes ...yes that's pretty much what is was like, but I don't mind if it helped Nina get her promotion."

"What promotion, Ben hasn't said anything about her getting a new job."

Melanie panicked as she realised she had just broken her first promise to Ratty.

"Well I don't expect Ben knows yet, I met Nina's new boss and he let slip that she was in line to work with him on this big new contract they've got, Stellar something or other."

"What d'you mean, let it slip? Doesn't Nina know yet?"

"I don't know, I suppose she does, although no, she'd have said wouldn't she... Oh I don't know. What does it matter?"

"It doesn't matter to me Mel, only I think it's a bit odd, this guy telling you before he tells Nina?"

"Well, that's drink for you Tim."

"So what, he was drunk, this guy, was he?"

"No, nobody was drunk (Only me, she thought). I just meant that after a few drinks people let out all their secrets. It's what drink does. You should know that ... after all you go down the Globe and after a few drinks you discuss our problems with Ben. What's that if it's not the drink talking?"

"Mel, the difference is, Ben is my mate, this guy doesn't

45

even know you. He's probably forgotten your name already and yet he was telling you stuff which was confidential, and he's a solicitor .... right? Just shows what I've said before, they're no better than us. All their fancy fees and bloody wigs but underneath they can't even drink a few beers without letting their tongues run away. They'd be no damn use in a real job."

"What, you mean like yours, fixing lorries?"

"Well, yes, if you like, what I do is hard work, it's a real job."

"Tim, what the hell has hard work got to do with this guy telling me things after we'd had a few drinks?"

"I hate the way you say 'Fixing Lorries'. You make it sound like it's beneath you, and all these people at the party. Mine's a trade Mel, remember that. I've got a trade! I did three years' apprenticeship before I became a qualified mechanic."

"I suppose he did a few years at University before he became a lawyer."

"So what are you saying Mel ... he's better than me?"

"Tim I'm not saying anything. I don't care all right! How's your steak?"

"Yea it's OK. Mel what did you mean when you said 'This guy was telling you things?' What other things did he tell you?"

"I don't know... nothing... oh I can't remember. Tim it's not important is it? I talked to lots of people; they were all talking about their work. They obviously enjoy what they do, just like I used to at the bank before I hit this crisis."

"What crisis? There's nothing wrong with you Mel. You just think you can't do something, but if you carry on like this, before long you'll find you really can't do it. You need to pull yourself together. Bloody hell, it shouldn't be too difficult... what you do. I mean, you've been doing it for enough years, you should be able to add up pages of figures with your eyes shut."

"Is that what you think I do? You think I spend all day adding up figures?"

"Well it is isn't it? I don't know what you call it, but it's still adding up."

"Tim, I talk to clients, I write reports, I manage my departmental budget, I have sixteen staff who report to me, I'm not just a bloody number cruncher. Got it?"

"Christ, I thought you said tonight was going to be different. Doesn't seem like it. I don't know the bloody difference between numbers and a budget. I'm a bloody mechanic in case you forgot. So if you've got sixteen people working for you is Rodders one of them? Rodders and his famous performing bow tie?"

"Rodney works in Internal Audit, nothing to do with my work at all. I work with customers and their banking details. He sees that the people who work in the bank aren't fiddling the books, milking the bank, whatever you want to call it."

"So who checks Rodders to see that he doesn't get his bow tie caught in the till? It's like I said before Mel, while you think you're running the bank they're actually busy checking on you. They don't even trust you after ten years of working there. How long's Rodders worked there? Five bloody minutes I bet, but he's one of the boys, probably Eton I shouldn't wonder with that bow tie. It says a lot for your devotion to the bank all these years, don't you think?"

"No I don't think any such thing. Of course the bank

has to have internal security. You've just got no respect for my position at the bank. To you it's just a joke. Well look at me Tim, Do you see me laughing?"

"Look Mel, lets start again shall we, this seems to have gone all wrong. It's my fault, I'm sorry. I didn't mean to quiz you about last night. I know Nina's your friend and I'm sure you just put up with that bloke for her sake but it's tonight now and he's pissed off back to wherever he came from. You've got me, and... you've got me all to yourself... all night. No Nina, No Ben, No kids, just you, me and a big double bed upstairs so shall we skip coffee and go straight for desserts?"

"Oh can we let our meal go down first Tim. I've got some of those mint chocolates that they serve in restaurants with the coffee. You've got to let me make the coffee."

"OK, after all the longer we wait the more we'll want it, won't we!"

Melanie was fighting back the nauseous feeling that threatened to choke her. You might want it more, she thought but there's no way I do. I don't even know if I can go through with this tonight. Tonight, what about any night? What is happening to me? First I have a crisis, and I want Tim to hold me, to help me get through it. Now I don't want him near me. What's changed? Melanie knew what had changed. Since last night her brain had returned over and over to the time she'd spent with Ratty. When she woke up, while she was cleaning her teeth, twenty times during the day, even while Tim had been rattling on about his crappy job as a mechanic. What was Ratty doing now she wondered? Had he thought about her since last night? Had he gone home and told his wife that he'd asked her to judge his speech next Wednesday? Somehow Melanie doubted that. What Ratty had found in Melanie was so special because he had planted it there. Until last night Melanie was convinced that she was hopeless. Ratty had revived her self confidence more in two hours than Tim had done in two weeks. He'd asked her to be at his big speech next Wednesday. He'd asked her to join him for lunch at the Hilton. When was the last time Tim had taken her for a meal anywhere? Tim would take her to the Globe for pasty and chips then invite Ben and his mates to join them. He'd never take her somewhere like the Hilton.

Melanie took the coffee in to Tim and put two mint chocolates on his saucer. She'd made it with boiling water. That way it would take longer to drink.

"Christ Mel", Tim said, spitting coffee down his best trousers, "This coffee's bloody boiling."

"Sorry Tim, I knew you wouldn't like it if it was cold."

'Well there's no chance of it being cold this side of the ten o'clock news.'

'Well, I'll be too tired by then Tim, so maybe we should put this off until another night.'

Tim burst out laughing. "Mel you always could make me laugh, I remember when we first went out together, that's what I loved about you, you were funny – not like other girls, in a rude way – you were just dead funny. You crack me up Mel."

Mel saw that Tim wasn't joking. She would have loved to say 'Tim I'm serious, I don't want to make love to you tonight.' She also knew if she said that, Tim would go crazy, things would be right back to where they were two weeks ago.

She knew what was expected of her. Tim was her husband, after all. He would depend on her to do her duty, to honour him with her body. She felt sick at the thought.

Tim was first to sit up in bed, "Sorry Mel."

"What do you mean?" she whispered.

"Oh come on Mel, I'm not stupid, I could tell you didn't enjoy it. I just didn't do it how you wanted. Trouble is Mel, if I don't know what you want how am I meant to do it?"

"You were fine Tim. It's me; I'm just not myself lately. I've told you, things are going on in my head, I think I'm losing it at work, I feel like I can't cope here at home. I'm going through one of those troughs they're always talking about in books and things. Tim, you might have to be very understanding for a while."

"Of course Mel, no problem. You know I've always understood. What's the problem?"

"Well I just told you... I just told you what the problem is... you never listen to anything I say!"

"Well, can you explain in a bit more detail, I mean it's difficult to understand when you don't tell me what's going on inside your head?"

"Tim, *I don't even know what's going on inside my head right now*. I don't think I'm going to be able to make love for a while... that's what I'm trying to say. I'm sorry."

"What do you mean, for a while? D'you mean like a week, a month... what's a while? Do we get to discuss this or is this like, your decision? I mean, 'The bank's decision is final Mr. Fisher. You can't have an overdraft and you can't make love to your wife either'. 'Mel, you can't just announce something like that, I mean.... we need to talk about it. I'm a reasonable man, you know that. I've always been reasonable, but bloody hell, it's like saying you don't really want to be with me. Is that what you're saying Mel? Is that it? Nothing makes any sense to me anymore. You wonder why I talk to Ben about our problems? Christ I didn't realise just how big a problem we have. OK, we had a row, I was a prat, I know that now and I'm sorry. But please can we forget all that and get back to how we were two weeks ago? After all, nothing's changed, has it?"

Mel had her head under her pillow. Quite a lot has changed Tim, she thought. Yesterday I realised that there is someone out there who cares about what I think. Someone who thinks my opinion is worth having. Someone who sees me as more than just a cook and a good roll in bed. Someone who makes me feel valuable, needed, someone who sees me as a woman ... and he arouses in me awareness, he makes me aware that I'm a woman.

"Tim, can we talk about this tomorrow. I feel sick at this moment."

"What you really mean is, you need to check with Nina before you can talk about our marriage problems, that's the truth of the matter. Well talk to bloody Nina, but don't act surprised because I take advice from Ben. Thank God he understands these things."

"No Tim, I won't be surprised."

CHAPTER THREE

Sunday morning at number four Willow Brook started as usual with the three children stampeding around the house in preparation for their recreational activities. Henry was a keen canoeist but this morning he was due to play football behind the village hall with his mates, one of whom was Alex, Nina's oldest boy from next door. James was the musical member of the family; he played the recorder as well as guitar and piano. Sundays was the only day when he and Guss (Nina's second child) and one of their friends could practice together in what they claimed was their band. Their problem was finding somewhere to make that much noise without attracting complaints, so often they spent more time planning where they could practice than actually doing it.

Amy wanted to do all the things her brothers did so she had her own small canoe and a recorder, from which she had so far failed to play a single tuneful note. She had a fondness for dressing up and spent hours trying on her mother's clothes and experimenting with her make up, all of which earned ridicule from her brothers.

Melanie was always up early on Sundays to get breakfast for her brood before taxiing them around. If Henry was canoeing she would have to take Amy as well plus two canoes. If James was playing at a school music club event he would expect his mother to stay and watch the performance, which meant that Amy would have to come too.

This Sunday Melanie was glad that she was required to provide transport for them, especially as James's performance was in a school hall twenty miles away. That would keep her out of the house until at least mid-afternoon.

Henry had already gone off to play football by the time she was preparing to leave and Tim was mooching about the house in a foul mood. For him last night's conversation with Mel had introduced a new set of problems into his already crowded bag. Just as he'd thought reconciliation was on the cards it seemed things had taken a turn for the worse.

Now they were all off out and he would be left to fend for himself for most of the day. Just for once, he thought, I don't want to fix anyone's car; instead I wish I could fix my marriage. He slumped at the kitchen table, his hands clasped around a mug of tea. All around him his family was rushing about with a purpose. James was spreading sheets of music across the table in preparation for his performance and Amy was trying to sort out the make up bag that she was taking with her.

While Melanie was upstairs getting ready, it dawned on Tim that he was the only one who had nothing worthwhile to do. He wasn't part of the mad scrabble to get to the next activity. He sometimes took Henry to football if Melanie was out with James but today he wasn't even needed for that, he was surplus to requirements, no one needed him, and he had no purpose to serve.

Melanie came into the kitchen looking as beautiful as ever. He knew that she'd been up for hours while he'd had a 'lay in'. She was a picture of perfection while he had simply thrown on his old joggers and a scruffy t-shirt. He hadn't even combed his hair or showered, for which he now felt ashamed. As he stared vacantly into the mug of steaming tea, he reflected on Melanie's importance to the family, he took a minute to see her for what she really was, a successful career woman, a proud mother to their three children, and most of all a very desirable wife.

Was it any wonder she'd called a halt to his marital rites? Tim looked down at himself and cursed silently for not getting up earlier, for not getting showered and for not getting dressed properly. He could have offered to go with them, spend the day with them. They could have eaten out at a pub somewhere after James had finished his music session.

Now it was too late. They were already carrying their stuff out to Melanie's car. Amy ran back and kissed him before chasing out to catch the others, James shouted, "Bye Dad." Melanie briefly looked back and asked, "Will you be wanting an evening meal tonight Tim? If not I thought we'd stop off at McDonalds on our way back and get something."

"No, I'll be OK, I'll get myself something," he said miserably. "Have a good time." He wanted to say more but they were already gone. The car door slammed and Melanie tooted, probably to Nina next door.

He didn't even know where they were going. If only he'd shown more interest he could get washed and dressed and catch them up. Not as good, going in two vehicles as going together, but it would be better than spending the entire day alone. It would be too embarrassing to ring Mel and ask her just minutes after she'd left and, anyway, she wouldn't answer while she was driving.

Maybe Nina was in her front garden, if so she'd have seen them leave, she'd know where they were heading off to. He was ashamed to admit it but Nina knew more about his family's activities than he did. How could he explain going round to ask her? ...it was so obvious that he was only going after them because he was lonely. What a pathetic mess I am, he thought, as he studied himself in more detail, trying to picture himself as Melanie might see him. She used to be so proud of her 'big lad', her prize mechanic who could fix anything. She used to joke that no one should go on safari without Tim. He could make a nut and bolt out of a bucket of sand, she boasted. He'd fixed her Dad's car not long after they started seeing each other. Soon he was called upon for advice on all manner of mechanical things. When anyone in the family wanted a new car they would consult with Tim first to get his advice on what was or wasn't a good model to own. That seemed years ago. It was ages since anyone in the family had asked his advice on cars. In fact, he reflected, it was ages since anyone had asked his advice on anything. He stared at his big hands, his dirty finger nails, ingrained with engine oil. It wasn't that he wasn't clean, but it took ages to scrub the oil off his hands and the next day it was back again. Of course, he would always try to get scrubbed up, as Mel called it, before they went out anywhere together.

When was that? When was the last time he'd taken Mel out anywhere, to dinner or to the theatre? He tried to remember the last occasion on which they'd gone out together. He struggled and it became more difficult as he went further back through the year. Where had this year gone? Eventually he conceded that he hadn't taken her out at all this year and it would be July in another three days.

Was it any wonder she'd decided that they wouldn't make love any more? Soon she'd be insisting that they sleep in separate rooms.

Tim went upstairs to the bathroom and looked in the mirror. What he saw worried him. I'm a slob, he decided, a scruffy shambles of the man I used to be. I come and go every day always thinking I'm doing a good job, supporting my family, but the truth is Mel earns more than me and she could support this family on her own. I'm like a lodger in this house. He stared down at the dirty clothes he'd left on the floor yesterday when he'd got himself ready for the all important meal last night. If he was honest, he hadn't even made much of an effort for that. Yes he'd showered and splashed some aftershave on, but was that really enough for a woman like Melanie? These days she was working with big city accounts. She often dropped their names in conversation but he'd never paid enough attention to remember any of them. These were successful men, they wore £500 suits and Rolex watches and they used exclusive men's fragrances. Was that what Melanie wanted? Some bloody poof who drove a Mercedes and wore designer clothes?

Tim stood there for several minutes clutching the wash basin with his left hand while running his right hand across his chin. Decision number one, a new shaver was needed; in fact a major overhaul was needed. He stepped onto the scales, fifteen stone plus, three stone more than he was when he first met Melanie. He had to bend slightly to see the scales because his belly obscured his view. Four or five pints most nights in the Globe had been the main contribution to this unwelcome overhang. A cloud of depression engulfed him as he struggled to think clearly. Had he left it too late?

Had he lost the only woman he'd ever loved, mother to his kids and the most essential ingredient of his life?

What could he do about it? He could go next door and seek help from Ben! If Melanie found out – and she would, Nina would see to that, then he would appear even more pathetic. No, he had to sort this one out on his own. First he needed to shower and scrub himself until not a trace of oil remained and then he'd set about clearing up the house for Melanie. He'd start with his own things which were left all over the place then he'd put all the kids things away before preparing a meal for them. That's it ... I'll ring Melanie and say don't bother with McDonalds, I'm getting a lovely meal ready for when you come home. That would give him an excuse to speak to her. Maybe he'd be able to tell from the tone of her voice how she was feeling about him. If she rejected his offer to make the evening meal it meant she couldn't face sitting down to eat together, which probably meant their marriage was all but over. If, on the other hand, she enthused at the idea then there was still time to put things right.

He wouldn't bring up the subject of making love for as long as she wanted. He'd act as if everything was just fine. The perfect husband, that's what he had to be. Melanie wasn't a snob; she'd never been one to be impressed by money or material things. She would appreciate a single scented red rose more than a huge bunch of roses. She'd never be influenced by a Rolex watch or a Gucci suit. How often had they laughed at the holes in their jeans in the days before they'd been blessed with Henry? Even when they'd bought this house on Willow Brook they'd made fun of themselves for living in such grand surroundings. On the day they moved in they'd looked out of the front room window and made jokes about the 'posh bird' next door. Nina appeared to be posh in lots of ways, a snob even, but she was a good sort and she soon became Mel's best friend. Was she really Mel's best friend? Surely *I've* always been her best friend, he thought.

Tim spent the next two hours getting everything right before plucking up the courage to phone her and suggest the evening meal, together as a family. The phone rang and rang. Tim tried every ten minutes for over an hour. Maybe they'd been in an accident? No, he was sure that one of them would have been able to phone home in that case. Maybe she was in a bad area for the phone signal, that would be it. Blast... that meant she would go straight to McDonalds before he could reach her. Frustration was driving him so hard that his earlier inhibitions were cast aside. Within seconds he was next door, knocking on the kitchen window as he always did when he went round for Ben. Nina opened the door without acknowledging him and shouted up the stairs. "Ben, Tim's here!"

"Actually Nina it was you I wanted."

Nina turned to face him. She looked quite shocked. "Me?" she said. "I don't want to play pool Tim and I couldn't bear the thought of spending the afternoon in the Globe."

Tim smiled politely despite the sarcasm, but the deeper meaning wasn't lost on him. Nina was hitting out at him over the row that had dominated his life for two weeks. She made no attempt to hide her loyalty to Melanie.

"Nina, I was hoping to drive over to join Mel, and watch James playing his guitar but I've forgotten which school she said it was at. I was hoping you could help me."

"Tim, you've also forgotten what instrument he's playing, maybe you didn't notice that James didn't take his guitar with him? He's playing the piano at Westcombe School. It'll take you the best part of an hour to get there." She looked at her wrist watch. "I'd say you're too late... it'll be finishing by three at the latest. You'd probably get there just in time to meet them coming home."

At that moment Ben appeared in shorts and an old tennis top. "Give me five minutes Tim, I've just got to shave and get changed. Where are we going, the Globe or the King's Arms?"

"Sorry Ben, I can't stop. I'll see you later." Ben watched with astonishment as his friend headed rapidly back to his house.

Tim was unable to think straight as panic took over. He drove off in his red van, heading for Westcombe with no idea of what he was expecting to achieve. The traffic was heavy, as the Westcombe Road was also the shortest route from town to the motorway. The warm weather had brought out hundreds of cars, some with caravans, and some with boats, all intent on taking the motorway south towards the coast. His normally calm driving style was lost in a mixture of anger and frustration as he moved barely half a mile in twenty minutes. He cursed at the horse box in front of him. It was an hour and a half before he drove into Westcombe School.

The car park was almost empty. He flicked the button to lock the van as he ran towards the school entrance. Two women were walking slowly away from the main entrance, obviously engrossed in their conversation. Maybe they could tell him if the music club had finished. In truth he didn't need them to tell him, it was obvious from the lack of cars. His face brandished the pain of his disappointment when they said it had finished an hour ago.

"My lad, James, was playing the piano ...I so wanted to be here but the traffic was bad. Now they'll have gone for food and I need to find them." A sudden thought hit him. "McDonalds," he demanded, "Where is McDonalds?" ...as an afterthought he added, "please."

"Well, I expect they'll have gone to the big one by Sainsbury's, that's the one we always use, you can't never park at the one by the station," said one woman to the other, ignoring Tim.

"Please... can you tell me the quickest way to get to it?"

The woman began again, still addressing her friend rather than Tim.

"Well, I'd go out of here and turn left, down to the roundabout, go right round, then down past B & Q and turn into the car park for Sainsbury's. Or he could go along the dual carriageway and over the railway; he'll see McDonalds then, won't he?"

"Thanks". Tim left before they could debate the relative merits of another route.

He drove out of the school, turning left as instructed. Two minutes later he was at the roundabout. Did she say first turning? Go right round she'd said – what does that mean? I'll end up going back the way I came. Just then he saw a Sainsbury's lorry coming towards him, so that had to be the road to go down. Within seconds he saw McDonalds. Frantically he searched for his wife's white Mondeo, but it wasn't there. He hurried inside, desperately hoping to find them, but he already knew they'd left.

Despondently he trudged back to his van to start the journey home. The Westcombe Road traffic was just as bad in the homeward direction. What had started out as a rotten day had steadily deteriorated into a disaster. His sense of loss at having missed James's piano performance and missing out on eating with them now made him inconsolable. He tried Mel's phone again but it went straight to answerphone. He felt sick at the thought of spending another hour to get home. He'd succeeded in wasting a day, a precious day he could have spent with Melanie, with James and with Amy and instead he'd spent it alone. He hadn't even made it to the playing field to watch Henry kick a ball about with his mates.

At ten to six he walked in the kitchen door, starving hungry and as fed up as he could be. The Mondeo was on the drive, so at least he could spend the rest of the evening with them. He forced a weak smile when he saw Melanie.

"Good of you to show your face before you disappear down the pub," she said.

"Hey slow down Mel, I've had a terrible day, at least let me explain."

"Explain what? Did Ben beat you at pool or something, I suppose that's where you've been all day, right?"

"No, wrong actually Mel, wrong, bloody wrong, listen ...please! After you'd left I wished I'd come with you. Nina told me you'd gone to Westcombe – this was after I'd cleared up the place a bit – so then I drove over to the school hoping to get there in time to hear James play, but the traffic was horrendous. Then I went to McDonalds to look for you, you know, the one by Sainsbury's, but you'd already left and then I got stuck in the bloody traffic again trying to get home. I'm totally pissed off but at least we're together now."

Melanie knew by the look on his face that his anguish was genuine. She felt a small measure of compassion for him even though it was entirely his fault.

"We didn't go to McDonalds. I wanted a few things in Sainsbury's so we ate in there. The traffic was bad but we've been in for over an hour, so you were much too late to have seen James play. He was brilliant. His music teacher is recommending him for a big schools concert in London later this year. You should've been there, I was so proud; honestly it brought tears to my eyes."

This was just what Tim didn't want to hear. Not only had he missed the performance but it was a very special performance. He sank into his arm chair and reflected on his day. What now? 'I'm so sorry Mel, I wish I'd got up earlier, I wish you'd asked me to come with you.'

"Tim, I've asked you fifty times, but you're always too busy fixing someone's car or doing whatever it is you and Ben do on weekends. Don't try to blame me because you're missing out on seeing your children grow up."

Why was it everything he said to make things better simply brought a response from Mel that made him feel worse? Couldn't she see he was already upset enough?

"Please Mel, don't rub it in. I'll change, seriously I mean it, you see if I don't. I'm going to give all of you more time. I'm going to make you proud of me as a dad and as a partner, and not ashamed of me. Look at my hands Mel, not a trace of oil. Oh, and can you get Nina to look after Amy this week because I'm taking you out for a really special meal one night, what about Wednesday?"

Melanie couldn't believe what she was hearing. She

actually had two men wanting to take her to two different restaurants on Wednesday. She'd have to watch it she thought, if she wanted to stay a size ten.

"Well, I'm not sure about Wednesday Tim, but I'll ask her. If not we can always do another night, unless of course Wednesday is the only night your not playing pool with Ben?"

"Mel, listen to me will you? I'm going to change; I won't go down the Globe with Ben if it makes you unhappy. I'd rather stay in with you every night than have you thinking I don't care about you or the kids."

"I don't think you don't care Tim... and I couldn't stand you under my feet every night, so you carry on seeing Ben, but maybe it would be nice to see a bit more of you, I know the children would like that. You could perhaps do a bit more of the running them around, that would help me a lot."

"OK I will, I promise... but I'm going to book us in at The Walnut Tree on Wednesday night and if Nina can't look after Amy she can go over to your Mum's or even my Mum's. We're dining out, in style, proper like. I'm going to give you a night to remember Mel, that's a promise, and just to show I mean everything I've said I'm going to stay in with you tonight. We can curl up together in front of the television, just like we used to when we were first married."

"Sorry Tim, I've already promised Nina I'll go round to hers tonight for a glass of wine and a chat. We've got loads to catch up on. But still, I've got Wednesday night to look forward to haven't I?"

"Mel, I feel like you're deliberately making this hard for me. Look, I've said sorry, I want things to be different... but

I can't do it on my own …I can't stay in and have a cosy night with you if you prefer to go out and spend the night with someone else."

"That someone else is Nina, my best friend. So don't give me a hard time just because Ben is doing something else tonight Tim. I've spent hundreds of nights on my own while you've been down the Globe with your friends, so don't make me out to be a bad person… all right?"

"Christ Mel, being nice to you can be a real struggle, but I suppose you do have a point. Do I have to make an appointment to spend an evening with you? I could get to see you easier if I opened an account with your bank. And another thing, you insist on calling Nina your best friend but shouldn't that be me?"

"Yes it should be, Tim. That's part of the problem."

"What problem? Why is everything in riddles? I need a bloody interpreter to talk to my own wife. This is crazy. I don't know what I'm meant to do."

"You've got an interpreter… Ben, remember! No doubt he'll be able to explain everything for you later on at the pub. Oh by the way, was Wednesday his idea?"

"No it bloody wasn't. I haven't talked to him about us for days. I told you I'm going to sort this mess out and I meant on my own."

"So you think it's a mess do you?"

"Well, don't you, Mel? I mean… if it wasn't we wouldn't be talking like this would we? You'd be happy for us to spend the evening snuggled up together on the settee, not making excuses because you'd rather be next door talking about me instead of talking to me."

"Tim, don't shout, I'm receiving you loud and clear. I'm

not changing my plans for tonight and I'm not letting Nina down. I accept your invitation for Wednesday and I'm looking forward to it. Now I need to get going."

With that Mel picked up her cardigan and flounced out through the kitchen door. She knew if she'd stayed another minute she would have lost it altogether with Tim. She didn't want another row; for one thing she was afraid of what she might say.

Nina was describing the latest exploits from her office even before they'd sat down in the lounge. She shoved a glass of white wine into Mel's hand and sat right next to her on the sofa.

"Mel, I've got loads of gossip from work, and it's better now that you know the people after the other night. I thought I might have heard something about you chucking wine over Miss Highnam, but not a word's been said. She's already the butt of most of the jokes at work anyway and if that got out she wouldn't be able to walk in the office without someone mocking her."

"I'm really sorry about that Neen. I hope it doesn't cause you any trouble with her."

"Don't even think about it. I just wish I'd seen it, or better still chucked it at her myself. She's not exactly popular you know."

"Sam, our office manager told me today that Ratty has booked some big wig from your bank to attend his corporate do on Wednesday at The Hilton. You know that your bank has been trying to get our business for a while? Apparently Ratty has spoken to your Divisional Manager about getting this guy to his event. I suppose you'll find out before Wednesday who it is?"

"Well …actually, Neen, I already know!"

"Oh do you, is it anyone important?"

"No… Neen, no one important, and it's not a he… it's me."

"Mel, I don't know who told you that, but I think they're winding you up. Sam told me that Ratty was absolutely insistent about the person he wanted … Oh my God! Mel… are you saying what I think you are? I've been slow to catch on, haven't I? Friday, here on this settee, you didn't just talk about interest rates did you? I saw you fall asleep on him but I thought that was because you'd had too much to drink. Mel you're moving faster than the speed of light… what the hell is going on?"

"I don't know Neen, that's the truth, honestly I don't know."

"There are at least a dozen bare waisted twenty somethings wearing tiny thongs half way up their backs just queuing up to take him coffee or to do his filing. He's a lady magnet, although I have to say so far none of them has managed to win a response. But you… you've got him drinking out of your slipper and booking you for his seminar, all in less than two hours. You do realise he's going to be talking about contract law, don't you… it's not exactly spellbinding stuff, although half the girls in our place would happily swap places with you."

"Yes I know that. He's going to talk about tortuous liability and duty of care among other things."

"Christ Mel, you're talking like a bloody lawyer and you've only 'slept' with him once, and that was on the settee in front of twenty other people! Does Tim know that you're doing this seminar on Wednesday?"

"No Neen, and he doesn't know that we're going for lunch afterwards either!"

"Well bugger me with a pitchfork, Melanie Fisher... you take the biscuit you do. And to think I didn't bother to hunt him down because I thought I was too old for him. You're a year older than me! You'd better give me a few tips, just in case he has a younger brother!"

"I was as surprised as you, Neen, when he asked me. I don't know what it was but something happened between us here on Friday night, something that shook me deep inside. Neen, I have to tell you something really terrible about that night after I met Ratty. You know what I'd planned for Saturday, with Tim? Well I didn't want to go through with it, but in the end I had no choice. Instead of being the fantastic sexy night of passion I told you it would be ... it turned out to be a real damp squib, and it was all my fault. I couldn't fancy Tim. Can you believe that? You know I've never as much as looked at another man, but after Friday I went into meltdown over that flipping raving loony lovely Ratty."

"Mel, I told you he was gorgeous, but I didn't tell you to fall for him the first time you set eyes on him ...and anyway, before you get too carried away I'd better tell you ...he's married; Sharon ...that's his wife's name, Sam told me. She's another one doing detective work in the hope of closing him down. Wait till I tell them that my best friend has pulled him! Christ Mel you've made me quite proud."

"Neen, I haven't pulled, I'm simply giving him advice on his seminar, that's all. And please... don't tell anyone, can you imagine the effect this would have in our house if Tim found out!"

"Mel, you are the limit. You ...are advising Rattani, our new super lawyer, recruited at enormous expense to strengthen our legal team, and *you... you* are bloody advising *him?*" "I doubt if he'd ask my advice and I've been practicing for ten years."

"Sorry Neen, I didn't do it on purpose. We just got chatting and he asked me if I'd listen to his speech. He told me a bit about what he was going to say and he said he wants me to tell him if it was interesting or if it bored the pants off me."

"He obviously intends to get the pants off you Mel, and if he can't do it by boring you he might just try some other means. He's certainly got the physique for it. You are the luckiest woman in Elmthorpe ...that's what you are."

"There's more Neen. On Wednesday evening Tim is insisting on taking me out to dinner at The Walnut Tree. I'm going to be well fed if nothing else."

"Mel, The Walnut Tree costs a fortune; you're talking two hundred pounds for a three course meal for two. What's he after, *Tim* I mean?"

"He wants us to be best friends again, just like we used to be."

"Mel, I think he's after a bit more than that. In fact I think they both are. You're going to have to wear your chastity belt on Wednesday if you intend to remain a decent upstanding woman of this parish."

"Well maybe I don't!"

"I wish I could swap places with you Mel. God... fancy having Ratty and Tim take you out in one day. I think you'd better buy lottery tickets on Wednesday. You can't lose!"

Melanie found it hard to act normally as Wednesday

drew closer. She went through the usual routine of motherhood at breakfast and banker throughout the day but she stopped short of being a lover at night. Tim stuck fast to his new resolution, refusing to go near the Globe or even to go next door to talk to Ben. He completely engrossed himself in his new role of doting father and caring husband.

Melanie observed the change in his habits and had to admit he was doing everything he'd said he would. He pampered her constantly until she longed for him to go and play pool and give her the space she was accustomed to. She hinted that it wasn't fair on Ben to drop him like a stone and that she'd really be glad of a quiet night on her own to read but Tim was having none of it. His reckoning was along the lines of 'a little affection is good' so a lot of affection must be even better.

After spending five nights a week without Tim it was simply too much to have him in every night. On Tuesday evening she faced the realisation that she would not only be spending Wednesday evening in the Walnut Tree with Tim, but that he would probably press her for his reward when they arrived home.

She confronted him as he sat watching the early evening news. 'Tim, you are going round to Ben's right now, and you will take him to the Globe and play pool with him, OK! If you don't, then I'll go round and drag him down there and I'll play pool with him. So go ...now!'

Faced with such determination, Tim decided to do as he was told. Melanie breathed a sigh of relief, but it soon gave way to concern for what surprises the following day might bring. She knew she'd find out soon enough.

The morning started well and Roddy remarked that he

couldn't remember seeing her look so happy. He'd heard about her booked appearance at Rattani's seminar and was warm with his congratulations. 'I don't know how this guy found out about you', he said, 'but he's no fool to want you at his show. Good luck to you Mel, you deserve a break.' She was to remember his words more than once in the weeks ahead.

Four times she had dressed and undressed this morning, before finally deciding on the black trousers that caressed her backside like a glove, topped off with a pale pink silk blouse buttoned down the front in a way that flattered her 32B bust to perfection. The short, open, black jacket sat squarely on her shoulders, in sharp contrast to her top. Three inch heels helped make her legs look longer than they really were. The overall effect was stunning.

As Melanie followed the other delegates across the marble floored foyer of the Hilton Hotel her stomach was in knots. She made her way to the front of the conference room and sat almost dead centre in the front row. He did say, 'sit at the front' and this was as near the front as it was possible to get. Gradually the room filled up and she was pleased to see that the delegate sitting on her left was a woman, not a fat or unfashionable one but a very shapely and exceedingly well dressed one. After a few seconds a terrible thought crossed her mind, could this be Sharon ... his wife? Maybe she'd decided to hear her husband address the cream of local society at his Hilton debut seminar. No doubt she was very proud of him, why shouldn't she be?

When he appeared on stage she pushed her head down in a feeble attempt to hide. It was a pointless gesture as he had already focused on her, beaming at her with that fabulous smile she'd pictured a hundred times since the party. She glanced discreetly to her left and saw that Sharon was smiling back at him. Had he really invited her here simply to be humiliated? Was it too late to escape? A quick look round indicated that the doors had been closed at the back of the room. If she stood up now she would attract the attention of a hundred pairs of eyes, mostly male.

A Senior Partner from Nina's firm went to the lectern and introduced Ratty. "We are of course delighted that Rattani Naziree has chosen to join Osborne Melrose Law. He brings enormous experience and immense skill in technical matters of law. Rattani is going to talk to you for the next hour on the history and background to contract law and I'm sure you'll want to give him a very warm welcome." Without further prompting everyone in the room raised their hands to applaud the newcomer.

"Hello, good morning ...and welcome ...in that order." Ratty's huge smile lit up the room like a firework display. Another ripple of applause rang though the gathering. "In the short time that I have been with Osborne Melrose Law I have been tremendously impressed by the high standards maintained by my new colleagues. As you all know the firm is long established and has an excellent reputation. I am pleased that I will have the opportunity to represent some of you in the months ahead and I am delighted to be able to say that I have already started making friends with some of you." He looked straight at Melanie as he spoke.

There could be no mistake. His eyes were fixed on hers as firmly as an exocet missile locks on to its target. Well, she thought, if Sharon hasn't realised yet that he's talking to me then she soon will. Visions of a cat fight breaking out in the front row entered her head. She imagined Sharon tugging her hair out in bunches and screaming 'slapper' to her as the men around laughed and cheered. She recognised that it would be dangerous to turn and see what expression Sharon was wearing, but she also knew she couldn't stop herself.

Amazingly Sharon seemed quite happy and not at all put out at having to share him with the woman next to her. If he was my husband, I wouldn't sit here and watch him making eyes at another woman in front of half the town. But he isn't my husband, he's hers, I've got a husband. She hadn't heard a word Ratty had said in the last two minutes and she was meant to be assessing his performance as a speaker.

"Whenever I'm sitting where you are, waiting for the speaker to get started I wonder if I'm in for an hour of agony or sixty minutes of scintillating speech and fortunately, more often than not, I've been lucky enough to enjoy the latter. I've sat through some exhilarating speeches from master orators from many different backgrounds. One of the speeches that sticks in my mind was about the three minute rule, and this is how it went: The Three Minute Rule says that when you meet someone new you probably decide if you like them or not within three minutes. Actually he said, you more likely decide within thirty seconds. He also said that research has shown that Jury's have been asked when it was that they made up their minds about the guilt or innocence of the accused, and most of them said that they had decided within three minutes of seeing the accused, usually even before they had heard them speak. Now it's not yet three minutes but already I've decided I like every one of you and although I can't promise you a speech as good as those I've referred to I hope when you leave here today you will know a little more about the history of contract law than you do now. And most of all, I hope you will enjoy the experience." Again his soft smile shone down on his subjects. They loved it, their response was radiating around the room like an electric charge. It was pure magic.

This is cabaret, Melanie thought, I love it.

Ratty talked about Lord Denning, Master of the Rolls, Head of the Appeal Court and one of our most celebrated judges. "Today we accept it as normal that women should sit in our boardrooms and even lead political parties."

He looked straight at Melanie as he said, "We respect the women in our society as our equals in every sense of the word. Alas, it wasn't always so ... Lord Denning often spoke about the influence of the Church on canon law and later into common law and how two hundred years ago the legal existence of a woman was suspended during marriage. The husband was provided with the right under common law to keep her by force which meant that he could beat her as long as it wasn't in a violent or cruel way. The yardstick by which such force was deemed reasonable was that the stick used to beat her should not be thicker than the man's thumb. I wonder, is there anyone in this room would dare to agree with such a view today? ... No, I thought not."

"It wasn't until 1891 that the courts gave women the right to come and go as they pleased and this was as a result of a case where a husband took his wife prisoner after she had left him. Fortunately for the young woman, a writ of habeas corpus was brought and the court ordered her release. From that day forward it has never been in doubt that a man has no right to restrict his wife's liberty." Melanie found herself looking straight into Ratty's eyes. He has deliberately written his speech for me, she thought. He's sending me a clear message that I can see him if I so choose to.

"If we fast forward two hundred years to 1976 we can see how the law finally moved to protect battered wives with the Domestic Violence Act of that year. Not only that, but now a man's mistress was also able to receive the protection of the law through a mechanism now referred to as a 'common law wife'."

"Lord Denning was to take charge of a very famous case involving two young ladies who needed little protection; Christine Keeler and Mandy Rice Davies. Indeed it was the *government* that needed protection from *them*. I refer of course to the Profumo Case, a scandal which rocked the government in 1963 after the Secretary of State for War, Mr John Profumo, admitted having an affair with one of the girls. The affair forced the resignation of Profumo, and many people believe that it led to the resignation only weeks later of the Prime Minister, Harold Macmillan. Rumours at the time linked a number of senior officials to the girls, who can truly be said to have had a hand in writing the political history of that decade."

His ability to tell stories was like nothing Melanie had experienced before. Ratty had the complete attention of every ear in the room as he slipped one joke after another into his dialogue of fascinating but factual accounts of legal history.

Ratty moved into areas of law more akin to the daily business of most of the delegates gathered in the room. He explained the Anton Pillar order which, for the first time, allowed the courts to order the seizure of pirate tapes and records. He then explained Lord Denning's role in the origin of the Mareva injunction, which allowed creditors to seize assets which were almost certain to be disposed of contrary to the creditor's best interests, through the means of an interlocutory injunction.

Melanie was enjoying the history of English law and she was basking in the attention he was giving her, as time and again he aimed his smile directly at her. She was by now convinced that everyone in the room had noticed his declaration of affection for her. It was like they were having a private seminar, as if he was talking to her, and the rest of the people in the room were eavesdropping on them but still Sharon didn't seem concerned.

"Before I finish I want to tell you about another remarkable speaker I had the privilege of listening to and indeed meeting recently. His name is Khotsu Trinity. When I met him he was about to make his first public speech on his first ever trip outside his own country, Lesotho in Southern Africa. I talked with him for some time and was impressed by his humanity and sincerity, but when he began his speech I also realised that he was a gifted man with very special qualities."

"His role within the charity is to teach people in his country how to farm with one cow or one goat and to use the manure to nurture crops and to be self sufficient. We've all seen and read about poverty in Africa recently, thanks to the G8 concerts but you may not be aware that Lesotho has even more problems than most other African countries, and those problems have a strong connection with contract law. Many thousands of men from Lesotho worked in the South African gold mines, but they have recently been made redundant. Another ten thousand workers were employed in the rag trade, making clothes for the big brand names, names in fact that some of you are wearing today. But, the contracts to make these clothes offered little in the way of long term protection to the factories in Lesotho and when those brand owners found that they could get their clothes made for even less money by using lower paid labour in China they dumped their workers in Lesotho and left them to starve. If only the late Lord Denning could rule on such an unfair contract the outcome would be in no doubt, but sadly English law cannot help these people."

"Now I'm going to stop short of asking you to boycott these big brand names, although some of you might feel like doing so, but I am going to ask you to help me to raise a few pounds, here, today, for that charity. To get you started I am going to offer a full day of my time to any firm in return for a thousand pound cheque for the charity. I think you all know what a day of my time would cost if you had to pay Osborne Melrose Law, but this will be a day of my holiday so don't worry, they won't lose out." He said this with his usual smile, and to the obvious amusement of everyone in the room.

"Thank you sir." Ratty pointed to a man sat just behind Melanie. "Well, I didn't have to ask twice did I? Thank you. Can I ask others of you who would like to help this cause to write a cheque, or a pledge on the back of your business card will do just fine, and pass it to one of the staff members by the doors as you leave, and can I thank you all for being a great audience. I hope you have enjoyed my exploration into our legal past and I hope to have the privilege of working with many of you in the future. Thank you."

As Ratty closed his speech Melanie hurriedly looked at

her watch, convinced that less than half the allotted hour had passed. Not so, in fact Ratty had overrun by ten minutes.

The entire audience rose to their feet and gave Ratty a tumultuous round of applause. It was like he was the star of a West End show instead of a lawyer explaining legal history. They loved him, that was for sure, and so did she. Maybe it was the atmosphere of the crowded room coupled with the almost obscene knowledge that she had just had a very personal relationship with Ratty in front of a hundred people, one of whom was his wife, but she felt very much in need of some time alone with him!

As people started to trickle out she waited at the side of the stage in case he came down to speak to her. She tried not to make it too obvious and she never took her eyes off of Sharon. To her surprise Sharon was making her way towards the back of the hall and the exit. She certainly wasn't showing any interest in tackling her adversary. Melanie began to feel like the victor in a jousting contest. Her rival having been well beaten, was now slinking off to hide and lick her wounds, while she, Melanie Fisher, waited to claim her prize. When she took her eyes off of the retreating figure of Sharon, Ratty was standing beside her.

"Well, how did I do?"

"As if you don't know, Ratty," she said, "You were fantastic. I loved it, everybody loved it, you must have known from the response you got at the end just how well you'd done? I was really proud of you for raising money for those poor people in Lesotho, but did you really meet that man, the way you said?"

"Yes I did and I suppose if I'm honest I did think it went rather well. Are you ready for the lunch I promised you?"

"'There's no need now is there? You only wanted to take me to lunch so that I could tell you how well you'd done, but you know the answer to that, so I can head on back to work if you want."

"Is that what you want, Mel?"

Melanie didn't answer. Instead she turned slowly left and right on one foot and gripped her small pink handbag demurely, whilst looking at her shoes.

"You have just answered my question Mel. You couldn't bring yourself to say no, could you? I've thought of practically nothing else this week except Wednesday and lunch with you. I've just finished a talk which was entirely for you; even though those other people seemed to think I was talking to them. Why are you being like this…? Are you really so afraid to have lunch with me?"

"What is Sharon going to say about you taking me to lunch instead of her?"

"How do you know about Sharon? Oh of course… Nina. Melanie, do you know where Sharon is now?"

"Probably waiting for you outside I should imagine, that's the way she was heading."

"You've seen Sharon, have you?"

"You know I have, for God's sake, I was sitting next to her wasn't I?"

Ratty burst into laughter and put his hands around Melanie's waist. He pulled her towards him and pecked her nose with his lips. "You thought that woman was Sharon, my wife? …actually, my ex wife!"

"What, you mean she wasn't Sharon… and Sharon isn't still your wife? You've split up?"

"Yes, two years ago. We still speak to each other; we're

still friends ...at a distance. She's moved on; she'll probably marry again soon."

"And what about you, Ratty, have you moved on? Are you about to be married again?"

"I'd love to think so, but I haven't asked the girl in question yet."

His smile disarmed her as he lifted her two inches off the ground. She was experiencing something called happiness; happiness of a kind she had forgotten existed.

Ratty whispered in her ear, "I might ask her during lunch, but then again I might not, after all it's a bit soon ...don't you think, on our first date?"

She laughed happily at him.

Ratty had booked a window table, the best in the restaurant. It overlooked the river and part of the city with magnificent views of several church spires, as well as the park that led from the high street, near her office, down to the river. In the bright sunshine Melanie could see office workers taking their lunch breaks, spreading themselves out on the grass. It was like staring at a Lowry. Matchstick men and women scurrying around inside the picture frame of the window. It was quite the loveliest view of town she'd ever seen. She was enthralled, not for the first time today.

When Ratty spoke she was reawakened.

"The oysters here are quite special, I can recommend them."

"Aren't oysters an aphrodisiac?"

"So they say, but I doubt if the effect is so powerful that we will lose our self control here in the restaurant, do you?"

"No ...yes, I mean, yes I'd love to try the oysters."

"Then we'll both have them... maybe that will double their effect."

"Is that what you're really hoping for?"

"No, and yes, to use your words. No I don't intend to pressure you, but yes I would be less than honest if I said I didn't want to seduce you. But Melanie, every red blooded man between here and Land's End must feel the same."

"Well, none of them have mentioned it," she said sarcastically, "at least not lately."

He laughed at her. "That's what I love about you; you can keep me in order so easily. I admire that quality. You are in absolute control all of the time, I find that very attractive, as I do every other asset of yours."

"Have you been studying my assets, Ratty?"

"Possibly... but you weren't supposed to notice."

"Ratty... I know absolutely nothing about you. Can I ask you a question?"

"Of course, I would love you to interrogate me for hours. I want you to explore every detail of my past until you know me like you know your own hand, and then, when you have finished, I want to do the same to you. Is it a deal?"

"Well, I'm afraid it won't be for hours, I've got to get home early tonight, I've got something on this evening. She wished she hadn't mentioned that, in fact she wished she hadn't even thought about it."

"So, what is it you want to know Mel... please, I'm willing to tell you everything."

"Well, where did you come from? I mean where did your parents come from? Not England, not originally at least."

"Where do you think they came from?"

"I don't know, somewhere in Africa, Lesotho perhaps, or maybe India or Pakistan?"

"Well I'll tell you before you name every country in the

world, and anyway you were getting very close. I was born in London of Bangladeshi parents. I grew up in London and I met Sharon on a skiing holiday in France. I married her in London ten years ago when I was twenty-two and I divorced her there two years ago."

"That's quite unusual for a Muslim to divorce, isn't it?"

"Yes, it's unusual but not unique. Life is changing, for Muslims as for everyone."

"What do they do? Your parents... I mean your father; I assume he works in the City?"

Ratty laughed loudly and Melanie wondered what she had said to amuse him so.

"Yes, my father has worked in the City for years. They live in Brixton. He works at Brixton Bus Depot. He drives a number 159 bus up to Marble Arch every day." He was still laughing.

She smiled in surprise because she had assumed from his Eton accent that he was the son of a merchant banker or a QC. It was funny to imagine him as the son of a bus driver.

"Are you disappointed Mel, did you think I was the son of a warrior chief or something?"

They laughed together as they shared the oysters.

Melanie opted for Dover Sole as this would not lay too heavily on her stomach. She couldn't forget that this was only her first date of the day. In six hours time she had a dinner date with her husband. Ratty opted for the same main course as her. They were sharing an experience more intense than either had believed was possible.

"Where do you live now, Ratty?" Mel asked.

"If you lean out of this window and look about half a mile to the right you will see my apartment on the top floor of the new Quayside development overlooking the river, but I think its best you don't lean out so far because you may fall. It would be easier if I took you there and showed you it in person, maybe next time we meet?"

They made easy conversation until the coffee was served, when Mel glanced at her watch. It was a quarter past three. It was time to leave him, but just like last time she found every possible excuse to delay their parting.

It was Ratty who finally made the move. "Melanie, I have to return to my office to read some papers and file a defence before I can go home tonight, however I can't leave until I have extracted from you an agreement to meet me again, soon."

"Ratty, I feel like the accused in the witness box. Can you forget your legal speak and ask me properly?"

Fully a minute passed before Ratty uttered another word.

"Melanie, I think I'm falling in love with you. I realise you can't love me back and it's unfair of me to say such a thing, knowing as I do, that you're a married woman, but I can't pretend this time that I want to meet for any other reason than that I love being with you. Can I see you again, tomorrow or maybe the day after?"

It was Melanie's turn to be silent, shocked in fact.

"Ratty, I have it on reliable information that you have half the women in your office chasing madly after you. Young women, beautiful women, single women... I am eight years older than you, why me?"

"If I knew the answer to that, Melanie, I'd gladly tell you, but as yet my heart hasn't shared this secret with my head."

"Ratty, I should say no, I should thank you for lunch and leave now and yet I don't want to. You know I'm married, yet even so you may find what I'm about to tell you hard to believe. Tim and I have been married for eighteen years and he is the only man that I have ever slept with. For some strange reason I don't feel guilty for being with you, it seems so right, but I know I should be. You must accept that it can't go any further. If you really enjoy being with me, as I enjoy being with you then we can meet again, perhaps like today, but only as friends. Do you understand how difficult this is for me? After only two times together I have strong feelings for you, feelings that are not right. How am I supposed to feel when I go home to Tim, my husband? Tonight Tim is taking me out for a meal. I don't even want to go but he is trying hard to mend our relationship. We had a huge row a couple of weeks ago and we haven't been getting on very well since then. I'm feeling confused at the moment. I enjoy being with you, you can see that, but I can't betray Tim. He hasn't done anything wrong. He loves me and he loves our three children. You must see that I can never be anything to you; you're wasting your time with me. You'd be better to let me work things out with Tim and take out some of the girls Nina told me about, they're just waiting for you to invite them."

"Melanie, if it were that easy I would do as you ask. Since that evening at Nina's house you have never been out of my head for more than an hour, except when I sleep. When I wake up in the morning you are there, when I clean my teeth, when I eat my breakfast. All day long you pop in and out of my head. I am in love with you Melanie."

"But don't you see Ratty, you can't love me? I'm not free to love you back. You'll just end up hurting yourself. You may end up hurting me too."

"How can I hurt you Mel… unless, of course, you love me?"

"I didn't say I loved you. I can't love you. It's impossible, but I do like you… a lot. It would be better if we didn't see each other again and I think I should make this decision to save both of us from getting hurt."

"May I phone you Mel, at least you can talk to me can't you?"

"'OK, but that's all. You can phone during my lunch break, between one and two."

"Thanks."

They walked out into the sunshine together. Ratty gave Mel the kind of embrace usually reserved for old friends. They smiled at each other and then turned away to walk in opposite directions.

Five minutes later, Mel was back at her desk in the bank with her head still spinning. Roddy was the first to question her. 'How was your appointment Mel, did you do the bank proud, was the speech what you'd expected?'

'Yes Roddy, I think I did the bank proud and I think you could say it was a very good speech, but no, it certainly wasn't what I'd expected.'

CHAPTER FOUR

Melanie decided she would feel better if she changed her clothes completely before going on her date with Tim. It might ease her feelings of guilt for one thing. She found a white knee length dress which was drawn across from each shoulder to meet at her waist, a bit like an Indian sari. She knew it flattered her and she owed it to her husband to try to look her best tonight.

Tim arrived home especially early and was in the shower as she was preparing for their night out. He put on his best brown trousers and a cream open necked shirt with cuff links. She studied him briefly in her dressing table mirror. He looked smart but his clothes were in no way fashionable. Perhaps that was her fault, maybe she should insist on taking him shopping and helping him choose some decent clothes. Visions of Ratty filled her mind. She wouldn't have to show him how to buy clothes. His dress sense wanted for nothing despite being without a wife for two years. They were so different, Tim and Ratty. She sat staring into her dressing table mirror. Tim and Ratty, she said softly to herself, were there really two men in her life?

How could she be attracted to a man so different to the one with whom she'd shared the last twenty years. Had she changed that much? If this evening was to be a success, she had to put Ratty right out of her mind, yet that was like asking her to sacrifice a piece of herself, a piece that was growing day by day.

They went in Melanie's car, but Tim insisted on driving. He conceded that the van wasn't a great way to arrive at The Walnut Tree. She wondered if he was driving so that she could drink, or was it that he didn't trust her driving? She'd always expected him to drive when they went out together, but these days it was such a rare occurrence that she found herself resenting him for taking control.

The Italian Maitre de oozed charm from every pore of his body as he smiled softly and showed them to a table for two in a small alcove near the window. He leaned close to Melanie as he lit the candle and she enjoyed a hint of Chanel for men. He promised to send aux deuvres along with the menu. After taking their order for apéritifs he headed away to welcome another group of diners.

Melanie glanced out of the window, only to be gripped by panic as she saw a silver sports car park alongside her Mondeo. Was it an Aston Martin? She could ask Tim, he'd know what it was. There was no reason, outside her head, why she shouldn't ask, and anyway it would help to make some conversation, which they were desperately in need of in order to break the ice.

"Tim, what make is that car next to mine?"

"It's an Aston Martin DB7, she's a beauty, what I'd give to drive that for a day".

"You mean you'd swap your precious van for one of those? Surely not"! She was being sarcastic again and the poor bloke had only made a simple and quite reasonable remark. What the hell was wrong with her? She softened her sarcasm with forced laughter. "Tim, how would you carry all your tools in that?"

"He hadn't noticed that she was ridiculing him. He was happy, blissfully enjoying their evening out together."

"Well, perhaps I could tow a little trailer behind it for all my junk?" he joked.

She'd got away with that remark, but if this evening wasn't to end in disaster she had to start trying harder. The driver got out of the Aston and walked around to his passenger. He had his back towards her, but he was fairly tall and from this distance she couldn't be sure. Could it really be Ratty? What if he was eating at the next table to them? As he turned, her mind was on the woman he was escorting towards the entrance. Who the hell was she? As they got nearer she gave a sigh of relief as she saw that they were both complete strangers. Her heart resumed its normal rhythm. Her Dubonnet arrived along with Tim's beer. She picked up a menu and began to study it.

"I bet any money you'll have the prawn cocktail for starters." Tim said cheerfully.

"Actually I thought I'd have the whitebait, but you got the fish bit right! Let me guess what you're having... garlic mushrooms, yes?"

"Of course Mel, I always have garlic mushrooms, you know that."

"I know because you are totally predictable Tim, just don't ask for tomato ketchup or I promise you I'll get up and leave."

"If that's meant to be a joke, Mel, it's not funny. You seem a bit prickly tonight. What's wrong?"

"Well for one thing those trousers you're wearing. Look

around you Tim, look at the guy who's just walked in, look at his trousers and then look at yours. They are ten years out of date, they're the sort your Dad would wear."

"Christ Mel, I don't believe this. If you didn't want me to wear these then why didn't you say before we left home?"

"What was the choice Tim? Those or your bloody overalls I suppose. You don't take any pride in yourself any more. And what's that smell you've got on?"

"It's Brut, you know bloody well what it is."

"Yes Tim, I do and I expect everyone else in here knows as well. That's probably why he sat us in this corner and why everyone at that table is laughing."

"Why? What's wrong with Brut. You've always liked it up until now."

"No, I haven't liked it, Tim, I put up with it."

"Are you deliberately trying to spoil this night out Mel, because that's how it seems?"

"No, sorry I shouldn't have said that. Listen, tomorrow in my lunch break I'll go into Superdrug and get you a bottle of something decent, maybe Hugo Boss or even Chanel if you're lucky." She smiled in a valiant effort to get their conversation back on track. Why couldn't their relationship be normal any more?"

She began to quiz herself... what was normal? Sitting here in this beautiful restaurant with Tim wasn't normal. He should have booked them a table at the Queen's Arms. The food there was good and the prices were a quarter of what they were here. There he would have looked OK in his brown trousers and they could have gone in his van without looking out of place.

This would be a perfect place to dine with Ratty. He

would be completely at ease. She glanced towards the Maitre de, half expecting him to be looking at them and smirking. What Tim had succeeded in doing by insisting on bringing her here was to embarrass her. What if someone from the bank walked in? She thought about asking Tim to swap places with her, that way he would be less noticeable, but he'd go mad if she told him why she wanted to change seats.

"I'm going to the ladies," she said. She got up and made her way through the busy tables, among people who were clearly out to enjoy themselves. The noise in the restaurant was increasing, all from people having a good time. She washed her hands and dabbed her wet hands on her cheeks. "Sort yourself out Melanie," she said to herself, "...and go back to that table in a better state of mind. Be nice to him. Christ all he's done is take you out for a meal, a meal which is costing him half a week's wages and what have you done? Given him a bloody hard time ever since we got here."

After suitably admonishing herself, she slowly made her way back to their table.

She gave Tim a huge smile. He looked pleased.

"That's better, he said, for a few minutes just now I thought you weren't happy."

"I'm very happy Tim, and why shouldn't I be? I've got my gorgeous husband taking me to this fabulous restaurant and I've got three lovely children over at Mum's. I've got everything a woman could want." She hoped she sounded convincing.

The waiter arrived and she chose a pasta dish for her main course.

"Well, I've got to admit I got that wrong, I was sure you'd chose the Lemon Sole."

"I would normally Tim, but not twice in one day." Her heart missed a beat as she realised what she'd said.

"What d'you mean twice in one day? Tim looked nonplussed."

"I meant... what I meant was," she fought for time, time for her brain to extricate her from the failings of her mouth, "I didn't want fish again, you know after the whitebait."

He seemed satisfied and he ordered a fillet steak, well done.

They sat looking around, engaged at the sight of so many people enjoying the atmosphere, the laughter, the chatter and the sheer pleasure of each other's company. After several minutes they both spoke at once.

"No Tim, you go first. What I was going to say wasn't important."

"I was just going to ask if you'd had a good day."

"Yes I did. I went to a training course at the Hilton on contract law. The bank thinks I should know a bit more about it with the work I'm doing these days. It was fascinating. What about your day, Tim, tell me about what you did today."

"Why Mel? You wouldn't be interested, seriously... you wouldn't would you? I fixed an exhaust on one truck and did a full service on another. That can't really compare with your day, even I can see that. After twenty years it's hard to find anything interesting to say isn't it? I bet old Rodders from your place would have plenty to say, and if not he could always twirl his bow tie or stick his hands in his braces. I'm a mechanic, Mel, it's not exciting, in fact it's not even interesting. I sometimes wish I could do something else, something interesting like you do, but it's too late for that ... isn't it?"

"Tim, you're a good mechanic; skilled, experienced, and

really good at what you do. That's just as good as pushing figures around and doing all the stuff I do for the bank. It's just different, that's all."

"Mel, thanks for trying, but you're not even convincing yourself are you? My job is boring. I'm boring. You work with much more exciting people in the bank and you're fed up with me. I'm doing my best to be a better partner, that's what this was about tonight, but I'm a joke aren't I? My clothes aren't right; I don't have funny stories to tell about my work. Where do we go from here, Mel? I don't even know if I want you to tell me... because I might not want to hear what you're thinking."

Mel tried to cheer him up, but she recognised that, for once Tim had assessed the situation pretty much as it was. The awful truth was, he was right.

"Well, let me see, from here we go home. Then, tomorrow we get up and we do it all again. You go off to fix a few more lorries and I go and make a few more millions for the bank. Seriously, Tim, we can't change our jobs ... it's what we do, but maybe we could change our lives a bit. For a start we could book a holiday for when the kids break up. Let's be honest ...have you thought about what we're going to do in that six weeks? No, exactly, and nor have I. What did we do last year? A couple of day trips and running the kids to football events, music events, canoeing events. We did plenty of things with Nina and her kids, but how many of those did you come on? Hardly any, and why? You were always fixing someone's bloody car or else 'down-you-know-where' with 'you-know-who'. I'm going to book two weeks away somewhere. We are going to get right away from here and spend the time together, as a family, OK?"

"That'll be great Mel, I just hope I can get the time off, everyone else with kids will have booked the summer holidays so they might tell me I can't have it."

"Then tell them they can stick their job. I'm warning you Tim, I'm taking the kids away for two weeks with or without you. You'd better be with us, or else!"

"I'll fix it Mel, I'll fix it somehow, I promise."

They finished their meal and Tim paid the bill.

On the drive home they hardly spoke. Tim tried to evaluate tonight's success in terms of mending their marriage. All he had achieved was a huge bill and an ultimatum. What had he expected? At least she wanted him on holiday with her, with the kids, that was a plus. How would I feel now, he thought, if she'd said, "We're going on two weeks' holiday without you". No, looked at like that, tonight had been a great success. ... I'll have to get a few new togs though, just to keep her happy.

Mel was also analysing the night. A good meal in a good restaurant with a good man.... but no spark. He wasn't dressed right, he hadn't said anything that interested her, let alone excited her, and he hadn't exchanged eye contact or made her senses quiver. No, it had been a complete failure, a non-event. In fact her life was a failure, hadn't she said that to Nina only a few days ago. The only time her life was exciting was when she was with ... that's unfair she told herself. Life with the kids was still great, take last Sunday, when James got picked for that concert in London, that was exciting. It was just Tim, the time she spent with Tim was either boring, or they were rowing.

Tim let them into the house. "Would you like me to make you a drink, Mel?"

"No, I'm shattered Tim, it's been a long day. I'm going straight upstairs; I'll be asleep in five minutes. Her remark embraced a subtle warning to Tim not to get his hopes up."

He took his shoes off and shouted up the stairs to her, "OK love, I'll be up myself in two minutes."

"Don't bother," she muttered, under her breath.

Next door the Bowyer family had spent the evening on a war footing, as usual. Nina had accused Ben of being lazy and for good measure she'd added, shifty and worthless.

Ben had developed a hard crust of selective deafness, which filtered everything Nina uttered.

Her appraisal of his qualities went straight over his head as he made for the door on route to the Globe. Once there, he sat with the usual bunch of early evening drinkers, which tonight included Sophie, a blousy, well-padded girl who drove a parts van for a firm that supplied vehicle components. She sometimes took parts to Tim's haulage firm, so she knew him from work as well as from the pub, whereas Ben was just another regular at the bar. Sophie was a sociable creature by nature and one of the new breed of women, a twenty first century female, she was as happy in the company of a pub full of men as she was with the girls.

Her white T-shirt barely covered half her back and her low waisted jeans allowed her thong to spread its wings to public view. In the vast area between the two garments was a tattoo of a wasp, or was it a bee? Whatever it was she always warned 'would be' intruders that it stung, so look out! Her short, dark hair framed a face that was not unattractive. If Sophie had a weakness it was her lousy dress sense, but that appealed to some men.

Ben enjoyed her company, after all she was undemanding

and wasn't likely to criticise him for his many failings. Why should she, she didn't care if he had no job, no prospects, no income. He always stood her a pint of Stella, which made him a 'sound bloke' in her book.

"What's the latest with you, Ben, you got anything yet, cos if you haven't we got jobs down our place. I could get you a start tomorrow, one of our girls got the sack today, she pranged the van again. Fancy delivering car bits?"

"I fancy working with you Soph. Do I get to ride around with you all day or will I have to have a van of my own?"

"Bugger off Ben, I couldn't put up with you all day. Do you want me to get you in or not?"

"Well at least it would shut her up if I went back tonight with a job. Yeah, go on then, are you sure you can fix it?"

"I could ring Mick, my boss, now if you want? I know he's desperate and it'll be a tick in my book if I find someone quick for him, as long as you don't piss him about, Ben. You'd better bloody not, mind, or I'll mince you and send you back to your wife as cottage pie."

"You probably could Soph, you're a big girl. Go on … show me your muscles! He laughed at his attempt at a joke and was rewarded by a hard punch in the stomach, which winded him so he could hardly speak."

"Christ Sophie, that hurt", he said eventually, "I hope you don't intend to treat me like that every day if I come to work with you."

"That depends Ben, you muck up and I'll treat you worse than that, but if you do really well, then I'll just treat you… "

Ben was beaming from ear to ear. "Soph, I'm going to give this my best shot. Tell Mick I'm ready to start tomorrow morning."

Five minutes later, Ben was officially employed as a parts delivery driver. He returned home early to break the good news to Nina.

"I don't understand, Ben, you left here just over an hour ago with no career prospects in sight and now you're employed to deliver car parts? Has Jim put a Job Centre in the Globe?"

"No, but Sophie, you know, she plays in the darts team, I've told you about her before, she got me the job."

"Is this the same Sophie that swapped shirts with the captain of the other team when they won last season? That tart who took her top off in the bar? She's got you working with her now, has she? I thought you reached rock bottom Ben when you drove that laundry van, I didn't realise you could get still lower."

"I thought you'd be pleased. You've been telling me to show some initiative. She said they were a driver short and I said I'd do it."

"Ben, I don't care what you showed and I don't know what you said you'd do, but this had better be a proper job. I'm warning you I've have had more than enough. I hope you get my meaning Ben. This is your last chance."

Ben briefly thought about all the last chances she'd given him before, too many to count, but it didn't matter, because he intended to make a success of this job. None of the jobs he'd had up until now had the kind of prospects this job had. What was it Sophie had said? 'Make a good job of this and I'll treat you'. That was the kind of encouragement he'd been wanting for years.

Next morning he was out of bed early and spruced up for his first meeting with Mick, his new boss. Mick explained that they were a van short, thanks to yesterday's mishap, so Ben would have to double up with Sophie, but he also made it clear they'd have to cover both rounds until the replacement van arrived.

Sophie took Ben under her wing and showed him where all the regular drops were. They mostly went to the same garages and workshops each day, so knowing the locations meant that they could get the work done well within the day, even with the extra deliveries. Sophie revealed to him that the job was a 'piece of cake'. I could get all my drops done by eleven in the morning if I wanted, she said, but if Mick found out he'd just give me more, so I take my time and usually get back about half past three, just in time to load up for tomorrow.

One of their calls was to the yard where Tim worked. He was dumbfounded at the sight of Ben walking in with Sophie carrying the bits he'd phoned up for earlier. Explanations followed over a quickly arranged tea break. Ben relayed Nina's lack of enthusiasm for his new job. "That woman is never satisfied," he said, "I don't know what she expects." He turned to Sophie and between bouts of raucous laughter, "I've satisfied you, Sophie, haven't I?" then jumped back before she could land him another of her left jabs.

The day went well and Ben returned home just after six agreeably tired. For the first time in living memory he'd enjoyed going to work. This was going to be easy. Mick was a nice bloke, the work wasn't hard and Sophie made getting out of bed in the morning worthwhile.

Nina knocked the contented smile off his face in seconds. "So how was your day with that little tart? Did you get any work done? I see you're still wearing the same shirt as when you left this morning. Didn't you get her to swap, or did you swap back again later?"

"Actually, Nina, we've been flat out all day because we had to do double the normal number of drops. Mick's a van short, thanks to the bump that got me the job in the first place."

"I don't doubt for one minute that you and she have been 'flat out all day', in fact that is precisely what I was afraid of. I'd like to say I cared Ben, but truthfully, I'm not interested in your position either with Mick or, more often I imagine, with her. I'm going round to Melanie's tonight and I won't be cooking for you, so unless you've already shared a meal with her, as it seems you've shared just about everything else, then you'll have to eat at the pub. But then as she'll be there that should suit you fine."

"Anyone would think you don't trust me, Nina. Get a job you said, and that's what I did. You know you're trouble don't you ... you're never satisfied."

"Not by you, Ben, that's true, in fact you never spoke a truer word." With that she flounced out, intending to spend the rest of her evening next door with Melanie. She was disappointed to find that Mel was not alone. Tim was sitting in front of the television holding his cup of tea when Nina walked into the lounge, which made her feel a bit awkward. She wanted to share her problems with Melanie in private. Tim's presence was disconcerting to say the least, but she could hardly ask him to leave. Sensing her anxiety, Melanie came to her rescue.

"Tim, Neen and I would like to have a quiet evening in with a glass or two of wine, so that we can catch up on all the news, so why don't you take advantage of your good fortune and spend the evening at the Globe, with my blessing. I'm sure Ben would be happy to keep you company."

Seeing that protest was futile, Tim drank the last of his tea and picked up his jacket. As he closed the kitchen door he turned and addressed Melanie with a smile, "I won't be late, Mel."

"He means it too," she said. "He's trying so hard to please me, I feel sure I'll fall over him each time I turn around, Neen, he's driving me mad."

"Mel, I've got so much to tell you, I don't even know where to start". For the next hour she gave Melanie the sordid details, mostly from her imagination, of Ben's new job 'working for that tart Sophie from the Globe." Melanie did at one point suggest that Ben might have accepted the job in good faith in an effort to please her, but Nina wasn't prepared to consider that possibility. When Nina had exhausted her disgust with Ben, she remembered the most important news she wanted to share with Melanie. Her face lit up. "Mel, guess what ... I've got it, I've got the promotion I wanted. I am now officially in the team to support Stellar Haufman plc, and my new boss is none other than your good friend Rattani Naziree. Isn't that great!"

"That's brilliant news, Neen, I'm overjoyed for you, honest I am."

Nina looked at her for a few seconds, "You knew, didn't you ... you bloody knew, I can tell by your face. I expected you to be surprised, but you already knew. You knew before me. Bloody hell, Mel, was it pillow talk or what...? I'm sorry, I didn't mean that, but I can't believe he told you first."

"Neen, it slipped out accidentally when we were sitting together on your sofa that Friday night. He asked me not to say anything and I didn't. He was saying lovely things about you and how good you are at your job, which, if you remember, you asked him to do."

"So it was my fault, was it?"

"Of course not, but it was part of the praise he was pouring on you. As soon as he realised what he'd said he was sorry, and of course I had to keep his confidence."

Nina couldn't stay cross for long and, anyway, it was too big a triumph to let anything spoil it. Telling Melanie was the most enjoyable part of it in a way. It should have been wonderful sharing the news with her husband, but she hadn't even bothered to tell him. Mel, I really don't want him any more. I'm thinking of asking him to move out. After all, it isn't as if I need his money ... I've supported him for the last five years and the kids wouldn't care that much, and if they did, well ...I wouldn't stop them seeing him or anything. After all, I don't want him climbing on the balcony of Buckingham Palace in protest."

"Neen, think carefully before you take such a big step. It would change your life, it would change both your lives. How much thought have you given to it?"

"That's exactly what I'm hoping, Mel, I'm hoping it will change my life. At the moment my life outside of work is crap, so why shouldn't I want to change it?"

Melanie pondered over the irony that both people with whom she'd shared a sofa recently had divulged secrets to her. What was it about her that made people tell her things they wouldn't tell anyone else? Was it her or was it the sofa?

Knowing about Nina's intentions would sit heavily with her, after all her husband was Ben's best friend. If she didn't tell Tim, he would sooner or later accuse her of betraying him and if she did he would tell Ben, and then the shit would hit the fan, big time. For once she was trapped in a dichotomy not of her own making.

"Thanks Neen, I almost wish you hadn't told me. Tim'll go mad if he ever finds out I knew about this and said nothing. Anyway he'll know you talked to me before you told Ben. Oh, well sod Tim, if he gets upset about it too bad. After the shit night out he gave me yesterday, I'm buggered if I care."

"Last night wasn't a great success then ... not the highlight of your day?"

"Our meal at The Walnut Tree was a disaster. Tim looked like a bloody reject from Oxfam. He sat there munching overcooked steak like it was haut bloody cuisine. If I hadn't threatened him beforehand he would have covered it in tomato bloody ketchup. The waiters all looked at us as if we'd taken a wrong turning at McDonalds. The best part was when he got the bill ... you should have seen his face; he knew it wasn't going to be cheap but I was watching his expression as he picked it up. It was priceless. He was ready to protest, but he choked on the bloody mint. That was the only laugh I had all night."

"You are so hard on Tim, he's a great bloke compared to my lazy lump of lard, and don't forget that up until you met Ratbag, my loose lipped boss, you thought so too. Nina was in full flow now and beginning to slur her words. Melanie knew from evenings past that this would happen around her second or third bottle. They debated the respective qualities and failings of their husbands, but failed to reach agreement on which was the least attractive. As they neared the bottom of the fourth bottle they found it increasingly difficult to articulate clearly, but they reached an agreement. Both Tim and Ben were bastards who needed to be taught a lesson. They, after all, were intelligent, hard working women who had the right to deserve better. Nina made it back to her house with difficulty only to spend the night on the sofa, unable to make it up the stairs.

When Ben found her upon his return from the pub he tried waking her but she refused to co-operate and instead let loose a stream of expletives that were less than complimentary. Eventually he gave up the struggle to raise her and left her to sleep it off where she lay. She was awakened by the first rays of sunlight streaming in through the lounge window. With one hand raised to shield her eyes, she gradually regained consciousness. She tried making coffee but it was impossible in her condition. She dropped the milk saucepan before giving up. Ben came down at the sound of crashing utensils, intending to check on her well being, but he met with more abuse.

"Did you enjoy yourself last night with that slut from the pub? I hope you realise Ben that you've gone too far this time. We're finished, d'you hear me, I said we're finished.... it's over. I want you out. Out of here, do you understand? You want her, that's fine.... yes it is, it's fine with me, but don't think you can mess about with her and then come creeping back into this house when she's finished with you. Get your stuff and get out!"

Ben stood staring in disbelief at his dishevelled wife. He had never seen her so angry, nor for that matter so drunk. Nina could hold her drink normally, but this time she had over indulged to a point where she obviously didn't know what she was saying. He'd give her time to sober up and then try to reason with her. For a start, Sophie wasn't in the Globe last night... he hadn't seen her since they left work, which reminded him, he had to be there in an hour. There was no way that Nina would be fit for work today. He'd ring in and explain that she was unwell; after all it wasn't really a lie. He finished making the coffee that had caused her so much trouble and put a piece of toast alongside it next to where she was sitting, holding her head in both hands at the kitchen table. He looked at her and compared her to when they'd first met, all those years ago. She was still a good looking woman, she'd gained a few pounds, but she dressed well and outside of the bedroom no one would notice her extra weight. Her dark brown curly hair was still one of her best features, along with her strong classical features. Her dark brown eyes had once sparkled with affection, but nowadays they always flashed with anger. Either way they were beautiful, just a shame it couldn't be like the old days. OK, he admitted to himself, I've been a bit of a cad. I should have tried harder to hold down a decent job, but she always knew I was a bit of a lad, that's what she loved about me.

She lifted her head from her hands and stared at Ben as if she was having difficulty recognising him. This was no time for a sensible discussion about their problems, that would have to wait until tonight. No Globe tonight, he thought, this had to be sorted before it got any worse. Even Ben could see that things had reached an all time low. He got ready for work and slipped out quietly, leaving Nina gazing into space. He hoped she'd see sense.

When he and Sophie arrived mid-morning at Tim's yard they stopped again for a tea break. He told Tim, in front of Sophie, exactly what had gone on last night and before he'd left home this morning. It seemed necessary to beef up his side of the story, so as not to appear henpecked.

"When she'd finished telling me to get out, I gave her breakfast and told her to sober up. She accused me of having an affair with Sophie. I told her to get her brain examined. I said to her, Sophie and I are good mates for sure but we respect each other too much to take liberties, that's right isn't it Soph? There was no way she could drive into work. I phoned up and made excuses for her. She was so drunk she didn't know what she was saying. I told her I'd have a few things to say to her tonight, if she's sober by then."

Ben had hoped that Sophie would be indignant and she was. "Why did she say all those things about me? If she's jealous, that's her problem. She wants to look in the bloody mirror and see whose fault it is you don't want to spend all night with her bending your ear. Perhaps she should get her fat snobby ass down the Globe and try enjoying herself, then maybe she'd have a clue instead of being so bloody self righteous. I feel sorry for you, Ben. I don't know how you put up with all that nonsense, after all you are the man in the house, you deserve a bit of respect."

Tim listened in silence. He compared Nina's outburst to Mel's ultimatum of the night before. He might be the man in his house, but he knew he wasn't the head of the house. He'd lost that position somewhere along the way. He wasn't even confident that he was wanted any more. All this talk of women's equality was rubbish, women were running the world; certainly his world and poor Ben's too. Was it too late to stand up to them? He decided it was much too late for that. He went back to his work with a heavy heart.

Sophie refused to give up on the subject as they drove

around dropping off parts, and Ben revelled in her sympathy. He gave her every encouragement, until by mid-afternoon they'd reached an understanding in which Sophie would offer sanctuary to Ben if he got chucked out.

"Seriously Ben, I mean it, if that daft cow wife of yours tells you to get out when you go home tonight give her the fright of her life. Say, OK I'm off but don't think I'm gonna come crawling back when you want. I'll come back when you say you're sorry and you start treating me with a bit of respect. Then pack some stuff in an overnight bag and come round to mine. I'm not going out tonight. I'm staying in and washing my hair, saving my money for tomorrow night. I'm going out with the girls in town tomorrow night. Saturday night at the Ramp Club is brilliant, ever been there, Ben?"

"No Soph, a bit too young for me. Don't forget I've got more than ten years on you."

"You don't look old, Ben, and remember what they say about being as old as the woman you're feeling? Once you get in the Ramp and start dancing with some of my mates you'll feel at least ten years younger, no sweat."

Ben's head was filled with conflicting thoughts as the day wore on. He was nearing forty and his wife, who was a bit older than him, was giving him a seriously hard time. He was working with an attractive young woman who seemed to be saying that there was room in her life for him to shed a few years and start living again. He imagined himself as John Travolta dazzling all her mates with his gyrations on the dance floor. He conjured up images of young women asking him to take them out. He was still in this pleasant land of fantasy when he got home just after six. He walked in with a new air of confidence.

"Hi Neen, I hope you've sobered up since I left this morning. You were a mess, I think you know that, but I'll overlook it this time. What I find more difficult to excuse is the accusations you made against me and Sophie, who, for your information, is a decent girl and a damn good friend. I won't have you or anyone else speak about her the way you did this morning, so we'd better get that understood before we go any further." Looking into Nina's icy stare, his confidence began to wane. She didn't appear to be about to back down. In fact she looked like a bull about to charge. Maybe she could kill him with her bare hands. He stood rooted to the spot, not daring to encroach further into her space for fear of pushing her over the edge.

"How dare you! How dare you speak to me like that? How dare you even mention her name in my house? Your friend is she? Well get out and go to her, because you certainly aren't spending another night under this roof. Now get out!"

This wasn't going as well as he'd intended. She was supposed to shrink under the might of his authority; trouble was … she didn't recognise his authority. She was running this show and nothing had changed since he'd left this morning, except maybe for the worse. This left him with only one option. He would follow Sophie's advice, pack a few things and call her bluff. Maybe Nina wouldn't be quite so cocky when she saw he was actually going. Without another word he went upstairs and put his wash things together with a few pairs of pants and socks in a bag. He dragged a pair of jeans off the hanger and a couple of shirts. As an afterthought, he put in a dressy shirt which would look pretty good if he ended up at the Ramp Club tomorrow night. He was sure he wouldn't need it because he'd be back here tomorrow enjoying a making up session with Nina, once she came to terms with the fact that he was calling the shots. He left by the kitchen door whistling in an attempt to appear confident as he walked past her. "See you when you're sober and when you're ready to say sorry. Call me, OK?" He pulled the door to and left, quite pleased with himself, for Sophie's place.

Nina sat down at the kitchen table, shocked at what she'd just done, and shocked at his willingness to walk out on sixteen years of marriage. Was that all it meant to him? A couple of days spent with that little floozy and she'd lost him? Not that she cared, she didn't want him anyway. It just seemed so empty without his big frame taking up space around her at a time when she would normally be getting the evening meal. I'm being stupid, she thought, he hasn't been gone for five minutes and I'm missing him? As if! Yet deep inside, Nina had this niggling feeling that it wasn't quite the victory she'd thought it would be. She looked at the clock on the cooker. Too early to go round to Mel's. The kids had already had their meal, the housekeeper saw to that each evening before she left. They were upstairs doing homework, and by the time they'd finished it, it would be their bedtime. She'd go up now and kiss them goodnight, so that she could slip out in a while to go next door.

The children were intently discussing their father's words to them before he'd left the house. "What did Dad mean when he said he had to go away for a few days?" Gus was clearly concerned.

"It's this new job of his, love, he's got to do a long distance trip, but don't worry he'll be back before you can say, 'where's he gone'?" She hoped she sounded convincing. It seemed to satisfy Gus and the others didn't ask any more questions. She left them to get on and retreated downstairs. At a quarter to seven she couldn't wait any longer. She quietly crept out of the back door and made her way round to Mel's kitchen.

"Come in Neen, I'm almost finished clearing up after feeding my lot. Had a good day?"

One look at Nina's face told Mel she hadn't, and no doubt she would hear all about it in the next hour or two. "Neen, I'm not going to touch any wine tonight. God I don't know how I got to work this morning. I went in an hour late, told Sam the Office Manager that I had women's problems. When I got in the lift to go up to my office my head started spinning again and I did almost no work before lunch. I'm strictly teetotal tonight. What about you?"

"Well, I think I might need a drink. In fact, you might when I tell you what I've done. I didn't go in at all today; It was all I could do to stand this morning. Ben phoned in and said I was bad and I rang in at lunch time because I was supposed to be working on the first job Ratty had given me for Stellar Haufman. Good bloody start that was wasn't it? He must be well impressed. First day and I let him down. He's probably regretting giving me the job already. Luckily he was out when I rang, but I'll have to face him tomorrow. I don't know what to tell him."

"Tell him the truth Neen, he already knows anyway."

"How can he know? No one knows how pissed we were last night, except Ben and I heard him phone in. He just said I wasn't well. The only other person who knew what a state I was in was you.... Oh no, not again Mel. You have ...haven't you? You've bloody told him I got pissed and was too drunk to get to work on my first day in my new position. Great, absolutely bloody great. So, am I fired? What have you two decided? Wait a minute... when did you tell him this, have you seen him today?"

"Neen, when he was out to lunch he was with me. He called me and asked me to meet him in the wine bar on the quay and then he took me up to see his apartment in that new Quayside development. Oh, you should see it Neen, it's like something on one of those TV shows. You can't even begin to imagine how fabulous it is."

"Well I'm not likely to get an invite now am I? Why, why did you have to tell him? Come on Mel, you're my best friend and I feel like you've shitted on me. Why?"

"Neen, I haven't done any such thing. I told him how Ben was upsetting you, he was very sympathetic, I also told him how fed up I am with Tim. I told him about that stupid evening at The Walnut Tree and how Tim showed me up. I said we were both feeling pretty low because of our partners and how we had got a bit drunk together. I actually said it was my fault. I told him you were just helping to sort me out and my problems. He was fine about it, he said he'd do anything he could to help, either of us I mean. Neen, he is the most genuine person I've ever met. He couldn't be unkind if he tried. You've nothing to worry about, trust me. He was very concerned about me and about my being unhappy. He said I can go to his apartment any time, night or day, if I need to talk to him. He said he'll be there for me, no pressure, just a shoulder to cry on. I *can* talk to him, that's the funny thing; I can talk to him so easily, in a way I never talk to Tim. Why?"

"We were at his place for over two hours and I had to make another excuse when I got back to work, bearing in mind I was late getting in in the first place. Ratty is a great listener, he put his arms round me and held me. I felt as if all my problems had dissolved. He has this wonderful effect on me. He only has to put his arms around me and I'm relaxed, totally."

"So what happened then, Mel, you stood there for two hours like that?"

"No, not exactly."

"So exactly how did you stand?"

"We didn't stand."

"Jesus, Mel, you haven't slept with him?"

"No, I haven't, but we did sit in his big chair together... "

"That must have been very uncomfortable. Only got one chair has he?"

"Of course not, all he did was comfort me... he's so good at that, honestly... Tim would never snuggle me up the way Ratty did. He's a good friend and the way my head is lately I need a friend. It's lucky we met that night."

"Lucky for him... lucky bastard. I'm not sure I want to work for him after all. I can see what he's going to be like. I said he was beautiful, didn't I. There's going to be knickers all over his office floor... young girls from every department crying their eyes out as he casts them aside for the next one, and to think I actually fancied him. Mel you've been daft, but you can put this right if you stop now. Tell Mr Romeo Rattani tomorrow that it's over. Tell him you love your husband. That his affections caught you unaware in a moment of weakness brought on by the stress and anxiety of a problem in your marriage. Say you are willing to forgive him for taking advantage of the situation and that you trust he will have the decency to protect your good name, so that you can restore your marriage to its former status. Got that Mel? Tell him over the phone, but make sure no one's listening and then forget all about him. You've had a very close thing there, but thank god you've seen sense before it's too late. Tim is a wonderful man, Mel, he doesn't deserve this. You'd better hope he never finds out."

"Neen, I'm seeing Ratty again, tomorrow lunch time. I can't help it; honest, I know what I'm doing. I think I want him more than I want anything else."

"What a mess we're in... I've got no man and you've got two. Ben's got that overweight trollop from the pub, you've got my boss and all I've got is a bloody headache from last night. The funny thing is, Mel, I'm missing Ben. I can't believe it either, but I am. I'm frightened Mel, what if I've driven him off for good? I know I want him back. I can't go to bed tonight and stare at his pillow, knowing he's with her. I don't want to spend the rest of my life on my own".

With that, Nina broke down and cried. Mel put her arm around her best friend and in seconds she was crying too. What had they done?

CHAPTER FIVE

As Ben drove towards Sophie's flat he thought only about the consequences if she refused to let him in. It was a possibility after all. Had she been serious when she invited him to stay with her? The thought of returning home in less than an hour was pretty grim and would result in a serious loss of face, from which he could never hope to recover in the eyes of his wife. If Nina thought he was a 'waste of space' now, what would she say when she knew that, not only did she not want him, nor did anyone else. No, the idea of going back home tonight was out of the question. Sophie was more than a little surprised to see him at her door clutching his overnight bag, but he hardly needed to explain. "Come on then, come on in," she said in her usual cheerful manner. Ben followed her into the flat, trying to take in as much detail as he could without overtly invading her privacy. It was clear that the one bedroom flat wasn't the tidiest place on earth, but it was scrupulously clean.

She indicated with her left hand. "That's my bedroom and opposite is the bathroom. Through here is my lounge diner and at the back my kitchen. In short Ben, everything I need. Stick your bag down there and I'll get you a cup of tea. You'd better tell me exactly what's happened."

Ben related word for word the verbal exchange with his

wife which had resulted in him being here, in her armchair, in her flat. He took comfort from her sincerity and from her willingness to listen, but he couldn't help feeling that he was an intrusion in the organised chaos that was her life. Her clothes lay everywhere, a bra on the back of the settee and jeans and socks on the floor. One shoe lay in the middle of the room waiting to be reunited with its other half. There was a personal feel to this domain that was entirely different from the home he was used to. In his house everyone had their own room where items of clothing might be left lying about, but in the rest of the house, in the shared areas like the lounge, that would never happen. Although Sophie didn't seem in the slightest concerned at his intrusion, he felt distinctly uneasy. This wasn't how he'd imagined moving in with Sophie would be when she'd thrown the invitation his way earlier that day. She returned from the kitchen grasping two mugs of tea and offered him one. She sat down on the sofa and looked him straight in the face.

"Well Ben, do you think you can sleep on this OK? It's not as good as a bed, I know, but it'll do until she lets you back into your own little love shack".

Ben's mind was in turmoil. He'd walked out on his wife to live with the girl he worked with. But truth was dawning speedily and with startling reality. He had read more into her invitation than she'd ever intended. He was a guest, offered the sofa as a temporary respite from the war zone that he'd just escaped from. Was she waiting for him to make the first move? Would she think him wet if he stayed under her roof for a few nights without making a move on her? It might even be rude, like saying I don't fancy you, sorry, I don't mind shacking up in your lounge on your sofa, but sleep with you? No thanks.

"Sophie, I'm a bit confused right at this moment and I need to know where I stand. You're a hell of a good looking girl and you must have realised I fancy you rotten. I've just walked out of a heavy relationship that ended a long time ago. How long do you want me to sleep on your sofa? What I mean is how long is a respectable time before I can move my stuff into your room?"

Sophie burst out laughing. She certainly wasn't offended by anything he'd said and that could only be good. He waited for her to set out the timetable for their future together.

"Ben, you are a big oaf. I can see why she gets her hair off with you, but don't worry, I'm not about to scream and shout at you. Right, here's the way it's going to work."

Ben sat forward, leaning on his knees, his posture one of concentration, glued to her every word. This was what he had been waiting for, a guide to how married men glide effortlessly from the scorn of an angry wife into the bosom of a young and single woman.

"You are going to sleep on this sofa and eat at that table. Eat, that is, anything you make yourself in that kitchen through there. Once you've eaten you're going to wash up all your plates and saucepans and hang them up where you found them. I'm going to sleep in my room and we are going to share the bathroom. If you see me dashing about in the morning in nothing more than my knickers it's just because I'm in a rush and I've forgotten you're here. Just ignore me. As for moving into my room, Ben, that isn't going to happen. I have dozens of friends, Ben, lots of them crash out here from time to time, but I don't sleep around. You may think I'm an easy lay and it's obvious your wife thinks so, but that's probably because deep down she has no morals herself. I'm sorry to have to disappoint you, Ben. We're mates and I'll give you a roof while she's refusing to do so, but I won't be providing any home comforts of the kind you are missing already by the sound of it. Sorry, but those are the rules, Ben. Now make yourself at home."

Ben watched her disappear towards her room, harvesting items of clothing as she went. This wasn't turning out quite as he'd expected. He looked down at his six foot frame and compared it to the sofa. Any hope of sleep on that was futile. An hour or two maybe, if he was lucky. A good night's sleep? No, it wasn't possible. A sudden fear grabbed him as he realised he'd walked out of a lovely home where he had every comfort, well, except the love of a good woman, and into a flat where he was to be permitted to snatch some sleep on the sofa and make himself a snack, provided he accepted the role of kitchen porter into the bargain. The things that had initially attracted him to this move were turning into vapour. He couldn't stay here long, or he'd end up a hunch back, a very tired hunch back. He wondered if it was worth pointing out to Sophie the comparative dimensions of her sofa and his body. Maybe later. He turned on the TV and stared at the screen in a trance of bewilderment. He returned over and over to the moment when he'd issued his declaration to Nina. Perhaps I was a bit hasty, he thought; maybe I could give her a second chance. Her words resounded in his ears; he knew it was him who needed the second chance. Who was he kidding? He'd never been in control of this situation. All he'd done was make it easy for Nina to chuck him out. Getting back in would be much harder if not impossible. If he just turned up with his little bag of belongings she would probably refuse to let him over the threshold. She might have even changed the locks. God, how the tit tats in the street would love that; that bloody woman in pink two doors down who never missed a thing. She'd see him struggling to get his key in the door and then watch him turn away as it didn't fit. The whole street would be laughing in five minutes once they knew that he was a refugee. The situation was beginning to look bleak. He glanced at his watch, he hadn't been gone two hours and already he was sinking fast. Perhaps Nina was right, maybe he was useless, a waste of space. Is this how men start on the road to becoming a tramp, he thought? He pictured himself a year from now, a long beard, unwashed, and carrying the little bag, by then in tatters, and preparing to sleep under a hedge. Ben you're in a bit of a fix mate, he said to himself. Better sort this out and quick!

Sophie came out of the bathroom wearing a towel around her head and another wrapped around her bust, tucked in to keep it up. It wasn't long enough to cover her thighs and he couldn't resist sneaking a look at what she had already declared as forbidden territory, before turning away, frightened that she would see what he was up to.

"Do you have any plans for tonight?" she said, as if reading his mind.

"Well, I might go over to the Globe and talk to Tim. I'm in new territory here, Soph. I'm not sure what happens next."

"Just take your time and don't go back there bashing the door down or anything. That's just gonna make it worse, OK?"

"I won't, I'll think long and hard before I go and talk to Nina. At this moment I wouldn't know what to say to her."

He got up and headed for the door.

"Ben, wait, I'll get you a key. That way you won't have to wake me when you come in."

Half an hour later he was perched on a bar stool alongside his best friend.

"I don't understand Ben, what do you mean, she threw you out? Look at you, you'd take a lot of throwing out of anywhere, and Nina is a lady after all. If you left, you must have done it on your own two feet. What really happened?"

For the second time in two hours, Ben related the details of his row with Nina.

At the end of his story he owned up to having misunderstood Sophie's invite. Tim, I'm just crashing down there. I thought she was inviting me, well properly, but she's made it clear that her room is right out of bounds. I'm a good foot longer than that bloody sofa, Tim, how the hell can I sleep on that? I've screwed up again, out of the fire and straight into the bloody frying pan. Do you think Nina would listen to you? She's always holding you up as a paragon of virtue; why can't you get a proper job like Tim? Why can't you do this like Tim? Why can't you do that like Tim? Are you really so good Tim? I bet Mel doesn't think so." He smiled at the irony of their wives' views on their relative merits.

"I don't know, Ben, about Nina listening to me. I'll try, of course, but you know what'll happen as soon as she opens the front door. I'll get a list of all the things you've done wrong in the last twelve months and then get told to piss off. I'll be like a Christian to the lions. Do you really think it's a good idea? What if I just make matters worse?"

"Well I don't see how that's possible, frankly, Tim. I mean, I'm chucked out of my own house, sleeping on a sofa in a flat with a gorgeous bird who insists on keeping a wall between us. How much worse can it get?"

"OK, I'll see what I can do, but I'll have to tell Mel what I'm planning to do otherwise I'll end up upsetting her again and we're not exactly top drawer ourselves at the moment. I feel like a bloody tight rope walker with two women just itching to see me fall from a great height. It's Saturday tomorrow. I'm not working so I'll be around all day. I'm going to do a few jobs to keep Mel happy and I'm going to tag along wherever the kids are going, you know, violins, recorders, dancing, canoeing. You name it, I'm going to be there, right by her side. I'm a caring, doting father from now on. You should try it Ben, it might be better than sending me in as your envoy."

"Yes, but I can't dote or care if I'm not even allowed back in, can I? Please Tim, go round and talk to her tomorrow and tell her I'm not having an affair with Sophie, unfortunately ...so would it be all right if I came back. He laughed at the hopelessness of his situation. Tell her I intend to dote and care and point out to her all my good qualities. She's got to be reasonable about this after all."

Tim laughed at his friend. "Remind me again, Ben, what are your good qualities?"

"It's not funny Tim; I had a vision earlier of me, a year from now sleeping rough, like a tramp. Ring me as soon as you've spoken to her, please, and if she says I can go back tell her I'll pack up my stuff at Sophie's in two minutes and be on my way."

"I'll do my best, Ben, but don't expect a miracle."

On the walk home from the Globe, Tim examined the situation surrounding him. His wife was barely talking to him and his best mate had just got himself thrown out of his wife's best friend's marriage. Somehow he was expected to sort all this out, even though he rated a pretty low score with his own wife and probably a lot less with Ben's wife. To his surprise Melanie greeted him warmly as he walked into the lounge, where she was sitting alone.

"Nina's just gone back round. I suppose Ben's told you what he did?"

"Do you mean about Nina throwing him out?"

"That's just like you Tim; you're both bloody chauvinist pigs. He insulted her, he humiliated her with that hussy from the pub and now he's walked out on her, after all she's done for him."

"Well that's not quite the story Ben's telling me Mel. There are two sides to every story, right?"

"Right! ...Ben's and the truth."

"That woman is beside herself, Tim, I've had her crying most of the evening. She's crying for her husband who's walked out on her and for the kids who've lost the day to day contact they had with their father. He's an irresponsible shit and if you don't want to upset me still further don't come in here preaching his side of the story, or how hard done by he is."

"Mel, I'm not taking sides, I just want to get them back together. Ben is desperate to get back if Nina will just let him. He's not having an affair with Sophie, she is simply letting him stay at hers tonight, but he's on the sofa, Mel. He's asked me to try to talk to Nina. What do you think I should do?"

"Talk to her if you want, but if you think she's going to just say, OK he can come back, I think your dreaming. She was already fed up with him before he took off with that girl. Nina is convinced that Sophie is a trophy hunter and wants Ben as a notch on her bedpost. Once she's succeeded she'll throw him back to Nina, but there is no way she'll ever have him back then."

"Well I'm just glad I've got you, Mel. You know I'd never look at another woman, don't you?"

"Yes Tim, we make a lovely couple, right?"

Tim wondered why the look on her face didn't correspond with what she'd just said. It was so difficult to understand her. Even after twenty years she was a mystery to him more often than not.

Saturday morning started sunny again. Tim waited until just after ten before deciding it was now or never. He went around to the back door and knocked, before opening it just enough to call out, "Nina, are you about?"

Nina appeared from the lounge, surprised to see Tim holding the door open. "Come in Tim," she said, "I suppose you've come with news of my husband?"

"Yes, Nina, he's asked me to come and talk to you. He's told me pretty much everything and he wants you to know exactly what is happening. He's hoping that you'll let him come back."

Nina didn't say anything as she led him into the lounge and sat down. She motioned for Tim to sit and he did so. Nina had a way of making you feel like a client meeting the lawyer to discuss your case, he decided. She could be quite intimidating and she left Tim in no doubt as to who would control this exchange. They sat staring at each other. Tim waited for her to say he could begin but she remained silent. She was practised at interviewing people and she was accomplished in the court room. She was as good as any man at dragging evidence from reluctant, sometimes hostile witnesses. She wasn't about to capitulate to Tim's efforts to relate Ben's rather sordid little story.

He stuttered his introduction to his recital of Ben's unfortunate fall from grace. "You see Nina, he wanted to show you that he isn't weak. He knows you don't respect him and he thought that by just laying down and pretending to be dead when you were attacking him, you would lose what little respect you had left for him. He tried to be strong and to stand up to you, but now he wishes he hadn't. He knows he's just made things worse."

"So he's told you that I was attacking him, has he?"

"Well, I don't know if he used the word attacking, but he said you were pretty angry when you threw him out."

"Tim, you are an intelligent man, I've always thought of you as a lot brighter than my husband and certainly more capable, capable of working hard, thinking hard and using reason to work out what is right and what isn't. For example, I could never imagine you behaving in such a course or lewd manner towards Melanie as Ben has done to me. How, therefore, do you deduce that I threw Ben out of this house? Isn't it obvious to you that Ben left this house of his own free will?"

Tim could see where this was heading. She would destroy every argument he put forward in Ben's favour, logically, one by one, before finally throwing him out as well. This was going to be humiliating, and then to cap her victory she would tell Mel how she had made mincemeat of him.

"I said as much to Ben, Nina. I agree he went of his own accord but I'm trying to explain why. You made it impossible for him to stay and at the same time retain his dignity. What was he to do?"

"Tim, Ben doesn't have any dignity to retain.

Nevertheless, he could have behaved properly. He could have got a decent job like you. He could have held onto any one of a dozen jobs that he's had in the way that you have held onto your job year in and year out. He could have said no to that little tart from the pub who enticed him to go and 'work' if that's what they do, together, and finally he could have stood his ground and made some resolutions, some statement of his intention to be different. I warned him that this was his last chance."

"Nina, you need to know that Ben is not in any kind of relationship with Sophie, no matter what you may think of her. Yes, she's a bit... I suppose you could say common, but she has a good heart and she's taken Ben in like she would a sparrow with a broken wing. He's sleeping on her sofa. He told me himself, that she made that very clear when he turned up at her door."

"Tim, you are a much more sensible person than Ben will ever be, and definitely more sensitive. Surely you can see that no woman would tolerate what Ben has put me through in the last few days, let alone the last three years. Since we moved here, at the same time as you, how many jobs has Ben had and lost?"

"I don't know Neen, quite a few. Some of them he lost through his own fault, he would be the first to admit that, but some of them have been lousy jobs, jobs no one could hold down. If you give him another chance I can help him to get a job you'll find acceptable and I can help him to keep it. In fact Neen, I'll let you into a secret, one I haven't told Ben yet, mainly because the time hasn't been right, but there's a job going at our place; storeman. It's not brain surgery, but it pays quite well, the hours are normal and I would be able to keep an eye on him. If you'll take him back, Neen, I'll convince him to go for the job and I'll talk my boss into offering it to Ben. Then all I'll have to do is make sure he doesn't bugger it up, because if he does he'll make me look pretty stupid as well, but I don't think he will. He wants to be back here with you, Neen, and if you give him this chance I know we can pull it off, that is, he can pull it off with my help."

"Tim, you are a good man. Ben doesn't deserve a friend like you. I don't know what you see in him, but clearly you see some quality that I have yet to discover. I'll do it for you, because *you've* asked me to and Ben had better understand that it's only thanks to you that I'm taking him back. But can you also tell him that he'll need to be a very different man from the one who walked out of here two days ago. I don't need him financially, Tim, and if I can be brutally honest at a very personal level, he's not very good in bed. He's just about average as a father and he's less than reliable in all other matters of importance. He couldn't organise anything and he is not particularly good company. Can't you see, Tim, why I don't love him anymore?" Nina had lost her cocky court room attitude and was now slumped forward in a dejected manner.

"Neen, you know deep down you love him, you've spent all those years together, just like Mel and I have. You can't not love him, he's the father of your children and he's been in your life for that long, you know how it is, you're just going through a sticky patch, a bit like Mel and me. She moans about everything I do, it's never good enough for her, but I try to do my best. Do you know the other night I took her to The Walnut Tree? We had the most amazing meal and it cost me a fortune, but I was chuffed to bits to take her there. All she did was spoil it. She set out to spoil it from the moment we arrived there until the moment we got home. At one point she even said she didn't like my trousers and she used that as an excuse to get at me. I sometimes think she doesn't love me anymore, but then I think of all we've been through together and I realise she can't stop loving me any more than I could stop loving her."

Nina looked at Tim and started to cry. "Why is it so hard, Tim, to stay happy with someone? You do your best for Mel, but it's never enough. I've carried Ben for years but still he doesn't make any effort to please me". She got up and went to grab the box of tissues. Tim reached to get them for her and they collided. Nina reached out to stop herself falling and in doing so put her hand on Tim's chest. In the same second he put his arms out to break her fall. They ended up in a bear hug, but instead of breaking away in an instant they held on to each other. Nina put her head onto his shoulder and wept like a child. Tim put his arms around her waist and held her tight. He experienced a wonderful feeling of being needed, something he hadn't experienced in a long time.

They clung to each other with enormous compassion, one friend to another. After a few minutes of comforting they pulled away and looked at each other. "Thank you Tim she said, you are a lovely man. I just wish Ben could be more like you."

Tim made ready to leave. As he neared the kitchen door he turned and, with arms outstretched, reached for Nina again. She responded as friends do before a lengthy parting, but Tim only lived next door.

The next few days kept Tim busy as first he tackled his boss about employing Ben and then, with this arrangement secured, set about selling the idea to Ben.

"But I really love my job with Mick, and you know I'm pretty good at it. For once I've got a job I like and she wants me to give it up."

"Ben, you don't have a choice, not if you want to get back inside your own house again. I've arranged for you to start at my place as storeman. I can keep an eye on you and help you a bit. I don't want you messing up, because if you do it'll look bad for me. I'm trusting you to do well at it, OK? If you do this I've got Nina to promise that she'll have you back, but she did say you've got to change. What you need to do is send her a nice bunch of flowers, send them to her work, she'll like that, and everyone will see what a great husband she's got. That'll be worth a few brownie points and then you get cleaned up, get a haircut, do like Mel tells me to do, get some new clothes and a bottle of men's perfume and then whoosh, you're in. Back in the loving arms of your wife. You're a lucky man, Ben, do you know that? Nina's a great woman, if you just treat her properly. Not like Mel, who doesn't appreciate all the things I try to do for her."

Ben looked puzzled that Tim could even suggest that Nina was a great woman. "She's a monster more like. You don't know her, Tim, she is as hard as nails. She doesn't have a soft side, like Mel. She's like a stick of rock with 'hard' written all the way through".

Tim knew that wasn't true but it was pointless arguing with him.

"So do we have a deal? Can I go back and tell her you'll do it?"

"Couldn't you go back and try to negotiate a bit more, Tim, get her to let me keep my parts delivery job. You told her I'm not screwing Sophie, what more does she want?"

"Ben, I'm losing my patience with you. I've got the best deal from Nina that I could get. Now I'll either go back and tell her you'll take it or I'll go back and tell her I failed. Which do you want me to do?"

"Well, if you won't help me, then I've got no choice have I? I'll just have to chuck in the best job I've had in years to become a bloody storeman. I just hope I don't die of boredom."

"Do you know, Ben, you are an ungrateful bastard! I think Nina's probably right about you."

"I know you don't mean that, so you'd better go round to Nina and fix it up for me. I'll have to work my week's notice though. Give me a ring and tell me when it's OK to come back. Cheers Tim, I owe you a pint."

Tim looked at him in disbelief.

"So that's it, Neen, he's agreed to everything and I've fixed it with my boss for him to start as soon as he's worked out his notice at Mick's place. He's promised to change his ways. Look out for some surprises, Neen. I think you might have a few shocks to come from Ben."

"He doesn't move back in here, Tim, until he's out of that job and away from her, even though I accept that you are telling me the truth that they're not sleeping together. If I didn't, well you know I wouldn't even be discussing him coming back."

As Tim left, he gave Nina a big hug. She clung on to him for a few seconds and, with her head tucked in close to his shoulder, she whispered, "Thanks Tim."

He went home feeling elated. He had been more successful in mending Ben's relationship than he had ever thought possible. If he could do that for someone else's marriage, surely he could do it for his own.

Mel listened to his account of his efforts to get Nina and Ben living under the same roof again, tutting repeatedly at Ben's crass refusal to grasp the situation. "It's as if you just fixed his car, instead of fixing his marriage," she said. "Doesn't he realise how close he came to losing Nina?"

"No, he thinks he can balls up his marriage completely and then just get me to go round and sort it out. Honest Mel, you should have heard the way he said, 'I owe you a pint'. It was as if I'd just given him a lift to the pub or something. I sometimes think Nina is right about Ben. Even though he's my mate, I have to admit he's a bit of a burk."

For once they were in total agreement on a marriage in difficulty. If I could just swing this conversation around to our problems, this might be a good time to sort out our own marriage he thought.

"Mel, helping Nina and Ben has made me think about us, and particularly about me. There are some similarities aren't there? Like Nina, you're a clever woman with a top job, and you seem pretty fed up with me, sometimes... I mean, can we... can I learn anything from this, anything that will help us to get back to where we were just weeks ago?"

"Tim, there's nothing wrong with our marriage ... I'm just a bit stressed, that's all. You're OK, honest, take no notice of me."

With that Mel strode off to gather up kids and instruments for a music practice. To Tim it seemed that she had simply dismissed him, she was unwilling even to allow time to discuss their problems. How could she say there were no problems when she was refusing to make love, and endlessly finding fault with him? At least Nina had been willing to listen to him, how the hell could he ever get to sort this out if Mel wouldn't sit down and discuss it?

"I'll come with you and the kids, where are we off to? Are we going to eat out like you did last time?"

"Tim, there's no point in you dragging along, honestly, it's only a practice and you'll be bored silly. I shall be sitting talking to the other mums that I've got to know and you'll just wish you hadn't come. Do whatever it is you do on Saturdays and we'll see you later. We'll be back by five. I'll cook something for us when I get back. See you later."

With that she was gone, following James and Amy out to her car, without any attempt to kiss him goodbye. He stood in the kitchen for several minutes after they'd gone, trying to work out why it had all gone so wrong from the plan he had. He had intended, even wanted, to go with them, he'd told her all week that he was going to spend the weekend doing whatever they were doing and yet she'd pushed him to one side. He hadn't stood a chance. What to do next was beyond him. He strolled out into the front garden as if expecting to find them still there, but only the scent of the roses was there to console him.

"Not going with them again today, Tim?" He looked up to see Nina standing six feet from him on her side of the fence.

"It would seem not, although I wanted to, Neen. She just refused to let me go with her. I can't understand what's happening in this house. I feel like I'm her lodger instead of her husband. Neen, you probably know her better than anyone, even better than me these days, I'm ashamed to say. What can I do? What's going on? She's bound to have said something to you about the way she feels, just like Ben and I talk about these things. Please Neen, tell me what she's thinking. If you don't help me there's no one else I can turn to."

"Tim, I was about to make myself a coffee. Come round and I'll make us both one."

They sat in Nina's immaculate lounge, her on the settee and Tim in the armchair. They sipped at their coffee and made small talk about the hot weather.

"Nina, you know more about what's going on in Mel's head than you're letting on, don't you? Can't you see that my only chance of getting this mess sorted out is if I know what she's thinking?"

Oh no it isn't, Nina thought! If you really knew what was going on in Mel's head, and not just in her head, you'd probably kill her. She knew he needed help, but how could she help him when she was keeping a secret that would destroy their marriage completely if it got out. Thanks Mel, you've put me in a difficult position now for sure.

"Look Tim, you're a super bloke, you've helped me a lot, and you've proved what a good friend you are to Ben. I will always be there for you, Tim, just as I know you will be for me if I need you, but I can't tell you what's going on in Mel's head. I'm not sure I even know myself, but I do know that she's in a mess right now. What you need to work out is, what can you do to sort her out... right? Tim, if I knew, I promise I'd tell you, but I think maybe this is one of those things Mel has to work out for herself. Be kind to her, don't be afraid to tell her you love her, take care of all the little things that you know annoy her, but I don't know if that will be enough. You see I don't think you are the problem."

"Nina, if I'm not the problem, who is.... it's me she's fed up with, it's me she's horrible to every time I get near her. She's fine with the kids, there's no one else it can be. It has to be me."

If only that were true, Nina thought, I can't tell him any more, I've said too much already. This poor man is desperate to make her happy and she's got her head full of that Rat from work. She looked at Tim with pity, certain that he could see by her face that she was holding back on him. He looked so sad she wished she could do more for him, the situation was so unfair.

"Tell you what, Tim, I'm going to the garden centre to get a few things, why don't you come with me and then if I buy something heavy you can carry it for me. What I really mean is it would be better than sitting around here being miserable until they come back this afternoon, wouldn't it?"

"I'd like that, Neen, like you say I'll go mad if I sit around here all day on my own. Give me five minutes to get changed and I'll be with you, we can go in my van if you've got anything dirty to get."

"No, but thanks," she said, with a grin, "The Lexus will do just fine, and anyway I need to stop off at a couple of shops on route, you can help me choose a sun hat."

He smiled at the thought of her riding in his van. "You're right, we'll go in style."

Nina tried on twenty sun hats before she found one she liked. They laughed at a huge straw boater that would have looked good for punting on the river. In the end she settled for one that Tim chose, a pretty basic Nike cap, the sort a mechanic might wear. He told her she looked good in it and she believed him. After two hours of strolling around the garden centre on one of the hottest days of the year they were both exhausted. In the garden cafe they shared a plate of huge scones with jam and cream and a pot of tea. She looked at her watch. "Do you realize, Tim, it's three o'clock, we'd better be getting back if you want to be there before Mel and the kids get back."

"Actually, Neen … I do, what I mean is, I want to be there when she gets back. Would you mind if we don't say anything about being out all day together. I've really enjoyed today, if I'm honest, much more than I would have enjoyed being at James's music practice, but in the present mood I don't think it's a good idea to let her know that, do you?"

"You're right, Tim. We'll say nothing to anyone. This has been our little treat, and I want you to know I've enjoyed it too, really enjoyed it. You are such a good friend, Tim; I understand now why Ben finds it so hard to stay in with me at night when he can be at the pub with you."

She laughed happily and got up to leave. There was an awkward silence in the Lexus as they drove home. Their awareness of how much they'd enjoyed their time together shopping was intensified by the sharing of a secret. It made it difficult to know what else to say. As she pulled up on her drive she turned towards him, "Thanks, Tim, and remember, not a word, OK?"

"Our secret, Neen …thanks a lot for today."

The meal that Melanie cooked was nothing special, and despite what she'd said earlier the kids had eaten in McDonalds. Judging by the way she pushed her chicken around the plate he guessed she had as well. When it came right down to it he was really eating on his own, something that caused him enormous disappointment after her promising that they would eat together tonight. This was obviously one more attempt to put distance between them. He was less than half way through his meal when she pushed her plate away, her food barely touched. He couldn't take any more.

"So, not only can you not bear to sleep with me anymore but now you can't bear to eat with me either, is that it?"

"What are you going on about; I'm just not very hungry."

"I can see that, but why, after you promised me we'd eat together tonight, why did you have to go and eat in bloody McDonalds?"

"Because, Tim, the kids were starving, that's why, and are you telling me you haven't eaten anything today?"

"What do you mean by that?" he replied, rather quicker than he should have.

"Oh, touched a nerve have I? ...What I meant was, I expect you've eaten something too, but clearly there's something else I don't know about."

He was in a state of panic now. She could read him like a book and she would know instantly if he lied. He had to change the subject. "Mel, Why couldn't you just have waited so we could all eat together, that's all I was saying."

She stood up from the table and carried her almost full plate to the kitchen. With his hunger now ruined, he too stood up and followed her, putting his plate next to hers on the kitchen side. He tried to take her in his arms. He needed to hold her, to express his feelings for her, to experience the feelings he knew she must have for him. Instead of putting her arms around him she stood statue like in the middle of the kitchen. His embrace was not reciprocated and after a minute or two he let her go. She sank from his arms and turned away without a word to head upstairs. He felt totally deserted, it was like she'd left him, yet she was still here. He could see her, touch her, talk to her, he just couldn't reach her. He needed her to talk to him, to let him know she still cared. A moment later he stormed up the stairs after her into the bedroom, where they both stood looking at each other. That he was suffering was obvious.

"This can't go on Mel; you're hurting me like mad. I need to know what you're thinking. Please will you talk to me?"

"I can't Tim. No one can see what's going on inside my head at the moment. I'm sorry, I told you weeks ago that I was in crisis but you didn't believe me. Now you can see it, maybe you *will* believe me."

"I never disbelieved, you Mel, I just didn't understand. I still don't understand, but I do want to help. Please don't shut me out. I want to be a part of your life ... but lately I feel like you don't care if I'm here or not."

"Tim, people change. You think I'm still the same girl I was when we got married, but I'm not! We've both changed a lot since then. Maybe we are no longer as right for each other as we used to be. You must consider that as a possibility."

"Tim's eyes were filling up. She was trying to tell him it was over. He had never seriously considered that this was a possibility. Now it was happening and nothing he could say was likely to change her mind.

CHAPTER SIX

At the flat, Sophie's preparations for Saturday's clubbing night with her mates were in full swing. Ben watched with interest as she pranced about in a seemingly endless ritual of painting her face and swapping clothes. Each change of outfit resulted in Sophie wearing less than before, until she finally appeared satisfied with her choice. Could you call a small piece of white cotton which barely covered her breasts and a nine inch lime green mini skirt an outfit? Ben calculated that they covered no more of her than her shoes and handbag. He was shocked that Sophie could contemplate going out so uncovered, but she talked endlessly about her friends, who she was sure would be wearing even less than her. This aroused him sufficiently to tag along as she suggested. Given that his only other option was to sit in the flat all night with only the television for company, it wasn't a difficult choice.

His worry was that once inside the club she would disappear with her friends, leaving him to drink alchopops for hours on his own. Sophie assured him that her friends would want to meet him and that he'd have a fabulous time, but she expressed horror at his Levi jeans and Umbro top. "We need to make you a bit more dressy", she said, and with her kitchen scissors proceeded to cut holes in his clothes. She ripped the cuts so that his knees and chest were exposed.

Ben watched in shocked silence as she destroyed his clothes. He was experiencing a subdued and scary detachment from reality. She justified her actions by explaining that they probably wouldn't let him in looking like he did before she'd smartened him up, making him look like a regular clubber.

Feeling more like a scarecrow than a clubber, Ben followed her to the bus stop praying that he wouldn't see anyone who knew him. As the bus neared town, two of Sophie's girl friends got on and she introduced him. They looked him up and down briefly before proceeding to ignore him. His forebodings of a dreadful night to come were already materialising.

Standing in the queue for Ramps night club was a humiliating experience made worse by yet more of Sophie's friends effervescing around her, saying little or nothing to him as they chattered incessantly about people they knew and events that had occurred since last Saturday. Ben barely understood their jargon, but he translated occasional glances in his direction as astonishment at his appearance. They were probably wondering why he was here, but then so was he. He sidled along beside them, anxious to get into the darkness of the night club, where hopefully he would be invisible. He could then prop himself up at the bar and watch them dance.

The next two hours were pretty much as he'd expected, alternating between the bar and a balcony table where he sat alone watching his new friends gyrating wildly to deafeningly loud music. At midnight he squinted at his watch in the gloom of his corner. Minutes later one of Sophie's friends slumped down beside him without warning.

"I'm Beckie," she announced, before going on to explain

that after eight hours on her feet at the sandwich shop she couldn't dance any more. To Ben's immense surprise their conversation lasted for over an hour. He mentioned in passing that he was crashing out at Sophie's place, taking great care to avoid any mention of the mess that was his marriage. Sophie appeared several times in an effort to get Beckie back on the dance floor, but to no avail. Having exhausted their small talk, Beckie asked Ben a question for which he was completely unprepared; "Ben, do you want to come back to my place?"

Not wanting his new friendship to end as suddenly as it had begun he readily agreed and in seconds they were outside waiting for a taxi. Throughout the journey she clung to him as if they knew each other. She found the key and led him up the communal staircase to her flat. Once inside she kicked off her shoes and it was soon evident that her invitation extended to her bed as well as to her flat.

As the morning light shone in through the bedroom window, Ben lay there reflecting on how he'd come to be here. Steadily climbing out of bed, he stood up to his full height and stared at the attractive body lying naked except for the sheet pulled up to her waist. Either she hadn't noticed, or maybe she didn't mind, that he was fifteen years older than her and when he woke her with a coffee she was every bit as friendly as the night before. Had she been so drunk that she couldn't see him for what he was? Standing there in his ridiculous ripped jeans and with his t-shirt in shreds, he resembled a shipwrecked mariner. He certainly felt all at sea; he was to all intents and purposes shipwrecked... from a life which just weeks before had been orderly and predictable. He'd just spent two nights in two different flats with two different girls. This was a lifestyle he'd dreamt about in his late teens, a dream denied him then. Now, married and with three children, the dream was being fulfilled, but was it honestly a dream or was it a nightmare?

What should he do? Should he leave now or should he stay long enough to say sorry to Beckie for taking advantage of her when he knew she'd had too much to drink. Before he could reach a decision she sat up smiling and announced that they would be heading into town this evening for a concert on the Quayside, where one of her favourite bands was on stage. Not wanting to face Sophie and having no other options, he decided to go along with her plans. After a lazy day spent lounging around in the flat he once again prepared for a night out in his 'clubbing gear'.

Some of her friends from last night were there but thankfully Sophie didn't show. Beckie introduced him as if they were a couple and so gradually he began to believe that they were. After feasting on chicken and chips from a cardboard box they headed back to her flat for a second night. In the taxi Beckie decided Ben couldn't go any longer without a change of clothes. A quick instruction to the driver and they were off in the direction of Sophie's flat. "We'll get your stuff," she explained, "and then we'll go back to mine and have a DVD and a few cans."

He liked the way she organised him, she obviously didn't see any need for consultation. He'd never been a decision maker anyway, so that suited him perfectly. Sophie was surprised to see them together on her doorstep, but she offered no objection when Beckie explained the purpose of their visit. She watched with amusement as they gathered Ben's few possessions into his travel bag and left holding hands, convinced that neither of them had thought beyond the next twelve hours, but perhaps that was for the best. Back in Beckie's flat, Ben chose a DVD in preparation for a relaxing night but Beckie had changed her mind.

"Ben, what happened to your marriage?"

"How do you mean?"

"Look Ben, whatever you may think, I'm not stupid, OK? Even without the white mark on your third finger any woman would know you're married. I don't mind that but I think you should tell me what happened, especially as how I've taken on her role in bed."

"Say what you mean Beckie, why don't you..."

"Right Ben, if you want to share my bed again tonight you'd better start talking, OK? Did she throw you out because you hit her or did you screw her best mate?"

"I didn't do anything. Actually that was precisely what she accused me of, not doing anything. She's got this stupid idea in her head that I'm lazy, can you believe that? I mean, I'm creative, and that's my trouble, creative people often get mistaken for lazy."

"So what have you created?"

"What d'yu mean ... d'yu want a list or something?"

"No, just tell me one thing that you created."

Seeing no logical way out of this Ben decided to humour her. "Well I created a right balls up at the laundry when I delivered the towels to the wrong hotel" he quipped.

"Beckie laughed at his ineptitude but seemed satisfied. Secretly, she decided his wife was probably right, he probably was lazy, but he was good fun to be with and that was all she wanted."

Once in bed both of them forgot everything else until

the alarm went off at seven the next morning. Over a coffee Beckie asked him if he was coming back after work.

"I guess so," he said, "I'd rather be here than with Nina – that's her name by the way."

"But what about your kids? Don't you miss them?"

"Not really, Nina took them everywhere, did everything with them, it'll be weeks before they even notice I'm not there."

"So you were a lazy husband *and* a shit father? What have I landed here Ben? Not much of a bargain, that's for certain."

"Not true, Beckie. For you I could work my ass off and I could even pay my share of the rent."

"Is that some kind of a proposal Ben?"

"Yea, I propose we shack up until we get fed up with each other."

"OK, Ben, but no messing about. If I find you're screwing your wife or anyone else you're out of here so fast your feet won't touch the stairs on the way down."

"No sweat, Beckie, I'm a one woman man. You'll see."

The strange thing was, he meant it. He was enjoying Beckie, both in bed and out of it. She was full of life, full of fun, she didn't expect miracles from him and she took care to organise everything. She was very young, not long out of her teens, great for his ego, not that Ben ever lacked self-esteem.

After dropping Beckie at the sandwich shop on route to work, he had time to think about the job Tim had arranged for him as storeman. Stuff that, he decided, I'm happy working for Mick and now I don't have to please Nina I can do what I want. Mick had given him his own patch so he didn't get to call at Tim's place any more, which was a shame. He wasn't likely to be in the Globe for a while with Beckie planning his evenings. He'd miss seeing Tim, but Beckie more than compensated. In fact he couldn't remember a time when he'd been happier.

He thought back to when Nina had given birth to their first child ...wasn't that the happiest moment of his life? Supposedly it should have been, but he could barely remember it now. Was he even there? Funny how time softens the memory, even of important things. Guilt consumed him momentarily as he thought about other things he couldn't recall, like their wedding day, what her dress was like, what colour the bridesmaids dresses were. Surely most men wouldn't remember these things, so was he any different?

A nagging doubt crept in as he thought of Tim, he'd remember every detail of his wedding day. He'd have been with Mel through every minute of the births of their three children. The voice inside Ben's head refused to leave him alone, forcing him to argue fiercely in an attempt to defend himself. Why should I beat myself up over things that took place years ago? After all it was Nina who chucked me out, it isn't my fault I had to sleep at Sophie's place, and if I hadn't been there I wouldn't have met Beckie. No, this is all Nina's fault, he reasoned, she's got no one to blame but herself. Feeling better now he'd shifted the cloud of guilt to his errant wife he turned on the radio and sang along with it. His life was on the up, he'd landed on his feet with Beckie. As long as he didn't muck her about, they had a steady relationship, which suited him fine. There was a perverse pleasure in the knowledge that Nina had done him a favour when she'd sentenced him to the miserable fate of a lonely existence without her. It was mid morning when Tim called him.

"Ben, where the hell have you been? You haven't been in the Globe for days and your mobile's been on answerphone. Nina's going mad. You've got some serious explaining to do matey, I've tried to keep her calm but you need to get round there and grovel a bit... but ... the good news is... she'll have you back provided you say you're sorry and promise not to mess her about again. Let me know what time tonight you'll be there, I'll go round first to warn her so she's expecting you... all right?"

"Can't make it tonight, Tim, sorry, in fact I can't make it any night. Nina threw *me* out Tim, if you recall... well, I'm doing all right, in fact I'm very happy and I think Beckie is more to my style than Nina."

"Ben, what the hell are you going on about? Who's Beckie?"

"She's a friend of mine Tim, in fact we live together and we've got big plans for the future, well... Beckie has and I'm happy to go along with whatever she wants."

"Ben, have you had an accident? Are you suffering memory loss or something? There's a woman called Nina who lives next door to me and she's got three kids ... your kids. Stop being a prat and get round there tonight and sort this out before she comes looking for you, because if she does, you really will have an accident. Where did this Beckie spring from anyway, I've never heard you mention her before?"

"Met her when I was out clubbing the other night. We're living at her place in town until we can find something better. Tim, can you tell your boss thanks, but no thanks? I won't be needing that storeman's job now. Beckie's fine with me working for Mick and Sophie's her mate so she's OK with her as well. How are things with you Tim? Hello... Tim, can you hear me? Hello... sod him, he's hung up on me."

When Tim got home from work he was still angry with Ben.

"Do you know what he's done, Mel? He's only gone and shacked up with some friend of Sophie's, a girl called Beckie... reckons he's not coming back... what am I going to tell Nina? She thinks I'm sorting him out with a job and that he's coming home with his tail between his legs."

Mel was every bit as scornful as he'd expected, "Sound's to me like he's got his tail between *her* legs, whoever Beckie is. You'd better get round there after you've eaten and explain to Nina that you've cocked it up".

"What do you mean, *I've* cocked it up? It's Ben who's screwed it up, not me. I've had to go in to my boss and explain that Ben isn't taking that storeman's job... that made me look pretty stupid. I don't need this any more than Nina does. She'll go berserk when I tell her what he said. Do you think I should leave it for a few days? Maybe it'll all blow over with this Beckie and he'll come running back."

"And what if it doesn't, how are you going to explain that you forgot to tell her that you knew he was living with this Beckie and that he told you he wasn't coming back? You don't have a choice Tim, but you're right about one thing, she'll go mad when you tell her."

"Mel, do you think this might sound better coming from you?"

"Tim, this isn't going to sound better coming from anyone! He's your mate... you tell her."

At precisely seven o'clock, Tim knocked on next door's kitchen door and gently pushed it open.

"You there, Nina?"

"Oh hi, Tim, come in, you've some news on my truanting husband I hope? Do you want a cup of tea, I'm just making one?"

"Thanks, that'll be good... Neen, that's why I'm here, to tell you the latest on Ben."

"Go in the lounge, I'll bring the tea in." It sounded like a command.

Tim sat waiting as Nina poured the boiling water onto the tea bags. He heard the spoon clink on the cup as she stirred in the milk. She came in smiling and held out a mug to him. He could only delay this by a few more seconds at most. He sipped the hot tea and looked at her. Her expression was one of anticipation as she prepared herself for news of the imminent return of her man. She gave him a soft smile as she waited patiently for him to start.

"Neen... it's not good news about Ben I'm afraid."

"Don't tell me... he's lost that job you got him already?"

"No, it's not that Neen, he didn't take the job, he's still driving the parts van for Mick."

"But you said he'd pack that in, you said he would do it for *me*, like I asked... why hasn't he?"

"Neen, please don't get angry, he's met a girl called Beckie and he's staying with her in town. I phoned him today, otherwise I wouldn't know any of this. I haven't seen him for days. It seems he met her in a club and... and... I don't know what he intends to do now."

"Tim, what did he say? Did he say he's not coming home? Is that it, he's left me for this Beckie? Oh my god,

Tim, please tell me it isn't true. I really am alone now; he's never coming back now is he?"

"Neen, you know Ben, give it a few days and it'll all fizzle out. He'll come crawling back, begging forgiveness and in a few weeks you'll both be fine again."

"Tim, you know that's not true."

Nina stood up and clutched at the kitchen door, pushing her forehead into her arm to hide the tears that rolled down her face. She was whimpering pitifully and that upset Tim.

He instinctively went to her and put his arm around her shoulder, gently prising her from her hold on the door. She let him turn her until she was facing him, and he pulled her head into his shoulder. His arms surrounded her waist to stop her crumpling before him. She was weeping for something that was almost certainly over. Tim gently moved her, taking her head in both hands he held her like a child. Her eyes were filled with sorrow and in a desperate effort to stop her crying he pulled her face close to his.

He couldn't bear to see her like this, but then Tim couldn't bear to see anyone unhappy. With her wet face pressed tightly to his she was in his charge now, unable to do anything for herself. She was like a child, completely reliant on Tim to get her through the trauma she was facing. He pulled her body close to him as he cradled her head. He tasted the tears that were now wetting his face as well as hers and he became aware of his own desire to protect her, to make her better. There was something very good about the feeling that came from fulfilling the intimate needs of another human being. She needed his tenderness at this moment and he gave it, unconditionally. He gave her strength, injected from his body to hers by an abstract force he couldn't understand or explain. It charged them both with a burst of emotional energy.

Time was of no consequence. What was important was that he was sharing a physical experience with a woman who, until now, had barely been a friend. She was allowing him to nestle her body into his, submitting to his control. How strange that he should have so much power over Nina when at home he had no emotional influence with his own wife. When she was unhappy she pushed him away, demonstrating she didn't need him, making it clear that his attempts to caress and care for her were neither helpful nor appreciated.

Why then, was Nina absorbing his kindness so readily? Why was it that the woman of his best friend could accept his arms so willingly, surrendering herself completely to his protection? With Nina he was achieving the ultimate role of manhood, the way he imagined it should be, as he wanted it to be. In this jungle that was life, he was fending off the evil that was hurting her; he was taking on the role of her defender. She was willingly allowing him to take total responsibility for her well being. He was happy with this, after all this was the role he'd sought to provide in his own marriage since the beginning, but which had been rejected so often of late. leaving him to feel rejected and unwanted.

If he was giving Nina inner strength right now it was nothing to what she was giving him. His self esteem had spiralled overnight. He would be her counsellor, friend and protector with a willingness fuelled by deep feelings within, feelings he could not describe but which rewarded him with a pleasure greater than anything he could remember. He was caring for Nina because her husband had abandoned her.

He had picked her up from where Ben had cast her down. How could Ben leave his wife for a girl he'd known just a few days? Tim felt the warmth of Nina's body through his shirt. He didn't know how long he'd been holding her but he had no desire to let her go. Gently holding her face he moved her until just a few inches separated them. They stared into each other's eyes, unsure of how they had arrived here. Slowly he closed the gap until his lips met with hers. He was ashamed of what he was doing; frightened that her gratitude would turn to anger but instead of pushing him away she opened her mouth willing his tongue to touch hers.

Slowly they explored each other's bodies as if expecting to find something previously unknown but what they found excited them in a way neither of them had known in years. It was like the first time all over again, as neither of them had felt the hot flush of sexual gratification in a long long time. It was impossible to tear away now that it was engulfing them. They gave themselves willingly to what was inevitable, gradually Nina's tears of sorrow turned to tears of joy. They held each other tightly as they made their way upstairs and neither saw anything except the other. For two hours they pressed every inch of their bodies into each other in an outpouring of love and affection which required to be constantly re-consumated through more and more contact. They excitedly pulled at each other and gave themselves unreservedly. It was half past nine when Nina finally released Tim sufficiently to whisper, "You must go home, Mel will be wondering why you have been so long."

Tim pulled her to him once more and kissed every inch of her face before conceding to the inevitable. He would have to leave her. As they pulled on their clothes they still held on to each other. The feelings that had been aroused tonight were too strong to walk away from without pain and suffering. They made their way downstairs and stood together in the kitchen. Every minute now seemed worth stealing and they held each other a while longer as they readied themselves for the inevitable parting. They had hardly said a word since they had first consumed each other, but they both had a head full of things that needed to be said. Tim spoke first.

"Nina, please don't think badly of me after I leave. I couldn't help what happened tonight and I'm not sorry for what we did. In fact I'm happier at this moment than I have been in a long, long time. I've discovered myself tonight ... you gave me your body with more love than I could ever have imagined possible. This can't end when I walk out that door Nina ...please tell me that you aren't angry at what we've done".

"You know how it was Tim, I could hardly pretend that I didn't enjoy this evening could I? But think about our circumstances. Mel is my best friend. We may have feelings for each other but we can't do this again. We can't Tim, I shall feel terrible about this when I see Mel tomorrow, but I promise you I will never say a word. Thanks Tim, thanks for making me whole again. You've mended my broken heart and my broken body. I shall love you as a friend forever after tonight. Go now before I start to cry again. She softly pushed him out of the door and into the garden, holding onto him just long enough for them to exchange one last kiss before he disappeared out of sight.

Tim was glad that Mel was busy upstairs with the children; hopefully she wouldn't notice how long he'd been.

He put the television on and tried to feign interest in the programme ready for when she came down, but his head was full of what had happened next door. It seemed unreal, impossible even that when he had left this house almost three hours ago he could claim one hundred per cent fidelity to his wife and now he was an adulterer, but much worse than that, he had made love to his wife's best friend, and his best friend's wife.

On a scale of one to ten he had scored top marks as a bad husband and a shit friend. Yet he still felt secretly pleased with himself and his desire to return to next door was overwhelming. "Why don't I feel guilty?" he asked himself. If justification were all that was needed to absolve him from blame it was easy, his wife was treating him like shit and his best friend was bonking some girl he'd only known a few days. Why then, shouldn't he and Nina console each other like two old friends? Well, for a start Nina had never been very friendly to him, seeing him as an extension of Ben most of the time. The dichotomy was about to split his head when Mel's voice made him jump.

"Well, what did she say?"

He turned to where she was standing and gave her a scared look.

"Tim, what is wrong with you? For the third time, what did she say? You look awful... is she all right?"

"Sorry, I didn't hear you come in. Yes, she's fine... everything's OK."

Melanie looked amazed. "How can she be fine? You've just told her that her husband has left her for a younger model and yet, everything's fine. You've been round there for hours; will you please tell me exactly what she said?"

"Well, I can't remember exactly but she cried quite a lot and I tried to tell her not to worry. I said he'd probably come back in a while when he was fed up with Beckie and that seemed to satisfy her."

"Tim, you're hopeless... you've left her upset and miserable haven't you? I'm going round there to see how she is. I daresay you watched football on her TV while she was crying her eyes out, probably distraught. Who knows what she might do? I'd better go and pick up the pieces. I should have known you'd only make things worse."

"No, don't go round Mel, honest she's fine... all you'll do is start her off again. She was fine when I left. I think she's accepted that it's over and she's ready to move on."

"Well I'll see for myself, I'm not going to abandon my best friend when she needs me most, that's for certain, and with that Mel left by the kitchen door."

There wasn't time to ring Nina and warn her. She wasn't going to be expecting a visit from Mel so soon after what had just happened. What if she broke down and confessed everything? Mel would come storming back screaming at him and this time he would be the one getting thrown out. Should he go up and start packing? No, he'd go up and spend the next few minutes with the kids; after all he might not be seeing them for weeks if Mel barred him from the house. He tried talking to James about his forthcoming London concert, but he quickly realised that he was the only one who didn't already know what had been arranged. He kissed the lad goodnight and gave him a fatherly hug. Amy was already asleep and even Henry seemed surprised at his sudden interest in them.

"Am I taking you to football this Saturday, Henry?" He

hoped he could make an arrangement that would guarantee him access to at least one of the children this weekend.

"No Dad, I'm going with Garry, his dad's taking us. He never works Saturdays so it's better we go with him, then we're certain of transport, and his dad's a pretty useful player himself so he gives us quite a bit of coaching."

The gulf that Tim had allowed to grow between himself and his family was coming back to bite him. All those Saturdays spent messing about with cars and playing pool with Ben were now costing him any hope of saving his marriage. Why, he wondered, do you only ever see you're mistakes when it's too late. He hung around a few minutes longer, but the kids were all back into their own things and he was acutely aware that he wasn't serving any useful purpose by staying there. He made his way downstairs, dejected and frightened. Any minute now the door would slam behind a raging Mel, shouting at him to get out. Perhaps it would be simpler if he was gone before she returned, but then he would still have to face her sooner or later. He considered putting on a show of strength and refusing to leave, after all this was his house as well as hers. Sleeping on the settee would be better than sleeping in his van tonight and as long as he was in the house he had a slim chance of appealing to her to give him another chance. Before he could arrive at a decision she was back. She kicked off her shoes and slumped down in an armchair.

"Well, it seems you're right for once. She's taken it really well, so well in fact that I don't think she will have him back whatever happens. Only yesterday she was crying her eyes out for him, saying she couldn't face life as a single parent. I don't know what you said to her, but well done, Tim, I

obviously underestimated you. I'm about ready for bed...
what about you? I know I said we can't make love at the
moment but this latest upset has made me realise that I need
to try a bit harder to please you. What I'm trying to say,
Tim... is... do you want to make love to me tonight?"

He hesitated as he considered the madness of what was
happening to him. He'd gone for weeks without any passion
in his life, thanks to Mel's refusal to let him near her and
tonight, after he'd just made love to his neighbour for two
hours, Mel was seeking to do the same.

"Well, I thought you'd be pleased... but if it's that hard
to make your mind up we won't bother."

"Sorry Mel, of course I want to, it's just that you took
me by surprise after the way it's been lately."

He took her hand, turned off the TV and the light and
closed the lounge door behind them. As they quietly climbed
the stairs his head was in turmoil. Could he really make love to
Mel as if everything was normal, when an hour ago he'd been
in bed with the woman next door? To his surprise he found it
quite easy to meet Mel's expectations, but the episode didn't
excite him nearly as much making love to Nina had. He kissed
Mel goodnight and tried to go to sleep. He wished he was next
door in Nina's bed where his feelings had been so eagerly
aroused. If making love to Mel had proved anything to him it
was that he didn't feel the same excitement at touching her as
he did Nina. Sleep saved him from further deliberation.

When he arrived home from work the following evening
Mel was in a good mood. The smell of cooking was as good
as he'd been used to before their recent problems and she
was as chirpy as ever.

"Guess what I've done?" she said.

Tim tried to think but nothing sprang to mind.

"I've booked us two weeks' holiday in the South of France. I went to Thomas Cook's at lunch time and we've got a twenty eight foot mobile home all to ourselves on a fabulous site with a pool and everything. Amy can play tennis there and we can even go pony trekking. You just have to tell your boss that you won't be in for two weeks, OK?"

"Mel, I heard on the news that the Air Traffic Controllers are going on strike, which means we'll probably spend our first day at Gatwick and then get stranded in France when it's time to come home. I wish you'd told me before you booked it."

"Tim, I do listen to the news you know, which is why we're going by Eurostar and then by TGV all the way to St Raphael. Don't try to find excuses, Tim, I told you... we're going on holiday as a family and nothing is going to stop us. We're leaving on Saturday morning early, so make sure you put out everything you want me to pack for you. Tim, I'm so glad we're off for two weeks. We've got some serious catching up to do, you know what I mean!"

She winked at him and he knew exactly what she meant. Two days ago he would have been overjoyed at her sudden change of heart, but he couldn't get yesterday and Nina out of his mind. He needed to go round and see her. He'd have to find some excuse.

"I spoke to Ben today on the phone; I'll go round and update Nina later."

"Leave it Tim, she's getting over him better than I thought she would, you don't want to get her thinking about him again do you?"

"No I don't, he said truthfully, but I can't not pass on his message."

"What message was that, what could he say that she would want to hear for God's sake?"

The problem with lying was that it required you to lie more and more. He had to think quickly to come up with a message that Ben could have given him, but instead his mind went blank.

"So what was the message? Is he sorry for what he's done?"

"No, not exactly, but he did ask me to tell Nina that he's thinking of her and to remember him to the kids."

"Are you serious Tim? You can't bloody go round there and say that... She'll probably kill you ... Nina, your shit husband says that while he's bonking some teenage sex object he's thinking of you constantly and would you remind him of the names of his kids as he's forgotten them already."

"Mel, that isn't how it is at all. He does still care about them, even though he isn't with them. I'll be very tactful, I promise."

"Oh OK, but don't blame me if she sets about you."

"I won't Mel, but if she is upset I'll stay until she's OK, so I might be a while."

"Don't worry, I've got clothes to wash for Saturday and all the kids' stuff to pack. Don't leave her on her own until she's OK."

"I won't." And with that he slipped out to head for next door.

If Tim thought that his visit to Nina would be a re-run of the previous night he was mistaken. Nina was pleased that Tim and Mel were going off on holiday for two weeks and she made a point of expressing her hopes that this would rebuild their relationship. She never mentioned what had taken place between them and when Tim left he was more confused than ever.

Had Nina simply jumped into bed with him without it meaning anything to her? Yesterday that thought would not have been possible, after he had given her the strength to recover from the scars inflicted upon her by Ben. She'd taken his help willingly and at the same time filled him with a desire to give much more of himself. Why then was she now acting like it never happened. He wanted to ask her how she felt about him, but the mood wasn't right and he would have embarrassed both of them. After a few minutes their conversation dried up and he made to leave. At the door he gave her a kiss on the cheek, just like he would to a friend. She responded without any warmth, unlike he'd expected. A willing kiss would have confirmed their special relationship.

Confused and troubled, Tim arrived back home after ten minutes. What a contrast to last night. Had everything he'd felt been a sham? Had he imagined the racing of their pulses as they had frantically made love twenty-four hours ago? If this served to tell him anything it was that he would never understand the workings of the female mind.

"Nina's fine", he said lightly. "Didn't need to stay long, she seemed perfectly OK."

"You're a good man, Tim; thinking about her feelings and taking care of her when Ben seems to have forgotten she exists. It makes me realise just how lucky I am."

If there was one thing Tim didn't need right now it was praise for spending time with Nina. If she ever found out how last night's time had been spent, their relationship would be over faster than he could say 'sorry'.

He found it hard to concentrate on work the next day and

when he heard Ben's voice on his mobile he was filled with guilt. He was so certain his voice alone would confess everything. He said, "Hi Ben, how are you?" but in his head it sounded like "Sorry Ben, I slept with your wife the other night but it's over now and she doesn't even mention it any more".

Ben, though, was his usual carefree self and was only ringing with an update on his affair with Beckie.

"This is the real thing, Tim. I'm serious, we are so good together there's no way now that I could go back to Neen and her constant moaning at me. Beckie likes me the way I am. She isn't trying to turn me into something that I'm not. She's brilliant, which is why I'm ringing, you've got to meet her. How about a game or two down the Globe tonight?"

"Oh, I don't know, Ben, what will Nina think of me if I meet you and Beckie?"

"Who cares what Nina thinks? You know how she is. Anyway she always told me that she thought you were as useless as me, so sod her. Nina is the one who puts all those ideas in Mel's head. You should think about that. When they get together Nina doesn't just put me down, she puts you down as well. She hates men ...that's her trouble, she's cold blooded and bloody minded. You want to stop Mel going round there; it's her that's filling Mel's mind with all this stuff about you not being a good husband. She thinks every husband is no good. She's going to find out just how lonely it can get when she's got no one to turn to... and serve her bloody right. I'll see you tonight, about seven, OK?"

"OK, Ben, but I don't think you're entirely right about Nina."

"Of course I am, she's a bitch and I'm well shot of her. See you later."

Perhaps Nina is a bitch, after all she took me in the other night, made me think we had something special and then last night acted like she barely knew me. Christ, why are women so devious? Tim thought back to all the advice Ben had proffered on women and on marriage. It seemed he was right in most of what he'd said and he'd certainly got his own life sorted out with this Beckie. It would be interesting to meet her and see just what she was really like.

Over his evening meal he broached the subject of Ben and Beckie being in the Globe.

"I heard from Ben today."

"Why do you sound so surprised, he phoned you yesterday didn't he?"

Sod it; he'd forgotten last night's lie. "Yes, I just meant he phoned with something special to say today."

"Special? What could be special about that big creep?"

"Hang on Mel, Nina's not exactly without blame in all of this. If she hadn't treated Ben like shit he would still be living next door. She can change with the wind that one, nice to you one minute and ignoring you the next. I don't blame Ben for saying enough is enough."

"You've changed your tune haven't you? Two nights ago you spent an entire evening helping her get over that bastard and now you're singing his praises! The trouble with men is they're never consistent – you can't believe a word they say from one day to the next. I'd expect that from him but not from you. The best thing you can do is stay away from him, let him stew in his own bloody juice, let him rot with his floosy but whatever you do don't encourage him."

"Well that's what he phoned me for; he wants me to meet Beckie down the Globe tonight."

"You are joking... I hope! Why the hell would you want to meet her... or is she bringing a friend along for you to try?"

"Stop this, Mel, Ben's my mate and just as you like to spend evening after evening listening to all that propaganda from her-next-door about Ben, and letting her poison your mind about me, I want to spend some time with him, and if he's moved on from Nina then I don't blame him. I'm not going to turn my back on him because he's found affection with someone else. It's just a pity she hadn't kept her mouth shut every time he walked in the house and it's a pity she fills your head with the so called faults of mine. I know it's because of her that we've been struggling these past months. It should be *me* saying I don't want *you* going round *there*."

"Try it Tim, try telling me who I can bloody talk to. I thought you'd changed, I was looking forward to us going away together on Saturday, but how can I go away with someone as two-faced as you? We're right back to where we were two weeks ago, Tim, and it's your fault. I hope you're bloody pleased with yourself."

Melanie left her half eaten meal and slammed upstairs.

Tim sat staring at his plate and wondering how he'd got into this mess. He finished his meal, but now it was tasteless. He couldn't face going upstairs and having another confrontation, so he put his plate in the dishwasher, picked up his coat and closed the kitchen door behind him.

When Ben arrived with Beckie he looked as happy as the proverbial pig in shit. Not that anything ever got Ben down for long. He was so easy going problems simply went over his head. Was this a quality? It certainly saved him from getting stressed about things that would have Tim lying awake half the night. Tim moved his glance from Ben to the woman standing at his side. She was beautiful, that was undeniable, and young. She seemed to be as happy as Ben was and they had an air of togetherness that made Tim jealous. How could he be jealous of his best friend, a friend who deserved a bit of luck after putting up with the wife from hell for all those years? Ah yes, the wife he'd been pleased to sleep with just two nights ago. As he shook hands with Beckie he was aware of yet another physical contact, the touching of hands. It meant nothing to Beckie, but Tim thought how his hands had touched Nina and how she had touched him back.

"Ben's told me all about you", she said with a cheeky grin. "Well, probably not everything. I expect you've got a skeleton in your cupboard, like most men."

It was as if she knew about him and Nina, as if she was teasing him. He wiped the sweat from his brow and pretended to laugh at such a suggestion.

"Oh yes, I've got more skeletons than the British Museum."

Ben joined in. "What you? He's so squeaky clean, Beckie, that if a woman invited him into her bedroom he'd have to phone his wife first to ask her permission."

Ben chuckled at his own attempt at humour, but Tim was disturbed at the nearness to the truth.

"How's the job going?" he said, trying to change the subject.

"Oh great, better than being a storeman, Tim. Sorry mate, but I couldn't have stuck that for five minutes."

"That's OK. I'm glad to see you settled in a job you like. How's Sophie?"

"She's OK, she sends her love. She's off somewhere tonight. How are things with you and Mel? Is it still the same?"

"Well it did get better, briefly, but when I told her I was meeting you tonight she threw a wobbly and I'm right back in it again."

"Don't put up with it Tim, I'm serious. Come out clubbing with us on Saturday night. Beckie'll sort you out with one of her mates, won't you Babe?"

"Yea, no problem. A good looking bloke like you, Tim; they'd be fighting over you. You can always stay with us if it's getting too much at home."

Tim tried to imagine living in a tiny flat with Ben and Beckie, but it was too horrible to contemplate. "Yes, OK, I'll bear that in mind."

They played pool and talked until Jim shouted last orders. "We'd better be going," Ben said, "work in the morning."

They said good night and Tim set off for home with a heavy heart. He crept in and tried to use the bathroom without waking Melanie, then slid gently into bed alongside her.

"So what was Beckie like?"

"I thought you were asleep."

"I was, you woke me up."

"Sorry."

"Don't worry about it. What was Beckie like?"

"She's really nice. Very different to Nina."

"You mean she's half Nina's age, young enough to be Ben's daughter?"

"No, that isn't what I meant. She's a lovely person. They're very happy together."

"Invited you to the wedding, did they or will the christening be first?"

"Mel, it's their life, why can't you just be happy for them?"

"And are you happy for Nina?"

"What do you mean by that?"

"You know, Nina, lady who lives next door? Her husband just left her... what about her?"

Tim didn't like the direction in which this conversation was going. Melanie had spent the evening with Nina. Could she have said anything about Monday night?

"Nina will find someone else, Mel, that's what happens when people split up."

"Oh is it? So you think Nina will find someone else in two minutes flat do you?"

Well yes actually, he thought to himself. "Of course not, but in time she'll move on, just like Ben has."

"Move on? ... You use that expression as if it fixes everything. She's breaking her heart over a man who's walked out on her and her children and you can fix it all with three words... She'll move on. She's not a bloody bus stuck in a traffic jam, you idiot, she's a woman. She has all the feelings of a woman. You could never begin to understand."

"I understand her perfectly. She's upset now, but she'll get over it, she'll probably use anyone she meets for her own ends and then she'll eventually find some other poor bugger to fix onto, and then she'll start all over again. She's not as innocent as you make her out to be Mel. Trust me!"

"How dare you speak like that about a woman you hardly know. Yes you've spoken to her over the fence, you've listened to Ben telling you what she's like, but you haven't got a clue what she's like underneath have you?"

No seemed the only sensible answer.

"Precisely, and you need to think about that when you treat me like dirt, the way Ben treated her. I hope this Beckie hasn't given you ideas about trotting off with some lovesick teenager!"

"No darling, I'm hoping to go off to the South of France with you, if that's still the plan?"

"Of course it is, but don't think for one minute that I'd ever stand for any nonsense between you and another woman... OK?"

"OK love... good night."

CHAPTER SEVEN

As the Eurostar snaked its way through Clapham Common on its way to the Channel Tunnel, the Fisher family seemed incredibly happy. For Henry, James and Amy this was an adventure about to begin, new friends to find, new places to see. They explored the Kent countryside through the window before it plunged into the darkness of the tunnel, from which they would emerge in France.

Tim and Mel had travelled across France several times before, but not like this. Neither of them had journeyed on the TGV before. As the train reached one hundred and fifty miles per hour they lazily watched the French landscape flash past for hour after hour until the sun began to fall and the scenery took on the terracotta shades so familiar in the rocky landscape of Provence. Eventually they climbed down onto the platform at St Raphael and, after a short journey by taxi, they arrived at their holiday park at the end of a long day. If the children were tired they didn't show it as they pleaded to be allowed to explore at once. Top priority was the giant pool and waterslide, followed closely by the tennis courts. Melanie wanted to see inside the restaurant, but Tim suggested they have a drink first in the pub, which he knew boasted several pool tables.

"What a pity we didn't invite Ben," Mel said.

He gave her a wry smile but he couldn't help thinking he would have enjoyed Ben's company over a few beers and some leisurely days of pool in the air conditioned games bar. Wisdom decreed that he would keep such thoughts to himself.

The weather forecast was steady at thirty degrees for the week ahead, so their plan included trips to the beach and a day pony trekking. The mobile home was big enough for them to spread themselves out while, outside a wooden balcony extended out onto a rocky incline, providing plenty of room for sun beds and a fabulous view of the distant mountains.

After a good night's sleep they made their first trip into the town of Frejus and the hypermarket, which would become a frequent haunt for the next two weeks, as they shopped for food, wine and clothes. In the mall there were rows of smaller shops selling designer clothes, watches and jewellery as well as pizzas, pastries and coffee. The kids wanted to explore independently, which suited Mel because she had a burning desire to acquire some chic French designer outfits and this looked like a good place to start. They agreed that they'd all meet back at the coffee shop in an hour.

Tim was happy to be led from one shop to another, pouring out compliments on new and expensive outfits and agreeing grudgingly to be kitted out with designer trousers, shirts and shoes. He briefly considered the damage to his credit card when Melanie insisted he buy an expensive bottle of men's perfume, but he wasn't about to spoil a holiday that was looking better than he could have hoped for two weeks ago.

If he was worried about the price of the perfume, he

almost choked on the bill for five drinks and five pastries, but he said nothing. He watched Melanie fussing over her brood and at last it seemed like family life was back to normal. She was always attentive to the needs of the kids, but he had enjoyed her undivided attention as she'd chosen his new things. In return for this wifely devotion he would agree to anything they came up with and when Henry asked if they could spend the afternoon at the go cart track he was fine about it, even though it would dent his credit card still further.

As they waited their turn, James asked him which car was fastest, which pleased him. His son was acknowledging his mechanical skills and seeking out his opinion. He proudly suggested to James that he should head for the number four car and his advice proved sound when he beat his elder brother in two successive races.

After Tim had come last to all of them they headed back to their mobile home amid arguments about who was the best driver. Tim explained that his weight was the reason he couldn't keep pace, but the kids were convinced that their driving skill was the deciding factor and eventually he gave in and let them have their way.

Melanie cooked what she described as a French meal and, apart from Amy, who made faces in protest at the mussels, they all cleared their plates. The kids did the washing up while Tim and Melanie sat out on the balcony in the evening sun with a glass of wine. Tim had wanted beer, but Melanie had insisted he drink the local Vin Rose. Determined that nothing should spoil things, he yielded to her wish yet again.

Over the next two days Melanie shaped Tim's eating,

drinking and dressing habits in a bid to rid him of his old fashioned ways. He allowed himself to be moulded into stylish shorts and designer shades, while he sipped a Dubonnet before his evening meal. No point in protesting for a beer and risking spoiling her mood – after all, three whole days had passed without the slightest chastisement. His marriage was back to where it was before all the troubles of the past few weeks and he had no intention of rocking the boat.

On the third evening they were alone on the balcony after their evening meal, the kids having gone off with new friends to the concert stage where camp staff arranged nightly entertainment. Melanie had decided they were quite safe within the camp boundary so long as they came back by nine. On the first night Henry had got a concession till ten as long as he brought Amy back safely at nine, and James had slid off with Henry leaving Amy to complain that she was being victimised because of her age.

They sat staring up towards the mountains, which rose steeply in the distance, and they watched as lights twinkled in the distant villages. It was Melanie who spoke first.

"Tomorrow night we're going up to that village, she said, just you and me ... I've phoned and booked us a table at a little restaurant called 'Le Stable'. I went to reception earlier and got the number from the very nice Frenchman behind the counter, who described it to me in great detail. He told me it was very romantic with lots of atmosphere and very good French food. To be honest, Tim, the way he talked to me I wondered if he was offering to take me, his French accent was so sexy I would have had to say yes."

Although Tim knew she was joking, it jarred a little that

his blissful state could be threatened by a 'would be Latin lover', even an imaginary one. It bothered him that she'd had this seemingly intimate conversation behind his back. He made a mental note to keep an eye out for the amorous Frenchman. "What about the kids? We'll have to be back by nine for Amy."

"No we won't, I've made friends with the couple in the van next to us. They've got two girls around Amy's age and she'll stay with them until Henry comes in at ten. Terry, that's her husband, is going to drive us up to the village at six thirty and I've booked a cab to bring us back at eleven."

"How did you book a cab?"

"Francois, my Frenchman in reception, helped me. He knows a taxi driver who lives up in the village. He even got me a reduction in the price."

"So what else did Francois say? Did he tell you what we should eat?"

"Yes he did, he said that if we wanted the beef bourguignon we would have to order it the day before, so I asked him nicely and he did it for me. The restaurant is run by two old ladies; Francois says they are celebrated around here for their traditional French cuisine. He did the ordering because they don't speak a word of English. He's also chosen for us a red wine which he says will be a perfect accompaniment to the food. He's a gourmet of course, like most French men. The way he talks about food gets me quite excited. I don't suppose you'd understand that."

"What I do understand is that this greasy bugger breathed garlic fumes over you, muttered a few words in French and you had a bloody orgasm! I don't want to hear any more about Francois or what he's chosen for my bloody pudding. Christ, Mel, when you said this was to be a romantic night for two I thought you meant us two. This bloke's already done the romance bit, all I have to do is hand over my plastic and pay the bloody taxi. I don't want to go. Sod him. I'll choose a restaurant and we'll go where I choose tomorrow night, right!"

"No, Tim, wrong. Stop being so bloody jealous. All I did was ask for his advice on where to eat and he proved very helpful. I can't help it if he just happens to be fantastic looking with a sexy voice can I?" She laughed at him, knowing that he would have to give in to her.

"Well, all right, but next time you decide to go up for some advice, tell me first and I'll come with you, OK?"

"Of course, darling... after all it's only fair that you should meet your rival." For some perverse reason she didn't fully understand, she was enjoying Tim's discomfort.

He knew she was sending him up and his only defence was to join in her silly game.

"I shall challenge him tomorrow to a dual: Spanners at Noon – that's what mechanics do ... not as messy as swords. I shall bash his French brains out before your very eyes and he will rival me no more." He said it with the haughty accent of one assured of victory.

"Actually, darling, his t-shirt says he's a martial arts expert, so you might want to be careful, especially with your back."

Mel would always get the better of these exchanges and he knew when to quit.

"Then I shall poison the bugger. I'll put arsenic in his Perrier; that should fix his sexy accent once and for all."

They both laughed, but inwardly Tim was disturbed

that Mel found it so easy to communicate with a man in just minutes. Mel made friends with everyone; that was part of her charm, one of the reasons he loved her so much, just like she'd made friends with the people in the next van. If he turned his back for two minutes she was making friends with someone. Having a lovely wife who everyone wanted to be friends with was fine, but sometimes it seemed to Tim that he had to try harder than everyone else to exact his share of that warmth.

Surely he should be at the front of the queue, she should pour her personality all over him, let him feel secure in the knowledge that he was the most important person in her life? Why then did he always feel like he had to work harder than anyone else for her attention? He would have to talk to her about it; he'd try to explain over their meal tomorrow. Surely she'd see that it was right to put him first.

Terry was good company on the seven mile drive up to the village in the mountain, keeping them amused with stories from his ten years of holidaying at the park. On arrival in the village they weaved their way up through the narrow main street under the shade of huge spreading platan trees. A wide pavement on the left hand side was busy with tables and chairs all beautifully laid out for tonight's diners, some of whom were already sipping drinks in readiness for the meals to come. One of the two restaurants had yellow table cloths and napkins, while the other had red ones.

Melanie tried to see their names, hoping to work out which one they would be eating at. Terry slowly navigated the car up the crowded street. When he reached the end of the shops he turned right down a little alley behind the shops which led onto a boulevard lined with olive trees.

Because the road clung precariously to the mountain side it boasted a fantastic view across the hills towards the sea and their camp site. Terry parked the car and insisted on escorting them to the restaurant, explaining that they would have trouble finding it without his help. They walked back towards the main street alongside a low wall which separated them from a two hundred foot drop down the cliff face. Terry explained how the Romans had originally built this village in the mountains where it could be easily defended. While the two men discussed several old vehicles parked in the street, Melanie silently took in the hustle and bustle around her. There was a post office building as well as a few food shops and one with postcards outside. She saw pictures of houses in a shop window and wondered how an estate agent could survive in such a remote village. A quick look at the prices provided the explanation and she moved on with interest to the shop next door, which was a ladies' hair salon.

They crossed the road and made their way between the tables of the pavement restaurants. Melanie was surprised when Terry walked straight past the two restaurants she'd seen from the car. She sneaked a quick look at the menus, trying not to get left behind. The centre of the village was really quite large, with a relaxed, almost lazy atmosphere that was obviously attractive to the dozens of people who were milling around the focal point, a large, ancient fountain. Perhaps they had also come to this mountain paradise to eat because they certainly didn't look like locals. Hurrying to catch up with the men, Melanie found herself in a narrow back street with tall houses on each side. Most had their front doors open and wonderful aromas of cooking drifted into the street. From an upstairs window an old woman smiled down at her so she returned it politely, not wanting to stare. After a few right and left turns up streets too narrow for any kind of vehicle they came into a wide open square under yet more platan trees.

Across the square was a beautiful church, hundreds of years old but clearly still in use. Terry turned sharply to the right and on their right was a large old house which, like the other buildings in the square was tall and in desperate need of renovation. Over the open front door was a small wooden sign, 'Le Stable'. Melanie looked in amazement as Terry announced that they'd arrived. This was it, their romantic hideaway for the evening. He wished them bon appetite then promptly disappeared back the way they'd come.

Tim stared at Melanie in disbelief, but there was nothing for it but to venture inside. Tim had to duck his head as he went through the open front door into the dim space beyond. It was like walking into someone's home. At first they were embarrassed in case that's what it turned out to be. In the gloom they were met by the reassuring sight of three tables set ready for a meal, each with a small candle burning and a slim pottery vase of fresh roses. A tiny lady with a wizened face dressed all in black tottered out from behind a coat stand and greeted them with a welcoming smile. "Avez vous en reservation?" she asked pointedly. She looked so old and so frail that Melanie wanted to apologise for having troubled her. Instead she replied in her best Franglais.

"Mais oui, Madam, le nom c'est Fisher."

Still smiling, she beckoned them through an opening into a small alcove where a table was set for two. It was beautiful and intimate, perfect for two people in love who yearned to shut out the rest of world for the next two hours. The meal had already been ordered over the phone and in a while the wine arrived, along with a basket of freshly cut bread. Tim couldn't resist sinking his teeth into a piece of it, dropping crumbs from the crust into his lap. He washed it down with the red wine, which he had to admit was good. Melanie nibbled on her bread and looked into his eyes. She had planned this meal with great care – after all, it was to be the backdrop for what she was about to say to Tim. There seemed no point in putting it off any longer. She had rehearsed this a dozen times today, now was the time to get it off her chest.

"Tim," she started, "I've got something to tell you, something you'll like, I think, something that will help us get back to how we used to be." She knew this would get him on side, ready for the bit he wasn't going to like. This had to be handled with great care if it was to succeed, and it had to, if they were to get their marriage back on course.

He looked anxious as he waited for her to continue.

"We've drifted apart, Tim, I think we both know that. You've said lots of times how you feel like we live in two different worlds, me... working in the bank, meeting professional people, going to work in nice clothes and coming home tired but still clean. You've done all right as a mechanic, but you come home smelling of oil, covered in grease, always having to wear those stinking blue overalls... I think it's time you moved up the ladder, into something closer to the professions, something where you could go off in a smart suit every day, something that would mean you'd come home as clean at night as you leave in the morning, something that could make me proud of you again. I want you to meet the kind of people that I spend my time with, that way we could go places together some evenings. I'm not saying I want to stop you going down the pub or anything like that but we could spend more quality time together.

Tim looked like he'd been hypnotized, speechless. He picked up his drink as if by remote control. He hadn't expected this, that was obvious, but what was he thinking?

He was in shock, unable to think of anything sensible to say. On the one hand he was happy that Mel wanted to get the marriage back on track, but this announcement was too much to take in. Was she serious? "You want me to stop being a mechanic?"

"Yes Tim, I know it used to be good years ago, but we've changed since then. You don't need to do that kind of work any longer. It's hard, it's dirty and you're not getting any younger. You deserve a chance to do something better, something you can enjoy."

"I enjoy fixing trucks. I know you're saying this to help me, Mel, but I'm not sure I could do anything else. I mean … realistically... whose going to employ me to work in a suit and tie? What do I know about anything other than vehicles, unless I went for a job in vehicle management, but do you know Mel, most of those jobs pay a lot less than I earn as a mechanic. There's a desperate shortage of skilled men, which is why I earn what I do. If you're honest I bet I earn more than a lot of the people you work with, don't I?"

"Tim, that's probably true, but your work is physically draining and if you carry on like this you'll be a wreck in ten years' time. How many mechanics do you know who make it into retirement?"

"I know… most of them end up being pensioned off with

bent backs or stiff fingers, but what can I do Mel? I don't know anything else."

"Well, that's my good news, Tim. The day before we left I heard Martin Bateman, one of our Executive Account Managers telling Joe that one of his clients is looking for a personal assistant stroke security man. This guy is stinking rich and he wants a smart, intelligent man to drive him around and to be a bit useful in the event of any trouble. He owns a lot of property in London and elsewhere. He's not involved in crime or any of that stuff, but obviously because he's well heeled he could always be a target for some get-rich-quick thug. He's looking to pay one hell of a salary, much more than you make now, Tim, and you would get your designer suits provided as part of the package. I told Martin that you were the perfect person for the job and he's putting your name forward to this guy as soon as he flies back into London tomorrow. He's asked us to help him find someone. We often do this kind of thing for our very rich clients because they need to find someone honest without going through the usual agency channels, where they might end up with the wrong kind of candidate. When I talked to Martin about you he agreed that you are perfect for the job. You're big enough and strong enough to look after yourself and Simon Stonewood – that's the millionaire you'd be taking care of. He's a decent bloke to work for. You're completely honest and with my position in the bank that counts for a lot. This is a fantastic chance for you Tim, in fact it's probably the best job offer you're ever going to get. I've said I'll ring Martin tomorrow afternoon to see if he's managed to talk to the guy, and if he has, find out what he wants you to do next. Martin thought he'd probably want to speak to you over the phone, straight away, because he's a fast mover. He makes his decisions quickly and Martin said that with your pedigree, if he likes the sound of your voice he'll probably offer you the job over the phone. Just think, Tim, by tomorrow you might not be a mechanic any more."

This was going far too quickly for Tim.

"Mel, this is too much for me to take in ... you're talking to your mates about me as if I'm a bloody poodle at Crufts... they think I've got a sodding pedigree. For God's sake, am I supposed to bark or something? You take me out for a nice meal and then tell me that you are too bloody high class to stay married to me as a motor mechanic... that's what all this is about isn't it... your bloody friends look down their noses at me because I get my hands dirty? Mel, I realise now what this holiday was all about ... it wasn't about us getting away together, having a good time together with the kids ... it was about you re-designing me to be what you want ... the way that suits your friends. You choose my clothes, you choose this meal, you tell me what I can do. I even have to drink wine now because you're too bloody snooty to let me enjoy a pint of lager before my meal. And then you want me to baby-sit for some bloke I've never met. He'd probably want me to fly halfway around the World looking after him. No chance."

"Tim, he wants you to drive his car, not fly it. It's a Mercedes, not Chitty Chitty bloody Bang Bang. Grow up, will you? If you want to stay a grease monkey for the rest of your life that's fine by me. Find yourself some chick with a motorbike and tattoos who will probably appreciate it. I don't... OK? If you can't cope with improving yourself then stay right where you are, but don't expect me to stay with you. What's wrong with wanting to improve yourself? You used to have ambition when I first met you, but now you can't be bothered to spend any time with me, you do next to nothing for the kids and you think I should be satisfied. Well I'm not. I arranged this night out to try to show you how it could be, how we could plan things together, how I could help you. Yes my friends are different to yours... what's wrong with that? You could look at this differently and see that I've taken a lot of effort to try and get you a job that most men would give anything for, but you, no... you're too set in your ways. Well I want more from life than I'm getting from you, Tim; you need to decide whether being a mechanic and drinking with Ben and your mates down at the Globe is all you want, because if it is, Tim, I don't want to be a part of it. Let me spell it out for you, Tim, if that's what you want... then I want out."

Melanie got up and headed off to find the ladies, leaving Tim to stew on her uncompromising ultimatum. She was demanding a decision, one that would change his life, whichever decision he made. He had come out tonight expecting it to be just like any other night out together, but then they didn't often go out together – she was right about that, he didn't do much to make the marriage work. She definitely had a right to expect more from him than he was giving her. No woman worth having would accept what he was offering her and be happy. His head was spinning. Before she comes back to the table, he thought, I need to make my mind up about what I'm going to do. He looked out from the alcove. It was difficult to see much in the half light, but it seemed there were only seats for ten people in the place.

This was probably as much as the two ladies could

manage, for it was obvious they did everything; cooking, serving, the lot. From out of the gloom an old lady appeared, much heavier than the one who'd seen them to their table, clearly the other partner in the Auberge. She made her way slowly towards him. Her wrinkled face softened into a warm smile for his benefit... " Ca Va, toute bien?"

He had never been any good at French but he knew by her face that she was enquiring if everything was OK. Had they raised their voices? Had everyone been staring into their alcove, watching to see what would happen? Tim tried to replay their conversation to judge how loud they'd been.

Melanie was standing behind the lady, who clearly hadn't heard her return, waiting for her chance to regain her seat, but not wanting to push past. She coughed gently which was a signal for the old lady to turn and let her through.

The lady wants to know if everything is OK, Tim said.

"Mais Oui, Madam, ce'st tres bien".

The old lady, still smiling, gave her an understanding nod, as if she had seen this kind of thing before. Maybe French couples came here all the time to sort out their marriage problems.

"Deux minute". She turned and made her way slowly back across the restaurant towards the black hole in the wall, which led to the kitchen. Tim looked at Melanie; she had signs of tears, hastily wiped away while she was in the ladies. She was still clasping a tissue.

"You're right, Mel; I haven't been treating you properly. I couldn't bear it if you left me. I do want to be different. If you ring Martin for me, I'll talk to this guy on the phone. I will try to be the man you want me to be, Mel, but I may need your help."

"I will help you, Tim. That's what I've been trying to do... but maybe it's too much to ask, maybe you've been doing what you do too long to change?"

"You mean maybe I'm beyond help, is that it? Mel, you used to believe in me, you used to think I could do anything, now you don't even think I can drive a bloke around in a car... of course I can. You're right; it would be a brilliant opportunity for me. Do the phone call, Mel, leave the rest to me, I won't let you down."

He pushed his hand across the table and took hold of hers. She smiled back at him and he believed he had just saved his marriage. The old lady returned with two plates, which she placed in front of them. She muttered something about the food and then, still smiling, wished them bon appetite before leaving them to enjoy their meal.

The combination of delicious food and good wine soothed the situation and when Melanie spoke again she was totally composed. "This place is straight out of a history book," she said. "These two ladies must have been running this place when the Romans invaded. It's quaint beyond belief. You should see the toilet, the china is decorated like those on the Antiques Roadshow and on the way there you can see straight into their kitchen. It's just a normal kitchen; they've got big copper saucepans on an old gas range. Gordon Ramsey would have a fit if he went in there. Thank god they wouldn't understand a word he said."

Her attempt at a joke was a signal that she was trying hard. Tim knew her well enough to continue the conversation in the same vein.

"What about Keith Floyd, surely he must've found this place on his travels? He'd love all this old furniture and he'd certainly like this wine. You chose well Mel, even if you did have some help from Casanova at the camp."

"Tim, are you sure you don't mind the changes that I'm asking you to make? Are you saying yes because it's better than the other option?"

"Yes, of course I am, but I can also see that staying like I am, isn't an option ... I don't blame you for wanting more from me. I want us to stay married and to be happy... that's all I've ever wanted."

When the coffee finally brought the meal to an end, Melanie phoned the taxi driver to come for them. They thanked the two ladies, who insisted on hugging them both before letting them out into the square.

"What a fabulous place, what lovely people", Mel said, how old do you think they were?"

"Not a day under eighty I reckon, but that food, how do they make it taste so good? They must have a garden with all kinds of herbs; maybe they even grow their own vegetables."

"I expect they use Herb de Provence, after all, they would wouldn't they? But you're right – the taste was better than anything I can ever remember. I think that place could be our secret restaurant. Every few years we can come back again."

"Only if they both live to be a hundred," said Tim.

"Do you know which way we're going? If we get lost in these alleys we might still be here when we're a hundred? Where is the taxi waiting for us?"

"He spoke good English, he said to go to the big fountain in the main street and wait for him there. I remember seeing it when we came by earlier. What an amazing night out!"

"In more ways than one, Mel, that's for certain."

He caught hold of her hand as they headed back in the direction of the main street. The taxi was already there and within seconds they were speeding down the mountain towards the holiday park and the kids.

The next day was as hot as ever and they went to the pool for a few hours in the morning before going back to the van for a salad baguette lunch. At three o'clock Melanie phoned Martin back at the bank on her mobile. Tim listened carefully as she scribbled a phone number on her magazine cover. She thanked him and hung up. "He's done it, Tim; he's convinced Simon Stonewood that you are the right man for him. You've got to ring him as soon as possible on this number." She handed the magazine to Tim.

"I'd better get down and do it then, hadn't I, if I want to keep my wife!" He grinned at her, but she wasn't amused.

"Tim, you aren't doing this for me ... you are doing it for you, remember that, and whatever you do... remember that."

"I know, don't let's go there again... I've said I'll do it, and I meant it, OK?"

He dialled the number on his mobile and waited. "Hello, is that Mr Stonewood? My name's Tim Fisher. I think Martin from your bank has mentioned me to you... yes that's me, thank you for asking me to ring you."

Simon Stonewood was nobody's fool, he knew that Martin would only have recommended this guy if he had good reason. Martin had told him Tim's wife had been at the bank for ten years, he was a reliable chap, a mechanic, useful perhaps and he was built like a brick outhouse, just what he needed. "Why do you want to leave your present job, Tim?"

"My wife wants me to get a job away from the grease

and muck; I want to go to work looking smart and come home smelling of perfume, not engine oil. It's time I had a change."

"You're a mechanic, so you must be a good driver, right?"

"I like to think so, yes. Simon, would you want me to service the car as well as driving it? I wouldn't mind, after all it would be nothing after looking after trucks for years."

He heard Simon laughing at the other end of the line. What had he said that was so funny?

Eventually Simon got his laughter under control and spoke again. "You know, Tim, I like you... and you make me laugh, that's good. Didn't Martin tell you what car I drive?"

"Mel, that's my wife, said you've got a Merc..."

"Not any Merc Tim, it's a Maybach. Have you ever seen one? It cost me four hundred and fifty thousand pounds. I think we'll let the dealer service it, don't you?"

Tim was speechless.

"What does a truck mechanic earn these days, Tim?"

"I'm in the top link at our place, so I'm on good money – thirty thousand with my overtime. I often do a Saturday."

"Tim, I'll pay you half as much again, but I need you to start as soon as possible. When do you get back from your holiday?"

"We've got another week and a half here... and then I'd have to give a month's notice."

"Tim... phone your boss please, tell him you're already finished. Say sorry, but I need you as soon as you get back. Whatever he stops you in wages let me know, I'll make it up. Do we have a deal?.. Did you hear me Tim? I said do we have a deal?"

"Sorry, I was trying to get it into my head, everything

you've said... yes we do. Thanks Mr Stonewood, thank you very much."

"Tim, my name's Simon, except when we're in business company, OK? We're going to get on fine together. Ring me the minute you get back, have a great holiday and thank that wife of yours for putting your name forward. You must be proud of her. I'm told she's quite a somebody in the bank."

"Yes, I am proud of her, she's very special. Thanks Simon, for everything. This job is very important to me, I won't let you down."

"I know you won't, Tim. I hope you and your family have a good holiday."

Tim stood looking at Melanie. "I've done it! I've bloody done it! Mel, did you know what car he's got? You know you said he's got a Mercedes; it's only a bloody Maybach, only half a million pounds' worth of car. Bloody hell Mel, can you see me driving that?"

Mel could. At last she was making progress with her plans to get her life back on track, and in order to succeed she had to re-invent Tim, something she was well on the way to succeeding at. Just a month ago she had been close to a mental breakdown, convinced that she was starting the menopause, losing her faculties and unable to manage her job or her marriage. Suddenly her confidence had returned, she was helping the bank to keep one of its top clients happy by finding him the perfect personal assistant, and at the time she had moved her husband from a job she had come to despise into something she would be pleased to tell her friends about. The kids were happy – they always had been mind, they'd never noticed that their mother was on the point of cracking up. They were enjoying a fabulous holiday together in the South of France and, best of all, Tim was willingly embracing the changes she had sought to impose on him. Oh yes, there was one other thing.

She was also sought after by a partner in one of the bank's top clients for her advice on his public speaking. She hesitated at this thought, because it wasn't true... what he wanted was her. Her, as in, her body, her mind, and her, full stop. Ratty had made it clear he would be happy to take Mel on her terms, a prospect which she had to admit she had considered, even if only briefly. Fortunately, Ratty was now history, just a small blip in an otherwise blameless twenty year relationship that was now at an all time high. She thought about the moments she had shared with Ratty and smiled to herself. Yes of course it was wrong, technically, but all she had done was flirted with an eligible admirer. Was that so bad?

For all she knew, Tim might have pictures of half naked women pinned up all around the garage where he worked, and if he didn't you could bet some of the others did. Their mess room would be full of sleazy pictures of the kind of women who sold their bodies to magazines or tabloids every day of the week. Tim couldn't pretend he didn't look at these things, even if they weren't his. No she had done nothing wrong... really. Anyway, she was incredibly happy now and it didn't do her image at the bank any harm to let a few of her colleagues know that she was a sought after piece of 'Management Property'. They certainly wouldn't 'let her go' knowing how keen Ratty was to hire her services, and that because of her they might win an account they'd been chasing for some time.

Tim was just as upbeat about the changes to his life and

was actually looking forward to getting back from this holiday to start his knew job. He imagined his mate's faces when he told them what he was doing, especially when he told them what he was driving. My god, he'd be the envy of everyone in the Globe and he'd be talked about in every pub in the district. He would have celebrity status if he drew up in the Maybach. Not only did he have a new career to get stuck into, but his relationship with Mel was right back where he wanted it. They were married again, in every sense of the word. Last night she had made love to him with such enthusiasm that he was almost intimidated by her.

They strolled around the harbour at Port Frejus in the early evening intent on selecting the perfect restaurant, one that would be acceptable to the kids, but fine enough for their new found status in life. They never stopped talking about his new job and as they stared into the million pound yachts and cruisers packed into the harbour they imagined themselves being a part of this set. This could easily be their cultural home, among the rich and famous where they strolled with ease and contentment. Eventually they selected a restaurant which had a large outside area under a canvass roof, and settled themselves in the cane chairs with a bottle of Chardonnay. Melanie was so happy that she insisted Tim have a glass of 1664 lager. It was perfectly acceptable and, indeed, looking around it was definitely fashionable. Over a meal which included moules marineire, fillet steak and creme brullee, washed down with excellent wine, chilled to just the right temperature, they reflected on just how good life was. Secretly Tim was thinking that it was like he'd won first prize in a lottery, for it was only a few days ago that his marriage was on the brink and his future appeared to offer only emptiness and misery. It was amazing how you could get out of a rut, if you were prepared to put in a bit of effort, he decided.

They both determined that nothing would spoil the happiness they were now enjoying and it was in this mood that they saw out the holiday and returned to England in high spirits.

On their arrival back in Elmthorpe the first person to welcome them was Nina. No sooner had they opened the car boot to start carrying in the cases than she was hugging them and demanding to hear about everything they'd done for the past two weeks. One thing she knew for certain was that they'd had a good time. That much was clear from their faces, but even more obvious was the fact that Melanie and Tim were in unison, displaying togetherness unlike she'd seen between them for months. Something had done the trick for them on this holiday and she was glad. What had passed between her and Tim was nothing more than the flutter of a butterfly's wing in a force eight gale. She was resolute in her desire to see them happy together. If only she could go off on a magical holiday with Ben that would have them glowing with satisfaction at each other in just two weeks. She also knew that wasn't remotely possible. Ben was gone. Ben was living with another woman, a much younger woman, and he certainly wasn't coming back. She was set to spend the next few years at least without the love or support of a man. Maybe she would end her days alone, who knew? Seeing Tim so happy with Mel made it so very clear just what she was missing.

Nina helped carry in some of the wine, which they had bought in a French supermarket, and dumped it down in the kitchen. Melanie was about to follow James upstairs with one of the cases. "Stick the kettle on, Neen," she shouted. With the car unloaded, Tim slumped down on the settee, while Melanie started opening the accumulated post. "All bills and advertising rubbish."

Nina carried in two mugs of tea and then went back for hers. So... how was the holiday? She was itching to know what had got them so firmly back together again. Tim spoke first.

"Brilliant, Neen, absolutely brilliant. Guess what ... Mels's only gone and fixed me up with a new job, I'm a minder now, for a very rich guy with a fabulous car, which I get to drive, and that reminds me, I promised to ring him as soon as I got back. I'd better do it now." Tim took his mobile phone from his pocket and went outside to make the call.

"What is Tim going on about, Mel?"

"Exactly what he said, Neen, It's true, he isn't a mechanic anymore... he's got a proper job."

"Well, you've changed your tune. I remember when we first moved in here you thought Tim was the best mechanic on Earth and you told everyone so. Now it's not a proper job?"

Melanie detected a hint of resentment in Nina's voice which she didn't understand.

"I thought you'd be pleased for me. I've finally got him out of those filthy stinking overalls and into a smart suit, and instead of mixing with the likes of Ben he'll be working with people who are going somewhere, making something of their lives."

Nina put her hand to her face, she was starting to cry.

"I'm sorry, I didn't mean it like that, what I meant to say was..."

Before she could finish, Nina spoke over her. "Ben isn't rubbish, if that's what you think. Yes, he's a fool and he's left me for a girl half my age, but that's because I kept on at him all the time. I was always trying to change him, and all I succeeded in doing was driving him out, and where's that got me? I'll tell you where, I'm alone now, left to bring up the children on my own. I've been stupid and I've messed everything up."

Nina got up and headed out through the kitchen door. She passed Tim as he was coming in, but instead of speaking she pushed past and made for her house. Melanie ran up the path in a bid to catch up with her, but when she got to her she met with a hostile response.

"Leave me alone, Mel. You've got what you wanted, I'm happy for you. You don't have to attack Ben though. You have no idea how I'm feeling, do you?"

Once inside her kitchen door, Nina made to shut it behind her, making it obvious to Melanie that her company wasn't wanted.

"Nina, I'm sorry, I'm so sorry for what I said. Please let me come in. You are my best friend; I can't go home and leave you like this." She pushed the door open and went in. Nina had thrown herself down on her cream leather sofa, where she wept without reserve. Melanie squeezed onto the edge of it and put her arm around her friend.

"Nina, sweetheart, come on, we need to talk. I've never seen you get so upset before. There's more wrong than you've told me, isn't there? Come on, let's have the rest of it."

Nina laid there with her head buried into a cushion. Yes

there was more than she'd told Mel, but it wouldn't do to speak about it. Not now, not ever. She could hardly look up and say, "Well actually, I find your husband very comforting when I'm as down as I am now, and as you appear to be rather more fond of my boss than your husband I'd like to borrow him at times like this to make me feel better." No, that crazy moment with Tim was a fleeting moment in history. Tim had probably forgotten about it altogether, but then he was doing just fine. Mel was doing just fine.

Melanie stayed with her until one of the children came in from playing.

"What's wrong Mum? Why are you crying?"

"It's OK, Alex, Mum's just a bit upset, don't worry. You go on out and play. I'll sort Mum out".

Nina sat up and dried her reddened face with tissues. Melanie still had her arm around her and together they sat for a while longer before either of them spoke.

"It will get better Nina. I doubt if this thing between Ben and this girl will last five minutes. You know Ben, he'll be back and wanting you to let him off in no time. I'll ask Tim to go and find him, find out what he's doing, and then Tim can come round and put you in the picture. How's that?"

"Yes, that might help, but I think you're wrong about Ben, he's done a lot of daft things in the years we've been together, but he's never left me before. This is different, Mel."

After a short silence Nina spoke again.

"How is your thing with Ratty now?"

Melanie was shocked at the mention of his name.

"What do you mean Neen? Ratty's nothing to me. Never was. Only someone I had to put up with at that law seminar thingy for the sake of my work."

The dismissal of Ratty in this way confirmed to Nina that they had really made up on holiday. Even if Tim did come round with news of Ben, it wouldn't be like the last time he'd comforted her.

"I'll be all right now, Mel, you go back and finish your unpacking; I'll see you later when I've sorted myself out."

"If you feel down, Nina, come round to me, promise?"

"I promise, thanks Mel. Sorry I was a bit uppity just now."

"You were fine; it was me and my big mouth. I'll see you later."

As she started to cook a meal for five she reflected on the way Nina had acted. Quite unlike her normal self. But then things weren't normal, her husband had left her.

"Tim, you need to find that mate of yours and see if he's still got the hots for that young thing. I promised Nina you'd talk to him and then go round to her, hopefully to give her some good news on him coming back, try to cheer her up a bit."

Tim thought about the last time he'd cheered Nina up. His head filled with guilt as he looked at Melanie, sweet unknowing Melanie. God she must never find out what he'd done in a moment of weakness. He loved his wife more than anything in the world, always had. How then had he behaved like that, with her best friend of all people?

"I won't have time tonight Mel, I've got to get myself ready for tomorrow. Ready for my new job. I've also got to go down to the yard and collect my tools. That's gonna be a bit embarrassing. I've really shit on my firm. I go off on holiday and then phone up from France and say I'm not coming back. You know how hard it is to get fitters, they're gonna be well stuck until they can replace me."

"That's not your problem Tim. You've done what's best for you and for all of us. I'm proud of you." She moved close to him and put her arms around his waist.

He knew she was right; it hadn't been like this in a long time.

CHAPTER EIGHT

"Ben, it's Tim. I'm back from our two weeks in the sun, and I've got loads to tell you ... are you going down the Globe tonight?"

"I don't go down there much now, Tim. Beckie and I prefer to go into town but yea, OK, why not? I certainly wanna hear your news, and I've got some news to tell you."

"I'll be there about eight'ish. See you then?"

"Looking forward to it, Tim, see you later."

Tim pushed his mobile back into his pocket and went in search of Melanie.

"I've arranged it, Mel. He's meeting me at the Globe at eight. He also said he's got some news for me. Let's hope he's had enough of Beckie and is planning to get back with Nina."

"Did he hint at that?"

"No, he didn't. In fact if I think about what he said it's hard to fathom out what he's up to. He said they don't go to the Globe much because Beckie prefers to go into town. Maybe that's the key to it, she wants the clubs and her young friends, but he can't keep up the pace and misses his pool games and wants to get back to his old routine. After all, it can't be easy satisfying a young twenty something... can it?"

"I don't know and you are not about to find out, so take

that smirk off your face Tim Fisher and get back to satisfying this almost forty something before I find someone more capable..."

They laughed as Tim scooped her into his arms, easily picking her up. He carried her to the bedroom and pushed the door shut behind him with his outstretched foot, placing her carefully on the bed. "What did madam have in mind?" he enquired.

"Madam prefers to have a surprise."

They played for a while until inevitably the chemistry manifested itself into a frantic scramble to make love. They lay together for some time afterwards, Tim with his arm around Mel's naked body, confining her to his caress.

"You will grill him tonight, Tim, won't you? Nina needs to know when he's coming back; she's broken up at having lost him. Strange when you think of how she used to go on about him all the time. I often thought she would be glad to be rid of him; in fact I'm sure she said as much to me, but now she sees only loneliness for her future. She won't accept that she might meet someone new, someone better suited to her than Ben. Let's be honest, they weren't suited were they?"

"That's the trouble with women, you moan about us when we're with you, but it isn't until we've gone off with some young attractive enticement that you realise how lucky you were to have us. I can't help thinking Nina brought this on herself. I mean, I'm not saying I don't feel sorry for her, but she could have treated Ben a hell of a lot better than she did."

"Trust you to be on Ben's side. He's a shit and you know it. OK, so he's your mate, but I haven't forgotten how he nearly broke us up just weeks ago with all his phoney marriage guidance advice, which *you* followed to the letter. You gave me serious shit, Tim Fisher, thanks to that prat, and you are lucky that I didn't bugger off and leave you. Don't you ever try all that eating at the pub stuff again or I'm warning you this bed will go cold and stay cold."

Tim didn't like the way that the slightest mention of Ben stressed Melanie. This conversation was rapidly undoing the good work of the holiday and the subject needed changing fast.

"Well, tomorrow's my big day, my new career. What do you think I should wear?"

"Not too difficult a choice for a man with hardly any decent clothes. You could wear the suit you got in France or you could wear those bloody awful trousers that you wore to the Walnut Tree. If you do, your career with Simon Stonewood might end before it gets started."

"I don't know what you hate so much about those trousers. They weren't cheap."

"Remind me, Tim, who were you with when you bought them? Whose fashion advice did you seek on that momentous occasion?"

"You know who I was with. Ben and I went shopping after football… oh that's it isn't it, you hate them simply because Ben had a say in choosing them?"

"Tim, you can be quite stupid sometimes. You know my feelings on Ben, yet you insist on defending him. If you don't want a row, I suggest you shut up about him and take those trousers to Oxfam, got it?"

"Mel, it's a deal. There's no way I want a row with you about anything, especially Ben."

"Good, but I do want you to meet him tonight to sort him out and get him to go round and see Nina. Even if he won't stay get him to talk to her, promise?"

"Well, I promise to try, Mel, but please don't blame me if he's not ready yet. I'll do my best".

The pub was unusually busy for a Sunday evening. Tim saw Ben standing at the bar with Beckie. He observed them for fully a minute before making any attempt to go over and say hello. Beckie was quite stunning, a good looking girl ...was she a woman? She was certainly very young. She had her arms around Ben's generous waist in a display of affection intended primarily to let female predators know that he was hers. He remembered that he'd been sent here to persuade Ben to dump her and get back to Nina, but that seemed like an impossible task. She was smiling, bubbly and not the slightest bit embarrassed by the obvious age difference between them. How could he mention Nina in her presence? She didn't look like she was about to be separated from Ben, even for a second. He threaded his way towards the bar.

"So, Ben, how's it been?" Tim shifted his glance to Beckie, "Hi Beckie, you're looking good." She held out her hand and he took it without thinking, she shook it enthusiastically. She was full of life, brimming over with vitality. He could see how it would be fun to wake up with her every morning and go to bed with her every evening. He experienced a pang of jealousy at Ben's good luck. He knew every man in the pub was taking notice; he wasn't the only one who envied Ben.

Beckie finally let go of his hand and turned to her partner, "Tell him, Ben, tell him our news".

"OK, but I don't want to tell the whole pub, it's too important for that."

"OK, I'll tell him," she said and taking hold of Tim's shirt, she dragged him out of the pub to the roar of his mates... "Trust Fisher to nick her off you, Ben. You don't want to trust him with her. Five minutes outside with him and she won't want you back anyway." The raucous remarks continued, but Ben smiled and took a sip of his pint. He knew exactly where he was with Beckie.

Outside in the car park, Beckie was still holding Tim by his shirt.

"I know your Ben's best mate, he's told me loads about you, and so I want you to be the first to share our news," she said.

Tim was excited by her presence, by her hold on his shirt. Her relaxed attitude to intimacy was something he wasn't accustomed to and it had a profound effect on him. He was willing to listen to her, he would follow her command to the letter; he was under her spell and loving every second of it.

"Ben and I are going to try for a baby."

He was speechless. This was going to change his script entirely, the script in which he was supposed to reason with Ben about going back to his wife, that slightly overweight, respectable lady next door who made a hobby of moaning at Ben throughout her waking hours. He laughed inwardly at the thought of any man letting Beckie slip from his grasp in favour of Nina. Right now he would have thought about leaving Mel if Beckie had asked him to try for a baby. Christ, pull yourself together... he remonstrated with himself for having lecherous thoughts, thoughts about the girlfriend of his best friend, the best friend whose wife he had slept with just a couple of weeks ago. You bastard ... how can you even begin to call yourself his best friend?

"Well, are you happy for us? Ben said you would be made up at our news."

"I am, I am, I promise, it's just a bit of a shock that's all."

He hugged her, as was expected of him at a moment like this. She responded with exuberant enthusiasm by squeezing herself tightly to him. As he let go of her he wished he hadn't enjoyed the contact as much as he did. They made their way back inside with her leading him by the hand. The cheers began again amid innuendoes that they had been intimate in the two minutes they had spent outside. To Tim it felt as if they had been intimate. If only he could experience the same thrill from Mel, when she had something to tell him.

"Congratulations, Ben."

He was forced to hug his mate, although he knew if Nina or Mel found out how enthusiastically he had received this news he would be in it up to his neck. Ben leant forward until he was within an inch of Tim's ear. "This is it, Tim, this is the real thing. I love this girl, with her I feel like I can fly." Tim could understand that, he had been almost airborne just talking to her.

"Ben, you need to go and see 'her' ...you've got to mate. She has to be told, she still thinks you're coming back. She's in a hell of a state, crying and blaming herself for driving you out. I'm in the middle of it. Mel sends me round to convince Nina that you'll soon be back and Nina cries constantly... I'm running out of things to tell her. Please will you go and sort it out, you owe her that much". Beckie had heard most of what he'd said.

"Tim's right, Ben. Nina is your wife. You have to treat her with a little dignity at a time like this. We'll go there together and explain how happy we are and tell her what we're planning. Once she understands that it's over she'll be glad for you, glad that you're happy and that she can move on with her life. It's the uncertainty that is upsetting her, making her cry. I'd be the same in her shoes. She needs to know exactly how things stand and you'll need to work out access for the kids, that sort of thing. She'll need to be reassured that I'm fit to look after them when they come to stay. These things are crucial to a woman at a time like this."

Tim was trying to picture Ben and Beckie sitting in Nina's front room telling her their news. It was too bizarre to contemplate. Nina would kill both of them, her only difficulty being to decide which to kill first. Beckie seemed to think it would be tea and biscuits and a friendly little chat to sort out the details. She didn't know Nina. And if that wasn't enough to think about, he had to work out what he was going to tell Melanie when he got home. This was enough to stop her speaking to him for a month, and probably worse. Despite the problems that lay ahead, Tim couldn't bring himself to be unhappy for Ben. This was a good relationship, one in which they were both incredibly happy. He couldn't spoil this by any more lecturing of Ben on his responsibilities to Nina or his kids.

"Tim, you said you had some news for me?"

"Yes, it seems pretty unimportant now, after hearing yours. I've chucked my job at the yard and I start as a Personal Assistant tomorrow for a guy who's got more money than you or I could ever dream of."

"You're joking... you a personal assistant? What, you

mean like you do his typing?" Ben laughed at his joke and made typing impressions with his hands. "Take a letter, Miss Fisher, sorry Mr Fisher, will you..."

"Ben, please don't take the piss. This job means a lot to me, not least because it's got me and Mel back together again, properly I mean."

Beckie admonished him, "Ben, Tim didn't treat you that way when we gave him our news, you say sorry. I think its brilliant Tim; I hope you love your new job. I'm made up for you. She pulled his shirt again and reached up to kiss him on the lips then gave Ben a scornful look, "He is sorry, aren't you?"

Ben knew he'd overstepped the mark. His humour had fallen flat this time. He put a huge arm around his pal and pulled them together. "I'm chuffed for you, Tim, you know that. I'm glad you and Mel are sorted and this job sounds good. What *do* you have to do?"

"Well, firstly I drive him around. I'm also there to look out for him in case of any problems – not that I'm expecting any, he's a good bloke. I've spoken to him on the phone, and he sounds really nice. He's going to kit me out with some decent clothes, none of your peaked cap nonsense, it's not like I'm a chauffeur. I don't really know myself what I'll be doing but I do know he gets around in a Mercedes Maybach, half a million pounds worth of it, how about that?"

"You lucky bugger, Tim, give me a ring tomorrow night and let me know how it's gone will you?"

"OK, I will, and you let me know when you're going to go see Nina. Mel's expecting me to go round and tell her what I've found out tonight. I don't want to be the one to tell her your news, happy as I am for you two; you can see where it puts me, can't you?"

It was Beckie who answered. "Don't worry Tim, you find out what night Nina will let us visit and we'll go there together and tell her everything."

Tim wasn't certain how he could 'not worry' in the circumstances but he would do his best. They played a couple of games of pool before Tim said good night and returned home.

"So, what did he say? I bet he's sorry now, sorry he ever messed Nina about for some little tart he met in a night club. She's probably met six more since then... he's made a mess of it this time and no mistake. I hope you told him how lucky he is that Nina is prepared to give him another chance..."

"Mel, stop, listen will you? It's nothing like that. He is in love with Beckie and she is in love with him."

"Love? That idiot doesn't know the meaning of the word, unless it comes in front of beer or snooker. I told you what to tell him. It sounds to me like you've messed up and fallen for his daft talk. You're saying he's still seeing her then?"

"Mel, will you please listen? She was there tonight, with him. I saw it for myself, they are in love properly. He is never going back to Nina. She, Beckie that is, promised that they would go and see Nina together and explain everything, sort out things like access to the kids, and all the other stuff that they'll need to sort out."

"She'll sort him out, you're not forgetting she's a solicitor are you, Tim? She's handled loads of divorce cases, she'll put that bastard through the mincer, you wait and see. Access? He never even wanted access to his kids when he lived with them. She'll see to it that the next time he sees them they'll be driving their own kids around. God he's got a bloody nerve."

"Mel, I'm his friend. Did you want me to say, "Sorry mate, I can't wish you well, my wife is your ex wife's best friend?" He's a new man, you should see him... you should see them both. They look so happy together I think it's for the best. I'm as sorry as you for Nina, but she did treat him pretty badly. I know he was as bad... maybe they just weren't right for each other. This way she can move on, find someone closer to her in class, someone she can look up to. I think in a year or two you'll see that this was the best thing for both of them."

"Well I hope you're going to tell her all that, Tim, because I wouldn't want to have to. Just be prepared for her to crack up completely when you give her this 'good' news."

"I didn't say it was good news, I can't help what has happened, can I? All I'm saying is it'll work out for the best in the end." When shall I go round there? I suppose it'll have to be tomorrow night. I can't really put it off but I wanted to spend tomorrow night celebrating with you, I'll have loads to talk to you about, after my first day. What's do you think is best?"

"You're right, Nina knows you saw Ben tonight, you'll have to face her. Tell you what ... I'll feed the kids early and then do us something nice, you can tell me about your day over the meal and I'll tell Nina that you'll come round after. She'll understand. Come on, let's go to bed, I need to show you how cross I am with you..." She winked at him and turned off the lounge light before heading upstairs.

The next morning was bright and sunny, which matched Tim's mood perfectly. Despite last night's encounter with

Ben, his marriage was still intact. In fact, Mel had proved to him last night that she wanted him as much as she ever had. Now, with five minutes to go until he arrived to start his new job, the world was fine; everything was fine. He wished he'd had time yesterday to wash his van, as if somehow that would have disguised the fact of what it was, yet another of the things Melanie hated so much. This was another icon of his past that would have to go. As soon as he got his first month's money he would trade this in for something more in keeping with his new position. Perhaps he could pretend he'd borrowed the van, pretend it wasn't his. No that would mean starting on a lie, not a good way to start out. No he'd try to park it out of sight if possible and hope that no one would see it. Simon had given him instructions to get to his house and where he was to report for duty. Tim knew the area well enough, it was no more than ten miles from Elmthorpe, but Simon had told him the house was quite hard to find. 'I like it that way,' he'd said.

Tim drove through the village of Nempswell and about a mile out he saw the post box after which he was to turn left. The turning was easy to miss, unmarked and with high trees on either side allowing it to merge into the surrounding scenery. He slowly turned left and followed the lane until it split, taking the left split as per his instructions. Within thirty seconds he saw the sign, 'Nempswell Manor, Private Drive, Visitors only by appointment'. He pulled up to the large metal gates and got out under the observation of a CCTV camera, which followed his every step. So much for his hiding the van out of sight. Before he could press the button a voice spoke to him from the box mounted on the gate.

"You must be Tim Fisher?"

"Yes, you're expecting me?"

"That's right, Tim, Mr Stonewood gave you a password. Did he tell you to mention someone's name at reception?"

Tim knew he had, but he also knew he'd completely forgotten the name; this was his first failure, even before he'd even got inside the grounds. He tried desperately to remember the name but his mind was a blank. He'd better think quickly or see his credibility dissolve.

"Actually I was talking to Mr Stonewood on a mobile from France and it was breaking up really bad. I didn't get the bit about who to ask for, I'm sorry, but I do have plenty of ID on me. I brought my passport, driving licence, in fact, you name it I've got it with me. Does that help?"

"Tim, I'm going to open the gates, drive down to the house and then drive across in front of it, turn left to go around behind it. You'll see the garages and my office behind the kitchens. My name's Ian Mitchell. I'm Head of Security and your immediate boss. I'll see you in two minutes."

Tim did as he was told; trying as he did so to work out whether Ian Mitchell was friendly or not. Could he be miffed that he hadn't been included in the interview process? But then Simon hadn't even interviewed him. For a job involving security it seemed remarkable that it had all been done over the phone. A slight worry entered his head that this was not as straightforward as he had imagined. Was he going to be asked to drive the Maybach to Amsterdam and back, unwittingly bringing drugs into the country? He'd have to keep his wits about him if he was to avoid ending up in something nasty.

He turned in through the gates, going slowly up the long

curved drive under old horse chestnut trees until it turned sharply to the right and across a large well manicured lawn of an acre or more which led to a gravelled drive circling in front of the house to provide parking for at least twenty cars. The manor house was certainly grand, well hidden from the gaze of even the locals; it was a perfect hideaway for anyone wishing to stay out of the public eye, or perhaps out of the eyes of the authorities. As he arrived behind the kitchens an enormous man with the face of a career boxer blocked his path like a human roundabout. He pointed to a gap between two buildings.

"Stick it on the parking behind the laundry; at least we won't have to look at it all day then."

The van had made exactly the impression he had feared. Already he was down in Ian's bad books, he'd forgotten his instructions and he'd shown up in a shitty little van, not exactly the impression he hoped for. He parked the van as instructed and walked back to meet Ian, determined from now on to listen to every word, every instruction. He couldn't afford to muck this up; he had too much riding on it. What the hell would Melanie say if he blew it and had to go back to being a mechanic. It wasn't worth thinking about, this had to work.

Ian took his hand and after the customary introduction led him to his office overlooking the rear of the house. It was well equipped with expensive office furniture and a console containing ten monitors, each showing a view of the house, mostly the outside but at least one of the kitchen and another of a room presumably inside the house.

OK Tim, so let's see this ID and then I'll spend the next hour acquainting you with the house rules. Where you can go, where you can't, things like that. You don't smoke do you? He was clearly pleased when Tim shook no to the question. That's good, 'cos you can't bring cigarettes anywhere inside this office or the house. Mr Stonewood doesn't allow any kind of smoking.

Any kind? Was that a reference to drugs, Tim wondered?

If you see anything that looks unusual, you tell me at once, is that clear? If you think about doing anything without telling me first, don't... is that also clear. In the five years I've looked after Mr Stonewood he's never so much as caught a cold. That's because no germs would get past me... you know what I mean? I'm good at what I do. The bank spoke very highly of you. Welcome to my team.

"The bank? But I don't work for the bank. They don't know me at all."

"Tim, your wife works for the bank, has done for ten years; she's got promotion on several occasions, as I'm sure you'll know, she wouldn't have got that if the bank hadn't checked you out. Believe me, I've seen the records they have on you. There are details on there that you probably don't remember, which reminds me you should eat more for breakfast, it keeps your strength up through the day." Ian laughed and Tim wondered if he'd got that little snippet from the database or whether he'd heard his stomach rumbling. One thing he was sure of, this was no ordinary job.

"OK, so Mr Stonewood told you he likes to go up to town in his Maybach, yes?"

"Yes, he said I'd be driving it."

"You will, all in good time. First we are going out back in the field and I'm gonna show you a few tricks, driving

202

techniques you won't see in the Highway Code, but ones that would keep you alive if some bastard decided to take Mr Stonewood hostage for a ransom. He's worth a lot of money and he's a prime target for any scumbag who wants a big payday the easy way. The car has a lot of security built in and I'll run you through that later. Right now I want you to prove to me that you can drive out of any situation you might get into, better still I want you to prove to me that you won't get into a situation in the first place. The field contained at least a dozen cars, most of them dented – from previous sessions, no doubt.

Right, Tim, you take the Volvo estate, drive round the main track as if you're taking a normal trip. I'm gonna come at you in one of these vehicles and you must get out of my way. Whatever it takes don't let me stop you, do you understand? If I can stop your vehicle my thugs can take your passenger hostage. If that happens it's all over for you, probably with a bullet inside you, so unless you wanna put on weight suddenly, get your ass out of reach of me when I come at you, got it?"

"Ian, I'm a truck mechanic, I regularly drive all kinds of trucks. I'm used to being in the best seat when it comes to an argument on the road."

"Well I wish Mr Stonewood would let you take him up to London in a truck, I'd feel a lot better about that, but like most millionaires he prefers a car. Shame but that's the way it is. Let's go."

The volvo was tidy inside and worth ten times more than Tim's van. This seemed a shame when he realised that it was only used to practice 'road duels'. He drove around the track as instructed, watching for any of the other cars to start moving. On his third time around he saw a land rover coming up behind him. So that was it, Ian was going to push him from behind. Not now he was ready for it, he wasn't.

As he watched the mirror in anticipation of a shunt from behind he was suddenly aware that a black Ford had pulled out right in front of him, totally blocking his path. If he T-boned the Ford he would take his radiator out and probably disable the Volvo, then the Land Rover would close up on him, sandwiching him so he couldn't move. Game over.

He slapped the brake pedal to the floor and pushed the gear into reverse, with the clutch out and the throttle pedal hard down the car wheel span for a second and then shot backwards. He waited for the crash. He didn't have long to wait. The land rover gave a sickening squeal and a bang as it ejected steam into the air. He pushed the gear lever into first and swung a full lock to turn the Volvo around. Under full throttle he nudged his front nearside wing into the front corner of the Granada knocking it sideways and splitting the front tyre. The angle of the front wheel confirmed that the Ford's suspension was broken. That wasn't going to chase the Volvo today. As he headed away from the scene he looked back with pride at the devastation he had caused to two of the 'firm's' vehicles while only sustaining a bent boot and front wing damage to the Volvo. Ian was standing in the track as he came round again, signalling for him to stop.

"That was quite impressive, they are two of the best men in the business. Both ex-SAS, and now doing stunt work. I got them down here today to teach you a few tricks, but it seems like you already know how to stay alive. Well done."

The four of them went for tea in Ian's office, where they

discussed a lot more tactics to be used in the war on hostage takers. Although Tim knew a fair bit about defensive driving they were able to show him some useful 'tricks' that he hadn't seen before. When they stopped for lunch, Ian declared himself pleased with the morning's work. I think I'd trust you to take Mr Stonewood out and about after that, he said. It puzzled Tim why he always referred to him as Mr Stonewood when the man in question had insisted Tim call him Simon. No doubt the reason would become clear in time. After lunch Ian took him on a tour of the house, introducing him to each member of staff as he went. There were a total of ten members of staff, including Ian's wife who worked in Mr Stonewood's office inside the house.

It was part of the security that each member of staff knew the other's, so no intruder could try to pass themselves off as a new member of staff. There were passwords which could be used covertly in normal conversation to alert other members of staff to a situation. These words were banned from normal conversation, only to be used if needed. It was becoming apparent to Tim how seriously this household took security. He was now a member of a professional team, which meant he had to think security at all times.

"On your way to work in the morning you take a note of anyone following you. If you think you have a tail you drive straight past the gates and phone this number, which you save on your mobile under the name wife. If your phone gets stolen by no-goods that's the first number they'll ring. As soon as they do, we know we are on 'Red' alert. If you call the number, I'll ask you what's going down, but only after you've given me the codeword, so I know it's you and that you don't have a gun to your head. If you do have a gun to your head, you say whatever they tell you to, and I'll know you're in trouble. How long are you keeping that van?"

"Not long, why?"

"Every vehicle here has GPS tracking so I can watch it on screen every minute it's out of here. As soon as you get something you intend to keep, I'll get it fitted with a tracker. That way I can follow you if you get jumped. Look, don't worry about all this, the chances are nothing will ever happen, but the best way to make sure nothing can go wrong is to have a system in place to deal with it, right?"

What Ian was saying made sense, everything he'd done today made sense, yet none of it was what he'd expected. One thing was nagging at him though. Was this job putting Mel or the kids in any kind of danger? He would have to talk to Mel about it tonight, let her decide. It did seem as if Ian was professional and everything was in place to make it as safe as possible.

"Ian, supposing I am at home one evening, one of my kids answers the door and before I can say or do anything a guy with a gun tells us to do exactly as we are told. Now I'm not about to get brave, or stupid, with my wife and kids to think of am I? How do I let you know I'm in trouble?"

"Do you know, Tim, I've been hoping you'd ask me that question all day. It proves beyond doubt that you're the right man for this job, it proves I can trust you to be thinking, even in a difficult situation. OK here's what you do. You take this tiny black box which you keep in your pocket and press it, like this."

At once a shrill noise came from the control panel on Ian's desk and a red dot flashed on the centre of a map on one of the screens. That map is showing me where the red situation is, so right now it's showing here, see take a look, but this is also a GPS device so if I fix the control box up in your loft, one press of this button will tell me that you have got visitors. I can give you a second switch so you can hide it in another good location. Think of it as a panic button, keep it by the bed maybe, but it doesn't sound an alarm in your house, it sounds one here. OK, Tim, you've done really well, so now it's time to take you into town for your uniform."

"Hang on a minute, Ian, Simon, I mean Mr Stonewood told me there was no uniform. He told me I would be wearing a suit and tie."

"And so you will, Tim, which is why we are going to see Stefano, he's the best tailor in town, have you heard of him?"

"Never, where is his shop?"

"Shop? Stefano doesn't have a shop, he has an upstairs studio, not far from your wife's bank. His clients know where he is and he doesn't need to advertise, in fact most people have to wait a few weeks to get to see him. Mr Stonewood doesn't have to wait, hence when I phoned him just now he said to come on down, you ready?"

Apparently when 'Mr Stonewood' spoke people jumped. The bank, for example, had gone to great lengths to fix him up with one of their trusted employee's spouses. It seemed that the very mention of his name in high places would meet with an instant response.

"I suppose he doesn't have to book for a table in the local Bistro either?"

"Well seeing as he owns it, I guess not."

Ian drove them into town in his Renault Megane. They walked down the High Street until they reached the estate agent's building on the corner, not far from Melanie's bank. At the side door, Ian rang the bell and within seconds they were going up the stairs to the sound of Italian opera. Like so many artisans of Italian origin, Stefano was a character, expressive and assuring, happy in his work, for which he no doubt charged excessive amounts.

Before Tim could ask about fabric or colour, Ian had given Stefano his instructions. "The boss wants him to look the part, you know what he wants. When can we pick up the first suit?"

"I'll take a few measurements now and then I'll get my cutter onto it first thing tomorrow. If you can bring him back for a fitting on Wednesday morning I'll have him looking marvellous first thing on Thursday. That's the best I can do." He shrugged his shoulders and smiled. Even for Mr Stonewood my girls cannot sew any faster. Some things are worth waiting for. Mr Stonewood knows about quality, he understands that my work cannot be hurried too much or the quality will suffer. That would never do, so Thursday it is ...OK?"

Ian knew there was no point in pushing Stefano. He knew what was needed and, in any case, Ian wouldn't want to upset Mr Stonewood's favourite tailor.

"That'll be fine, do what you need to now and well see you again on Wednesday."

Twenty minutes later they were in the Renault heading back to Nempsall Manor. "Funny isn't it? You start work here and within a week your house will have better security than it had after your wife's ten years in the bank."

"I suppose the bank employ thousands of people in jobs like Mel's, they couldn't install security in all their houses could they?"

"Depends if they care enough about their staff? You will quickly learn that Mr Stonewood is a very generous man. Don't ever do anything to offend him and he will take care of you and your family like you were part of his family. He likes loyalty and respect, but in turn he gives the same to his employees. We all think very highly of him. You won't ever hear anyone bad mouth him for example, if you ever did do that he would know about it in minutes and you'd be history."

"Thanks for the warning, but I wouldn't do that. I've worked for my old firm for a long time and I've never said a bad word about them. When I rang to say I was leaving without notice I apologised and said I'd forfeit the money owed to me. They were very good about it, but I know they were unhappy at me leaving. I was their top mechanic for the whole fleet."

Tim's first day in his new job was almost over. It hadn't been a bit like he'd expected. They headed straight for Ian's office, where a fellow Tim had not met before was sitting at Ian's desk.

Ian spoke first, to Tim. "I suppose you're wondering when you'll get to meet the boss... and when you'll get to see the car?"

"Yes, I am if I'm honest."

"Well, the answer is now and in five minutes. Simon, this is Tim Fisher."

Simon Stonewood was nothing like Tim had expected, a small man, slightly bent over from rheumatism, with a slight hump on his back. He had a kindly face, sort of like Father Christmas, but not the usual fat one. Tim took Simon's extended hand into his and they smiled at each other like old friends. He had only spoken to Simon once before and that was from France.

Ian tells me you've done well today. He's got you sorted

out with something to wear – that's good. Tomorrow I need to go up to town so you'll just have to wear what you've got on. You'll be fine. Oh, and we'll be back by seven or thereabouts. Your wife will get used to our odd hours, but tell her not to worry, she'll see plenty of you. I won't keep you apart more than I have to, but we sometimes have to stay away overnight, you knew that of course."

"I kind of expected it," Tim said. I'm really looking forward to working with you and I'll give you one hundred per cent, you can rest assured of that."

"I know, Tim, I did a lot of checking on you before I asked them to get you to ring me. Well, I think Ian wants to show you the car, so I'll leave you to it now. Please pick me up at the front of the house at nine, once you drop me off in China Town you can go over to the Mercedes dealer where I've arranged for you to have a four hour course on the car. Your mechanical experience will be most helpful and I shall be reassured knowing you have been shown all of the devices on the car."

After wishing them both well, Simon departed and Ian led the way to the garage. This is what Tim had been waiting for all day. The next hour felt like ten minutes as Tim went over the car. It's got a V12 lump in it, develops five hundred and fifty horse power, goes like shit off a shovel, but take my tip, don't push it until you're used to it. This isn't like one of your trucks; this is more like steering a rocket, just watch you don't take off!"

Driving home was surreal. Five minutes ago he had been in the seat of one of the world's most expensive cars; now he was driving this excuse for a van. Tim wondered if Simon would ever let him take the Maybach home for the night.

Just imagine sticking that on your drive. It was half past six when he walked through the door and Mel was waiting to serve the meal, which had been ready for half an hour.

"If it's ruined you can blame your new boss, or maybe yourself. Do you think you could ring me if you're going to be late? Come on, sit down before you tell me everything."

"Well, for starters I'm off to London tomorrow, so I won't be back before seven; I'll eat in the day if you like to save you getting food at that time of night."

Tim related the day's events, proudly detailing how he'd shunted two cars to escape from an ambush.

"I've now got the best tailor in town, Stefano. He's just near your bank but I bet you've never even heard of him, right?"

"Wrong actually, Randy gets his suits there, reckons he knows more about cutting fabric than anyone outside of London. We all reckon it's because he likes having Stefano feel his crutch at the fitting. Did they tell you he's gay?"

"No they bloody didn't and anyway that's bullshit. Stefano's as straight as I am, I'd put money on it. Last thing tonight I met the man himself, not a bit like I expected. A nice guy though, I think I'll get on well with him, I'll soon know tomorrow."

"Well that's tomorrow, Tim, but tonight you've got another little task to take care of... remember?"

"Can't it wait Mel? I've had a long day and I need to be up early tomorrow. Nina can wait until the weekend. After all it isn't like I'm going to give her good news is it?"

"Tim, she knows you were going to see Ben last night, so if you don't get round there soon she'll be round here and I don't want to be there when you tell her what he's decided.

Please get round there and stay there until she's OK... you hear me? Don't just give her the bad news and then piss off back here, leaving her to cry all night. Your mate got you into this mess, you sort it out. I'll see you later, but if I'm asleep when you come in be quiet, you can tell me all about it tomorrow after work."

Tim put his shoes back on and begrudgingly made for the kitchen door. This was a task he could do without, one that Ben should be sorting out, instead of which Ben was probably out clubbing with Beckie while he had to break the news to Nina. Typical of Ben. At least she was pleased to see him and sat herself down next to him on the cream leather sofa. "Come on, Tim, tell me everything he said. Has he finished with that little tart yet?"

Tim felt a sense of revulsion at her description of Beckie. She was so bloody unfair, what did she know of her to call her a tart? He had spent some time with Ben and Beckie last night and he knew for certain that Beckie was not a tart, far from it. He wanted to say, 'She's a lovely, vibrant full of life young woman who's transformed Ben's life into something better, better than it could ever have been with you,' but there was no way he could say that and escape alive.

"Nina, it's not as simple as you seem to think. Firstly they are still together and I know you're going to be angry, but last night when I met Ben at the Globe he had Beckie with him. I promise you I didn't know he was bringing her."

"What's she like, is she still in school uniform?"

"Nina, she's at least twenty and I have to be honest with you... she's a nice person, I'm sorry, but she is. They seem really happy together. Nina, he isn't coming back, not at the moment anyway."

"Well, you've changed your tune. Some friend you've turned out to be, especially after what happened last time you came round, or have you forgotten?"

"Nina, I haven't forgotten that night. I will never, ever forget what we did that night. It was so wrong. I love Mel, as you well know, and I took advantage of you when we were both feeling low. I shouldn't have and I'm very, very sorry. I don't know what else to say except I hope we can stay friends. I would have loved to come round tonight and say Ben will be back next weekend, but he won't. What more can I do Nina?"

She was crying again, and not without good reason, given the news he had just imparted to her. He watched for several minutes, thinking that she had brought all this on herself. How could he have any pity on her? But as the minutes passed, it became more difficult to watch another being suffer, and she was suffering. Despite her part in driving Ben away, she didn't deserve to be so desperately unhappy. He placed his arm around her shoulder and she instantly pushed herself into his side, seizing the protection he was offering from the misery that was now her life, her life alone. She wanted the luxury of someone to hold her, someone to care if she was happy or not, but the strange thing was that she had never had either of these things when she was with Ben and she hadn't needed them. It was only now he was gone that she understood the pain of loneliness, of knowing he wasn't coming back, not tonight, not ever.

She clung to Tim, desperate for whatever affection he could spare her. She knew it would be hard for him to give her the support she wanted now that his relationship with Mel was back on track. She shouldn't even be thinking like that, but it was easy to be righteous when you had the love of a man; much more difficult when the only man who would share any time with you was the husband of your best friend.

It wasn't as if she wanted him to betray his wife, she wasn't after him for sex, she simply wanted him to hold her and be nice to her. She dreaded the moment when he would say he had to leave. Every woman is aware of the power she possesses and this was the moment for her to use it to best effect, even if what she was doing wasn't strictly fair. Who was making the rules anyway and what were rules for if not to be broken once in a while?

She slid forward, pushing herself closer to Tim and causing her skirt to ride well up her thighs. Tim would notice before long, she would see to that, but first she undid the top two buttons on her blouse, discreetly so he didn't see her do it, but so that the next time she moved he would be treated to the sight of more than just cleavage.

Tim's mind was far away, he was thinking about the drive to London tomorrow and wondering how he would get on with Simon once they spent some time together. He felt Nina wriggle in his arms and glanced down to see if she was still crying. He was met by a full on view of Nina's breasts with no attempt to conceal them. Could Nina really not know that her blouse had come undone? Was she so distraught that she didn't care that she was showing her legs – rather nice legs as it happened, right up to her knickers? He did the decent thing.

"Neen, sweetheart, your blouse is undone, it must have popped open when you moved, I wouldn't want you to think that I was looking without you knowing."

"I don't mind you looking, Tim, after all no one else is going to look are they? Let's undo all the buttons, what does it matter? She ripped her blouse open to expose her bra, pulling it off her shoulders and throwing it across the room. Look at me, Tim, am I so ugly that you can't bear to look, is that why Ben left, because I'm ugly? I always thought I had good legs but maybe they're not good anymore. I don't have cellulite though, look." And with that she undid her skirt and, taking her weight on her feet, she let it slip down past her knees before kicking it off completely.

Tim was acutely aware that Nina was sitting in his arms wearing nothing but her pants and bra, and these were pretty flimsy as underwear goes. He felt himself starting to sweat. His arms were now holding her bare flesh and she was willing him to hold her closer.

"Tim if you reject me then I know that I'm finished, I know that no man is going to want me now or in the future. Help me, Tim, please..."

"Nina, you are beautiful, I told you that before, when... you know ..."

"When you made love to me, Tim, is that when you mean? Why can't you say it?"

"Nina it was different then. You know how bad things were between me and Mel, but it's better now, we've sorted ourselves out. I couldn't do anything like that now; it wouldn't be fair to Mel... or to you."

"Let me decide what's fair, Tim, I need you now, I need you to convince me that life is worth living, that I am still a woman, a woman who is attractive. You know how it feels to be rejected, you were feeling it yourself only a few weeks ago, remember?"

"I'm sorry Neen, I can't do it... but I'll sit here with you for as long as you want. I'll cuddle you and help you to shake off this fear of being alone. I'm still your friend, Neen, that won't ever change; it's just that I don't want to be unfaithful to Mel."

Nina's womanly senses were as sharp as a razor; she had detected the first signs of weakness in his declaration of faith. He was weakening, once he started he would grow weaker still with her help.

"That's all I want, Tim, I want you to hold me, cuddle me, don't let me be alone, protect me, you're so good at that. Why is it I feel so safe in your arms? You have so much power over me. Do you feel it, the power you have?"

Tim wasn't sure if what he was feeling was power or not, but he knew for certain he was feeling something. He also knew that he was changing shape. Nina rested her head into him, then lifting her head she undid his shirt to place her head onto his skin. He couldn't deny he liked what she was doing; he enjoyed being a comfort to her. He was satisfied that he was doing nothing wrong, nothing that counted as being unfaithful. In fact he thought back to what Mel had asked him to do. 'You must look after her, don't leave her crying, stay there as long as you have to, but see she's all right'. Those were her words. Holding an almost naked woman was a test of his resolve, he knew this, but after all, he only wanted to do what she had asked of him. He must take good care of her. He felt his arms explore her body in an effort to comfort her, to comfort them both. She responded at once, moving to make it easier for him to access her. She let her hand wander to where she knew she would find the evidence of his growing excitement. She was pleased to find she hadn't been wrong. They stayed like that for several minutes, savouring the intensity of the situation, each knowing that soon they would progress still further. Although he wouldn't admit it, he had already submitted to Nina. He could only observe as she undressed him completely and then rid herself of her remaining clothes. He failed to protest as she slid across him and they slowly experienced everything that each had to offer before making sensuous love.

When Tim finally stood up to replace his clothes it was past midnight. He kissed her again and crept quietly out of the house. Back home, he went upstairs without using the light and silently got into bed alongside his sleeping wife. His mind was in turmoil at the enormity of what he had done, not once but twice now. Once again he tried to imagine having to explain his actions to Ben and Mel at the same time. He fell asleep dreaming of Nina and Beckie and Melanie.

CHAPTER NINE

Melanie was glad she'd booked yesterday as an extra day of holiday. She'd learnt years ago that it takes a full day to unpack, do all the washing and get back to normal. Tim was off to London on his first trip with his new boss, and wouldn't be back till gone seven so she had time to get home from work, have a relaxing bath and be ready to hear all about his day. The first day back at work after two weeks in the sun was sure to test her resolve but she was feeling more confident now, almost her old self again. Mentally she was taking stock of all the changes she had wished for, and achieved in just two weeks. Her husband had gone through his silly phase, it was almost a distant memory now, when he chose to eat at the pub rather than sit down to eat with her, and when she had come close to cracking up. She recalled with a smile the night she offered Tim a sausage sandwich for his evening meal, and the reaction it evoked. The row that had followed had nearly split them up. She had even reached a point where she no longer fancied him and had refused to satisfy his needs.

That chapter was well behind them now that she had re-invented Tim from being a boring lorry mechanic with dirty fingernails into a personal assistant to a millionaire. What a transformation in just two weeks. Yes, she had good reason to be confident, she could still get results and that was why the bank had promoted her more than once. They knew she was a decision maker, a results getter, in fact management material; who knew the next move could be to Senior Account Manager, or SAM as they were known in the bank. That would put her on the next floor up and push her salary up another four grand a year. Very useful with the possibility of university fees looming in the not too distant future.

If she played on her current strengths she was convinced she could be upstairs by Christmas, after all with two SAMs about to retire the bank needed her skills as much as she needed the promotion. It was all but in the bag. She put the large bag of Provencal sweets near the printer for everyone to share, in customary fashion after returning from a holiday. The next task was to work her way through two weeks of e-mails, most of which could be deleted without the need to read them. One that immediately caught her eye was from Jo, the Office Manager: *'Mel hope you had a great holiday, the Divisional Manager wants you in his office at eleven. Sorry don't know what it's about, but I wouldn't be late if I were you, Jo'.*

John Higgs, the DM, was something of a mystical figure in the bank. Although he was on the next floor up, along with the SAMs and Internal Audit, he was a very private man, a man of few words, and despite his three years at this office not much was known about him. His image as a secretive figure was enhanced by his secretary, a spinster nearing retirement age who also played her cards very close to her chest. Despite her earlier confidence, an audience with Higgs was sufficient reason to bring on an attack of the butterflies and as Mel made her way up the stairs to his office she was less convinced of her importance to the bank. All the old doubts came creeping back, so that when she finally sat across the desk from him she was expecting the worst.

"Melanie, you've been on holiday, France wasn't it?"

"Yes, how did you know that?" Her surprise at him even knowing her name was obvious.

"It's my job to know these things," he said, with a reassuring smile, "but actually I was involved in the matter of your husband being recommended to Mr Stonewood. Martin Bateman talked it through with me in a private meeting before we asked security to run the usual checks on you and your husband. Forgive the apparent intrusion, but you do hold a responsible position in the bank, Melanie, and these things are part of the price you have to pay for that privilege."

"Oh, I don't mind. Honestly I'm fine about it and, if you're interested, Tim, that's my husband, got the job. Great news for us, we're both very excited about it."

"Good, I'm glad it's working out well and I've got even more good news for you."

So, she was on her way upstairs, he must've read her mind as she drove to work this morning ... 'I must promote Melanie Fisher today, I'll call her up at eleven and tell her the good news, "Melanie, I want you to become one of our Senior Account Managers, you'll be personally responsible for some of the biggest accounts held by the bank" ...' She was still imagining what lay ahead when she noticed John Higgs was staring at her with a bemused look.

"I was very impressed by the request we had from one of the partners at Osborne Melrose recently for your services at a legal seminar at the Hilton. That shows how well you get on with our top clients and it puts you in a good position on my roadmap for future promotion. Anyway, this client, Mr Naziree has been on to us again. He wants you on secondment for a month, some big project for Stellar Haufman plc, which will involve us in providing substantial finance. If you pull this deal off, you'll be on this floor from the moment you get back from Poland."

"Poland? ... what the heck has Poland got to do with it?"

"Poland is where the project is centred. Stellar Haufman want to take over a former state owned company in Poland; an electronics firm who have apparently done some excellent R and D. They have huge production facilities which are now within the EU but which operate at less than half of the cost of a similar facility in the UK."

"Well, I'm very pleased for them but I can't go to Poland with Mr Naziree. Did you say for a month?"

"That's right, that's how long he expects negotiations to last. You'll be there to represent the bank in all of the dealings, but the intention is that we'll get the business for the entire Polish project of Stellar Haufman. We are talking about a figure that will make it one of the three biggest accounts in this division. You pull this off Melanie and your future in the bank is guaranteed, in short you'll have it made. You will be known throughout the bank and the industry. You'll be the one giving seminars to business people after this. I'm just glad I'm able to push you into this wonderful opportunity."

"Mr Higgs, I'm flattered at the offer, of course I am, but I'm a married woman, I've got three children, I can't go off to another country, leave my family for a month."

"That's a pity. Can I ask you to go home and discuss it with your husband? I'm sure he'll be supportive especially if you explain how important it is to your career."

"Are you saying that I'll miss out on promotion to Senior Account Manager if I don't accept this brief?"

"I think it's more a question of you retaining a position here in the Regional office if you refuse to carry out the instructions of the bank. This is a high profile customer and a high profile project. In other circumstances I would try to hush it up and send someone else, but the client has insisted you take this instruction, and if you refuse he could well take the business elsewhere. If that happens your career in management is over."

"But that's unfair... I'm a mother, and a wife, I can't just leave my family for that length of time."

"Ironically, Mrs. Fisher, your reason would have been accepted years ago. I would have been obliged to put someone else onto it and the bank couldn't have done a thing about it. That all changed, however, when your union negotiated equal pay for women employees. Part of the deal the bank agreed was that in return for equal pay, women would be required to carry out equal tasks, regardless of what those tasks might be. I suppose you could say that's perfectly fair. Look, I'm sympathetic to your situation, but I have to have your answer by tomorrow morning. I'm already coming under pressure to get it organized, but I couldn't do anything until you returned from holiday. We'll meet again at ten tomorrow, but be under no illusions about what I can do to help you. If you decide not to go you will almost certainly be out of here by tomorrow night. You know exactly how the bank operates in cases like this."

"Yes, I remember poor old Jenny crying herself sick after her five o'clock briefing."

"So do the sensible thing, get child care. The bank will pay all your reasonable expenses and your husband can surely live without you for four weeks, or are you saying you can't survive without him for such a short time?"

"Yes... well no... I love my husband, we've just had a brilliant holiday and got ourselves back on track. We were having a few problems, you know the kind of thing, twenty years of marriage and all that... it's just that it's not a very good time for us to be apart."

"Ten o'clock tomorrow then. I'm sorry, but after that it's out of my hands."

Melanie left his office gritting her teeth and clenching her fists... bloody Rat.

Rat by name and Rat by nature. He was doing this to get at her because she'd turned him down. So either she went off with him for four lousy weeks, or she got the sack. Devious Bastard!

Back in the office she found it hard to settle to the work, piles of it, two whole weeks' worth of it. Within minutes of getting back to her desk, Jo was hovering over her, itching to find out what the call upstairs had been about.

"I suppose you've got your promotion, you're off upstairs, is that what the meeting was about?"

"Well it is and it isn't, Jo. If I bugger off to Poland with Romeo Ratty from Snotty and Co I can have promotion, and if I say no I can have the sack. That's it in a nutshell."

"So what will you do? You can't throw away everything you've worked for in the last ten years, not when you're being offered a move upstairs... wish they'd offer me a month's holiday and a promotion. I'd phone Andy from here and say, 'Get your own bloody tea, I'm off for a month, and don't forget to wash the bath after you'. I know what you should do, Mel, and so you do. Jobs like that only come around once in a lifetime. Be honest, Mel, if you left the bank where could you go and get another job close to that salary?"

"Yes, I know, but that doesn't make it any easier, does it? What do you think Tim will say? Christ, a month? That's half a lifetime when you love someone, and how can I go a month without the kids? Get a child minder, the bank'll pay... that was John Higgs answer, as if it was that easy."

"Well, it does help, Mel, it means you can employ a nanny, the very best you can get, and it's not costing you a penny."

"A nanny? You mean have a young girl sleeping at my house for a month while I'm abroad? Oh yes, Tim would bloody love that, wouldn't he? Just like his fun friend Ben, he'd have her in my bed before I'd learnt to say 'Hello' in Polish. I wonder if the bank will pay for my divorce lawyer as well as the nanny. This is terrible, Jo, what am I going to do?"

"Why don't you take the rest of the day off, go home, search the yellow pages for a good nanny – by good I mean efficient but ugly – and then explain it to the kids. Get the new nanny round to the house today if you can, and then tonight take Tim out for a meal somewhere and explain the whole thing to him. He'll be fine about it, trust me."

"It's my only option isn't it? I suppose I should be glad they didn't say 'Outer Mongolia' and six months. She forced a smile and Jo responded."

"Look's like I'm going to have to answer all your e-mails

for the last two weeks and then for next month as well. I'm the one who should be complaining."

The kids were surprised to see their mother home from work at lunch time, so she decided to get that part of it over and done with. "Whatever you do", she said, having explained the situation in detail, "don't say a word about this to your dad. I'm going to take him out tonight and tell him over a big juicy steak. Promise?"

"We promise," they said in unison.

Her next call was to a firm called 'No Nonsense Nannies,' and that is exactly what they were. At four o'clock a young woman by the name of Trudy was standing at the door with a form in her hand.

"I've been sent by 'No Nonsense Nannies', here is my identity and letter of introduction. Her accent was that of a Scot and her manner was abrupt but friendly. After glancing at the letter, Melanie invited her into the lounge.

"Would you like a cup of tea Trudy, before we start to talk about why you're here?"

"I'll make it, don't worry, you just leave everything to me." Before Melanie could answer, Trudy was in the kitchen, the kettle was on and she was searching for the tea bags. She looked at the letter again and muttered to herself. I see what they mean about 'No Nonsense'. Best let her do it, she decided, no point in putting her down so soon into their relationship, and after all if she was willing to look after the kids this well, she'd have little to worry about while she was away ... or would she? She hadn't dared to say to the agency, 'I want someone ugly.' Somehow she doubted if you were allowed to say that, it was probably illegal under some European discrimination law.

Trudy wasn't ugly. OK, she would probably never grace the cover of Playboy magazine but she certainly wasn't bad looking, and her figure was... well it was twenty one years old, that's what it was; no spare tyre, no cellulite and no bloody stretch marks. Shit, this was the one part of the plan that had badly misfired. She would have to spell it out to her, 'Now look, you're a nice girl and I can see that you're going to be good at taking care of my three beautiful children, but, and this is a big but, don't shag my husband while I'm away!' No, I can't say that, she'd think I was paranoid, mad, she'd probably think I was off to spend a month in a stress clinic. What about, 'Trudy, you're a very nice girl but I want you to know I love my husband very much, even though I'm leaving him for a month.'

"Do you take sugar, Mrs. Fisher?"

"Ah... no, no, I don't, thanks Trudy."

"Here you are then, good and strong the way we like it in the Hebrides."

Melanie laughed at her. "We call it builder's tea! Is that where you're from, the Hebrides?

"Och aye, I'm only here for two days."

"Sorry, I thought the agency said you would be available for a month."

"So I can, I meant I'm only arrived here two days ago."

"Oh I see, sorry, right, well your letter is excellent, I'm sure you will look after my three babies for me and keep them safe and sound. Welcome to our household, I'll move James in with Henry so you can have his room. I want you to have your own room. I think that's very important – that you have a room where you can shut the door at night and be completely and totally on your own, don't you?"

"I don't understand, the agency said your children were all at school?"

"They are, that's right."

"But you said, 'your three babies'."

"Oh, it's a term of endearment. I call them my babies, I probably always will, even when they are out to work and having babies of their own. I guess it's a mother thing. We're a very close family you see, especially Tim, that's my husband and me. We are very much in love. It's going to be very hard, leaving him for four weeks, but I have no choice."

"I'm sure he'll be fine, don't worry I'll take good care of him for you."

That's supposed to stop me worrying, she thought!

"Trudy, if you are sure you're happy to work here for the next month, I'll get the children in and you can meet them. They're playing next door."

"Please, I'd like that, I feel at home here already."

Melanie went in search of her offspring, wondering if Henry was old enough to take on the responsibility of keeping his father and the nanny apart for the next four weeks. How can I explain to him that his father may be overcome by sudden urges to mate with the young woman who is caring for you, rather like Ben from next door has found solace in the arms of a girl the same age? I could say it's a middle-aged crisis. No he'd never understand, but I know who would.

Nina will be perfect for this; of course she knows how a middle aged man can go off the rails when left for a few minutes with a nubile young female whose only need is for experience. Yes, I'll talk to Neen, she'll keep the horny bugger in check if the bonnie lassie starts shedding her tartan in front of my husband.

She gathered up the kids and dragged them back to her house. Now you know what I explained earlier, well this is her, this is your nanny for the next four weeks. Please be nice to her and spend as much time as you can with her especially in the evenings when she might get lonely, being so far from home, got it? They said they would, but she knew they wouldn't remember after the second night. What a pity I don't trust Tim. I did until that row a few weeks ago, but thanks to my giving him such a hard time then, I'm not sure now. Back inside the house, the kids took to Trudy in seconds. She was at an age where she could relate easily to their interests and the conversation soon left Melanie behind. Social networks really weren't her strong point. Well, there I was worrying about deserting my family and they couldn't care less, my replacement has only been here ten minutes and she's got their total attention. All that remains is to break the news to Tim, but at this rate he'll probably offer to take me to the airport tonight. After all that bullshit I gave John Higgs about my family missing me, it turns out they don't mind in the least.

To say Tim was surprised would be an understatement. He arrived home to see Trudy eating with the kids as if she'd known them years. Not unnaturally he expected an introduction. She seemed a little old to be one of their friends and yet they were responding to her as if she were a long time friend. Their conversation centred on their plans for next week, the last week of their school holidays.

Melanie would no doubt explain over their meal. She usually made sense of everything, except there was no sign of her or of any cooking in the kitchen. Things were unusual to say the least. Tim found her upstairs in their bedroom getting ready to go out.

"Mel, there's a girl having tea with the kids. She's too old to be at school with them and she seems to think they're spending the whole of next week together. Who is she?"

"Tim, I'll explain a hundred things to you, but not now and not here. She took hold of him and planted a kiss on his lips. I said it would be good, you coming home clean and tidy. Come on we're going out, and I'm treating you to a meal."

It seemed like the only option was to do as he was told, and if the kiss was anything to go by, it looked like being a pleasure anyway. A brief goodbye to the kids and they were off. Melanie drove to the bottom of the road and then stopped, "Where do you fancy Tim? How about the Walnut Tree? Let's see if I can make up to you for giving you a tough time on our last visit there, what do you say?"

"Let's do it!" Tim was in paradise, his marriage restored, his wife adoring, and his new job better than he could have hoped for, life was so different to the way it was before they went on holiday. Putting on a suit in the morning had changed everything including his personality. He wasn't even thinking like a motor mechanic anymore. He was, after all, a Personal Assistant, a man with real responsibility, someone who had to think on his feet, always aware, so when Mel said the plans for the evening had changed, he took it in his stride."

The Maitre de welcomed them at the Walnut Tree. Yes of course he could seat them; indeed, it was always a pleasure to welcome them. Mel wondered if he remembered them from last time. If he did he was very discreet. This time they had a table near the bar with a view across the entire restaurant. Seated on a stool next to the bar was a middle-aged man, almost certainly of Mediterranean origin, his rugged features no doubt acquired from spending years in the sun.

Melanie was mesmerised by his physical charm as he sang ballads and gently strummed on his Spanish guitar. She'd wanted tonight to be special but this was exceeding even her expectations.

Melanie took Tim's hand. Time, once again, to explain what was happening, just like she had in the mountains of Provence. "Tim, I had a shock waiting for me when I got into work this morning. If I tell you I came that close," she held up her first two fingers of her right hand an inch apart, "that close to resigning, you'll get the picture. It has been a bitch of a day, all thanks to that bastard at Osborne Melrose, you know, the one Nina works for."

"Sorry Mel, can you start again? I'm not following this at all. Why would you resign from the bank over a bloke that Nina works for?"

"Because he," … she stopped, remembering just in time that she'd never told Tim about him asking her to attend his speech, she'd simply said it was seminar on legal matters. This would mean changing the story slightly, which wouldn't make her task any easier, but there was no option. "Right, let me start from the beginning. Mr Naziree, that's Nina's boss, has asked the bank to put me in charge of a colossal project to finance a new venture in Poland for Stellar Haufman. They're a major client of Nina's firm. It means the bank will fund millions for the project and I have to go to Poland to oversee the whole thing on behalf of the Bank."

"Poland? You won't be able to fly there and back in a day, Mel."

"Tim, that's why I almost resigned, I have to stay there for a month, that's how long they expect it to take to get the deal signed off."

Tim was lost for words until the realisation hit him, "You said you *almost* resigned? Does this mean you've said yes?"

"At first I said no, but then I was told if I didn't change my mind by ten o'clock tomorrow morning I could clear my desk, I'd be out of the bank, finished, career over. We can't afford that Tim, even if I was prepared to see my entire career go down the pan, we'd be struggling on just your money, even with your new job and just say… say your job didn't work out… what then? I don't have any choice Tim, you can see that can't you?"

"Is there no way round it, can't someone else do it? Why does it have to be you?

"Because this guy is insisting I manage the project."

"But why? Why does he want you?"

"He's heard that I'm good at my job, that's what Higgs told me."

"It looks like I don't have any say in it then, but I'll miss you Mel. Four weeks is going to seem like a lifetime. I suppose we'll manage, as long as you phone me every night."

"Oh, I will Tim, I'll probably cry down the phone for two hours every time I hear you or the kids. My trip to Poland is the reason for that girl, Trudy, being at our house. I got her from an agency, she's a nanny, and she'll be with you for the next four weeks."

"Well I'd be struggling without some help, what with the new job and everything, but I think we'll be fine. Just don't stay there a minute longer than you have to."

The singer wandered between the tables singing love songs. It was easy to see why this place was so popular, good food, a romantic ambience; it was perfect for two people in love. They ate their lamb shank with Mediterranean vegetables and enjoyed a Spanish love song. Mel watched Tim and knew that she had nothing to fear from Trudy. Tim was in love with *her*, he respected her, unlike that idiot Ben, who couldn't keep his hands off a twenty year old out on her own for probably the first time. What they had was special, the culmination of twenty years together, bringing up three children together. Four weeks would be like a moment in time in their relationship.

At ten o'clock Melanie was outside John Higgs' office. She knew that him keeping her waiting for five minutes was part of the corporate game; it was done to make her feel inferior, to emphasise the difference in their status. He would know that she was here to say yes; no one of Melanie's intelligence would wash away a lifetime's career for the sake one business trip. She'd made her protest, that was permitted under the rules, the unwritten rules that was, but by the time set by him, she must be back, ready and willing to do as she was told, and if that involved leaving the bosom of her family for a month then so be it. The phone rang and the secretary answered it, "You can go in now, Mel, Mr Higgs is ready for you."

I bet he is, she thought. I'd love to see his face if I told him to stick Poland and stick his job, but I can't and he knows that. He'll have checked our joint account, he'll know what our standing orders are each month, and our earnings, he'll know precisely why I have to do as I'm told, but I doubt if he'll know how bloody angry I am about it.

"Mrs Fisher, good morning. How did it go with your husband last night? I hope you explained to him the importance of your role in this project?"

"Yes, I did and he was most supportive, as I knew he would be."

"Good, he's a sensible man, that husband of yours; I've heard a lot of good things about him. In fact, I shouldn't really tell you this, but I had an e-mail from Simon Stonewood first thing this morning. He's very pleased with him, says the bank did him an enormous favour in recommending him. That's another feather in your cap. The fact is, if you pull off this Polish project successfully, your future is made. You'll go into a very small group of Senior Account Managers who are recognised for their special ability at Head Office in London. You are on the verge of becoming a name within the bank, and that's something very few of us ever achieve."

"So, when do I leave? I'd like to know a bit more about the project and what I'm meant to secure for the bank."

"Don't worry, as of now your normal duties will be assigned to someone else. I've convened a special meeting for twelve, over lunch. I will chair the meeting. Securities will be there as well as Internal Audit. Mark Standish from our overseas office in London is already on his way down here. We should finish by five. By then you will know what you can lend, against what security and at what rate. Once in Poland you will be 'The Bank' but don't forget I'm at the end of the phone if you need to talk any part of the deal through with someone. I'll give you my direct number after this afternoon's meeting."

Melanie noticed the shift in his tone, the change in his

manner towards her; suddenly she was getting respect where before it had been curt instructions. She had already been promoted in the minds of the bank's hierarchy. In spite of her reluctance to take the project on, she liked the new feeling of respect, she was already comfortable with the knowledge that while she sat through a five hour meeting on the top floor, her mates downstairs would be churning their way through the boring everyday paperwork, and one of them would be saddled with hers as well. This new sensation of power was something you had to experience before you could describe it, like a drug, powerful, satisfying and something you definitely wanted more of. Back downstairs Melanie had just two hours to clear up any last bits of paper and to tell them what was happening. She was the centre of attention in the office. The rumour mongers had worked overtime since yesterday's meeting, after which she had gone straight home.

She's been sacked, she's had a mental breakdown, she's been transferred to London. Only Jo, the Office Manager, knew the truth, but true to her position she had said nothing. Now Melanie told everyone where she was going, and why. Someone produced a bottle of sparkling wine and a toast was proposed to her success in Poland. She loved working with these guys and probably the only downside to her future was the knowledge that she would have to leave them behind when she returned to take up her new position upstairs. Randy took control of affairs and insisted that Melanie make a farewell speech.

"I've been very happy in this office and you've all been wonderful to work with. I've had good days and bad days, but never a day when I didn't enjoy the friendship of every one of you. I shall miss you if I move upstairs, but if I cock up this Polish adventure I might be back with you yet, so please wish me luck."

Randy cheered and raised his glass. "Good luck to Melanie in Poland, and here's to a successful project. Who knows? If she makes the bank enough profit on this deal we may all get a rise."

They all laughed and joined in the good wishes. Melanie wiped her eyes, aware that nothing like this had ever happened to her before. She reflected on how a month ago she had felt despair at her apparent inability to remain in control, she was close to losing her marriage and was convinced she was a total failure. Now her marriage was the best it had ever been, her husband had a fantastic job and she was at the pinnacle of her career, swamped with success. What a difference a month made. She spruced herself up and re-did her make up. She had to look the part for the twelve o'clock meeting. She would be observed by people who, until today, had never heard of her. She was to be the star of the show and, she told herself, "At twelve I'm going to make my big entrance and by five I will have to have given the performance of a lifetime. In four weeks time they'll be writing their reviews on me and I'm going to make certain they're the best."

John Higgs wasted no time as he introduced Melanie to the four others in the meeting. Now she was Melanie, what a change from yesterday when she had been Mrs. Fisher. The others were comfortable on first name terms, but for Melanie board room meetings were breaking new ground. She struggled to call him John, thinking instead how she would prefer to address him as Higgs. One day, maybe?

"Some of you may know, he started, a few weeks ago Melanie was asked to provide a report on a seminar given by a senior partner from Osborne Melsose Law, a highly respected firm of lawyers. Clearly it was a stunning report because that same firm have now requested, I should say insisted, that Melanie represents the bank in negotiations for a major client of theirs, a firm you will all know, Stellar Haufman plc. This requires Melanie to work at the negotiating table in Poland for the next four weeks and, if successful, we will be writing a very substantial amount of business. In addition, we look likely to win the Osborne Melsose account itself. The delegation to Poland will consist of Mr Rattani Naziree, Mr Hugh Ballantyne, Major Projects Executive of Stellar Haufman plc and our own Melanie Fisher. They are booked into the Park Hotel, Poznan, where most of the negotiations will be held. Whilst there they will visit the production facilities of Praza at a number of locations. Praza is the former state-owned information and communications technology company that Stellar Haufman is seeking to buy for a client. Because of the continuing problems caused by Air Traffic Controller strikes you will be leaving from Waterloo on Friday Morning, to Brussels where you will take the connecting train to Cologne. There you will board the German ICE train, on which you will have lunch during the five hour trip to Berlin. From there you take the Berlin-Warsaw express to Poznan. The hotel mini bus will be waiting to take you and all of your baggage to the hotel.

Melanie was struggling to absorb the vast amount of information that was being crammed into this five hour session. In the centre of the table sandwiches sat in neat little triangles, minus their crusts, on a silver platter. French pastries overflowed from another and there were jugs of coffee and fruit juice. This was life on the top floor, better get used to it, she thought.

One by one they set out the requirements of their departments in the making of the deal. She was given top secret numbers for contacts at Head Office who could advise on any aspect of the deal at pretty much any time of the day. Melanie was given details of her expenses account and told to use it however she saw fit in order to keep the delegation happy.

When Melanie confirmed that she was happy with the details, she was told to take the rest of the day off as well as Thursday. "This will give you time to pack and to spend a day with your children," John finished. "If you need to buy clothes for the trip please do so using your expense account. We must have you looking your best."

That evening Melanie handed over her home responsibilities to Trudy. She told her what date the kids started back at school and went through a list of the things they would need for the new term. There was a lot to think about; four weeks was a long time in a household with three school children and Melanie couldn't go until every detail was written down for Trudy to follow.

What instructions should she give in respect of Tim? Feed him once a day, wash his clothes but leave everything else for me to sort out when I return. Deep down she still wasn't entirely happy at leaving them to share the house together.

On Thursday night she cried bitterly, and wished she hadn't agreed to go, convinced that the house, the kids and

Tim would all be gone in four weeks' time. Tim was good at times like this and his big arms enveloped her as he whispered gently, "You'll be fine, we'll be fine, and in four weeks' time you'll have loads of stories to tell us about your trip. We'll miss you, of course we will, but you can phone us every night, the bank can pay for that, and a month will pass in no time at all."

She wished she could be sure that he was right, but at least it was nice to have him giving her so much attention. How ironic, she thought, that just as their marriage was back to where it should be they were to be separated. She woke up twice during the night and spent long periods trying to get back to sleep while thinking of all the things that might go wrong in the next few weeks. What if one of the children was ill? What if they had an accident? What if...? When the alarm went off it was as if she'd never been to sleep. She got up, showered and made breakfast, for she was determined to remain in control until the minute she left. When that moment arrived, the kids all kissed her dutifully and then Tim took her in his arms. "I love you, we all love you, be safe, call me every day, and come back soon, love you forever."

She kissed him but words were out of the question. Tim placed her two large cases in the taxi and closed the door on her. His last view of her as she drove off was with a tissue covering her eyes. Only then did he succumb to the tears that had been beneath the surface since he awoke.

They got through the day thanks to the mobile phone. "I'm on the train", "I'm in Brussels", "I'm in Cologne", "we're having lunch on the ICE train, it's fabulous Tim, like a five star restaurant travelling at a hundred a fifty miles per hour", "we're almost at Berlin; I'm frightened, I wish I was back home; we're on the Warsaw Express". "Tim, we're crossing the border at a place called Frankfurt Oder, across the girder bridge that was the scene of so many battles in world war two, I recognise it from those old war films." And then, "I'm at the hotel, it's dark now so I didn't see much of Poznan, but it's a lovely hotel, my room looks out onto a huge lake and there are lights, hundreds of them reflecting across the water. In the morning I'm going to get up early and go down to see the lake before breakfast. I'm tired, I love you Tim and I miss you so much, goodnight, kiss kiss."

Tim went to bed as exhausted as Melanie. He felt like he'd travelled half way across Europe, but now he had to try and sleep in an empty bed and that would be hard. He always reached out for her before he went to sleep. She'd say, "move your arm, I'm too hot," or she'd turn away to get more space, but he knew she'd find it just as hard as he would to sleep alone.

In her hotel room, Melanie put her clothes into the cupboards. It was like she was moving in, she thought. Thank god it was a nice room and a nice hotel. Four weeks in a grotty hotel would have been a nightmare. She finally climbed into the double bed and pulled up the covers. Maybe it was that she hadn't slept the night before, or maybe it was the excitement of the journey, but within seconds she was fast asleep until the sun shining through the curtains woke her. There was no better awakening than to the brightness of the summer sun. It washed away the fears and tears of the darkness and made everything perfect. Her mood was still happy as she showered and prepared for her first day of business. She hadn't said ten words to the other two on the journey, there was no need. They'd been deep in conversation and she was too busy watching the scenery and phoning home.

Today she would have to face them, and in particular Rattani Naziree. If he thought dragging her a thousand miles from her home and her loved ones was going to make her friendlier towards him he was in for a nasty surprise. She arrived in the restaurant to find the most fantastic array of food imaginable. Cold meats, cheeses, breads, cakes, jams, the huge centre table was awash with mouth watering dishes. To one side was a hot covered pan with scrambled eggs and sausages. At its side were fresh oranges and a juice machine. Coffee, tea and jugs of fruit juice were lined up ready for the morning's diners. All she had to do was eat, what a wonderful way to start the day.

The view from the picture windows was of the lake. Dozens of people were already out exercising on foot, on bikes and on roller blades on the six kilometre path that surrounded the lake. She hurried her food so that she could get outside in the sun and take a closer look at this huge park with its lake. Once on the path at the water's edge she turned right and could see in front of her a dry ski slope and a toboggan run constructed on a huge purpose built hill. That had to be investigated, she thought and within five minutes she was at the foot of the ski slope. A couple of food bars and gift shops were preparing for a busy day, while on the slope men were working on the chairlift. The whole thing was so exciting, so unlike anything she had expected that she found herself falling in love with the place. On the lake teams were rowing encouraged by a trainer in a motor boat. Was she watching their Olympic team in training? A couple of motor coaches arrived and emptied upwards of a hundred young children into the park; a sea of happy faces, they at once turned her thoughts to home and her three offspring. They would be getting up about now. Would Trudy take proper care of them, making sure they had sun cream on before she let them out? Get a grip, Melanie, she told herself, they'll manage just fine, you just make sure you do the same.

Back in her hotel room, she plugged her laptop in and checked out some of the stuff she'd been given, all the notes from the meeting were here so she could refer to them before going into a meeting. When they arrived last night, Rattani had told them to meet in the hotel foyer at ten. An hour yet, should she ring home? Tim would be getting ready and the kids might still be asleep. Better wait until tonight she decided. Right now she had business to attend to. Large, brown leather sofas made the huge foyer a good place to meet and tables of fresh flowers made waiting pleasant. She observed the comings and goings of the guests, 'people watching' as Nina would call it. Coaches were bringing new German tourists in, while another group were dragging their cases towards the glass doors to leave. Saturday was probably change over day for most guests.

She didn't see Rattani until he sat down next to her. She moved along to put distance between them.

"Is that how it's going to be for the next month?" He said it quietly and with his usual smile.

"I don't know what you mean; I'm here to do business for my bank, that's all."

"Of course, and I'm sure you'll do it very well. That's why I asked for you."

"You didn't ask for me. You insisted on it being me, you threatened the bank that they wouldn't get this business unless I came with you, you blackmailed them and they fell for it, but I know why I'm here and so do you. I'm a happily married woman and as long as you remember that we will get the work completed without any trouble."

"And if I forget, what then?"

"You bastard, I've told you I love my husband, is that so difficult for you to understand?"

"You know it is, and you know why. Have you forgotten how you sat next to me at Nina's party and told me you didn't love your husband? You told me lots of other things as well. You made it clear you had feelings for me. I told you the truth then, nothing has changed... I love you Mel and I want to be with you. In Poland, in Portugal, I don't care where as long as I'm with you."

"Ratty, you're a nice person deep down but I said those things when I was drunk. It was my fault, I was going through a lot of shit with Tim at the time, I even thought we would split up, and yes... I did enjoy your company, you helped me at a time when I was pretty low, but I'm through that now, Tim and I are stronger than we've been in years. I'm sorry if I used you, I never meant to lead you on, you were just there, and in the wrong place at the right time, I guess. Do yourself a favour, Ratty, stop loving me and find yourself a younger woman, one who will appreciate all the things you can give her. If you go outside you'll find hundreds of lovely girls busy taking their morning exercise around the lake. You might have trouble keeping up with them though, unless you're good on roller blades." She laughed in a feeble attempt to lighten the atmosphere between them. Ratty wasn't a bad person, he just wasn't the right person, not for her. She had her right person back home and the sooner he realised she meant it, the better for both of them.

He gave her that caring smile she had liked the first time she met him. "Have you had breakfast?"

"Hours ago and I've been out and explored the lake and the ski slope as well."

"Good, I think you'll like it here."

"Have you stayed here before?"

"Yes, a few times. There's a great deal more I want to show you around this beautiful city, but there's plenty of time for that. First we have some work to do and you have to make a few millions for your bank so that you can go back a hero."

"Ratty, I'm finding this really hard, being away from home and the kids, please don't make it any harder."

"I will do everything I can to make it easy for you, I promise."

"That's what I was afraid of."

Chapter Ten

Tim was standing watching over the Maybach in a street just around the corner from Trafalgar Square. Simon owned several properties in China Town and was particularly good friends with the tenants of the one he was visiting today, a Chinese family who had run it as a restaurant for years. Simon Stonewood was on first name terms with most of his tenants and there were a lot of them. His property portfolio extended to more than a dozen cities across the UK and a few dotted across Europe. He had been left a few run down buildings when his father died, but with hard work and a shrewd understanding of good timing, he had bought when prices were low and sold when prices were high, so that he now owned over two hundred properties, including restaurants, hotels, warehouses and shops. Sadly, his wife had been unable to have children and although he'd always remained faithful to her, their relationship had never been fulfilled as he would have wished. These days his first love was his property and he made sure he visited each of them at least once every year.

Tim was talking to the traffic warden. Funny how a ten pound note and a smile could solve even the most difficult parking problem. Simon kept him supplied with a wad of notes for the purpose, because he liked to have the car and his driver close by. In the Golden Dragon, Simon had been obliged to eat with the family so as not to offend them. They held him in great respect and his visits were always regarded as a special occasion. Eventually, when they had eaten their way through a dozen different dishes and updated him with their news, he was able to leave.

"Here he is," Tim said to the traffic warden, who had seemed glad of some friendly company to relieve the boredom of his turn of duty.

Tim opened the rear door for Simon then with a last farewell to the warden, he headed off to the next property on Simon's list.

"Wonderful people the Choy family," Simon said. It was nice, the way Simon talked throughout the journey, discussing the matter of rents or tenants with him. It was as if he needed someone to share all of this with. Simon had already explained that his wife had no interest in the business; "She doesn't even care about the money," he said, "she potters about the Manor garden and fills her day directing staff and arranging dinner parties. We share a wonderful life together at the manor, but all of this is of no interest to her. We could eat in a different restaurant every week for a year, all of them in places we own, but she refuses. "Rather have a few friends round for dinner at home," she says. So while I spend my days meeting up with my clients, most of them old friends, she spends hers in the garden or in the kitchen. I wish it could be different, but I know she'll never change." Tim sensed the disappointment in his voice at having so much to share, but having no one to share it with.

"Our next stop is with Harry, one of my first ever tenants. He's a proper Cockney, serves good food, but no frills. I need to talk with him about repairs, the place is falling down at the back but we've had problems over access. While I'm talking to him get some food inside you, ready for the drive home."

It was gone seven when Tim got home and, although he'd eaten well, he was missing the thought of the family meal and the faces that meant so much to him. This job would mean a lot less of those, which was a pity as he'd promised Melanie he'd spend a lot more time with them from now on. That was before she'd taken off so suddenly on a mission to make more money for her bank. Once home, he saw that Trudy had fed the children and was busy organising games with them, something they were obviously enjoying. Maybe they were pleased to see him, but they didn't see the need to break off from their game and he couldn't raise the enthusiasm to push his way in.

He rang Ben, hoping for an evening of pool and gossip at the Globe. "Sorry mate, Beckie's got tickets for a concert in town tonight, what about Monday night?"

"Yes, let's do that, it's getting to be a rarity for us to spend a night at the pub. I'll see you there about eight. With nothing planned for Saturday or Sunday, Tim began to realise how hard it was going to be to get through the next four weeks. He heard the kitchen door open and Nina's voice, "It's only me," and with that she appeared in the lounge.

"There you are. Have you heard from Mel, is she OK?"

"I'm expecting her to ring soon; I don't want to ring her because they could be meeting over a meal. I don't want it to look like we can't manage without her, she'll only worry."

"Have you eaten, Tim?"

"Yes, at lunch time."

"Well that's no good, you need an evening meal inside you. Melanie gave me strict instructions to keep you fed until she gets back. Come on, we'll go round to mine and I'll fix you something."

"Thanks, Neen, but I can't go out until Mel has phoned and, anyway, I'm not hungry. You know why, I'm missing her, missing her like hell and it's only day one."

"All the more reason to let me take care of you. She won't want you moping around while she's making millions for her bank over a five course dinner."

The thought of Melanie having dinner every night with a group of businessmen wasn't helping him to overcome his melancholy. They would no doubt find plenty to laugh about between the serious business; they'd become good friends, spending so much time together. This train of thought wasn't going to help him deal with nights spent eating on his own.

"I'll tell you what we'll do, you stay here until Mel phones, give her my love, and then come round and I'll make you some supper. She's bound to ring before the kids go to bed, so if you're not round by nine I'll come and drag you round."

Tim knew she wouldn't let go and what she said made sense. He wouldn't bother to get himself supper and if he sat here all night with no one to talk to he'd go crazy. Mel's call was shorter than he'd expected; she told him she was doing fine, they were, as he'd thought doing business over a meal and she'd had to dash out between courses to phone him. How were the kids? Could he call them down quickly so she could speak to them? In a few minutes it was over, she was gone, back to her meal and her precious meeting. Tim experienced uneasy resentment that she couldn't find time after working hours to talk to him properly. He'd been looking forward to her call all day, it was to be the highlight of his evening and it had lasted two minutes. He'd have it out with her tomorrow night, explain how important it was for them to talk, how much he wanted to hear her voice, to hear about her day. No, he couldn't take four weeks of this, he'd ask Nina what she thought, and she'd agree that what he was asking of her was perfectly reasonable.

"How was Mel? Did you send her my love?"

"I didn't get a bloody chance, Neen, she said hello, said she was OK and then spoke to the kids. I feel pretty pissed off about it. I thought she'd be desperate to talk to me, but obviously she's having such a good time that she isn't missing home at all."

"That's not how it is and you know it. She's there to do a job, and lots of business is done in the evening over a meal. You'll have to get used to this, Tim, once she gets her promotion."

"What do you mean? Are you saying this is the first of many trips abroad?"

"I'm not saying anything, Tim, except she'll be expected to entertain the bank's clients over dinner from time to time."

Entertain? Tim wasn't sure he liked the sound of that. In twenty years of marriage they'd hardly ever been apart and this was proving to be more difficult than he'd imagined. He kept going over the things she'd said when she told him about this trip, the night she'd taken him to the Walnut Tree, and after the meal how she'd entertained *him*!

"Neen, why did Mel make a point of telling me that it

was your boss who organised this trip, how would he know Mel anyway...?"

"They met round here, that night I had a few friends from work for drinks and you took Ben off down the Globe, just before he went forever."

"But why did he want Mel for this project, I mean there must be loads of people in the bank with more experience of this kind of thing than her. I know she's good at her job, but she's never been in charge of anything this big and certainly never any foreign deal."

Nina tried to contemplate the outcome if she didn't concoct a good story in the next two minutes. She remembered precisely the way that evening had ended; Ratty and Mel entwined together on the same sofa that they were sitting on at this very minute. She recalled how she'd got rid of Tim at the door when he and Ben had arrived home while the party was still going strong

"Well, he's new to our firm and to the area, so I don't suppose he knows anyone else at the bank."

"But would that matter? Come on, Neen, honestly... you work with this stuff all the time, you must know, wouldn't it be more usual to let the bank choose who went on a job like this?"

"I suppose so, but the danger is that he could end up with someone he really doesn't get on with, so if he knew one person in the bank who he felt he could get on with he might put her name forward. What does it matter?"

"It's probably just me being silly, perhaps I should try to get my head around the fact that Mel is incredibly good at what she does. In essence that was what she told me when we had that enormous row. I said I thought she spent her day adding up numbers and she went ballistic."

"I should think so, Tim. She's well thought of in the bank, I can tell you that. So what do you think I do? I suppose you think I get people off parking fines, do you? You are a bit of a pot-bellied chauvinist porker, Tim, admit it... the idea of women being good at something gives you a problem, doesn't it?"

"That's bullshit, Neen, I'm not like Ben, that's his philosophy for sure, he thinks women are only good at one thing, and we both know what that is. I respect you for what you do, same as I do Mel, but it's hard for me to understand your work or hers. How can I when I've only ever worked with motors?"

"Don't take it to heart, Tim, I don't think you're like Ben. I just wish he was like you – sensible, trustworthy, and *here*."

That last word sounded a warning bell in Tim's head. It was time he headed back home to the safety of his empty bed. "My God, is that the time?" he said, a nanosecond before looking at his watch, "I have to be up early tomorrow, I'd better be off."

"But I've got some lasagne warming in the oven for you. Eat that first, please?"

"OK, but then I must get to bed; I can't afford to be late on this job."

"It's a deal, Tim, lasagne and then bed." Nina was on her way to the kitchen; she turned and laughed dismissively at her remark."

"That's not funny, Neen. I'm not proud of what happened the other night and it must never happen again. We both know that."

Nina put the plate on the dining table and sat down

facing him. She watched as he eat his food. There was something very satisfying about feeding a man, having him praise you afterwards, maybe showing his appreciation. She had the measure of Tim's resolve tonight; he was in no mood to compromise his emotions towards Melanie. She would have to wait until he was missing her more, until he was suffering the pain of loneliness as much as she was.

"Are you ashamed of what we did, Tim? Are you ashamed of me?"

"No that's not what I meant, but we both know it should never have happened. It would kill Mel if she found out that her husband and her best friend had got it together."

"But she never will find out, not from me anyway. Tim, we must have needed each other or it couldn't have happened. Sometimes people need each other in a way that ordinarily wouldn't be right, but in that special moment it is right."

"No, Neen, what we did was wrong. I blame myself. You weren't to blame for what I did. I'm sure you would have stopped me if you could but I lost my self-control, and my self-respect. I have to live with the knowledge of what I did, but at least I know for certain that I'll never do anything like that again. I hope you can forgive me for using you like I did."

"Never...? That's a long time, Tim. Stop being so hard on yourself, I don't feel used at all. On the contrary, you made me feel like a woman... something Ben didn't do in years."

"Thanks for the food, Neen, it was nice, and nice of you to get it for me. You're a good friend."

"Well, promise me that I can be a good friend to you until Mel gets back; let me look after you will you?"

"I will, thanks for everything. I'll see you tomorrow. Tim was on the way out, no hint of hesitation in his stride for the door, no friend's kiss on the cheek as he left."

Nina cleared the plate away and tried to make sense of her feelings. What was she trying to do? Did she want to coax Tim back into her bed? Did she genuinely only want his friendship, companionship? Surely her friendship with Mel put him off limits. Most women would black ball her for what she'd done and she was prepared to let Tim think it had been all his fault. The fact is, she thought, he's going back to a cold empty bed and I am going upstairs to the same. Somewhere in Poland, Melanie is having dinner with the Rat and he wants her so much that he has orchestrated her presence there for one reason and one reason only. After seeing the effect he had on her here in two hours, can she seriously maintain her defence for a month? The fact is, she explained to herself, Rattani has got what he wants; four weeks of Mel all to himself, and time to work his magic on her. Why then should I feel guilty for helping Tim get through the same period without his wife? By taking him into my bed, I'm not only protecting him but I'm doing it for Mel as well. She smiled at her contrived conclusion; she had judged the case against herself and found herself entirely innocent. It was clear that her motive for seducing her best friend's husband was above reproach. She had asked the question and was satisfied that she was doing it for all the right reasons. She just had to convince Tim.

Tim's nightly visits became a ritual in the week that followed Mel's departure and each time the pattern was the same. Nina would pour Tim a glass of beer before sharing a meal with him. He would eat it and compliment her on her

252

cooking, while telling her about his day, his new job, the new people he was meeting and the new places he was going. Once, after he'd met a celebrity at one of Simon's restaurants, he was excited, eager to share his news with her. Nina in turn listened attentively to every word, asked the right questions and made sure he knew that she was interested in everything he told her. She would carry on the conversation from where it had been left the night before, proving she'd remembered where he was going that day and who he was likely to meet. As she began to learn about his boss and his work it became easier for her to encourage him to tell her more. She, in turn, told Tim snippets of gossip from her day, carefully chosen bits of information that he would find interesting but easy to understand. No point in boring him with heavy legal stuff, better to keep to the human details, and in a firm the size of hers there was always something worth relating. Tim looked forward to the meal and the exchange of news; they also talked about their feelings. It constituted a kind of intimacy, the sharing of private details, things he would normally have only revealed to Mel but, Mel wasn't there and Nina was very easy to talk to.

Whilst guarding the car outside a restaurant in Oxford, Tim reflected on how much he'd told Nina during the past week; highly personal things, things that belonged to Mel and him, but after a couple of beers and with only the prospect of returning to his empty bedroom, he became increasingly willing to share his innermost thoughts with her. Why not, he reasoned, after all... who else is there to tell? It's not my bloody fault that my wife has gone off with Nina's boss. He sat contemplating all that had happened in the past month. There was an uneasy pang in his stomach. Mel, his wife, his lovely wife... he loved her to bits, where was she? What was she doing right at this minute? She was somewhere in Poland. Was she thinking about him, missing him as much as he was missing her? If she was, she'd leave for home right now. He was missing her so much that at this minute he considered driving the Maybach to Dover then across Germany straight to wherever she was in Poland. He ached to see her, to touch her; he tried to picture her face and was scared when he couldn't. He couldn't see his wife's face; instead he was seeing Trudy and his kids sitting around the family dinner table, just as he did each night when he got home. There was something else that wasn't right; Mel's phone calls to him each night. OK, she'd talked to him for quite a long time on a couple of nights, but she didn't say much about what she was doing out there, about what she was doing each day and, more importantly, what she was doing each night. Each evening he told Nina all about his day, but he knew nothing about what Mel was doing. She always asked about the kids, asked him how he was, even asked how Nina was, but she never spoke about her time there. Why? What was it that she didn't want him to know?

He was sweating so much he had to open the car window. The cloud of anger around his head was suffocating him, drowning him in a fog of not knowing, not knowing what she did every night in Poland. He was getting himself into a panic, he needed to calm down, he opened the car door and stood outside in the fresh air and stamped his feet. Clenching his fingers open and shut should help to control his physiology, help to stop his brain from running wild. He needed to get back to his normal state before he went mad.

As quickly as the attack had started, it stopped while he paced up and down taking deep breaths. Thank God, he had got himself right, he saw his boss returning and tried to put the episode out of his mind. Simon chatted away as usual on the drive home and he listened as always, but today he heard nothing. When eventually he became aware of Simon's anxiety he snapped out his shell in an effort to act normally. "Sorry Simon, what did you say?"

"I asked you how your wife was getting on in Poland; in fact I asked you three times... are you OK, Tim?"

"Yes, of course, I was just concentrating on the road, that's all."

"No you weren't, Tim, you nearly hit the curb on that last bend. I think you'd better tell me what's worrying you. It's to do with her being away isn't it? Are you finding it hard to manage the children? Would it help if I gave you a few days off?"

"Thanks Simon, that's kind of you, but honestly they're no problem and the nanny, Trudy, she's doing a great job with them. I don't think they've noticed Mel's gone she's so good."

"But you have... noticed she's gone, is that it?"

"Yes, I'm missing her, missing her like mad if I'm honest."

"That's good, Tim, that's proof that you have a sound relationship."

"Do you think so?"

"I'm absolutely certain of it, and what is more, for you to feel like that you must both be very much in love with each other. I don't doubt that she is missing you every bit as much."

"I hope so, I really hope so."

"Tim I could fly you out to Poznan this weekend if you want? You could surprise her. You'd have to fly to Berlin and then get a train to Poznan. I've done the trip quite a few times. I have several properties in Poland. Sadly, as yet, I haven't acquired anything in Poznan, but I will, in time."

"Is it a nice place?"

"It's a wonderful place, Tim, she'll be enjoying the city and the food I'm sure. Ask her if she's been to the zoo, you know my love for animals, Tim, I visit zoos wherever I go and Poznan has an excellent one. If she likes animals she should make sure she visits it."

"I'll ask her," Tim said, instantly thinking, who would she go with...? She wouldn't want to go to a zoo on her own. Would she go with her work people? Why not? He fought against the imminent reoccurrence of another panic attack. What the hell does it matter if she goes to zoo with her work mates. It matters because she does everything with them; she works with them, eats with them... he stopped short of saying she sleeps with them.

Somehow he got them safely back to the manor and then drove home as fast as he could. He barely said hello to the kids and cut Trudy short when she started to tell him what they'd done earlier in the day. "Sorry, can't stop, tell me later, thanks," and he was out the door.

He walked straight into Nina's kitchen. It was force of habit now, and it would have seemed ridiculous to knock first. She was ready for him, same as every evening, smiling, reassuring. Tonight the smell of her cooking affected him the way lavender might an over-active child. He felt strangely calm for the first time in hours. He was bursting to tell Nina what had happened to him, to explain to her the crazy thoughts that had invaded his mind today. He needed to unload all that stuff as soon as possible. Nina would listen, she'd understand, she would help him through this. He downed his beer in seconds before attacking the food like he hadn't eaten for a week.

"Are you all right, Tim? You look like you've just escaped from Alcatraz. Are you going to tell me about it?"

"That's the thing about you, Nina, you can read me like a book. You understand me perfectly. I've had a terrible day; I wanted to get back here to tell you about it. Neen, I think I'm losing it."

"Go and sit down on the sofa and I'll bring you another beer, then you can tell me what's upset you. Whatever it is we'll talk it through, you'll be fine, trust me."

He did as he was told. He did trust her, she was the only person he could trust. He couldn't trust Mel, not at the moment. Where was she, what was she doing? Why hadn't she ever mentioned the zoo if it was such a big thing there, what was she hiding? He sat down, almost unaware of where he was, his mind was returning to the state he was in earlier; so many questions, so many things he needed to ask Mel, but where was she? Why couldn't he ask her? And that was another thing... why did she insist on always ringing him? She had made it clear that he should only ring her if it was an emergency. She would decide when they could speak, how long they could speak for, she decided everything. She'd probably intended to be picked for this trip, she'd said she didn't want to go, talked about resigning, but that was rubbish. Even as she'd told him how upset she was, she was telling him she'd decided to go anyway. It was a ruse, a plan to pull the wool over his eyes; he'd been a fool to even think she didn't want to go. All that stuff about their marriage being back to how it used to be... she'd said that when they were on holiday, but on her first day back at work she'd announced that she was off again for a month. She knew all along... it was so obvious... how come he hadn't seen it at once? Nina sat down beside him and passed him another beer.

"So, come on, Tim, out with it, what's upset you?"

"It's Mel; I don't think she's told me everything... I'm sure she planned this trip, she wanted to go with him, your boss, after you told me about that night here it was obvious. She hasn't told me about the zoo; why not? And why would she keep that a secret if she hadn't been there with him?"

Nina was confused in more ways than one. Had Tim found out what really happened that night when Mel had got too close for comfort with Ratty? How could he? He didn't know anyone who was at the party except herself and Mel. She'd admitted they met here but she hadn't hinted at any impropriety, and what was all this about a zoo? Had someone else put ideas in his head? She decided to find out more before she gave too much away.

"I don't understand Tim, what's this about a zoo?"

"Mel's bound to have been there, Simon told me. He knows Poznan well, he said everyone goes to the zoo. She wouldn't have gone alone, she went with him, but she never mentioned it to me, that's proof that she's up to something, isn't it?"

"I don't think so, Tim. I don't think it proves anything. You don't even know for sure if she's been to the zoo. Why don't you ask her? Has she phoned yet tonight?"

"No, well not when I left home."

"So you might have missed her call? Why don't you go back home until she calls and then come back and tell me what she said? We'll probably find you're getting upset about nothing."

"No, bugger her, I won't be told that I can't phone her. Why shouldn't I if she's got nothing to hide. Tim took his phone from his pocket and dialled the number Mel had saved into his phone."

Nina could hear it ringing. He looked pathetic, like a little child she thought, like those you see at the beach when they've lost their Mum. His expression exuded panic. Melanie's voice sounded anxious, as well it might be – after all, they had agreed he would only ring her if there was an emergency.

"What's wrong, Tim, is everything all right?"

"Yes of course it is... well no, actually, it isn't. I'm fed up with you lying to me about what's going on there. Have you been to the zoo?"

"Tim, you sound a little crazy, have you been drinking? Are you with Ben? He's put you up to this hasn't he? I might've known he'd be causing trouble before long with me not there."

"Well that's the trouble, you're not here, I'm here on my own and I've had enough Mel, do you hear me? I've had as much as I can take. I don't know what you're doing or who you're with. Why don't you tell me anything? Who are you with now? Is he listening?"

"Who's he exactly?"

"Nina's boss, she told me how you met at her party. You knew all about this bloody trip before we went on holiday didn't you...? All that bullshit about nearly resigning, you couldn't wait to bloody go, and I fell for it, every word of it."

"Tim, is Trudy there? Can I speak to her please?"

"No you can't. I'm round at Nina's."

"Then I'll speak to Nina, now Tim, please."

He handed the phone to Nina, "She wants to talk to you."

"Hi Mel, I'm sorry about this. Tim came round half an hour ago. I gave him something to eat but he is really distressed. I'm trying to find out what's upset him but he's in too much of a state at the moment. He's going on about the zoo; it seems to be quite important to him."

"Neen, he's just said that you told him about Ratty and me meeting at your party. Why? Why did you tell him that? That's bound to make him think something's wrong, and just in case you're wondering, nothing is wrong, especially on that front. This trip is business, that's all, so please make sure he understands that, will you?" Her voice was verging on anger.

"Mel, it wasn't like that, I can't explain now, I'll speak to you later, ring me at work tomorrow."

"OK, but are the kids all right? He hasn't gone and sacked Trudy in a temper has he?"

"No, they're fine, she's doing a brilliant job with them. You chose well with her and no mistake."

"Nina, this trip is hard enough without a phone call like this; I want to be back home with Tim and the kids. I've cried myself to sleep for the last two nights, but I have to stay here until it's all signed and settled and that won't be for a while yet. Please, Neen, can you look after him? Tell him the way I'm feeling."

"It might be better if you told him, Mel, it's you he

wants to hear it from, not me, but I'll do my best."

"Thanks, Neen, put him back on and I'll try, but it'll only make me cry again."

Nina handed the phone to Tim and then left the room.

"Tim, I love you, I promise you I didn't know about this trip until the day I came back to work. I want to come home just as much as you want me to... she started crying, uncontrollably... Tim, I'll talk to you tomorrow." Unable to say another word she rang off, leaving Tim holding the phone and feeling as confused as ever.

He put his head in his hands and wept silently. How had they come to this? They couldn't even talk to each other now without shedding tears. What had she said to Nina? Was she in on this game that didn't include him?

Nina came back and sat down next to him. He turned to face her, "What did you mean, Neen, when you said, 'It wasn't like that'? You said you couldn't explain now. Why not now? Because I'm here? Is that it? You said, 'Ring me tomorrow at work.' What's going on Neen? Are you a part of this conspiracy? I thought I could trust you, I really thought that I could trust you, but you're in on her dirty little secret aren't you?"

"Tim, love, I'm not in on her little secret. She didn't know about the trip, of that I'm certain. You can trust me," she put her arm around him and pulled herself tightly into him, "please believe me. I only told her to ring me tomorrow because I knew she was about to cry. If you really think I'm scheming against you then you'd better leave but if you do I shall be the one in tears. I'm here for you Tim, if you want me, that is?"

He turned and hugged her, letting all his desire for

261

human comfort explode in an effort to rid himself of the fears that had torn him apart all day. She was warm in his arms, willing, always willing to give him love when he needed it. She was a real friend, she wasn't at all selfish like Ben had always made her out to be. He just didn't treat her properly; if he had he would've discovered that he was married to a fantastic woman, a woman who would give everything to make him happy, not like Mel, who cared more about the bank than him. That had always been her bloody problem.

"Do you know, Neen, there are three of us in my marriage. That's why it will never work?"

"Three? Who's the third person, Tim?"

"It's not a person, it's a bank. She loves the sodding bank more than she does me. If she loved me she wouldn't have gone, would she? She'd have said stuff your bloody job, I've got a husband, but no, they said go and she said 'when'? I'm not stupid, Neen, I've known for ages that I was second to her bloody career. You've got a brilliant career as a successful lawyer, but it didn't stop you loving Ben, did it?"

"I don't know, Tim, maybe it did. I never thought he was right when it came to mixing with the people from my work. He simply let himself down, and he used to let me down, that's why I asked you to keep him out that night when I had my work people round for drinks. Maybe I'm a snob, Tim, but although Ben wasn't good enough for me, it doesn't stop me missing having him around."

"Do you still love him?"

"I don't think I've loved him for a long time, but he was part of the furniture, part of my life. I got used to dusting around him, putting up with his drinking and the fact that he couldn't hold a job down for more than five minutes.

Does that make me a selfish cow? That's what he called me in one of our last rows."

"You're not selfish, Neen, you are the least selfish person I've ever known. Tim put his head alongside hers and felt her arms around him. You've given me the most precious gift a woman can give a man, Neen. You wouldn't have done that if you were selfish. You've given me love when Mel was too busy to bother about me. I owe you, Neen, I owe you so much."

"If you believe that, Tim, take me one more time, make me feel complete, give me the love my husband should be giving me, please ... don't make me beg for your affection."

"I won't, Neen, you won't ever have to beg me for anything, and even if Mel and I get this sorted out I owe you too much to ever let you be unhappy. l want you right now as much as I ever wanted her."

They went upstairs and stayed there, together. It wasn't until six the next morning that Tim woke up with the sun streaming in through the curtains. He was completely naked alongside Nina, who was the same. He climbed quietly out of bed and went downstairs. When he woke her, it was with coffee and toast, and kind words.

"Nina, sweetheart, wake up. I've made us some breakfast, then I've got to get showered and off to work. He leaned across and cuddled her to him. I meant everything I said last night, Neen, you are a lovely person. I always want us to stay friends."

"We will, Tim, I promise you, whatever happens we'll be friends."

Simon noticed the difference as soon as he set eyes on Tim.

"You look a hundred times better this morning; did you

ask your wife about the zoo? Just talking to her has made all the difference hasn't it? You look your old self again, which is just as well because we're going to have to stay away for two nights. I've had a call from a tenant in Edinburgh; a few problems that need sorting out. We'll call round to your house when we leave here and you can pick up a few clothes. Maybe I'll get to meet your children, I'd like that."

Tim was also surprised at how good he felt, he was on top of the world, yet nothing had been sorted with Mel.

"We did talk, but not for long, and I asked her about the zoo, but she didn't seem to know what I was talking about. I don't care anyway. I feel good about things this morning. I won't be taking up your offer to fly out to see her, but thanks, it was very kind of you."

"Tim, when I asked you to take this job, I wanted more than just a driver, and I think I got more. I like to think of you as a buddy, Tim, someone I can share my property problems with. I suppose you think that's a bit strange, people tend to think that because you're well off you want for nothing. In fact nothing could be further from the truth. Yes, it's true I can have anything that money can buy, like this car, like the Manor, but Joan, my wife, has always been a very shy, private person. Nowadays she enjoys giving dinner parties at home but you still won't find her making speeches or coming out of the shadows. She prefers to leave it to me to do that sort of thing, while she watches from the sidelines. The truth is, Tim, I don't have many close friends. We're very happy together, but I miss having someone to share my business interests with. She doesn't want to meet the people we visit on these trips, yet most of them are fascinating people who look forward to my visits as much as I look forward to seeing them. Having someone to share the journey with and experience the welcome which awaits us is a pleasure in itself. It adds enormously to my enjoyment. You've a good head on your shoulders, Tim, and you're easy to talk to. Your wife is a lucky woman and I bet she knows it. Four weeks is a long time to be away from someone you love and I bet any money that she's hurting, just like you are, but she'll be back before you know it and then you'll appreciate each other all the more. Anyway, I intend to keep you extra busy until then, my way of helping you to get through it, OK?"

"Thanks Simon, I count myself very lucky to be working with you."

By the time they reached the Scottish border, Simon was asleep in the back. Tim turned the radio off, preferring to have some quiet time to examine the thoughts that were filling his head. He thought about what Simon had said. Even with all his money he needed something he couldn't buy; friends. Yet Tim had made two in as many weeks. Simon was a dependable man, one his father would have called, 'Officer Material', unlike Ben who could fairly be described as totally unreliable trench material. What about his other new friend? She had been in his mind all day, unlike yesterday when it had been Mel who occupied that space. The strange thing is, he thought, I should be feeling guilty but I don't, instead I feel a sense of relief. I actually feel perfectly at ease with what we've done... what we *are* doing... no to hell with it, I'll say what I mean ... what we intend to do. 'Look Mel, you're in Poland, you've barely found time to speak to me since you went there, you've shut me out of your life there, I don't know what you do or who you do it with.

There must by fifty people who know more about you at this moment than I do, waiters, taxi drivers, hotel staff, I bet they're all laughing at me and thinking, 'If her husband could see her now, enjoying herself like she's a single woman. Why? Why Mel? In the past we've shared everything, told each other everything. You've hurt me on this trip and I don't know if I can ever get over that. When you come back what are you going to do? Sit down for four hours and tell me everything that happened in Poland? No, of course not. It'll be, 'Oh I can't remember now'. All the events of this four weeks will be a secret shared only with Nina's boss and the rest of your cronies.' In his anger Tim forgot that this conversation was meant to stay inside his head.

"Well sod you; I've got a secret of my own!"

"Tim, what is this secret that is making you so angry? Would you feel better for sharing it?"

"Sorry, Simon, I was thinking out loud, I thought you were asleep."

Simon laughed, "I was, Tim, until you woke me up. Come on old chap, you're upset about something, that's obvious. I'm very discreet. I was brought up in a family where honour was paramount. My ancestors were tortured by the Roundheads, but preferred to die rather than betray the King. I can't promise quite that degree of loyalty but anything you tell me will go no further."

"It's a bit complicated, Simon. I don't even understand what's happening, so I doubt if you could."

"But I'm looking at the trees from a distance, Tim, unlike you; you're standing right in the middle of the forest. You're afraid that your wife might be tempted while she's away, aren't you? It's the most natural thing in the world to

266

feel that way because deep down you see it as a risk, a risk that you might lose the most precious thing in your world. Tim, I have a lot of influence, that's the one thing money does give me. Do you want me to make some enquiries at the bank about how the trip is going, that sort of thing?"

"Thanks Simon, but no. No one in the bank is going to say if she's found solace in the arms of Nina's boss. He's the one who arranged to have Mel go on this trip. That's the bit I don't understand. Why her? There must be people in the bank with more experience of this kind of thing than her. I found out from Nina, that's my neighbour and Mel's best friend that Mel met this guy, Rattani Naziree, at a drinks party Nina held a few weeks back, but she never said anything about him at the time. Then, all of a sudden, he's whisking her out of the country for a month. Doesn't that seem odd to you?"

"Tim, I'm your chum but I don't know your wife, so I'll try to be truthful without embroidering the facts to create a story which we don't know even exists. I've heard of Rattani Naziree. In fact, a few weeks back I went to a seminar at the Hilton, which he gave on contract law. He knows his stuff and he's highly thought of in the legal world, but that tells us nothing about his private life, does it? There are two ways we can handle this Tim. One, you let me hire a goof to follow her around in Poznan, he'll soon tell us if Naziree is coming on to your wife, and in the very unlikely event that she has fallen for his charms he'll give us proof; photos of them together, that sort of thing... or alternatively... you can trust her. The good thing about the first is that you will know the truth, for certain, but the bad thing about it is that you will always feel guilty for having checked up on her behind her back, and if she ever found out it might do immeasurable harm to your relationship. That is a decision, Tim, that only you can make. Why don't you think on it, let me know tomorrow after you've slept on it, OK? Good man."

I've only told you half of the story, Tim thought. I wonder if you'd still think I was a good man if I told you the rest?

"I will, I'll think about it." In fact he knew he'd think about nothing else.

It was Thursday before they arrived back, and as they parked the car at the Manor, Simon briefed Tim on his duties for the following day.

"Tim, I'm glad you decided not to have me hire someone to tail Melanie. I think you would have felt bad about it when she gets back, and I'm certain the answer would have been to say there's nothing going on, nothing at all. I want you to take tomorrow off, spend it with your kids, they're back to school soon aren't they?"

"Yes, I think so, I haven't been taking much notice, I've left it all to the nanny, she's been brilliant. I couldn't have got by without her."

"Well, take them all out somewhere and while you're at it, let her see she's appreciated. Have a lovely weekend and I'll see you here on Monday. We're up to London, but only for the day."

"Thanks Simon, for everything."

"Don't mention it, Tim, that's what chums are for."

At soon as they set eyes on him, the kids went wild, pleased to see him despite his dismal attempts at being a caring father during the past few weeks. Amy threw herself at him and even Henry hugged him. Trudy was doing a great job, but they were missing their mother, and Tim was the next best thing. He determined to spend the evening with them, perhaps the cinema, and he'd let them choose what they did tomorrow. Above all, he wanted to prove to himself that he could be a good parent;, not like Mel, who was willing to desert her children for the sake of her job. Whether he knew it or not, his actions were born of pure resentment, papered over by a facade of parental love and responsibility. He wasn't ready to face the fact that his resolve had disintegrated under the strain of being left to fend for himself. Not only was he happy to be manipulated by Nina, he was convinced that it was he who was steering that relationship. Trudy was delighted at the chance to cook for Tim as well as the kids and Tim was pleasantly surprised at how good she was, it seemed that she was good at everything, including being father and mother to his children. When he suggested they all go to the cinema they were immediately enthusiastic, each suggesting a different film. Once they had decided which it was to be they got changed and Tim drove them in Mel's car. It made him uneasy at first; the sight of her gloves on the passenger seat and the familiar smell of her car air freshener – Mel was fastidious about things like that. It felt really strange to see Trudy sitting in the passenger seat. Mel liked him to drive when they went out as a family and she'd often put her hand across to rest on him while he was driving. He missed those little intimacies, those unspoken moments that were worth a thousand words. Trudy was so excited, just as much as the kids in fact, at the prospect of an evening out. It was like he was spending his evening with four kids. He realised how lucky he was to have them.

It was gone eleven when they got home and after kissing

him goodnight the children went up to their rooms. Tim watched as Trudy made herself a hot chocolate. She sensed that he was uncertain of himself, missing his wife and trying desperately to make amends for his shortcomings as a doting father.

"Would you like me to make you a drink, Mr. Fisher?"

"Thanks Trudy, can I have a white coffee?"

"Of course, go and sit down and I'll bring it in to you."

"Tim did as he was told. He sat in *his* armchair, in *his* lounge and wondered why he was obeying *her* command. But then, that's what he did; Tim Fisher obeyed commands. He obeyed his wife; if she said stay here and look after the house and the kids while I skit off on 'business' – that's what he did. He obeyed Simon's commands, but that was fair enough; he was his boss and a good one at that. Did he obey Nina? No, surely Nina was the one taking commands from him...or was she? She helped him to believe that he was in control, but was it just an illusion perpetrated to make him feel better? And now he was taking orders from Trudy, a girl who had moved into his house two weeks ago and was already making most of the decisions for his children. Who obeyed his commands? No one. Tim was a foot soldier. He wasn't officer material, not like his wife. She was a commander in every sense of the word. Christ, he couldn't stand much more of this, it was driving him mad. He was a sucker, that's what he was, a bloody fool who couldn't see an inch beyond his nose. Trudy gave him his drink and then sat down opposite him.

"This has been quite hard for you, Mr. Fisher, hasn't it? I've watched you trying to manage without your wife. You two must be very much in love. I hope when I find a husband he's as nice as you, and I hope I have children as nice as yours. They are wonderful. You should be very proud of them."

"I am Trudy, and I appreciate all that you've done. I haven't said much to you since you got here and I'm sorry, I was a bit too busy feeling sorry for myself to think about you and what a brilliant job you're doing, but anyway... thanks."

"I don't mind, I've seen how distressed you've been without her. It's very natural. She'll soon be back and then I'll have to go... I shall be sorry to leave this house; you've all made me feel welcome. I'm also a long way from my home and my family... so I know just how you're feeling."

"Do you have a boyfriend back in, where is it," Tim was ashamed to admit he didn't even know where she was from, "Glasgow?"

"I'm from the Hebrides, but I've been down here for a year now and no, I don't have a boyfriend, there or here. I never work in one place for long enough to make friends."

Tim looked at her and compared her situation to his. She was away from home, all alone and with no one to turn to and yet she was managing perfectly, coping with not only her problems, for she must have some, everyone does, but also with his problems and those of his family. What qualities this girl must possess to be able to take on such responsibility and then to be told, after a few weeks, thank you but we don't need you anymore. Jesus, how cruel was that? Yet despite that she had arrived in his house and smiled every day from the minute she arrived. She never allowed anyone to see the sadness she must be feeling, not being able to see her family or to stay in one place long enough to get to know people.

"Trudy," he started, "you are a bit special you know, watching you caring for us has made me realise just *how* special you are. I owe you so much for taking care of my children at a time when I'm having trouble looking after myself. I'll be really sorry when you leave this house."

"Thank you, Mr. Fisher, I prefer not to think about that time yet, or I might cry and we can't have that, I have work to do."

"Trudy, will you do me a favour?"

"Of course, Mr. Fisher, what is it?"

"Please call me Tim. "

"If that's what you prefer, Mr. Fisher, but in most houses it is not permitted to call my employers by their first names."

"Trudy, in this house you're one of the family, one of us, in fact at this moment in time you're more like family than my wife, who has opted to take herself out of here for a month."

"But that wasn't her choice, Mr... Tim, she told me all about it when I came for my interview. She was forced to go or she would have lost her job. I know how it is to be forced to go away to work; I think she's a brave woman to do that for her family."

"Except it wasn't like that, Trudy, she wanted to go, no one made her go, she went because she cares more about her job than she does her family. She's enjoying herself in Poland... with a man she met before she went. In fact, Trudy, you might as well know... I think she might be there because of this man, not because of the job."

"Is that why you've been so unhappy this past week? Have you had some news that you would have preferred not to hear? I'm really sorry... Tim, I had no idea that you were in such a bad situation. If I can help, you only have to ask me, whatever it is, I'll do my best for you."

"Thanks Trudy, you're already helping me by caring for the kids the way you do."

"I'm tired now, would you mind if I go to bed?"

"No, of course not, and Trudy... thanks again for everything."

"It's not a problem. Goodnight, Tim."

He watched her leave and thought how lucky some man would be to marry this lovely girl and share children with her. Kind and caring, she would never run off and leave her family to fend for themselves. She was the very best kind of woman, better than Mel would ever be. She understood the meaning of loyalty. He wondered if Mel had phoned. If she had, she'd have wondered where they were. His mobile was off in the cinema, so she would just have to wonder until tomorrow. Maybe he would be out again tomorrow, play her at her own game, and give her something to worry about. Sod her, why should he sit here waiting for her to call when it suited her? No, in future he would make it difficult for her to reach him. She might take the hint when she found that he didn't care if he spoke to her or not, she might just realise that he was worth more than someone to be treated like a puppy that you can leave with friends or put in kennels while you go off on some foreign trip. His thoughts strayed to Nina. He'd told her he would see her tonight, in fact he'd promised her, but it was almost midnight, and she'd be asleep. He couldn't go round there and expect her to make him welcome at this time of night. Knowing that sleep was impossible until he sorted his head out, he opted to take a walk outside. Maybe the cool breeze would help to clear his thoughts. Making sure he had his keys, he slipped out, quietly catching the door behind him. From the front path he could see Nina's house. It was in complete darkness, just as he'd expected. He thought about ringing her. Could he at this time of night?

Before he could come to a decision a familiar voice came from the darkness.

"I expected you earlier, Tim. When I saw you drive off with the kids and the nanny, I supposed you were treating them to a McDonalds."

"Cinema actually, we had a really good night together."

"Good, give them as much time as you can."

"I was a bit anxious because of my promise to you; I didn't want you to think I'd forgotten."

"I didn't and, anyway, I saw you come back half an hour ago. I knew you'd be round as soon as they'd all gone to bed. Come on, let's get inside."

Once inside, Tim questioned her. "Neen, do you think I'm using you?"

"Probably," ... she laughed, "exactly like I'm using you. What's wrong with that, Tim? We need each other, we give ourselves to each other, we use each other. I want to be used by someone who appreciates me, and I know you do. Ben used me for years and never ever appreciated me, *that's* what makes me resentful."

"Have you heard from Ben?"

"Not a word... you?"

"I phoned him, I'm meeting him in the Globe Monday evening."

"Please will you find out what you can about his plans. I mean his plans for me and for his children. You might have to show him a picture of them; he's probably forgotten them by now."

"Nina, do you still love Ben? Do you still want him back?"

"I thought I did, but since I've been seeing you, the way we've been, I'm not sure. Why do you ask?"

"You'll think I'm crazy if I tell you."

"I already think you're crazy, tell me!"

"I think I'm jealous of Ben. See, I told you it was crazy."

"It is crazy and I'll tell you why. If he wanted me as his wife, as his lover, and let's be honest that's a pretty big if, given that he's shacked up with 'Little Miss Pretty', then he should be the one who's jealous, not you. You're the one whose sleeping with his wife after all. And you are the one I want most. That would be two good reasons for most husbands to be jealous wouldn't it?"

"When you put it like that I guess I'm the lucky one. I want you and I've got you, it doesn't get much better than that."

"It's good now Tim, but what happens in a couple of weeks' time when Mel gets back? You and she will soon make up and then I'll be out in the cold, on my own, the forgotten lover. You should always remember, Tim... lovers are for life, not just for Christmas!"

"The way I feel about you, Neen, I can't begin to think of not wanting you. We promised each other we'd always be friends, I meant it then and I still do."

"So what are you going to say to Mel? I won't be long love, I'm just going next door to knock up your best friend. Tim, when she gets back it's over. Don't think I don't know that. I understand the rules, but I also know I'd sooner have you for another two weeks and then lose you than not have you at all."

"Then it's like I said before, I'm just using you."

"Yes you are, think of me like your village post office. Either use me or lose me... so stop arguing and use me."

She took Tim's hand and smiling they went upstairs to bed.

CHAPTER ELEVEN

Poznan was experiencing hot, sunny weather, quite normal for August and perfect for enjoying the lake complex with all its sporting facilities. The Park Hotel was full, mainly with German tourists who knew its reputation for high quality food and its five star service. In the two weeks Melanie had been there she'd never once had a lager that wasn't cool enough or a meal that wasn't perfect. The staff were friendly and helpful, all of which eased the pain of separation from her family and her home. On the first day she had been extremely uptight, spoiling for a fight with Mr. Bigshot Naziree, determined that he would see the error of his ways. She'd rehearsed her lines to ensure the maximum effect. What was all that stuff about the pen being mightier than the sword? She believed profusely that the sharpness of her tongue would prove mightier than any pen wielded by Ratface Naziree. He'd better not start sending her memos... memos demanding this or that, Christ if he dared she would tell him where he could put his memos. At the first meeting of the delegation she was introduced to Hugh Ballantyne, Major Projects Director for Stellar Haufman plc. She liked him from the first handshake; his mature, no nonsense approach oozed confidence. In appearance he reminded her of Richard Geer, the slightly silvering hair, the gentle smile, the certain knowledge that he didn't have to try hard to impress.

"I've heard so many good things about you, Melanie, but I hope to get to know you a little better so I can make my own judgement. I'm certain it will be every bit as satisfactory as your reputation has led me to expect." His words were delivered through the ever present smile that served to warn her, she could be putty in his hands. He was the kind of man that women dreamt about, ideal to spend time with, but she was here to work. Best not forget that, she reminded herself sharply. He'd know how to treat a lady, and of course, he'd know a lady when he met one. She'd make certain he couldn't doubt her credentials in that department.

The unexpected pleasure in discovering Hugh Ballantyne made it all that much easier to be horrible to Ratty. She watched him, silently observing her, and for his benefit she responded to Hugh with far more intimacy than she would normally, or indeed than she was feeling. She was simply taking advantage of a gifted opportunity to put the knife into Ratty from the start.

"Hugh, I shall do my best to satisfy you at every turn," she said, treating him to her come to bed smile, normally reserved for Tim, and only rarely to him of late. Her eyes twinkled like tiny stars.

Sensing chemistry in the atmosphere, she embellished her welcome still more.

"I'm at a disadvantage, having heard very little about you except your name until today. I hope you'll take every opportunity to set right that omission and enlighten me with all of your experience. As you know, Hugh, I'm away from home without the benefit of a chaperone and in a country with which I am unfamiliar. May I seek your protection at times when I am unsure of myself? It would be so reassuring to know that I am safe, in the hands of a gentleman, someone I can trust. She swung hers eyes across to meet Ratty's, and was delighted to see that he was fuming."

"Melanie, you have my undivided attention, do not hesitate to call me whenever it pleases you. I look forward to being at your service."

She smiled graciously then turned to Ratty and muttered under her breath, "so stick that in your pipe you bastard and smoke it." She gave him a huge smile that was patently false. She hoped it might piss him off even more than he was already.

In that mood the meeting got underway, each of them outlining their brief from their respective firms and how they saw their part in the ensuing proceedings. Melanie made a point of agreeing with everything that Hugh said, while stalling Ratty constantly with phrases like, 'Sorry but can you be more precise,' or 'Could you make it clear what point you are trying to make'. By the end of the session Ratty's mood was foul; he shoved his laptop into its case and left the table without a word. Hugh gave him time to get out of earshot.

"Melanie, I need to know exactly what is going on here. Please don't treat me like a fool. You have just given Naziree one hell of a bad time. If it's part of your game plan then it was highly successful, the man has gone away in an extremely bad mood, but as we are all supposed to be 'on the same side' in these negotiations with the Poles I am more than a little puzzled. Please explain."

Melanie was shocked to discover that her performance hadn't gone unnoticed by Hugh as she had hoped. If she wasn't careful, Hugh would think she was a complete amateur and ship her back to the UK with instructions to despatch a replacement at once. All that would spell was an end to her career. Perhaps she had done enough to put Ratty in his place, so now she had better get things under control. First she had to decide what to tell Hugh.

"Hugh... I sense that you are a man of the world, sensitive, observant and at the same time discreet. May I be frank with you?"

"Our relationship will fall apart very quickly if you are ever anything less than. My position in Stellar Haufman doesn't allow me to make mistakes, nor does it allow me to watch while others do so."

"Ratty and I know each other slightly, we first met at a party given by a mutual friend and then we met a couple of times after that. Ratty wanted our friendship to go further than I was expecting. You see, I am a happily married woman. When I told him I'd never meant to give him the impression that we could be more than friends he... well, I suppose you could say he didn't like losing. He told me he wanted me, and the next thing I know I was seconded to this project. I want to be sure that he knows I'm not his plaything."

It was fully two minutes before Hugh spoke, but his smile never wavered.

"Do you want me to believe that you wouldn't have been chosen for this project if Naziree hadn't got designs on you?"

"Yes, I suppose I do."

"Then should I ask the bank to replace you with someone more suitable?"

"If you do that, Hugh, you will end my career and destroy me."

"So I have to decide between my professional competence and the charm of a rather flattering young woman?"

"Young might be an exaggeration as well!" She laughed at him, despite the knowledge that her future was hanging on a knife edge.

"Melanie, I can believe that Naziree wants a relationship with you; probably half of the men who ever met you also feel the same, but I've known him for several years. I was instrumental in getting him into Osborne Melrose Law, which in turn led to them winning the contract to work for Stellar Haufman. If his only motive for including you in our team is personal then he's behaved like a fool, but he isn't a fool and you would do well to take that on board. I know him well enough to say with certainty that if he chose you for this project it is because you are the best that the bank possessed. If you stay, your future is safe and your career can only do well. Welcome to the team."

She knew she had just been given her first lesson in trying to be clever with men who were accomplished at knocking metaphorical lumps out of each other. She had been stupid, outside of her comfort zone, in an area of business where she would need all the help she could get, and she had managed to humiliate the man who had given her the opportunity in the first place. Maybe, just maybe, she should give him the benefit of the doubt.

At the afternoon meeting they met their opposite numbers from the Polish Company Praza, all of whom spoke excellent English. Ground rules were established and some preliminary papers were exchanged. An itinerary was set out which included visits to nine production and research facilities across Poland. Hotel reservation details were discussed and transport arrangements were agreed. Although it was a productive meeting they had not touched on the real issues on which the deal would succeed or fail.

They agreed to reconvene in the hotel's board room at nine thirty the next morning, then with hand shakes all round the meeting ended and the Poles departed.

The three of them gathered up their papers and laptops in silence until Hugh decided enough was enough. "We'll meet in the restaurant at seven and discuss our strategy for tomorrow over dinner. Until seven then." It wasn't an invitation, it was a command, and it left no room for dissident abstention. Before the other two could acknowledge him, he was gone, deliberately leaving them to talk.

"I suppose you want me to say I'm sorry for earlier?" she said.

"And I suppose you want me to say sorry because I insisted that the bank sent you?"

"Shall we call a truce?"

"I thought a truce was something that occurred when two warring factions agreed to peace. I have never been at war with you, Mel; I made that clear to you weeks ago over lunch, when, as I recall, you were much friendlier towards me than you are now."

"Ratty, a lot of dirty water has gone under a lot of bridges since we first met at Nina's. Perhaps I led you on, gave you the impression that I was 'up for it' as you might say. The truth is I was a married woman going through a domestic crisis at home. I was vulnerable and weak. You were kind, charming and treated me like I was made of cut glass. I wasn't used to being treated like that, husbands don't bother. You must know that – and so I welcomed your attention. When Tim and I went on holiday we sorted everything out, and we're great again now. I had to put some distance between you and me before it became serious and stuffed up my marriage. I'm sorry, but that's how it was... then I came back from holiday to find I was booked to leave Tim and the kids for four weeks, just when we'd got everything sorted. Can't you see how bad that made me feel?"

"Yes, of course I understand and you should understand that I would never say 'you were up for it', or use some crude expression which demeans you. Have you forgotten that I told you I love you? So... you've sorted out your mess of a marriage, but for how long? If, after twenty years, you still haven't got it right then it must be time to call it a day, get out, and try something different, someone different."

"You make it all sound so easy, Ratty. You seem to forget we have three children."

"I will take you and your three children, I will care for them as I would my own. They are of you so I cannot do otherwise than take good care of them."

"But Ratty, don't you see, they love their dad, they want to stay exactly as they are, in their maternal and paternal family. You are kind, too good for your own good, but it's not going to happen. I told you before, Ratty, I have it on good authority from Nina that there are plenty of good looking women in your office who would welcome your attention. Don't waste your time on me."

"Melanie, time spent with you is never wasted. The happiest moments of my life are those I spend with you."

"You're hopeless, Ratty, What am I going to do with you?"

"If you can't love me, then at least humour me, pretend to love me, just until we go home. What harm can it do?"

"I don't want to. I have a husband. It isn't right. Doesn't your faith have something to say about women who commit adultery? I think stoning to death is the usual price a woman has to pay isn't it?"

"I am not a fundamentalist, nor for that matter devout. I went to school in London with children of many different religions and I learnt to respect the faith of others whilst not becoming too committed myself. Every religion claims to understand love, but to me love is wanting to be with someone so much that it hurts when you cannot be with them. That's how it is for me with you. I wake up in the morning thinking about you and I go to bed thinking about you."

"You are crazy."

"Funny, that's what my father said when I told him I was going to be a lawyer and not a bus driver!"

They laughed together at the absurdity of the situation.

"So what happens now?" Ratty asked.

"Now, I am going to lie down for an hour before I shower and prepare for dinner."

"You know that isn't what I meant... are we friends?"

"Of course we are. Thank you for loving me, it's a compliment, but please, can you try to fall in love with someone else? It would make things so much simpler."

"I can try, but it would be like trying to fly unaided, like a bird, it's not possible."

"Grrr... Ratty *you're* impossible. I'll see you at seven."

Melanie headed back to her room and looked out of the picture window onto the lake. The never ending stream of roller bladers and cyclists flowed along the water's edge, while on the lake crews of oarsmen were practising for competition. She wished she could get out there and join them. It looked a lot more fun than having dinner with two men who would talk business all night. She picked up her mobile and dialled home, too early for Tim but at least she could check that Trudy was still taking care of her offspring. The kids confirmed that she was doing a brilliant job. Nothing to worry about on that score then. She'd have to try and ring Tim later; difficult once they started dinner though.

As she'd expected, the talk initially was confined to how they would approach the negotiations, what tactics they would use to arrive at the most favourable deal. Hugh was in charge of the project and he set out his ideas on how they would react to proposals put forward by the Praza team.

"We'll listen to them, let them have their say, but we must never show any emotion. Don't look pleased when they show us a profitable factory, even though you know it's working at less than half the running costs of a similar plant in England. The Poles are very good negotiators; they will be looking to measure our reactions. They'll pick up at once on what their strong points are and which aren't. We need to keep our powder dry until we sit down to discuss figures. That's when we'll list the negatives, in a bid to pull the price in our favour."

"Won't it seem rude if we don't show some enthusiasm at what we are being shown? Imagine if you were showing a potential buyer around your house. You'd expect them to say 'What a nice bathroom,' or something, wouldn't you? If we appear to be unimpressed they may lose interest in us. Do they have other interested parties?" Mel addressed her argument at Hugh.

"Melanie you are very perceptive, despite your lack of experience. You're going to be a formidable player in this game."

"Is it a game?" she responded

"I like to think so, yes. As a child I played monopoly with a friend. We used to play for hours and I would sit there hoping he wouldn't notice that I had just landed on his Mayfair plot plus hotels. What we are doing here is playing 'real' monopoly, with someone else's money of course, but that means we can't afford to lose, not if we still want careers afterwards."

Ratty interjected, "What about the documentation? We've agreed that it will be in English and subject to English law, that's fine, but there'll be hours of reading necessary to study all the papers they are going to submit. We'll need to instruct a Polish lawyer to report on title for the properties included in the deal."

"No problem, you can do it tomorrow. You can miss some of the trips to look at factories if you need more time to study the papers."

Melanie wondered how Ratty would feel about being left behind while she and Hugh went off for a couple of days on a trip across Poland. His face gave nothing away. The arrival of the food brought conversation about work to a temporary halt. It was over coffee that Ratty suggested a walk around the lake. Hugh declined, indicating that he had to write up his notes on Day One before e-mailing them to London.

"I can't wait to see the lake close up," Melanie said, so after a quick change into jeans and trainers they set off around the lake.

The dry ski slope was closed now, as was the 'Cresta run'. There were still plenty of people out enjoying the lake though and tented eating places serving barbecued meats and other delicious looking treats. The smell was divine and Melanie made a resolution to eat here the next night. They agreed to walk right around the lake, a distance of at least six kilometres.

Ratty spoke for both of them; "So, we are alone at last."

"It would seem so, wouldn't it? Ratty, what do you intend to do with your life? You've got this top job in Nina's firm, but is that your ultimate aim or do you have a dream to go still higher?"

"Until recently my ambition was to go right to the top, wherever that is, but now I can't see me leaving Osborne Melrose, because that would inevitably take me away from you. Success without you would have a bitter taste."

"But you don't have me. I've told you, you never will have me, so why not keep trying for the top and see who you meet on the way?"

"But I do have you, at least a small part of you. You remember that night when we met? You fell asleep on me, you curled yourself into me, and you were completely at ease in my arms. I knew then that I had found the person I want to share my life with and for an hour or so we did just that."

At the half way point on the walk they sat down on a bench which looked across the lake directly at their hotel. The light was beginning to fade and the lights from the hotel were reflected in the water, creating the most magical effect.

"You were so trusting, so giving, so incredibly lovely, and for that hour you were mine. Now that I've tasted Appellation Controllee I can never be satisfied with Vin de Table. If I have to wait, that's too bad, but much better than to settle for second best."

"Is that what you think I'm doing, settling for second best?"

"We both know it, but you have good reason to hesitate before leaving him, even I can see that. You are a woman of quality... refinement. He... he is a mechanic. Does he care about fine food the way you do? Does he follow your career with genuine interest? Does he stimulate you in conversation? Melanie laughed, "He likes his steak well done, preferably with ketchup, hates my career and the last time we ate out I was bored senseless". Does that answer your questions?

"Of course it does. You deserve the very best. Someone with whom you can share everything, his success and yours. It makes me cringe to think of him putting his oily hands on you. I know plenty of guys who are mechanics around Brixton, I meet up with them whenever I go to see my parents. They work with oil and grease and it never comes off. They even smell of oil when they go out for the night after having washed. This isn't what I want for you."

"What *do* you want for me?"

"I want you in these arms, in these hands. He put his arm around her waist as if to illustrate his point. She made a token gesture of pushing him away, but he persisted. I want to give you everything I have, I want to give you love, make you know how much I value you, how much you mean to me, how intense my feelings for you are."

"I think you might stifle me with so much love."

"No, I would never restrict your freedom, you are like a

beautiful butterfly, I want to see you fly, to see the colour of your wings in the sunshine, or... like now in the moonlight."

He moved his hand under her T-shirt until it covered her breast. Either she hadn't noticed or she was being kind, he didn't mind which. Right at this moment there was an emotional current surging between them, one that didn't need words to help define it. He pushed his hand gently to lift her bra so that he was holding her in his hand, bare of the fabric that had maintained her modesty. She made no attempt to stop him. They stayed like that for a while until the fading light took the hotel from their view. Only the lights indicated its existence across the lake.

"We'd better start walking," she said. She pushed his hand away and put her bra back where it was meant to be.

"Yes, he said, we should, it's a long way yet."

Ratty knew the moment was over, but what a moment it had been. He had held the woman he loved in his arms, in his hands. He'd felt the warmth of her skin and she had allowed him to take a tiny piece of her and make it his, for a few minutes... precious minutes. He kept his arm around her waist as they walked on around the lake. There were fewer people now and as the occasional roller blader sped towards them in the dark she was frightened that they might be mugged. She was glad of his strong arm around her; she said nothing when he slipped his hand inside her waistband so that it was holding her bottom. She was happy to stay as close as possible to him as they synchronised their steps together. It was a comforting feeling to have him there, knowing as she did how much he cared for her. At the hotel foyer she broke away from him.

"Someone might see us," she said.

He laughed at her. "How many of these Germans do you suppose know us?"

"You know what I mean. It's one thing out there in the dark, but here it's different."

"Let's go up to the terrace bar and have a drink, before we turn in for the night."

"OK, but only one. I'm tired and I'm supposed to have typed up my notes of the meeting on my laptop."

As she sat there sipping her wine and looking out across the lake, with it's shimmering reflections in constantly changing patterns, she thought how different this was turning out to be against what she had expected. She thought about home and what they would be doing now ... "Shit," she said out loud, "I forgot to ring Tim. He'll be worried sick. I wonder if I should ring him now." She looked at her watch. Eleven thirty. Christ, what could she say? Sorry Tim, I went for a stroll with Ratty around the lake and clean forgot to phone you. Not the best move. Better to leave it for tonight and speak to him tomorrow. I need time anyway, to think up a bloody good excuse, she thought.

"He knows you are going to be doing business over dinner some evenings, I'm sure he won't be worried." Ratty tried to placate her.

"Ratty, if your wife went away and didn't phone you on her first night away would you worry?"

"I would never let her go alone to begin with. The woman I intend to marry... one day... is far too precious for me to risk losing, so if she has to go abroad I shall be at her side."

"It wouldn't work, Ratty. I've told you before, it would never work."

"I think it would because I would dedicate my life to making it work, to making you happy."

She smiled at him; she knew he meant every word of it. He was very much in love with her. She finished her drink. "I'm off to bed... alone." She'd read the expression on his face. "Good night, Ratty, and thank you for a wonderful evening. I enjoyed it."

He took her hand in his and kissed her gently on the cheek. He let her go, following her with his eyes and with his thoughts. At the doorway she stopped, turned and smiled. His heart was pounding; he was engulfed by the most wonderful feeling in the world.

During the following week there were several evenings on which no meetings took place and on each of these they walked around the lake together, like before. Melanie made sure she phoned Tim before they set off around the lake, but she found it hard to know what to say. She was missing him, of course; she was missing the children even more, although she couldn't say that. She remembered to ask him about his new job, but he seemed agitated whenever she rang, not wanting to talk about what he'd done or where he'd been. Oh well, he'd tell her all about it when she got back. It could wait. The days passed quickly in Poland, much more so than she had imagined possible at the start. From the moment they finished breakfast they were off, either to a meeting or on a train journey to see a factory somewhere. She loved the views from the train windows, miles of fields, full of corn and with red poppies and blue cornflowers around the edge. Sometimes she would see a deer running across the open fields. This was a country she could fall in love with, which was why she wasn't missing home as much as she'd expected.

What she didn't realise was that this feeling of contentment from the beautiful countryside in which she found herself showed in her voice. Tim had been expecting her to say she hated it there, but she didn't. Her calls home were lackluster, detached, emotionless, giving nothing away.

With two weeks of the project left, Melanie was unusually happy. She woke each day to the sun reflecting off the lake and a busy schedule of meetings. She'd managed to catch up on her notes and she was confident now in her ability to manage the business for the bank successfully. She was tasting success as a Senior Manager, she was tasting success as a woman and nothing would be the same after this, she knew she could never be happy in the confines of the office the way she had been the last ten years. Her life was evolving. She wasn't the same person who'd left England two weeks ago, angry and frightened by what might lay ahead. She was still confident that her marriage was repaired and that she and Tim would go on parenting their three children, but it was far less intense now, a relationship that worked well in the background, while the best of her life, away from motherhood, was work. She'd made her peace with Ratty. Not yet enough to totally satisfy him – he would always want more, more than she could give – but he seemed content to take what small scraps she gave him and wait for the day when, he was certain, she would turn to him. She actually enjoyed their trips around the lake together. The place was heavenly; watching night fall over the lake was an experience so sensual that it gave her goosebumps just thinking about it... and then there was Ratty; he was an integral part of the walk, so much so that she couldn't imagine doing it with anyone else, not even Tim. Tim belonged in England, where they would spend their lives together as man and wife. He wasn't part of this experience, he never could be and she forced herself to admit that Ratty had got hold of a small part of her and made it his. It was the Polish bit of her, a bit that in two weeks time would dissolve into her past, just a memory. But for a little while longer it was real and she wasn't sorry that there were still two weeks left before it would be over, for good!

At dinner that night the three of them discussed the events of the day. It had been a fruitful meeting during which the Poles had put forward, at last, their detailed financial proposals for the take over.

They had each looked at the documents, briefly, with the Poles watching on. They knew at once that the figures were much better than they had dared to hope for, but not one of them gave a clue in their expression. Hugh had thanked them, promising to make a formal response when they met in two days time. This would give Hugh time to work out a counter proposal, while Melanie checked the securities required by the bank and Ratty perused the contract details. All the indications were that they were going to pull off a deal better than expected, and on time. If they did, all three of them could expect a healthy bonus from Stellar Haufman plc, as well as increased respect at the most senior level of their organisations. Hugh put into words what each of them was thinking.

"We are on the brink of the most successful project imaginable, but we must keep our nerve, not let the Poles see for one minute how happy we are with the deal. It's not time for champagne yet, but at this rate it soon will be. I'm glad to see that you two have worked so well together. I must admit you had me worried at the beginning, but I'm warning you both now, I shall insist on having you in my next project team." He smiled across the table.

Ratty beamed at Melanie, and then turned to face Hugh. "Is there another project in sight Hugh?"

"There's always another project with Stellar Haufman. They make billions each year and they have a policy of continuous expansion. I have two junior project managers working flat out developing ideas. They are currently doing some exploration work. Antonio is fact finding in Italy and the other, a talented young woman called Jacqui is in Germany buying land for an industrial site for our land bank."

"Where do you think you will be heading next, when this one's wrapped up?" Ratty persisted.

"That is too confidential at the moment even for your ears, Ratty. Only three people in our organisation know the details. It is imperative that the company we are stalking don't get wind of our plans until we make a formal offer. At that time we'll launch a project similar to this one and you will be there; you too Mel."

At that moment Mel's mobile rang, she looked scared.

"It's only a phone, Mel, aren't you going to answer it?" Hugh said kindly.

"I told Tim only to ring me in an emergency," she blurted, before grabbing the phone and heading out of the restaurant.

"She looked rather worried over a call she hadn't even answered," Hugh said.

"Maybe she doesn't feel like talking to him right now."

"Why do you think that is? Does she have some news for him, news he isn't going to want to hear?"

"No, unfortunately she doesn't have any such news."

"So it is true? You are in pursuit of her affection."

"How do you know that?"

"Ratty, my friend, I would have to be stupid to sit here each evening and watch you two at dinner without seeing the chemistry between you. Your desire to get away after the meal for your lakeside walk tells its own story. You are a predator, she is vulnerable. She is also married with children. I hope you know what you are doing?"

"Hugh, I need to be honest with you ...I trust you ...completely."

"It seems that everyone wishes to bestow their secrets upon me lately. OK, but the whole truth, Ratty, or nothing!"

"Of course... Hugh, I'm in love with Mel."

"Is that it? Dear boy, I realised that the day we arrived, but does she love you? I got the impression that she was quite upset in the beginning at you having dragged her out here, though I've also observed that her mood has softened considerably since then."

"She says she doesn't love me, she says we can never be together, properly, yet she doesn't completely push me away. I cling to those precious moments in the hope that one day she will want me as much as I want her."

"That's fine, Ratty, and very honourable, but what if it takes years for this to happen?"

"Then I'll wait years. I'd swim an ocean to be with her forever, Hugh. I love her more than anything. I'd give everything I own to have her, to belong to her."

"What if you wait years and it doesn't happen? Then you will have lost the chance of happiness with someone else. Have you considered this?"

"How can I make a decision to abandon my love for her when there is even a one per cent chance of her loving me, one day?"

"Maybe Melanie should make the decision for you?"

"No, I don't want her to walk away from me. I don't think I could survive without the hope that she instills in me."

Hugh Ballantyne was pensive, his smile camouflaging his thoughts. This was a love affair too intense on the one side and too complicated on the other. The only certainty in such a situation was that there would have to be a loser, eventually!

"Supposing that one day Melanie realised how much you love her, supposing she decided that she was in love with you as well, so much so that she chose to spend the rest of her life with you. What do you think her husband would do?"

It was Ratty's turn to think before speaking. "I've never met him, so it's hard for me to say, but nothing in life is forever, he must know that, and anyway, from all the things Mel has told me, he doesn't do nearly enough to deserve her. He's a mechanic, an oily; she's worth more, much more."

"In your esteemed valuation of human worth a mechanic is less useful than a lawyer... is that what you think? I suspect that most of the people who break down on the M1 prefer a mechanic. Don't you think it's a bit arrogant to determine your worth to her in terms of your profession?"

"That's not what I'm saying. He simply doesn't have the ambition to get on in life, to give her the things she deserves. I could give her much more, that's what I'm saying."

"Ratty, love is not about material wealth, two people can

be as poor as church mice, yet love each other deeply. I know you love her, and obviously her wealth is not important to you, which is how it should be... what I am asking is ... have you thought that she might apply those same standards in her quest for love? You will only win this competition for her affection, if that's how it is, when she wants you as much as, and for the same reasons, as you want her."

"But how do I make her love me the way I love her?"

"Ratty, you can't make her, but if you show her that through thick or thin, in good times or in bad, you are always going to be there for her, then she will at least see you in your true light. I've also enjoyed Melanie's company since we arrived here and I can tell you, Ratty, if I didn't respect your feelings towards her I might be making overtures myself. She's a very easy woman to fall in love with. You might go years before you meet a woman as lovely as her. She has that rare quality in a woman; she is totally unaware of how lovely she is, unlike so many who believe in their own desirability even when it scarcely exists. Ratty, if you want to spend the rest of your life with her, be a friend to her, a true friend, one she can trust no matter what, and one day, maybe, you will become her best friend!"

"Thanks, Hugh, I'll always be there for her, no matter what."

"Good luck, Ratty."

When Melanie returned to the table she looked upset. The phone call had obviously gone badly.

"What's up Mel" Ratty asked, "Not bad news is it?"

"No... no, it's just Tim, he's upset. I think he's missing me. I can't think why." She tried to put on a brave face and attempted to smile. She joked to hide her concern, "I've left

297

him a young and attractive nanny, and my best friend Nina, your Nina, from next door to fuss over him and still he misses me. He must be mad."

Ratty sprang to his defence, "No Mel, he's not mad, he knows how lucky he is."

"Ratty, would you mind if we don't walk around the lake tonight, I'm not in the mood. I think I'll go up and type up my notes and then get an early night... see you both in the morning." She got up and left the table.

"Ratty, your face says it all, as if I didn't already know... you look like you've just been told there's no Father Christmas."

"I was so looking forward to our walk. It's the happiest hour of the day for me. I'm dreading the day we go home. I probably won't get to see her at all then."

"What did Melanie mean when she said, 'Your Nina'?"

"Her neighbour, and best friend, well best woman friend anyway, works in my department on your firm's account. I'm surprised you haven't heard of her, she's a promising talent in contract law. We talk a bit in work; it's my only way of finding out about Melanie, although she's very tight lipped on that subject, doesn't approve of my interest, but then, she thinks all I want is a cheap affair with her friend. She has no idea what love is. She's married to some prat who's just gone off with a girl barely out of her teens. From what she's told me about him I'd say she was better off on her own."

"I try to make it my business to get to know everyone who works on the Stellar Haufman account. When we get back I shall make a point of meeting Nina. She sounds like an interesting person."

"Not your type, Hugh."

"How could you possibly know what 'my type' is, Ratty?"

With you going all around the world on Stellar's business you must meet some fabulous women, Latin American, Caribbean, French, Italian... how could you find a local woman good enough to compete with those?"

"Well, Ratty, it seems that you did, and my reason for meeting her is business. Unlike you, Ratty, I can keep the two quite separate."

The next day was spent examining the detail of the Praza proposal. They took turns in making assessments of it and flagging up bits of it which required a closer look. The bank's role in this was limited to ensuring that the proposition was a sound long term investment. Melanie knew it was sound, whatever the outcome of the bid to squeeze extras from the Poles at the negotiating table tomorrow. "If it's OK with you guys, I'm going to get some fresh air. You don't need me for a while. I'll see you back here for dinner tonight, OK?"

Hugh could see she needed some space. She hadn't entirely recovered from the effects of last night's phone call. "Sure, go out and take in some sunshine and we'll see you at dinner."

"Thanks, Hugh, see you both later."

Melanie made straight for the reception desk, where a smartly dressed lady was in charge.

"Please can you tell me if there is a zoo in Poznan?" she said.

"But of course, Poznan has a wonderful zoo. If you walk this way, clockwise, around the lake," she pointed straight in front of her, "you will arrive to the Malta restaurant which is also the station for the little railway that will take you to the zoo." She smiled pleasantly, "It's a lovely day for visiting the zoo, enjoy your trip."

Ten minutes later she was once again walking round the lake, but in the opposite direction to the way they walked in the evenings. She mingled with the crowds of people who incessantly circled the lake in search of exercise until she reached the station restaurant. The sound of a train's whistle announced the arrival of the small steam train and after buying her ticket at the office she joined the queue to board it. Sitting in an open sided carriage with twenty excited young children made her homesick for the first time since she had arrived. Happy faces talking non-stop, regardless of whether anyone was listening, was universal when kids were on a day trip like this. The parents – or were they teachers? – seemed just as excited. She felt sadness at not knowing what her children had done this holiday with Trudy. Sure, they'd told her a few details during her nightly call, but they must have had lots of fun in the last couple of weeks, all of which she had missed out on.

The zoo was enormous, more of an animal park than a traditional city variety, where caged animals stare out from behind bars. After three hours of wandering around, gazing at animals who were unconcerned at her presence, she boarded the train again. Her head was telling her it was time to go home so that she would have time to change before dinner.

Home? Where was home? Right now the Park Hotel was home, but two weeks from now I'll pack my things and head for that other home, where who knows what awaits.

As the train headed back, she glimpsed a sight of the hotel across the lake and thought about Ratty and his determination to be her lover. He really was a kind and caring man. It would be very easy, here away from the pressures of family life to give in to him. But she would hold true to her marriage. Well almost. She smiled to herself.

Back at the tiny station, she drank a cold Lech lager at a table under the shade of the trees. She needed time to think before going back to the hotel. Tim's phone call was still heavy on her mind. He was angry. He wanted her back. Now! What do I say to him when I phone tonight? And what do I say to Ratty when he asks me to walk around the lake? She lost track of time as she sat there watching the trams on the main road, milling backwards and forwards to and from the town centre and disgorging their cargo of commuters before clanging noisily onto their destination. Sparks hissed from the wires above the trams as they sped along the busy track, but these were nothing to the sparks that would fly tonight. I've never known Tim to sound so pissed off as he did last night, and all that stuff about the zoo, how did he know Poznan has a zoo? He's been doing some research, but god knows how. He'd never read a book and he doesn't know how to use the internet. Maybe I should have a long talk with Nina, ask her what is going on inside his head. I need her to get closer to him to find out what he's thinking. If I'm going home to face a storm at least I'd like to be prepared.

As Melanie walked the path alongside the lake, she resolved to make that her next task. She dialled the direct number for Nina at work and was relieved to hear her voice. "Nina, it's Mel, can you talk?"

"Of course I can, Mel, how's Poland, I've been watching the European weather forecast, sounds like you're having even better weather than we are. How is my oversexed Senior Partner? Is he behaving himself?"

"Ratty has been a perfect gentleman, Neen, at least he's given me no cause for complaint."

"I'm not sure which way to take that, Mel, should I be worried for you?"

"Of course not. Everything's fine here and we're making good progress on the project. I absolutely love it here, Neen, I'm coming back next summer. I want to bring the kids here, they'd love it, and Tim of course. Neen, I wanted to ask you about Tim, he sounded really odd last night on the phone. He wasn't making any sense at all, wanted to know who I'd been to the zoo with. Where the hell did that come from?"

"He is a bit down, Mel, but nothing for you to worry about. The kids are doing fine and Trudy is a marvel; you don't know how lucky you were to find her. I'm booking her to look after mine as soon as I can get some time off, and as soon as I can find someone to take me away somewhere."

"Still no news on Ben then? He hasn't been in touch?"

"The only thing he's touched is little Miss Muffet. No, I've come to terms with it since you've been away, Mel, he isn't coming back and I don't even know if I'd want him back now."

"What's changed? When I left you were devastated that he was with her, now it sounds like you don't care.'

'Well what's done is done, Mel, let's face it he wasn't exactly the pick of the crop, even at his best, was he?'

"Neen, tell me honestly, do you think I'm coming back to an angry husband, because if so I'd rather know beforehand, and exactly what it is that's eating him. That way I can try to have my answers prepared before he asks the questions. I know you're not Tim's biggest fan, but can you please get close enough to him during the next week to get to bottom of his problem? Clearly he does have a problem with me and the trip, but he's not going to share it with me, at least not until I get home, then I'll probably get it, both barrels."

"Well, I'll try to get as close as I can, Mel, I've been cooking for him most nights anyway but he doesn't say a lot about you or the trip. Tonight I'll go to work on him, find out what's inside his head, if anything..." She laughed nervously.

"Thanks, Neen, I'm relying on you."

"OK, you take good care of my boss then, see if you can get me another promotion, be very nice to him."

"I thought you didn't want me to be nice to him. I'm a married woman, remember? I'll gladly tell him that you're looking for an opportunity to impress him upon his return if you want, that should get him excited."

"Like bloody hell it would, I could attend the morning briefing in my pants and bra and he wouldn't notice, but if I mention your name his face lights up like Blackpool bloody Tower. I don't know what it is you've got, Mel, but I wish I could get some."

"It's called 'being unavailable', it always adds to the attraction. Your only problem is you spent too long with Ben. Seriously, once he's out of your head you can let your hair down and start looking for someone special. You're a lovely person, Neen, you've just got to believe in yourself and I bet you could entice any man under your duvet if you just tried."

"Do you really think so? I'll give it a try, and at the same time I'll find out as much as I can for you."

"Thanks, Neen, speak to you soon."

Melanie put the phone back in her pocket. Perhaps she was worrying about nothing. Nina hadn't seemed overly concerned about Tim's state of mind and she'd seen him most nights, so she would know if he was in a 'state'. Good old Neen, she was always willing to do her bit to help, even though she had enough to think about with her own marriage problems. By the time they met up for dinner she'd brightened up enormously, so much so that she was full of life throughout the meal, enjoying being the centre of attention to two handsome and attentive men, a situation that didn't go unnoticed by other diners in the restaurant. But tonight, instead of feeling guilty, Melanie was revelling in her good fortune. There hadn't been that many occasions when one good looking man had dined her and paid her compliments, so having two men lavish attention on her was the icing on her Polish cake. The men were clearly enjoying her company tonight; perhaps it was the result of a long, hot day spent pouring over documents, but they were like two school boys on their first date.

Hugh was in sparkling form, as always. "So Ratty, tonight it must be my turn to escort this lovely lady on her walk around the lake."

"What do you mean?" replied Ratty, "I don't think that's a good idea."

"On the contrary, it's an excellent idea, especially if we are to preserve her good name, after all being seen with the same man on too many occasions could lead to gossip."

"Except of course there's no one here *to* gossip."

"You only suppose that ... for all you know her husband might have paid one of these Germans to spy on his wife. I've been watching that twenty stone fellow over there, he's never taken his eyes off of her.

"If you're determined to persist with this foolish notion I think we should ask the *lady* to decide who should escort her tonight."

"Why don't you both escort me? That way honour will be satisfied all round."

"Because, my dear Melanie, Ratty would not be happy with such an arrangement, is that not so dear boy?"

"Hugh, you've already said you want to meet my charming assistant Nina upon your return. Don't compromise your chances by trying it on with her best friend."

"I can see you're not happy with Mel's suggestion, Ratty. Ordinarily I would be forced to challenge you to a duel at dawn, but as I know you don't like early mornings I'll concede to you on this occasion, but remember, you owe me."

The intensity of their bid for her attention was bliss to Melanie. She was enjoying it as much as they were. It was like the trip had become a party that went on and on. She found herself dreading the day soon, when this would all end and she would return to a life of washing, ironing, cooking and cleaning with the odd moment of romance with Tim on Saturday night, after the kids had gone to bed. Ratty kept telling her that there was more to life than she was getting with Tim. She supposed he was right, but it wouldn't work with Ratty, they'd get fed up with each other, she'd still have underwear to wash, it would just be his underwear instead of Tim's. You'd better face up to it, Mel, she told herself, once this trip is over your life will be back to the same old boring routine that you left behind. Nothing will have changed except you girl. Better enjoy this while you can. After the coffee Ratty looked at her with that puppy dog look that said, 'Come on... walkies'. She read his expression and stood up from the table.

"Come on then, Ratty, the lake awaits us."

They set off together in the direction of the ski slope and before they had reached it he took hold of her hand. They strolled along in a state of perfect contentment, willing this walk to last forever. At the half way point they looked across the lake at the hotel as usual. Ratty led Melanie up the grassy slope until they were some way from the path, then he slumped down onto the grass, gently pulling her down with him. She didn't resist. He took hold of her and lavished her with cuddles. She succumbed to his embrace readily, making no effort to restrain his enthusiasm. Soon his hands were inside her clothes, one hand seeking the soft flesh of her backside while the other went around her waist. She relaxed and let the moment take care of itself. She couldn't pretend that she wasn't happy, or that she wasn't enjoying having him close to her. Their intimacy was something special, something they shared only when they had each other to themselves. A moment in time that would probably not happen again and before long would be impossible to re-create against the backdrop of her life back home. He gently lifted her bra and held her in his hands. His hands were soft, softer than Tim's, and he took more care not to hurt her. She knew that he would rather die than hurt her, yet in a way that's what he *was* doing; she would hurt later when she had to face either the guilt or the end to moments like this. His hand was inside her skirt, inside her pants...

"Stop, Ratty," she said, grabbing at his hand and easing it back to her waist. "I can't you know that. I've told you it's impossible, I have to go back to Tim. Try to understand."

"You don't have to go back to him, Mel, we can be together forever, and it can be like this every night of our lives. I want to touch you, feel you, hold you, love you. I want to make you mine and most of all I want to be yours."

"He's bound to question me about my time here with you and Hugh. I'm already going to have to lie. I couldn't face him knowing that I'd let you."

"Then don't face him. Let me go and see him, let me tell him that we have decided to spend the rest of our lives together. I'll be friendly, I'll offer him financial help if he needs it, and I'll ask him if we can meet to make arrangements over access to the children."

"Ratty, he's got some pride ... do you seriously think he'd accept your money, knowing that you had defiled his wife?"

"I guess he wouldn't, but I could give you money which you could give to him. You could make sure he had enough to buy a place of his own. He knows you're earning well these days, you could convince him that it was your way of saying sorry to him."

"But that would be lying to him, wouldn't it? I don't want to lie to him, and I don't want to see my kids for only half of their lives. Please get it into your head, Ratty, it can't happen. I have to go back to Tim and you have to try and forget me. Come on, let's go, it's getting cold."

Melanie was up and walking. He knew the moment had been almost within his grasp, but once again it was gone. He was thrilled that she had let him share this moment of intimacy, it meant she had genuine feelings for him. She wasn't a woman who could let a man touch her unless she loved him, at least a little bit. But he was filled with sadness too, at the impossibility of the situation back home where the demands of her children and her husband made it impossible for him to give her all the love that he was aching to give her. Back at the hotel they took drinks on the balcony lounge overlooking the lake. It reflected the hotel lights in a way that was as beautiful as the experience. He sat her on his lap and in silence they stared across the lake to the place where an hour ago they had lain on the grass and she had in part given herself up to him. He tried to make light of their escapade.

"Can you see the spot where we flattened the grass?" he said pointing.

"Yes, I think so," she said. "Do you think we'll ever find that spot again?"

Ratty knew it was a reference to them and not the location.

"I hope so Mel. You made me the happiest man in the world tonight. I wish it didn't have to end when we finish our drink. Come back to my room for a drink and let me hold you again, like before but longer, let me hold you until morning. It hurts me to let you go."

"I know, Ratty, I know how you feel about me, but I wish you wouldn't. I can't give you what you want. I'll come back for one drink but then I have to go and get some sleep, OK?"

"Of course, let's go."

Chapter Twelve

Monday evening in the Globe was usually busy and tonight was no exception. Ben held his pint high above his chest to avoid spillage in the jostle to get away from the crowded area by the bar. Once safely in the corner where Tim was sitting by the window, he eased himself into a wooden arm chair and took a sip of his drink.

"Just like old times, Tim, you and me and no women to bugger our evening up! I've missed these nights. That's the only thing I have missed though since I moved away from here."

"Not missing Nina then?"

"Are you kidding? Nina gave me hell for all those years and I never realised it. It's only now, now that I'm in a happy relationship that I can see just how crap those years were."

"Come on, Ben, it wasn't all bad, surely?"

"Well let me think... no... I'm sorry, Tim, but I can't remember any good bits, and do you know why that is? ....cos there weren't any."

"Ben, you spent a long time with Nina, you've got three kids together, don't you feel anything?"

"Oh yes, relief, Tim, relief at never having to go into that house again and have her stinging me with her spiteful tongue. Christ, Tim, you don't know the half about that woman. She can curdle milk with her scowl and strike fear into a Rottweiler with her tongue. You wouldn't want to spend more than five minutes with her Tim, trust me."

"So what happens now?"

"'Now... well I know everyone is saying there's too big an age difference between us, but sod em, Beckie and I are happier than either of us have ever been. I know it sounds corny, Tim, but I love her and she loves me."

"Love, that old chestnut, don't talk to me about love."

"Things gone pear shaped again with Mel?"

"I don't know, I haven't seen her for weeks."

"What?' Ben choked on his beer. 'Where is she, she hasn't left you has she?"

"She might as well have. In a manner of speaking she has left me, she's gone to Poland with a couple of blokes from work on some project for the bank. Nina's boss is one of them; he's the one that made her go. I'm well pissed off about it."

"Why did you let her go then?"

"Ben, she didn't ask me, she told me, that's why. Do you seriously think she'd take any notice if I said, 'Sorry Mel, but you can't go'? She's due back in a week's time, but I'm so pissed off with her I'm going to be struggling to say hello to her when she gets back."

"Big mistake Tim. Your Mel wouldn't do anything she shouldn't, you know that. She's probably spent every night crying her eyes out for you and the kids. Don't screw it all up by being horrible to her, welcome her back with some flowers, that sort of thing, take her down the Walnut Tree like you did before. Show her you've missed her."

"I don't know if I can, Ben, I'm too upset at the moment,

she's hardly phoned me since she got there. What kind of a wife does that make her?"

"She's a bloody sight better than Nina, that's for sure. How's the new job going?"

"Brilliant, better than I could have hoped for. Simon, that's my boss, he's a millionaire, mind you, he's a gem, terrific bloke. He's the best person I've ever worked for, looks after me like a brother, we've become really good mates."

"What's it like driving that car around? I bet you get a few looks don't you?"

"I should say, and because Simon insists on me wearing a good suit – he even bought it for me, – it looks like it's my motor. I tell you, when I park up somewhere on my own and get out people open doors for me, even had one guy call me sir."

"So, Mel did you a big favour getting you that job and making you pack in at the yard then?"

"She did, but don't forget why she did it. She just wanted me to have a snob job like she has. She didn't know that Simon would turn out to be such a decent bloke, I doubt if she'd have cared, as long as I came home without oil on me at night."

"That's not fair Tim. She could see you were going nowhere. Ask yourself, what would you have been doing down at the yard in say, five years' time?"

"I don't know."

"Yes you do ... the same as you were doing the day you left, mate, crawling under trucks, bumping your head, splitting fingers on sharp bits of engines and getting covered in shit and grease. If you can't see that she was right to get you out of there you need contact lenses. She's bright, your Mel, had the sense to see that you couldn't go on doing that job forever, got you out just in time."

"Maybe, but I still wish she hadn't pissed off to Poland. I can tell you one thing for certain, I won't be letting her go off anywhere else after this little lot, and if she kicks up a fuss then so will I."

"Good for you Tim, let her know who's the man in your house."

"Is that what you do with Beckie?"

"No need mate, she's too clever anyway to be fooled by that kind of thing. I let her make all the decisions, she's better at it than me, and anyway she wouldn't go to Tesco without me, let alone go to Poland. We're like that, we are." He crossed his fingers to illustrate the bond between them.

"She let you out tonight on your own though?"

"It was her idea. She said I shouldn't drop my mates completely. She's having a drink with Sophie at the wine bar in town. Does Nina still ask about me?"

"Not much, not any more. I think she accepts that you've made other plans, plans that don't include her. Maybe she's got plans of her own."

"What are you saying, Tim, has she met someone?"

"Oh, I don't know, do I? I just meant she might be thinking about looking for a new relationship, after all she can't wait forever for you to come back can she?"

"No, especially as I'm not coming back. Still it sounds a bit strange, like, hearing you say she might have another man in her life. I don't know if I like that idea much."

"Ben, do you seriously think she is going to wear black and take a vow or something because you dumped her?"

"No of course not, but it's a bit soon isn't it? I mean… I've only been gone a few weeks."

"Ben, you didn't die, you pissed off with another woman!"

"That's not the point, if she'd loved me that much she would still be too upset to think about going with another man. You don't think she has do you? I mean you don't think she's actually, you know, done anything like that, do you?"

Tim felt his face reddening, his lungs refused to take in oxygen, his breathing would have indicated to anyone that he was suffering intense discomfort, embarrassment, guilt even. Anyone except his best mate, Ben.

"You all right, Tim? you look like shit. You're probably as shocked by the thought as I am, but I suppose it's possible. Christ you live with someone for all those years, you think you know them, then you turn your back for a couple of weeks and they're at it with some other bugger. Well she can piss right off if she thinks I'm paying bloody maintenance, she earns twice what I earn and more. If I have to climb on the balcony of Buck House dressed as Batman to protest then fine, but they won't get one bloody penny out of me."

"You can't stand heights, Ben. You wouldn't even get over the wall."

"OK, fair enough, but you know what I mean. I'll go on the dole first."

"Wouldn't be the first time, Ben, would it?"

"No, Tim, it bloody wouldn't. Anyway, I told you before, we're trying for a kid of our own. We'll have a struggle to pay for that one, let alone paying for hers."

"When you say hers, Ben, don't you mean yours?"

"I suppose so, but Nina always told them what to do and when to do it. She never trusted me to take them anywhere or do much with them. I doubt if they've missed me much, to tell you the truth. It'll be different with Beckie. We'll do everything together, like it should be."

"That's nice, Ben, very nice. So what do you want me to tell Nina, any message?"

"Tell her that seeing as how she's having it away with another man he can pay for the kids."

"You're a crude bugger, Ben, I can see why she chucked you out."

"Well tell her she did me a favour, will you?"

"No, Ben, I won't. I think Nina deserves a break, she's had a lot to put up with over the years, come on, be honest. You were never going to be runner up for 'Husband of the Year' were you?"

"You don't get it, Tim, it's not about winning medals for being a shining example of a husband, it's about simple things, like looking out for each other, showing a bit of affection. Beckie is all over me like a rash when I come in at night, lets me see how much she's missed me since the morning, that's what it's about. Nina wouldn't know how to be affectionate if her life depended on it."

Tim's thoughts raced back to last night ... and the night before. He could easily have argued Nina's case with the benefit of his first hand experience, but he couldn't risk Ben knowing what was going on with his ex-wife, no, not ex-wife, *his wife*.

"So, will you be going for a divorce soon, Ben?"

"Don't know, I'll probably leave it to Neen, after all she's a bloody solicitor, she can get it cost price, or even do it herself I suppose. I can't afford solicitors' bills and anyway Beckie and I aren't that bothered about paperwork and stuff. We've got each other, that's what counts."

Although frustrated at Ben's simplistic view of life, Tim envied the way he could be happy with nothing more than a bedsit relationship with a girl half his age. But then Ben had never worried about anything, and in a funny way that was his strength. Tim had heard enough about Beckie for one night. He couldn't cope with more questions about Nina's possible infidelity, the conversation was getting far to close to his own involvement with her.

'We'd better play some pool before I forget which end of the cue to poke the balls with,' he said.

Jim rang the bell to call time promptly at eleven, said he couldn't be doing with all night opening, needed his sleep too much for that. They finished their game and promised to meet up again soon. Walking back from the pub Tim had time to reflect on things. It was complicated, a real mess. He was being unfaithful to Mel, his lovely wife, the woman he'd treasured for twenty years, he'd just lied to Ben, his best mate, and he was using Neen, someone who'd offered him friendship, but from whom he'd taken so much more. He looked up at the dark sky, full of tiny stars, one bright one shone out, much brighter than all the others. He tried to figure out where it was, it seemed to be in the East. Could that star be looking down on Poland, looking at Mel and at him and keeping an eye on both of them? He thought about Ben's words. Ben was right about Mel, she was probably lying in her bed right at this minute crying herself to sleep. He thought about how good it had been when they got back

315

from France, how happy she'd been at him getting that job. He should have trusted her, never doubted her, all he'd done was upset her even more and she had a hard enough time being apart from him without that extra pressure. The time had passed when he could have second thoughts about getting involved with Nina; he couldn't undo what had already been done.

What a pity it was too late to ring Mel. It would do her good to hear my voice, to have her know I'm thinking of her, tell her not to cry but to try and get through the next week until we're together again. He saw Nina's light on, she'd be waiting for him. She'd told him to let himself in whatever time he got back, she wanted an update on Ben and his 'grubby little affair'. But what about their affair? Wasn't that grubby? What should he do? He stood on the pavement looking at the two houses – this path or that one? It seemed symbolic somehow, like it was a defining moment in his future. This path led to his own bed, his and Mel's bed, his home, his kids home... this path led straight to Nina, and the comfort she could give him as he tried to get through another lonely night, struggling to get to sleep until first light, then sleeping for a couple of hours until he was forced to get up for work. At least with Nina he would sleep, after a while. In his bed he would be lucky to get two hours' sleep. What if he fell asleep at the wheel tomorrow, that wouldn't help Mel, would it, or the kids? No, it made sense to go and talk to Nina for a while. He probably wouldn't stay, he'd just talk with her until he was tired and then slip back to his house for some sleep. Nina welcomed him with a hug and a smile.

"Did you have a nice evening, Tim? Did you see Ben? I'm

glad you're back, I'll make you a hot drink before we go up to bed."

"Thanks, Neen that'll be lovely."

He knew he couldn't go back to his house tonight. He'd known that before he stepped onto her path. Why had he pretended that he could make that decision? He wasn't strong enough to do the right thing? He'd have to end this before the week was out, He'd tell Nina that he'd made a mistake, one he was sorry about, but he had to do what was right. She'd understand, but it could wait a few more days. They went up to her room and in minutes she was cuddled into him, only the duvet covering their modesty.

"What did he say? Did he ask about me?"

"Not really, Neen, he said that him and Beckie are trying for a baby. Actually he told me before but I didn't tell you, I thought it was just Ben talking rubbish, but he means it."

"Well good luck to her, I hope he gives her three and then walks out on her, like he did me"

"I asked him if he plans to divorce you."

"And... What did he say to that?"

"He reckons it'll have to be down to you, you being a lawyer and all that."

"Oh, I'll see to it all right. I'll see to him as well. I'll extract every penny from him, not that he's got many to start with. If she wants him she can have him, but she'd better get used to supporting him because he'll never be able to afford to look after her. I should know, I kept him for all our years together."

"Neen, do you think that's fair? "

"Fair? What's bloody fair, Tim? He walked out and left me with three children, his children, was that fair?"

"Of course not, but he's gone, you earn loads more than he does, you don't need his money do you?"

"That's not the point, why should he get off scot free? Why should he spend what he earns on that little trollop when I'm left here alone?"

"You're not alone now are you?"

"That's only thanks to you, Tim, I rely on you more than I ever did that useless good for nothing."

"Neen, what are we going to do next week, when Mel gets back?"

"That's up to you, Tim, but if I have to lose one of you as a friend I'd sooner it was her. It's a hard thing to say and it would be even harder to do but I've got used to this, Tim, I would miss you terribly."

"But, Neen, we both knew it was only while Mel was away didn't we?"

"Yes, I knew that, of course I did, but I didn't know then how much I would come to need you. If you remember, Tim, you and I weren't the greatest of friends before this were we?"

"That was because you only saw me as Ben's mate. You assumed I must be useless, like him."

"Well now I know different, I like what I know now. We'd have to move, Tim, that is if you did decide to stay with me."

"Yes ... but Nina I can't throw my marriage away just like that, because of an indiscretion, can I?"

"What you really mean is, you can't leave her just because you've been screwing her best mate for a couple of weeks. Don't let's try to make it sound less dirty than it is by using nice words Tim. You've been glad to come round here every night and have what you wanted, to screw Ben's wife. I bet you forgot to tell him that tonight, didn't you?'

"Nina, I'm sorry, I'll go. You're right, I am disgusting, but if it's any consolation to you I am disgusted with myself for what I've done to you, and to Mel and to Ben. I'm deeply ashamed."

He got out of bed and tried to find his clothes in the dark. He felt stupid standing there naked, groping around for clothes that he had discarded so easily just minutes before. How a mood could change so swiftly. His thoughts centred around Mel's return. It was obvious that Nina's anger with him would result in her telling Mel everything. That would be the end of his marriage, not to mention his friendship with Ben. What a mess he'd made for himself.

"Tim... get back into bed!"

"What? You just said I was ..."

"I know what I said, you made me cross. Don't worry, I'm not going to say anything... that's what you're thinking isn't it? Let's not fall out now. After all, if we don't ever say anything about this no one will ever be any the wiser. We might even be able to carry on as we are from time to time, what do you think?"

Tim thought that keeping Nina sweet was his best plan at this moment. This was not a good time to tell her he was intent on discarding her completely as soon as Mel was home.

'If you're sure, Neen.'

"I am sure, anyway Mel told me to get as close to you as I could. Well we can't get much closer than this can we? Now get back into bed and prove to me that you meant all those nice things you said last night." Tim did as he was told.

On the drive to London the next day Tim had little to say, but Simon was keen to know how things were with Melanie. He tried a few times to draw him into conversation, but without success.

"I'm getting the feeling, Tim, that you are on the defensive. Have you had words with her over the phone?"

"No, we don't talk for long enough to have words. She rings, asks me what sort of a day I've had and then asks to speak to Trudy and the kids. She talks to Trudy for longer than she does me."

"Hey, come on Tim, that's natural, she's a mother. Trudy is looking after her kids, taking over her role in the home, she's probably jealous of her actually."

"I don't think so. They seem to be talking for ages about everything, whereas she doesn't have anything worthwhile to say to me."

"That's probably because you're giving her a hard time, you see the trouble is you don't know you're doing it."

"If anyone's getting a hard time, Simon, it's me, not her."

"Well here's a bit of news to cheer you up, or not as the case may be. I've booked the wife and me on a flight to Florida the day after tomorrow; you can take us to Heathrow first thing. We're going to visit a few friends over there and hopefully play some golf, you know, relax a bit."

"What will I do while you're away?"

"Ha, you're worried you won't get to drive this beauty about all over the place, is that it?"

"No, I was thinking I'll miss our journeys and the time we spend talking."

"That's nice, Tim. Thanks, but don't worry, you'll still

be driving about and you'll have someone to talk to, well, listen to more like. Here's the not so good news; my sister flies in the day we fly out. I'm not saying she's difficult exactly but we just never really got on that well. Veronica, that's my sister, lives in Brisbane, which, to be honest, suits me fine. The snag is once a year she comes over here, usually with almost no warning. Coincidentally, if you get my drift, she usually arrives as we're about to leave for Florida, or anywhere for that matter. Its better that way, we'd only fall out if I stayed. Our parents left me the Manor house and some property in London and they left her some land in Australia. At the time she was very angry about it and threatened to challenge the will. When she found out she couldn't she went over there vowing she'd get the Manor off of me one way or another. Under the terms of the will she is free to stay here whenever she wants; she has her own rooms which we simply clean and maintain for her. I've tried over the years to placate her but she refuses to make up, even though she has done very well down under.'

"What are my instructions, Simon, while you are away?"

"Just do as she asks, old boy. Much better that than have her sue me or worse. She'll give you hell I'm afraid, make you drive her to see friends at two in the morning, that sort of thing, she's a bit mad like that. Humour her and hopefully she'll have gone by the time we get back. If you want to talk to me I'm only at the end of the phone, Tim, use my office. It'll be kept locked while I'm away but I'll give you a spare key. Just keep her out of it, that's all I ask. I'll call you every few days, just to get an update on what she's been up to. When's your wife due back?"

"She seems to think they'll be back on Saturday, but that

depends on whether they conclude this deal or not. I'm worried that Naziree fellow will try to keep them out there longer. Mel must be desperate to come home by now, I know I'm desperate to see her."

'You'll probably need to spend most of Thursday hanging around in London after we leave and while you're waiting for Veronica. Her flight isn't due until the evening but it won't be worth driving back home in between. You know most of my restaurant tenants in London, go to any one of them you fancy and have a super meal, put it on my account. Have a nice day in London, do some shopping maybe, get a present for your wife.'

"Thanks, Simon, that's a good idea and God knows, I'm pretty short of those at the moment."

The kids were pleased to see Tim when he got home, but he could only keep them amused for a few minutes before their attention wandered and they drifted back to what Trudy was up to. They seemed to find helping her clear away the dishes more fun than talking to him, which, although he tried to hide it, caused him more resentment. Now he was being rejected in favour of the nanny. Why was it that the family he'd loved for all these years could have such scant regard for him? He was getting a subliminal message, we don't actually need you. He'd got exactly the same from Melanie during their phone calls. She'd talk to him if it was absolutely necessary but she couldn't wait to have the phone passed to the kids or even to Trudy. Did he really mean so little to them that a newcomer in the house was worth more than him? Try as he might to dispel such thoughts, it still hurt. No point in sitting here half the night waiting for a phone call that's not worth having. Five minutes later he was sitting on Nina's sofa listening to her complaining about her job.

"Since Rattani's been away there are no new contracts for me to draft. I'm sitting there with nothing to do half the day, bored out of my brains, but I daren't tell management or they'll find me work off the Stellar Haufman account and I don't want to be in the middle of something else when they get back. I might miss out on all the work from Poland. How's your day been Tim?"

"Interesting, definitely. Simon's off to Florida on Thursday morning and I've got to sit around in London all day waiting to pick his sister up from Heathrow. She's arriving from Brisbane. Apparently they don't get on, so when she says she's coming he ships out… bit odd but that's moneyed people for you."

"Tim, why don't I take Thursday off, meet you in London, we could do some shopping, have lunch and then do a matinee before I catch the train back and you go to the airport?"

"Sounds better than spending a whole day on my own."

"Well, thanks Tim, that was one hell of an acceptance, if you were intending to make me feel excited about it you just failed miserably. If that's really how you feel then sod you, spend the day on your own. I'd sooner be bored in the office than in London with someone who doesn't appreciate me."

"Sorry, Neen, I never meant it to come out like that. I would love to meet you in London, and to prove it I'll take you to one of Simon's best restaurants. He's already told me to put the meal on his account, I'll show you the best food in London, how about it?"

"I'll think about it."

"Oh come on, Neen, you know I want you to come. I can't help it if my mouth doesn't always consult with my brain."

"OK you smooth talker. I'll get the nine thirty, it's a lot cheaper after the peak period and I can get any train back after six thirty, should work out well."

"What are your plans for tonight, Neen?"

"I didn't know we had plans in the evenings. I thought we just followed our instincts, up the stairs and into bed. Why? Have you got a better idea?"

Of course not, it's just that I didn't want you to think I was taking you for granted, not after last night.'

"Tim, with so few nights left, I'm happy for you to take me for granted., in fact why don't you do it now instead of waiting till after the news?"

"Sounds like you did have a plan after all, come on then!"

He pulled her up and steered her towards the stairs. They no longer had any inhibitions with each other and within seconds of starting to kiss she was pulling his clothes off. He felt the excitement of her passionate attack and wondered why Melanie never wanted him this badly. Maybe it would be different after four weeks apart.

He tried to imagine himself with Melanie as Nina eagerly explored his body. If Melanie did behave the way Nina did, like some sex hungry creature intent only on making their loving deeply passionate, he would want to know why she had changed. He knew if she was this keen he would be suspicious, wondering what had brought about the change in her appetite for sex. Maybe I'm just hard to please, he thought.

Thursday Morning brought no change in the heat wave and as Tim headed into central London after dropping Simon and his wife at Heathrow, he found himself admiring scores of beautiful women wearing their lightweight summer attire. The pavements were awash with people who had discarded all but the most essential items in an attempt to stay cool. Tim parked in his favourite underground car park just off The Strand and then set out about finding Nina.

She was due to emerge from the underground station at the end of the road any time now, so he settled for a coffee at a window seat in a bar on the corner and enjoyed the view of passers by. If Nina followed his instructions to the letter he would shortly see her on the opposite pavement. His mind drifted to thoughts of Saturday, the big day, when he would meet Melanie for the first time in a month. What would he say? Should he practice his lines? How would she look? Would she be overjoyed at their reunion or would she grasp hold of the kids and ignore him?

If their meeting was to be a success, and god knows he wanted it to be, then he would have to put aside his petty squabbles and consider her thoughts. Of course she'd head straight for the kids, what mother wouldn't? And anyway, what about his behaviour since she'd been away? Could he really blame it all on her and her lack of interest in him? Wasn't the truth that he had used her absence to behave badly?

If he were to stand any chance of getting away with this he would have to be nice to Melanie and even nicer to Nina. If she lost her temper in a fit of jealousy and spat it all out he was finished.

As he stared at the busy street outside he suddenly saw

her, anxiously looking at her watch. He left quickly and dodged between the traffic to get to her.

"I was just beginning to think you'd stood me up," she said.

"Sorry, Neen, I was staring out of the window, but my mind was somewhere else. You ready then?"

"Tim, I've been ready for ten minutes, let's go."

They walked towards Oxford Street, stopping first at Liberty, where Nina raved about a double bed that was on display, priced at three thousand pounds. 'What about that Tim? She said enticingly, "do you think we could make use of that?"

"What, now?"

"No, stupid, at home in place of my old one. After all I shared that bed with Ben. It's not very nice for me is it?"

What the hell was she going on about? They had talked about this. It was to end tomorrow. Mel would be back on Saturday. Was this her way of telling him she wasn't about to end it as they'd agreed?

"Neen, you haven't forgotten that Mel is due back on Saturday, have you?"

"Thanks Tim, I needed that. We've got just two days left to spend together and you are already thinking about her. Do you have any idea how hard this is for me? Can't you let me enjoy myself until then. God knows I'll have to face up to it soon enough. How do you think it's going to be for me, seeing you two enjoying married bliss together, while I sit next door alone? You are a thoughtless bastard sometimes, Tim, you know that?"

Sorry seemed the only appropriate word, but it was fast becoming the one with which he started every sentence. He wished fervently that he'd never started this affair with Nina. It was obvious she wasn't about to let go.

After two hours of shopping they ended up almost where they'd met. "Nina there's a great rib bar on the corner of the street where I parked the car, perfect for two hungry shoppers, what d'you say?"

"I say, lead on Tim."

Over two full racks with chips and two cold beers they discussed which show they should see. They settled for Mamma Mia, which would only necessitate a short walk from where they were eating. "So is this one of your boss's places Tim,?"

"No, but I've eaten here before, and I love the food. And just look at that view of the people below us, unaware of how we can look down on them as they scurry back and forth. This is people watching at its best.' After a few minutes silence, he added, 'Neen, I'll probably be too late back tonight to come round to you."

"So you're telling me we're finished, is that it? Is that why you let me come up here today? So you could dump me, well away from home. Do you think that's going to change anything? Do you think that's going to make it easier? Don't forget, Tim, that Mel will be expecting me to be there as part of her welcome home party. She'll think it damn strange if I'm not. You'd better get it into your head that we're in this together and I don't like the idea of it ending here, now, in London. Do you seriously think, after all we've done, it will make any difference if we have tonight together or, for that matter, tomorrow night. What do you think Mel would say if she knew? 'Oh well I didn't mind you sleeping with Nina, Tim, as long as you didn't do it the night before I got back'? Get real Tim, whether we get caught tonight, tomorrow night or one day last week the outcome will be the same. The shit will hit the fan, the volcano will erupt, and if it does, you are sitting right on top of it."

On that sombre note they left to make their way to the theatre. At six they were back out in the street again. Tim rang the airport to check on the Brisbane flight. "Neen, the flight is delayed, not expected in until seven thirty tomorrow morning. I'll have to put up in one of the hotels over at Heathrow to be on hand for the morning. What train do you want to catch? I'll get you back to the station."

"No you bloody won't. I thought I'd made it clear we are spending tonight together. Book a double room and in the morning I'll get across to Paddington for the train home. Tonight we can have a fabulous time in a luxurious hotel'. A perfect way to spend our last night together."

Her determination made his thoughts of protest futile, out of the question, so they got the car from the underground parking and joined the mass of traffic heading west to Heathrow.

Tim booked them into a top quality room. Simon was picking up the bill. He wouldn't mind as long as Tim spent the next two weeks making sure his sister had nothing to complain about.

They showered before taking dinner in the hotel's restaurant, but Tim was finding it hard to be good company tonight. Visions of Saturday kept flooding his mind. He saw Melanie, all smiles and happy to be back in the arms of her loving and faithful husband, except that he wasn't.

Would Mel take one look at him, see deceit in his face and ask him outright? She'd know something was wrong, she'd managed quite well without him for four weeks, and as soon as she'd extracted his confession she'd be calm but resolute. 'That's it for us Tim. I cannot believe what you have done. I never dreamt that you were capable of throwing twenty years of our lives away on some cheap and sordid affair with, of all people my so called best friend.' What would she do then? Demand he hand over his keys? Throw him out of his own house?

He could hardly complain that she was being too hard on him. Where would he go? Next door? Oh yes, that'd be great... that would guarantee any chance of reconciliation was stubbed out before it began. You idiot... why did you ever start this?

He looked up and straight into Nina's gaze. Was she reading his mind?

"You look like you've got a lot on your mind, Tim. Would it make it any easier if we shared it?"

"Neen, you know what's on my mind; Saturday, Mel, you, this, us being together, what have we done, Neen?"

"We've made love Tim, not once, or twice but lots of times. We've enjoyed each other, in every sense of the word, and do you know something, Tim? If things were as perfect between you and Mel as you are trying to make out, it wouldn't have happened. Be honest with yourself, it's the only way in the long run. Did you and Mel really find true love again on that holiday, or was that how you wanted to see it through your rose tinted glasses? You know, things were pretty bad between you before you went and yet after two weeks in the sun it was like you were young lovers all over again... No, Tim, what really happened was that you had a holiday romance ... with your wife!"

"Neen, I went with you because I couldn't stand being on my own while she was away. I was jealous, jealous as hell that she was spending her days and, who knows, maybe her nights, with another man. I was angry, confused, lonely ... any man would have gone off the rails in my situation."

"No, Tim, many happily married couples have to spend time apart, but they don't fall into bed with the woman next door simply because they can't have their own wife. You slept with me because you fancied me, because I fancied you, because we both knew that we had more to give each other than you and Mel do. Face it, Tim, you and Mel are never going to find lasting happiness together. You and I? Yes, we could make each other happy, we proved it this last four weeks, and not just in bed, but talking together. You said yourself that you couldn't talk to Mel the way you do me. You said she isn't interested, she's got other things in her head; she even had more to say to Trudy than she did to you, remember?"

"What about my kids, Neen? Am I supposed to forget them as well?"

"Your kids and mine get on great together, we can have all six of them to stay whenever Mel wants and for holidays. If we want a week away on our own she might take mine round at hers. Once she's got over the shock of 'us' I think she'll get used to it."

"Neen, please listen... two months ago Mel and I weren't speaking, you know that. I felt like there was no woman in my life, in fact I was sure of it. Now ... I have two women in my life. What's happened?"

"Us, Tim, that's what's happened. You're scared ... scared of the confrontation with Mel, the inevitableness of it. It's not the splitting up that frightens you, it's having to face the music, owning up, seeing her anger when you tell her what's been happening, but once it's out in the open, a few days and life will get back to normal."

"Normal? What's normal, Neen ?"

"Normal will be you and me Tim, and it'll be better than it's been in years ... I promise." Nina shared the last of the wine between them and hoped that she was getting through to him. For her the last four weeks had been a fresh start, not with a stranger, but with a man she'd known for three years and yet never considered except as a neighbour, as her friend's husband, her husband's friend, someone to nod to over the fence or say good morning to but absolutely nothing more. How could she have been so close to him for three years without realising that they were right for each other? How could she get him into her bed so conveniently so soon after her own husband had left for pastures new? Was she fooling herself as well as him? She was endeavouring to make him see that they had a future together, but how could she be so sure after just four weeks of ... of what.... lust? He was lonely, he'd said so, but she was lonely too. Was that all it was, two lonely people providing comfort to each other? Could he now go back to Mel as if nothing had happened? Perhaps nothing had happened ... maybe that was the answer they needed. After all, if they could convince themselves that nothing had happened then Saturday would be a breeze. They could hug Mel, smile, ask her about her trip, laugh at her stories ... everything would be like before, as if nothing had happened ... but that was for Saturday.

"Tim, please take me to bed, for the last time, if it has to be. Let me feel your affection for me once more. Whatever you decide, I'll go along with it, but don't shut me out tonight ... please."

He owed her this at least. Hadn't he promised her that he would never leave her? Tim Fisher was a man of his word; he would do what she asked like he was a knight of the realm on a white charger, rescuing her from the darkness of her lonely existence. This would be his good deed for the day. He could be proud then instead of ashamed.

"Come on, Neen, I'm going to take good care of you and to hell with Saturday. We'll worry about that tomorrow."

Her eyes were saying thank you. She had the look of someone who had just received good news. There was something special about dishing out happiness, a nice warm feeling inside, a satisfaction unique to giving, like when you threw a pound coin in a beggar's hat, or at Christmas when you saw someone open your present. This was much more than that though; this was giving someone your body, because they wanted it, because they needed it and only your body would do. It was like giving the most precious thing you owned, yet when he looked at her face and saw how much she wanted him he knew it would be worth it. She needed him at this moment and he needed to be needed.

Once safely tucked up in their room they did what came naturally. They were, after all, quite used to taking each other's clothes off, but tonight was extra special. If this really was their last time then he would make sure she experienced the maximum pleasure. Giving would be his pleasure tonight. He held her tight throughout their lovemaking, giving her the reassurance she sought. She was safe in his arms, wanted, valued and respected.

But no sooner was the excitement of the act over than a new desire washed over him. The desire to move away from her, to get up and wash, to distance himself from the taint of their bonding. He turned and slipped his arm from her but she clung to him, not satisfied by the pleasures already experienced, but wanting togetherness, commitment, affirmation of his sincerity ... wanting more than he could give. He heard her mutter "Please, Tim", but that only made him more sickened at his willingness to do her bidding, knowing how wrong it was. The soft glow of moonlight creeping through a chink in the curtains was like a beam calling him to leave now, but he daren't. To do so would provoke her anger such that she might do anything.

A woman scorned, and all that, my god, he'd used her, but now, what now? He had no use for her. Only one thing was important to him now; Saturday, his meeting with Mel. It had to be a success. This shameful feeling which engulfed him was proof that he loved his wife, wanted her. He'd had to use Nina to discover his true love for his wife. She'd never understand it, she must never know of it, but that meant keeping Nina on good terms. As he lay there, he explored every aspect of his folly, chastised himself for every bad move he'd made, but there was no chance to do it differently. What was done was done. A cold fear gripped him as he explored the possible outcomes of his meeting with Mel. It was a sobering realisation, but he was frightened of meeting his wife. Perhaps he could feign illness if she questioned him, claim weakness from lack of sleep, worrying about her, hence his pale colour, his lack of appetite, his vagueness of mind, distraction caused by a month of concern for her safety, her well being. If Nina even hinted at their time together he was finished, the game would be up. He was sweating as he contemplated a sudden and tearful end to his marriage, all because of this wretched affair, this woman who even now was clinging to him like some parasite. He tried to ease himself away from her until he was in danger of falling off the edge of the bed. Why couldn't she just accept that it was over, why couldn't she be reasonable, was that really too much to ask? Eventually sleep took hold. When he woke a bright shaft of sunlight had replaced the moon's subtle glow. He got up at once, before she could try to stop him. A shower would help cleanse him of what had taken place between them. He was dressed and watching the morning news when she woke.

"Nina, I have to be at the airport in less than an hour, can you have breakfast on your own and then get a cab to the station?"

"Whatever, Tim."She turned and went back to sleep, he slipped out of the room, heading for the car with almost indecent haste, like a fugitive escaping the scene of a crime.

He would have to face her later, tonight; he had to make his peace with her, check that she wasn't going to trash him to Mel tomorrow. Like it or not, Nina held the key to his future, he had to be nice to her, whatever 'nice' meant.

Veronica wasn't like he'd expected from the mental picture drawn by Simon. Instead of the red faced, ruthless character that Simon had portrayed, she was in fact quite ordinary. Ordinary in the sense that in a department store, choosing lingerie she would look as normal as the next woman, whereas Tim had conjured up visions of a tough skinned woman in leather clothes, with corks dangling from her hat and brandishing a whip. Instead of a gravel dashed voice demanding instant obedience, she issued her instructions politely with a hint of a smile.

I suppose I've got the right person, Tim thought as he drove them west towards the Manor. Simon always liked to talk when they were driving and, indeed, often sat alongside him, so, deciding to take a chance, he endeavoured to engage her in conversation.

"Should I call you Veronica or Mrs. Stonewood, Mam?"

"Well, Tim, as I've never got close enough to a man to contemplate marrying him I think Mrs. might be wholly inappropriate and I can't stand these modern mamby pamby creations like Miz. In fact where I come from, Miz is a call in a card game, so that just leaves Veronica. If it was good enough for my parents it should be good enough for you, OK?"

"That's fine, I didn't want to cause any offence, so I thought it best to ask."

"What's Simon been telling you? I suppose he said the Ogre from Down Under is coming, did he?"

"I don't think he put it quite like that."

"You're very loyal, Tim, a great quality and damned hard to find nowadays. I'm not entirely wrong though about Simon's description of me, am I?"

"I sensed he feels a little intimidated by you. Something to do with things that happened a long time ago?"

"You mean the will. My father left all his property in England to Simon. We fought all the time as kids and even into our twenties. Dad thought it was serious, but it was sibling rivalry, nothing more. Quite healthy even. In a way Dad made it worse. Every time we all met he would start out by saying, 'I don't want to hear you two arguing.' That always prompted one of us to say, 'It's not me it's him,' and before you knew it we were at it again. He decided that if he left me a load of land in Australia I would make a life out there, marry a tough, handsome man who would look after me and keep me in line. I was upset when the will was read. I was being sent off round the world to make something out of what I saw as the outback, while dear brother sat comfortably here on his ass in ready-made luxury. I had a right to be angry; all Dad had done was make things worse between us."

"I'm sure Simon felt guilty at having got the cushy end of the deal, but we didn't speak much for a few years and then, later, when we did we had this gulf between us which had got bigger during the time we'd been apart. In fact, the land in Brisbane has mostly been developed into what we call Riverside and Southbank, and is probably worth more than all of Simon's portfolio put together, but I stopped caring about the money side of our dispute a long time ago. I buried my resentment soon after I settled out there, but I don't think Simon knows how to. He was too 'old school tie', too formal to just call me up and say let's put it behind us and be friends, so we just went on getting further apart. That's all there is to it. Not so ominous when you know the truth is it?"

"Why didn't you call *him* up and say those things to *him*, you know, Let's put it all behind us and be friends?"

"I don't know, Tim, and that's the truth. I guess I felt that he was the one who'd had the best of it and I was the one who'd had the raw deal, therefore it wasn't up to me to say sorry for it. But, you're right, I could have done so.

Maybe I could have ended this feud, if that's what it is, all those years ago. A shame because actually I always liked my brother when we were kids. I used to boast about him to the girls at school. It was only to his face that I was horrible. Maybe I was to blame for what happened. Maybe Dad saw in me faults that I didn't know I had, which is why I never got the chance to put them right. I wish he'd said it to me, Veronica, you need to stop behaving like a jerk, stop being such a hoity little bitch and start being a real person. That's all it would have taken then, but no he just pushed me to the other side of the world. He never could stand any kind of conflict, he was a timid man, a lovely father, just too kind to get involved in our row I guess."

"Anyway, it's too late now, so I'm here visiting the few friends I still have in England and Simon's scuttled off to Florida rather than face me, just like Dad. That's what he would have done in the same situation. Sorry, Tim, I didn't come all this way to bash your ears matey, it's just that I haven't talked to anyone for twenty four hours and you're a good listener. I'll shut up now and let you drive.'

"Don't worry, I like talking when I'm driving, it makes the journey seem much shorter. Your brother and I talk a lot when we're in the car, not about you mind, but he always asks about my family and that kind of thing. He's a good man, he's good to work for, and yes, I do feel loyalty towards him, but this feud is nothing to do with me. My loyalty to Simon extends to his family, and so that includes you."

"Thanks for that, Tim, I shall look forward to our little chats as we hunt down my few remaining friends. I wrote to lots of people back here after I settled in Brisbane, but one by one I've lost touch, so now I don't have many. The internet helps of course, but there's no point in writing messages to someone if you never intend to see them again, and yet, you know, deep down this is still home to me. I'm a compulsive talker, Tim, just tell me to be quiet if I get on your nerves. I'm a long way from home, at least I'm a long way from the place I've learned to call home. What about this family of yours, the one Simon always asks about? I wouldn't mind hearing about them if you care to share your stories with me. Maybe you can patronise me a bit, help me to feel welcome here."

"Of course, I'd be pleased to tell you about my family, although it's all very complicated at the moment."

"Hell, Tim, families are always complicated. There's no such thing as an uncomplicated family. In fact, they're like the dodo, and they died out years ago."

"Well, mine's a bit of a mess at the moment. My wife's been working in Poland for the last month, she's due back tomorrow and I'm nervous about seeing her after all this time apart. The kids have been looked after by a nanny and she seems to be closer to them than me, and Mel, that's my wife, has been distant on the phone, almost like we didn't know what to say to each other. I can't wait to see her, yet I'm dreading our meeting. Does that make any sense?"

"Perfect sense, Tim. Of course she was distant on the phone, she was in Poland for Christ sakes. She probably missed you like mad and hearing your voice made her want to cry. That's how women are, Tim, even I know that and I've never had to deal with love and sentiment, but I bet she's counting the minutes until she sees you again."

"Do you think so, honestly?"

"I'd bet my ranch on it. Just you make sure you get the

biggest bunch of roses she ever saw and you take hold of her and let her know she's home, safe to you. I wish I could see your faces tomorrow. Who knows it might even get me crying, and that hasn't happened since my horse came second in the Australian Derby. Do you know, Tim, I can see why my brother treats you like one of the family, but I guess as he's not around for a couple of weeks, you're going to have to make do with me."

"That's fine by me, Veronica. I'm relieved you're not like I thought you'd be. I had visions of you wearing jeans, a hat with corks and brandishing a whip."

"Well, back home that's exactly how I dress, but as I'm on holiday I thought I'd dress like you lot. She laughed and Tim found himself joining in."

"Can you believe that I was petrified of picking you up this morning, after everything Simon told me about you?"

"Like I said, Tim, Simon doesn't know me because he hasn't taken the trouble to sit down with me and talk since Dad died. Do you realise you and I have talked more on this journey than Simon and I have in years. How daft is that?"

"It's not only daft, it's a shame, Veronica, and whatever you might think, I know your brother and he's a lovely man. You two must get it sorted out, before it's too late."

"Maybe it's already too late, Tim, he's a stubborn old fool is Simon."

"He's not a fool, Veronica, daft maybe, but well intentioned and kind to boot."

"Has my brother moved you into one of his houses, Tim, or do you live in at the Manor?"

"Neither, Mel and I bought a house three years ago on a posh new estate, Willow Brook, in Elmthorpe, not too far from the Manor. Mel earns good money. She's got a top job at a bank, which is why she's off to Poland instead of being at home looking after us."

"Sounds like you don't approve of women having successful careers, Tim?"

"Only if means they can't have a successful family too."

"Tim, I'd like to meet your family while I'm here, God knows I've precious few friends, and I could do with some new ones. Would you and your wife come over for dinner one evening? Bring the kids of course."

"I'd like that Veronica, but in the circumstances, you know with her being away and all that, I'll need to check with her. If everything's OK when she gets back I'm sure we'd love to."

"Why wouldn't everything be OK, Tim? You seem a little apprehensive about her impending return. I would have expected you to be over the moon, is there likely to be a problem?'

"I hope not, Veronica, it's a bit delicate and not something I want to talk about. Please don't take that the wrong way but it might be something Mel and I have to work out between us."

"Why am I getting bad vibrations, Tim? If it doesn't work out, you're going to have to tell someone. If you want an ear or a shoulder I'm around, well for two weeks at least, OK?"

"Thanks, Veronica, that's exactly what your brother would say if he were here. You two have a lot in common, and that's meant to be a compliment in case you were wondering."

"That's exactly how I took it, Tim. Don't forget, any trouble, call for some Aussie assistance."

Her laugh was so infectious that he joined in despite his worries.

Having safely delivered Veronica to the Manor, he set off for home and a rendezvous he would have preferred to avoid. With around fifteen hours left before he would see Mel again there was still the issue of Nina to deal with. What had started out as a simple neighbourly friendship had turned into a torrid affair based on loneliness and lust. Like a huge fire ignited with a single match, this relationship which had been so easy to start was proving incredibly difficult to extinguish.

Unless Nina was willing to sit down over a glass of wine and promise to forget everything that they had done together these past four weeks, his marriage to Mel was finished. He could blame her for leaving him at home and lonely, but she would never accept responsibility for what had happened once her back was turned. Her back had been stabbed not just by him, but by the woman she had considered her friend. Once the truth was out he would be an outcast, from his home, his family, maybe even from his job – after all Simon was a man of traditional values, this might prove to be too much, even for him.

Why, he kept asking himself, why did I throw everything away for ... for what? A romp with a good looking woman who never had time for me until her husband left her? Her husband ... my best mate... he'll never speak to me again. I've blown it ... I've lost everything ... unless, unless Nina will promise me...

In the kitchen Trudy was busy preparing the children's evening meal.

"Hi Tim, do you want to eat with us, I've made plenty. You'd better go and talk to the kids. They are excited like I've never seen them, counting the minutes until she arrives."

"Oh, thanks Trudy, I'd love to, but first there's something I've got to do, urgently."

"Go round to Nina's, I suppose?"

"Yes ... what do you mean, 'I suppose?'"

"Well, let's be honest, Tim, you've spent more time there than you have here since Mel went. Anyway, Nina came round earlier for a bit of a chat and, she asked me to send you round as soon as you got in, like you wouldn't have anyway."

"Trudy, we're just neighbours, friends... she's just lost her husband, well not lost in that sense but you know what I mean. She's been very upset with him going and everything. Mel asked me to see she was OK ..."

"Well that's good, because according to Nina, Melanie asked her to look after you. There's been a lot of looking after done this past four weeks, so you should both be fine for when Mel gets here in the morning."

Was she being sarcastic? Was she telling him that she knew what was going on? What had Nina said to her? If she knew, then there was even less chance of him getting away with it. If he asked her outright, it would be telling her what she might not know. Maybe she was just a bit suspicious. She'd never dare tell Melanie anything without proof and she had no proof. No, Trudy wasn't a problem. Best thing was to get round to Nina and find out what she'd said to Trudy, to make her so touchy.

"Keep mine hot please Trudy, I'll only be half an hour, at most. Tell the kids as soon as I get back we'll plan our welcome for the morning."

"That's good, they'll like that."

Right now seeing Nina and extracting the promise of

her silence was too pressing to wait another minute. He went straight in without the cursory knock, which had become his usual method of entry to her kitchen.

"Come in Tim, I'm in the lounge."

He walked straight through the kitchen and into the lounge, where Nina was sitting, waiting for him. She was perched on the edge of the sofa in what could easily have been a pose for the cover of Vogue. She had on a purple silk night-dress with tiny straps, which fell enticingly across her breasts. Her legs were crossed so that her thigh was exposed in all its beauty. She looked regal as she rested her elbow on her knee and held her wine glass in one hand, with the other tantalisingly across her bare leg with her fingers apart as if to emphasise the power she possessed right to the tips of her fingers.

Tim stopped in his tracks. He was taken aback at the overt beauty before him. Was this her way of thanking him for the friendship he'd offered since she had been deserted by the man whose duty it was to protect her? The role Tim had taken on, reluctantly.

He had never seen her look so stunning. What was different about her today ... or was it him, seeing her for the first time as a woman. She was perfection. Her form was generously moulded, like a sculpture, a masterpiece. She was a vision of beauty. Here, in front of him, a work of art on private display for him and him alone.

After what seemed an age she spoke.

"Sit down Tim, here, next to me ... we've so much to talk about."

He threw his coat onto a chair and placed himself next to her as commanded. He'd come here hoping to hear the words that would set him free from the torment of the last twenty four hours, but now his mind was focused only on the next few hours.

Nina took Tim's hand and placed it on her bare thigh, pulling him closer. His blood was pounding around his body. He was experiencing an uncontrollable fever of emotion. It was too strong to fight.

He looked down at his hand which was cupping her bare body beneath the silk gown. Nina stretched out flat on the sofa, her eyes closed as she relaxed in his grip. He kissed her, softly at first, then more intensely until they immersed themselves in the ultimate act of love making. After they had exhausted their emotional energy they lay naked on the carpet, clutching each other tightly.

Three hours passed in what seemed like minutes. Tim suddenly recalled his words to Trudy. "Oh my god Neen, I promised to be back in half an hour, I promised I'd help the kids sort out their welcome for Mel, they'll be going to bed by now."

"Then you'd better go. You've given me everything I need for tonight. You can go now."

"Nina, you do mean ... for good, don't you?"

"What do you think, Tim? Wasn't it just as fantastic for you as it was for me? Are you saying you can walk away from what we did tonight and never look back? I don't think you can, Tim, any more than I can. We both know that there will always be something very special between us."

"Neen, please tell me that you won't say anything to Mel. It'll destroy her, and me... please!"

"I don't want to destroy you Tim, you mean too much to me for that. Go home and help the children prepare for the morning."

"But I need you to say you won't tell her, can't you see it's written on my face that I'm guilty?"

"Trust me, Tim. She kissed him softly on the lips and then, still naked, steered him to the door and home."

The short walk back did not give him chance to sort his head ... as he walked in he was a mess of confusion and fear for what he'd done, again.

Trudy regarded him with disdain, contempt even. She must know now that he was a devious two timing monster. She was a woman after all. She addressed him via the children to avoid any verbal contact with him.

"Your father's back kids, and just as you were about to go to bed, you can have an extra half hour to sort out the morning and then bed. I don't want you being tired when your Mum arrives."

He couldn't fail to miss the way *she* had granted permission for them to stay up longer to see him. His children now needed *her* permission to see him and he needed her permission to play the role of father. How had he got to this in just a few weeks? The answer, he knew, was next door, and it was pretty obvious that Trudy knew as well.

CHAPTER THIRTEEN

A door slammed somewhere on the hotel landing, causing Melanie to wake with a start. The heavy curtains gave no hint of light, no indication of time, no clue as to whether it was day or night. In the room something seemed unfamiliar as she lay staring at where the door should be. It wasn't there. Still half asleep she turned to see if it was on her other side, and it was then that her arm encountered a body. In seconds her brain recalled the sequence of events that had led to her present confusion.

She'd shared a drink with Ratty in his room as agreed. A vodka, Polish vodka, very good vodka, especially with apple juice, a common combination in Poland. She'd had a second as they talked about their work back home and the work they'd completed here, then the conversation moved to families, her family, her husband, her relationship. The apple juice ran out and so she had vodka with vodka. She revealed to Ratty the problems within her marriage. Tim's inability to listen to her, to show affection of the kind a woman needs, kindness, caressing and understanding.

She knew Ratty understood, his strong but gentle arm around her was testimony to this. He didn't pressure her, he simply made it possible for her to find solace in a way that was impossible with Tim. She helped herself to another vodka and relaxed into his arms. He was everything her husband was not, this was a moment in her life she refused to hurry, savouring it instead, as if it might disappear at any minute. Her head was swimming with the effects of the vodka but she knew only too well what she was agreeing to; the inevitable.

That had been hours ago. The noises emanating from around the hotel were a positive indication that people were getting up, showers were being taken and doors were slamming as guests headed for breakfast in the restaurant downstairs.

She climbed out of bed, taking only a brief look back at the still sleeping figure of her lover. She dressed quickly and carried her shoes as she silently let herself out onto the landing. Her head was still in a whirl but now was not the time for reflection, rather a hasty shower back in her room followed by a quick breakfast and then a taxi to the station.

She managed to avoid meeting Ratty at breakfast, scoffing it down in record time before racing back up to her room to get her cases. One last look from the hotel window, the lake making her heart beat faster as it had done from the very first day. She'd fallen in love with this place, the hotel, the lake, the city; she turned from the window and thought about the man she'd left sleeping in the room along the corridor... had she fallen in love with him?

She looked across the lake to the opposite bank and saw people cycling on the path at the waters edge. She searched the grass further back until she saw a spot of grass that might be the place where they had spent an evening together. This was a magical place. She would return, of that she was certain, but who with...?

She took the small case in her left hand and pulled the larger one on its wheels with her right hand using the long handle to steer it. She made it to the lift where other people were waiting. At reception she had only to hand back her key and say goodbye and thank you to the lady who had helped her several times over the past few weeks. Goodbyes said, she took a last look at the double doors which led straight into the restaurant, but there was no sign of Ratty. It was better this way. The porter opened the front doors and took her cases to the waiting taxi. This chapter of her life was over; the next one might prove more difficult.

The taxi ride to the station was done at breakneck speed in an old Mercedes which stalled at every set of traffic lights. She watched with amusement as the driver cursed it each time as if it were the first time it had happened.

She thought of Tim driving his wonderful new Mercedes for Simon Stonewood and that brought thoughts of home tumbling into her mind. She determinedly closed the door on those images, preferring not to think about home until she was back on English soil.

She had several hours on the train to Berlin, plenty of time for self explanations and recriminations. From Berlin she had a flight booked to Heathrow, from where she would get a taxi and another train home. If everything went to plan, she should be walking up the front garden path around one thirty.

Once on the train, she was forced to think about her imminent arrival. Should she ring Tim and ask him to pick her up from the station or should she get a taxi? She decided that she couldn't face a twenty minute car journey, possibly alone with him. Not yet anyway. Better to return to a group welcome, one where everyone would try to talk at once, offering her protection from his questions, his searching eyes, looking for tell tale signs of her guilt.

Until yesterday it had been simple, there was nothing to hide – well nothing of any consequence. All right, she'd sat at the lakeside a few times with Ratty, she'd even let him touch her intimately once or twice, but on the grand scale of things she could deal with that. What happened last night was different, and what made it unforgivable, if Tim ever found out, was that she'd asked for it to happen. Yes of course she'd said no at first, but Ratty was a decent person, if she'd said no like she meant it he would have respected her wishes. She heard herself saying no, just as she had last night, except it sounded more like yes. She thought about the way she'd dealt with his moves. She practiced saying no to herself and each time she said it she knew that she'd really invited him to overrule her.

That was what she'd wanted him to do and he had obliged willingly. What had happened next was truly wonderful and she refused to tell herself that she wished she hadn't let it go so far. She had only good memories of last night and the hardest part, she knew, would be saying no to Ratty the next time he asked. The secret was not to find herself in a situation where it was possible. The hotel room had been a perfect opportunity. A double bed, a locked room, a mini bar stocked with vodka, a man she'd spent a lot of pleasant time with already, a man who had declared his love for her although she'd repeatedly told him she would never be his.

The problem with Ratty she thought, is he never takes no for an answer. The problem with me is I don't know if I want to say no. The train manager announced the approach of her station. She had very little time left to get herself organised for all the smiles, the reunion, the hugging, the kissing, and at the end of the day no doubt, matters of a more marital nature.

She lugged the cases for one last time across the platform to a waiting taxi, then gave him the instructions that would take her to her door. It was like being inside a space shuttle before take off. She imagined the world outside counting down, waiting for the big explosion that would be the start of her next voyage. Much as she was desperate to see the kids and to question Trudy about everything they'd done, every scratch they had, every trip they'd made together, she was dreading the first moments face to face with her husband. What was it her mother had always said? 'Absence makes the heart grow fonder'.

Maybe I don't have a heart, she thought, maybe I'm heartless, a heartless cow, that's what I am, returning to my family to smile and give them all the presents I bought in Poland, whilst hiding the truth of my infidelity, my treachery, my attempt to destroy the love and loyalty upon which our marriage has been based for twenty years.

Twenty years, is that how long I've waited? Waited for a man to hold me with feeling, with tender love? No wonder I jumped at the chance to share myself with Ratty. If only you could learn to love me like that, Tim, then, maybe ... just maybe we could have a relationship that would satisfy us both.

"Here we are then". The taxi driver must have realised she needed to be returned to the real world in time for her grand entry, hence his announcement that they were turning into her road, as if she wouldn't know that. But he was right, she'd seen nothing on this final leg of her long journey.

The road was empty. She hadn't phoned them because it would have made it even worse, as if she were saying, be ready, sound the fanfares, I'm back, when all she wanted was to slip quietly back into her home and into her old routine. Maybe they would all be busy. Tim might have had to work, Henry might be off playing football, James might have a music session. Please, that would be the perfect homecoming. She paid the taxi driver and started up the path skillfully towing her case behind her. She pushed the kitchen door open ... still nothing. She let go her cases and pushed open the door into the lounge ... Suddenly there were screaming children on every side, so overcome with excitement that they shouted above one another, drowning out individual voices so that conversation was impossible. Nina's three children had waited in hiding with hers, to witness the moment. Trudy, Nina and of course Tim stood behind the children, smiling and waiting until the crescendo subsided sufficiently to make their words worthwhile.

A banner across the wall said, 'Welcome Home Mum'. Helium filled balloons stood up on ribbons from the chairs and from everywhere that they could fix a drawing pin. If she had ever doubted the warmth of welcome awaiting her, this dispelled those thoughts completely. Fully five minutes passed before the children let her go, they wanted to know what it was like, where she'd been, had she missed them and then they each gave her a present, things they'd made for her, or in Amy's case, a picture of Poland that she had painted from a book.

At last the children allowed the adults a turn and it was

to Trudy that Mel turned first, after all she had been the one who had kept these children safe and well and amused for four weeks. Trudy affirmed their good behaviour and excellent health, laying to rest any fears Melanie might have had.

She turned her head to the only two people left in the room to whom she had not yet spoken. Nina and Tim stood side by side smiling like two book ends. They had patiently waited their turn and that turn had now arrived.

Nina spoke first, "Welcome Home, Mel. It seems a long time, you must be tired out. We must sit down and have a good long chat. There's so much to tell you and I want to know all about your trip, but first ... you need a chance to recover from your journey. I'll go and put the kettle on and give you a chance to talk to Tim. He's been like a fish out of water these last few days."

She made her way through a room full of children towards the kitchen.

Melanie looked into Tim's eyes, she saw that they were staring back like beacons from a lighthouse, searching, searching through the fog for any missing clues to their difficulties. Without a word being exchanged they both knew that the sparse conversations between them over the past four weeks would have to be explained. Reasons would be required, fears would have to be allayed, but first they would have to say something to each other.

"Tim, you look more tired than me, have you had trouble sleeping?"

God, what sort of a question was that? He thought about the past two nights and felt the sweat forming on his forehead.

"No, not too bad, but I've been anxious, anxious to see you arrive safely home, the kids have been ..."

"What have the kids been, Tim?"

He didn't know what the kids had been. He'd hardly seen them in the time she'd been away. He caught Trudy staring at him, as if daring him to speak about the children or what they had felt. She looked ready to torpedo him; she was angry and it showed. He mustn't let Mel see her looking like that or she would want to know why.

"I was going to say the kids have been so happy with Trudy, she's been wonderful with them."

"That's kind of you," she said unconvincingly. Already they were struggling for something to say to each other ... this was the proof, if proof were needed, she thought that their relationship was struggling.

'How's the job going, Tim?'

'Great, honestly, it was the right thing to do. I'm glad you pushed me into it. Simon's a good boss and so is Veronica.'

"Who is Veronica?"

"She's Simon's sister, she's over from Australia on a short holiday."

"Short or not, you seem to have got to know her quite well?"

'I only met her yesterday when I picked her up from Heathrow. I just meant she's a nice person, is that a problem?'

"No, sorry Tim, it's me being a bit prickly. I was at Heathrow recently too, it would have been nice for me to be picked up by a man, one who instantly thought I was a 'nice' person."

"Mel, I could have if you'd phoned and asked me, but you

chose not to give me any details of your journey home. Did you come back on your own or with him ... Nina's boss?"

"He has a name, Tim, he's called Rattani, but most people call him Ratty, and yes, in case you're wondering, he is a nice person, just like Simon's sister."

"I wasn't wondering at all."

"Liar ... you said Nina's boss, as if some stigma was attached to him. You couldn't bring yourself to say his name!"

"Well, you seem very keen to defend him, being as he's a lawyer I would have thought he could do that for himself, without your help."

"That's your trouble, Tim, you think."

"Mel, I haven't seen you for four weeks, I've been looking forward to this moment, please don't let's spoil it with silly arguing."

"Sorry, Tim, you're right. We should be all smiles from here on, look, like this." She stretched her cheeks into an exaggerated smile. It would help her to deal with the niggling irritation that Tim was propagating simply by being there.

"So ... Have you made any plans, Tim? Are we all eating out somewhere tonight to celebrate our being a family together again?"

Shit ... why hadn't he thought of that? It was so obvious, so blatantly the thing to do, but he'd been too busy with other things to get today organised.

"Sorry Mel, I didn't know if you'd be too tired, first day back and all that. I'll get on the phone and book something now, where do you fancy?"

"Why don't we try the Walnut Tree? Maybe third time lucky?"

Tim's recollection was that their last visit there had been a success, unlike the first one, but he wasn't about to argue.

"I'll ring them now, how many of us, Mel?"

Melanie turned to her friend. "Nina, you and the kids will join us tonight for a meal won't you? Help us celebrate all being back together."

Nina was delighted at the suggestion, "We'd love to Mel, what time?"

"Seven thirty?" she shouted to Tim, who was talking to the restaurant,

"OK," he said, acknowledging her at the same time.

"Seven thirty, Neen."

He put the phone down and made an announcement. "Right everyone, we're eating at the Walnut Tree at seven thirty, my treat, we'll leave here at seven. I booked the table for ten, OK?" He looked towards Trudy as he spoke, making it clear that she was included. He had some work to do to get Trudy on-side and tonight's meal would be a good start. Nina wouldn't say anything out of place in front of the children and so he could relax and enjoy the evening.

Melanie spent the remainder of the afternoon with the children before they got ready to go out, which meant that she had almost no time to talk to Tim. This suited her fine, though she had no idea that it suited Tim even more.

The Maitre de welcomed them as always, seating them on a large round table in the centre of the restaurant. Tim sat next to Mel, who sat next to Trudy. The kids all rushed to grab seats so that by the time Nina got to sit down she had to sit next to Tim. The irony of the situation was not lost on either of them, as one furtive glance confirmed. On his left Tim had his wife; on the right he had his lover.

As Melanie was busily engaged with Trudy in settling the children, Nina whispered in Tim's ear, "Bon appetite". She smiled and left him to contemplate the meaning behind her words.

Eventually, when they had all chosen and their order was taken, Tim became acutely aware that he needed to pay a great deal of attention to Mel tonight if this was to work.

"How does it feel, Mel, to be home, eating with us lot?"

"It feels good, Tim. At least tonight I won't have to talk business through and after the meal."

"Is that what happened in Poland, you talked late into the night?"

"Yes, most nights. Sometimes I walked around the lake in front of the hotel. It was so beautiful, I fell in love with that walk. I want to go back and spend more time there, see more of the city and for that matter the country."

"I'd have thought you'd have had enough of Poland after a month. After all, you didn't even want to go there when they asked you, if you remember." The acidity in his voice revealed the resentment he still felt for the time she had spent in Poland and away from him.

After twenty years of marriage his tone wasn't lost on Melanie.

"So do you have a problem with me liking Poland?"

"No, I'm just surprised that's all. I thought you would have hated it because it kept you away from the kids ... and from me."

Melanie felt her anger rising so much that she wanted to say, 'In your dreams Tim', but that would bring the meal to a disastrous and premature conclusion, not a good idea.

"Well in the beginning that may have been true, but after all, it wasn't the Country that kept me away, it was my work."

"So you hated the work then?"

"No Tim, I didn't, OK? I'm sorry, I know you want me to say that but it isn't true. I enjoyed my work. I was appreciated by the members of our team because I have qualities which make me good at what I do. They see me as someone who is capable of a lot more than just ' number crunching,' as you described it, and they believed in me. They believed that I could carry on negotiations for the bank and do a professional job. You know how hard I worked to build a career, to get on in the bank, all those nights I spent at night school and then taking exams, well this makes it worthwhile. It's great to be seen as someone with a lot to offer.

Tim was fuming at her overt defence of her trip. This wasn't what he wanted to hear. He wanted contrition, he wanted to hear her say she never wanted to do anything like that again. It was becoming clear that she'd be off tomorrow if another project were offered to her. He couldn't stand the thought of this all over again.

"What do you mean, the team appreciated you? There were only three of you ... and it was this Ratty guy who chose you, so you mean he appreciates you, is that it?"

"Yes, Tim, you've got it, he appreciates me."

"Well, Simon appreciates me but when he goes off to Florida for a month he doesn't drag me with him, expecting me to leave my family, he finds someone out there to do the job."

Melanie's fuse was about to blow. "Yes, Tim, but you're

a taxi driver. I expect he can get one of those anywhere."

Tim pushed his chair back hard against the wooden floor, the screech of wood on wood causing everyone in the room to stare across at his table. He stood up so fast he nudged his plate and tipped his wine glass over. Without looking back he headed for the toilets where he could splash his face with cold water and try to calm down before he erupted and caused a scene that would be remembered at the Walnut Tree for a long time to come.

Of the children, only Henry noticed the manner in which his father had left the table. He looked across to his mother to measure her reaction. She put her finger to her lips to signal that he should say nothing. The adults couldn't fail to observe his departure and wonder precisely what words had been exchanged to precipitate such a dramatic exit. Nina attracted the children's attention to the food with a story about the famine in Africa, explaining that children there had little or no food and that this meal would be a month's food for them.

Trudy gave Melanie a concerned look, "Is everything all right?" she asked, knowing full well that it wasn't.

"Yes, its fine, Tim's just a bit overcome at having me back; he'll soon be right as rain."

Inwardly she doubted that, thinking instead that things had reached a new low between them, but she felt none of the concern she had felt a couple of months ago when the same thing had happened. Then she was willing to take the blame and do anything to regain Tim's respect, whereas now she was ambivalent. She had changed while in Poland, she had regained her confidence, no longer a doormat for Tim to wipe his feet on. She knew there could be no going back to her old conciliatory ways. Subservience and submission were traits of the past. If Tim wanted them to have a future he would have to accept her for what she was, a successful woman with opportunities of her own making, ones which might not always include Tim and ones which he might find hard to live with.

Tim's return to the table was met with silence. The children were at last all quietly eating and the adults preferred not to speak until they knew what he was going to do next. He gave a weak smile, said he had choked on his fish. Might have been a bone, he explained, though nobody believed him. Conversation was strained now and the happy atmosphere in which the meal has started was gone. When it was time to leave, no one was sorry, the children had eaten their fill and couldn't wait to get out instead of having to sit quietly while the adults finished theirs. They decided to skip coffee and make for home.

On their way out to the cars, Nina caught up with Melanie. "Mel, why don't you put the kids to bed and then come round to mine for a drink and a chance to unwind?"

"That's a good idea, Neen, I can't face Tim in his present mood. I'll say good night to the kids and then let Trudy put them to bed, after all she's had plenty of practice."

On the drive home, Tim struggled to make amends for his outburst. "I'm sorry about that Mel. I'm just a bit tense, you know, having not seen you for so long."

"Do you think that can excuse you from ruining the meal and embarrassing Trudy and Nina? I wished we had never gone out. I can tell you one thing, I will never go there again. The Maitre de was looking at us for the rest of the meal. We lowered the tone of the restaurant, everyone saw what you did, and you not only showed yourself up but all of us as well. That was the worst night out I have ever had. I think it best if we don't speak about it. I'm too upset to talk to you anyway."

"So does that mean that when we get home you still won't talk to me?"

"What you really mean is, will I sleep with you tonight, right...? what do you think?"

If Tim was feeling bad already, things had just got a whole lot worse. After a month apart she was refusing him the very essence of his relationship with her. He was desperate to be intimate again. How could she punish him like this. It was unfair. His behaviour hadn't been all his fault, she had provoked him, she had goaded him to react as he had. She had better change her mind or he would really get angry. He had put up with enough. He'd let her go to Poland, but now it was time she did what he wanted for a change.

"Mel, I've put up with a lot lately, please don't push me too far or ..."

"Or what Tim ...? What will you do? Leave me like Ben left Nina, or will you start having your meals at the Globe again? Tim, listen carefully, I don't care, OK?"

Melanie bundled the kids into the house. Trudy had ridden in Nina's car and she took charge once inside the house. Melanie kissed each of the kids goodnight and then turned for the door.

"Where are *you* going?"

'I'm going next door, don't wait up.' With that, Melanie slammed the kitchen door and was gone.

Nina sat her down on the sofa and, after filling two glasses with Chardonnay sat beside her.

"Are you all right?"

"No, Neen, I'm not. We had a blazing row on the way home in the car. He's got a bloody nerve, thinks he can order me to do whatever he wants, like sleep with him tonight. Not a chance, not after the way he's behaved."

"Tell me about your trip, Mel, there must be loads of things to tell. How was that boss of mine? Amorous as usual?"

"Yes he was, but he's a man, a real man, he knows how to treat me, he makes me feel like a lady. Tim makes me feel like shit. God, I can see now why I found it so easy to spend my evenings with Ratty, we're on the same wavelength, we like the same things, same food, same wine, same books, same plays. What do Tim and I have in common? Nothing!'

"Well, you have three kids, Mel; I suppose that's something you have in common."

"I have three kids; Tim doesn't do anything for them. On the phone I kept asking Trudy if he was spending time with them, No she said, he's too busy at the moment, that was her reply every day. Too busy. He'll always be too busy, out with his mates or working or finding some excuse not to bother with them. No, Neen, he did his bit when they were conceived, he opted out after that, his hard work was over then; the rest of their lives are down to me. He only thought I would have sex with him ... after the way he showed me up in there. He must be joking. I'd rather sleep with the cat than sleep with him."

"So Ratty was the perfect gentleman? I'm surprised, I was sure he'd use the opportunity to try it on with you."

"I never said he didn't ... I said he knows how to treat me, treat me properly."

"So he did try it on?"

"Of course. I would have been shocked if he hadn't, I'm not that unattractive I hope."

"And you said no, of course?"

'Did I? Let me think ... yes, most of the time I said, 'No Ratty, I'm a married woman, behave yourself'.'

"Most of the time? What about the odd time when you didn't say no?"

"Then I said yes."

"Christ Mel, are you serious ... are you saying you slept with Ratty?"

"What if I did, Neen, is it such a big thing? I'm a woman, he's a man, we needed each other. Maybe we can't satisfy those needs except together. I don't regret what I did if that's what you want me to say."

"I don't want you to say that, of course I don't, if he made you happy I'm pleased for you. I'm just shocked, that's all."

Nina's head was spinning with this news, what an opportunity to confess her affair with Tim. It would have to be said one day. She couldn't live with a lie forever and somehow it seemed that Mel was far more concerned with Ratty than she was with Tim.

"He made me happy, Neen, I know it's not right and all that....but I spent one whole beautiful night with him. I've never experienced such a lovely feeling in my life, a feeling of being wanted, and after we'd made love he held on to me. He wouldn't let go of me, he cuddled me until I fell asleep. I don't think I can find it in me to sleep with Tim for the moment. I need to sort my head out first."

"So you liked Poland?"

"I loved it, Neen, I'm definitely going back there, to the same hotel, to the lake. I want to take the children there.

There's so much for them to do, it's amazing. Anyway I could bore you for hours with talk of what we did out there, but tell me what happened here, when Tim was going on about the zoo and all that. Did you talk to him?"

"Yes, I spent hours talking to him. I listened to him going on about you not being here, where, according to him, you should have been. He was round here most nights for food. He was getting home too late to eat with Trudy and the kids, so I cooked enough for two. One night in particular he was very upset. I thought he was about to fly out to find you. I had to ply him with drink to talk him out of it."

"Thanks, Neen. God it would have screwed things up for me if he'd shown up there. Can you imagine how Ratty and Hugh would have reacted to a jealous husband disrupting our negotiations?"

Nina laughed. "I've never heard it called 'negotiations' before. So what was Hugh Ballantyne like? I've spoken to him on the phone at work but I haven't met him yet, he's pretty high up in Stellar Haufman. He doesn't mix with the likes of me, I'm mere pond life in his world."

"Hugh is a lovely man, fabulously mature, looks a bit like Richard Gere, definitely a man you couldn't say no to. Unfortunately he never asked me."

"Just as well, sounds to me like this trip was one long orgy."

"It was certainly better than a holiday, Neen, it was a fulfilling experience, one that changed me, gave me the chance to find out who I am, what I am ... I'm not the same person I was when I left."

"Where does that leave Tim?" Nina had more than a passing interest in her answer.

"I don't know. Before I left we were right back on course, Tim had just started his new job, got out of those dirty stinking bloody overalls at last, we were even good in bed again, but I don't feel the same now. Perhaps I need more time to adjust ... or maybe it's more serious than that."

Nina filled their glasses again, conscious that Mel was in no hurry to go home.

"Have you heard anything from Ben? Still with Beckie is he?"

"Oh, very much so, He's a part of my past now, Mel, We won't be getting back together."

"Sorry, Neen, sounds like you don't want to talk about him?"

"About who... ?" She laughed to underline the finality of her relationship with Ben.

"I suppose I'll have to go home sooner or later, to whatever awaits me? Mel emptied her glass and stood up."

"We'll talk again tomorrow, Mel. Try to get a good night's sleep."

They hugged each other and said goodnight.

Melanie pushed the kitchen door open. At least he hadn't locked her out. She slipped her shoes off, turned out the kitchen light and crept up the stairs. The bedroom light was out, maybe he was asleep. But that thought was quickly dispelled.

"I'm glad you're back ... please let me say sorry for earlier."

The pleading in his voice made Melanie more sympathetic than she'd intended.

"It's OK, I know you've been upset while I've been away. Let's get a good night's sleep. Tomorrow things might look a little better.'

If Tim had hoped for more, he knew he had no chance, but at least she was talking to him. She was saying it might be all right tomorrow. Might be? She wasn't saying it would be; only maybe, perhaps she was playing for time, trying to get through until the morning when she would tell him she was finished with him. Why had he behaved so badly? His wife had come home and within hours he had screwed up big time.

Tim was up early preparing breakfast for the children while they watched TV then, taking coffee and toast up to Melanie, he tried to act as if nothing was wrong. She could hardly be cross with him for bringing her breakfast in bed. She seemed content as he sat on the bed and made conversation with her while she dispatched the toast and coffee. He was doing his perfect husband routine, they both knew that, but even if she didn't buy it, it was preferable to another argument.

"What would you like to do today Mel? We could go out somewhere. I could give you a real treat and take you out in Simon's car. He wouldn't mind and, by the way, Veronica, his sister, wants us all to go over to the Manor for a meal one evening. I said I'd have to ask you first, but it would be nice, don't you think?"

"I think it would be lovely. You fix it for any night you want, and as for my plans... well I've only got one plan right now ..."

"What is it?"

"To get you into bed and discover what I've been missing all this time."

She knew this would set Tim up for the day, which in turn would make the house a pleasant place for the children,

Trudy and herself, but there was another reason she wanted him to make love to her ... she needed to know if she would feel the way she did before she'd gone away. It was imperative and urgent that she should know if her body would feel what her head wanted from her husband. This was the only way she would find the answer.

"Tim looked at her as if he'd just won the lottery."

"Shut the door," she said, "and get in here." She peeled back the covers. Tim did as he was told, afraid to hesitate in case she changed her mind. After last night this was not at all what he'd expected.

She pulled her nightdress up over her head, giving him the full view of her naked body. He responded by taking off his clothes and climbing in alongside of her. He put his arm around her and set about seducing her.

Melanie tried to relax and give Tim time to achieve the desired result, but her frustration mounted as she accepted it wasn't going to happen. She encouraged him until he completed his task, but the physical act was nothing without the emotional fulfillment she so desired. She gave no outward sign of her disappointment, preferring to let Tim think she had been suitably aroused by his efforts.

Not discerning her disappointment, he assumed he had succeeded. He knew however that he had failed to find the excitement and sensation that he felt each time he'd made love to Nina.

As the day wore on both of them reflected secretly on partners who were more in touch with their sensual side, neither aware they had the same problem. Melanie blamed herself for Tim's inadequate performance, while he was sure Melanie was still affected by last night's troubles, so both determined to try harder next time.

Monday brought the first rain for weeks, but nobody complained at the much needed water. Melanie drove to work in depressing weather conditions which matched her mood. Once at the office it was entirely different. She was welcomed by John Higgs, who took great pleasure in showing her to her new office, on the top floor, as promised before she'd set off for Poland.

"Well done, Melanie," he said, "you pulled it off rather well, just as I expected. Stellar Haufman are delighted with your work, which has justified the exorbitant fee we charged them for your services. Hugh Ballantyne has written in glowing terms about your input to the project, a mention that will not go unnoticed at the highest level of the bank. In short Melanie, you've made it, you've arrived. In addition, Mr Rattani Naziree of Hoggart, Smith-Adams has also confirmed that you made suggestions and recommendations which have been incorporated into the final contract. Praise doesn't come any higher than that, heaped on you by these two gentlemen. You must have made an exceptional impression on them both, for they have also indicated that you will be requested on all future projects for Stellar Haufman."

"In case you don't know what that means, let me explain. It tells the bank that they want you as much as they want this bank. It means you couldn't be fired even if you tipped coffee over the CEO's head. It means if you moved to another bank, Stellar Haufman would move with you. It means you are impregnable. Very few of us ever achieve that distinction Melanie, all I counsel is that you use your power wisely."

Melanie looked around her new office with wonder. Two months ago she was convinced she was a failure, she was cracking up, she even expected the bank to sack her. Now she had her own office, a desk that rivaled Heathrow's third runway and a salary the like of which she had never dared dream of, and she was being told she was impregnable. A knock at her half open door brought her back to reality. A fashionable young woman clutching a notepad stood with one foot inside the door, as if afraid to enter.

"Mrs. Fisher?"

"That's me," she said happily.

"I'm Rachel, your temporary secretary. I'm from the agency. I'll be with you for a month or maybe more, that is until you appoint someone permanent. I've actually been here a week already handling your mail and setting up your diary for the coming weeks, I'd like to go through your appointments with you as soon as you're ready.'

"Well Rachel, there's no time like the present and since I didn't even know I had a secretary you'd better tell me everything else I don't know, like what's in my mail and who these appointments are with."

"Firstly, Mrs. Fisher, can I ascertain what holiday plans you have for the rest of this year, I'd like to get them in the diary as soon as possible."

"Rachel, I'd really like it if you called me Melanie, or better still, Mel OK?"

"Of course and can I say I'm really happy to be working for you. I've heard a lot about you in the past week, you're a celebrity within the bank, but I'm sure you already know that."

"No I didn't know that, but I'm slowly coming to terms with it, Rachel. When I left these offices four weeks ago for a mission to Poland I was a complete unknown working downstairs, ten years in fact downstairs and then, thanks to my being selected for this job I've been catapulted to the top floor and stardom in the eyes of the bank. If I seem a bit shell shocked, that's the reason."

"Well, with my help we'll get you nicely organised so that you know exactly what you're doing and when, and what is more I'll try to find out as much as I can behind the scenes before each of your meetings. That way your stardom will remain untouchable."

"How long have you been a PA, Rachel?"

"Ten years, Mel. Ten long years in which I've learnt most of the tricks of the trade. I've been PA to some very big names; in fact you'll be flattered to know that I was pulled off another job to come to you. Someone in the bank is working hard to make sure you succeed. Do you want me to find out who head hunted me?"

"Thanks Rachel, and while your at it can we strike a deal on you staying, being my permanent PA? I'm already beginning to feel nervous at the thought of losing you in a month or so."

"I'd like that Mel. We'll make a good team." She offered her hand and Melanie took it willingly. Their handshake lasted fully a minute and in that time a bond was forming which they knew would make working together a pleasure.

"Right Rachel, tell me all about these appointments and then we'll go through the mail together. We should be done with that by twelve and, unless you've got anything else planned, I want to take you out for lunch. I'm celebrating the first day in my new role and who better to share it with than my new team mate?"

"I'd love it, and you can safely bet we'll be ready for twelve."

Across town at Hoggart, Smith-Adams, Nina was preparing to make her first acquaintance with her boss for over a month. She'd kept his in-tray under control with the help of his secretary and dealt with the few minor legal issues that had occurred during his absence. She was thankful that nothing major had blown up because if it had she would have been forced to deal with it, and if anything went wrong on her watch she would have been bottom of his Christmas card list. The first thing Ratty did after checking his post and his appointment list was to call Nina in.

"How's it been Nina, I've heard nothing from you, not even an e-mail, that must mean it's been very quiet at Stellar Haufman."

"Don't knock it, Ratty, we've done everything they've asked of us and what with your triumph in Poland, they have every reason to be pleased with us. I've talked to Mel so I know how good a trip you had. I suppose I should congratulate you." She gave Ratty a be-knowing smile.

"Nina, I'm not sure what Melanie has told you or what you feel you need to congratulate me for but let me assure you that since I met Melanie, at your house party, I have never done anything that could hurt her. Quite the opposite in fact. I hold Melanie in great affection, I count her as one of my best friends as well as an indispensable colleague. I trust we understand each other?"

"Perfectly Ratty, you're telling me to butt out... right?"

"Not the phrase I might have used ... but, in the circumstances... quite appropriate."

"Ratty, I know you're my boss and I know you could destroy me if you had a mind to, but all I'm saying is don't destroy Melanie. She's also my best friend."

"Nina, you have nothing to worry about on that score, I would rather die than hurt a hair on her head, I promise you. Anyway, I've got some good news for you, news that might make you decide to thank me instead of reproaching me."

"You're doubling my salary?"

"Better than that Nina, I'm recommending you to Hugh Ballantyne, Projects Manager for Stellar Haufman. He wants one of our staff to be based in his new office in town. Until now he's worked out of their London office but he's been so successful that they've let him choose where he sets up his office and he's decided to base himself here in town. There'll only be him, a PA and yourself to start with. You'll still be working under my direction but you'll assume more control than you do now and you'll get to work on much bigger projects, always assuming you pass his scrutiny."

"What does that mean exactly, Ratty?"

"It means he wants to take you to lunch this week and over foir gras and champagne he'll decide if he can work with you. It's as simple as that."

"Ratty, I'm not sure if I like the idea of being shoved out of these offices. We both know how it could work out if he shuts his office in six months' time, I'll be out in the cold. Why don't you send one of the young dynamics out into the battlefield and keep me back here in the fort."

"Because, Nina he wants experience, maturity, and because you are a very good lawyer. I told him this when I was selling you to him."

"Oh thanks Ratty, like a slave? Do I go in chains to him to do his bidding?"

"Nina, when you have met him, come back and give me your decision, OK? Until then just go along with my request and keep an open mind and everyone will be happy."

"I wish I felt happy about this, I've seen what happened when you requisitioned Mel remember!"

"Nina this is different and, anyway, you are not Melanie."

Nina refused to cooperate in Ratty's plans, refusing to phone Hugh Ballantyne as instructed and leaving it instead to Ratty's secretary, who wasted no time in fixing their meeting for the following day.

"You are to meet him in the Orangery at the Copthorne Hotel at noon tomorrow," she announced.

"I'll see if I can make it" Nina said defiantly, knowing that she wouldn't dare be late, let alone not turn up, but she was satisfied to have displayed a measure of disobedience to Ratty and his damned wishes.

Still harbouring feelings of resentment at being shoved into this meeting, she hung around outside the hotel until a minute before Noon, then with all the airs and graces of a duchess she waltzed into the Orangery. The head waiter stopped her in her tracks, and having discovered her identity led her to the best table in the restaurant. It was perched up on its own terrace under an enormous potted palm and waiting at the table was Hugh Ballantyne. Upon seeing her, he stood up and offered his hand, which she accepted with all the graciousness of royalty.

If Mr Ballantyne was super confident, so was Nina. After all, she reasoned, she was very happy in her present office, she didn't need this 'promotion' and she didn't care if she passed muster with him or not.

Her self assurance was not lost on Hugh Ballantyne, but then he liked a feisty woman, much better than some subservient young creature who would shake every time he issued an instruction. He discreetly looked her up and down. She was every bit as nice as Ratty has described her, a woman in every sense of the word, but more importantly, she was apparently a damn good lawyer.

"Ratty has told me so many good things about you I wanted to meet you, and lunch seemed a good way to get to know each other," he said.

"Ratty is rather given to exaggeration. I'm afraid you may find me a disappointment."

"I think that unlikely, Nina. You don't mind me calling you by your first name?"

"Of course not, if I may call you Mr. Ballantyne?"

"You may if you so wish, though I'd much prefer it if you called me Hugh."

Knowing that she was weakening in the face of this charming, almost edible man she backed down gracefully.

"I'll call you Hugh."

"I'm glad we sorted that out so easily, I'm sure we are going to get on with each other, and as members of the Stellar team. Nina, this is a very good opportunity for you, not just in terms of salary but in other ways too. For a start you'll get the chance to travel all over the world with me on major projects, if you wish, and only if you wish, and furthermore Hoggart, Smith-Adams will regard you as top drawer once you are based inside Stellar Haufman."

"Hugh, I know it's a fabulous offer but I have three children, I can't just take off around the world at the drop of a hat. And what if you close this office, say a year from now? I'll be surplus to requirements in our practice."

"Nina, this office won't close. I'll give you a contract – you can even draft it – which ensures you have at least five years here. What more can I do to make you say yes?"

"You can tell me why you want me"

"Nina you fit the profile I need, with your background in contract etc, but you're right to ask and, yes, there is another reason. I want someone alongside who I can work with, someone I can trust. By chance when Ratty was describing you, I can't remember why, honestly, but I knew from his description that you were perfect for this office. Now that I've met you I'm even more certain. What more can I say or do to convince you?'

"Nothing ... I accept."

"He reached across the table and took her hand in both of his. Nina you won't regret this move, I promise you. Now let's celebrate in style."

Back at the office, Nina broke the news that she was being outposted to Stellar Haufmman's new office. Her husband walking out had been a major change to her life, this move would be the second in two months. She thought about Tim and wondered if there could yet be a third.

No sooner had Nina finished her evening meal than Melanie arrived.

"Neen, you'll never believe what happened when I got into work this morning. I've only got my own PA, Rachel. She's a treasure. Everything that I was promised before that trip has materialised. You know it was the best thing that's ever happened to me in my whole career and I owe it all to Ratty. It was him who made it happen. I should thank him really."

"I thought you did, in Poland."

"That's not fair Neen, what happened there was bound to happen. I've told you I don't regret it even though it's making it very difficult to settle down with Tim, you know, in the passion department."

"You mean in bed?"

"Yes, we can't seem to find our old desire for each other at the moment. I suppose it's bound to take us time to adjust after being apart for a month."

"Yes, maybe that's it. Mel I haven't told you my news yet, and mine is also thanks to Ratty's involvement. What is it about that man that makes him interfere in our lives so much?"

"What news, what's he done now?"

"He set me up with an interview with Hugh Ballantyne, that's what. I met him at the Copthorne for lunch. He's setting up an outpost office for Stellar Haufman here in town and he wants me to be the in-house lawyer. The package he's offered makes me very well off but it also means I get the chance to travel as well, probably on the same trips as you in the future. We could be going on some all expenses paid holidays. All I have to do is find someone like Trudy to look after these three."

"I'm keeping Trudy on, she's agreed terms to stay permanently. She's so good with the kids and they adore her. Basically it means I can bugger off any time Ratty asks without a care in the world."

"Except for Tim. I don't think he'll let you go again. He'll chain you to the sink first."

"Then I'll just have to take the sink with me. I'm not going to blow my career in order to keep him happy. I realised in Poland that my career gives me more than my marriage. I'm not including the kids in that, you know that, they come first every time, but they're getting older and the day will come when they have their own lives to live. If I let my career go now what will I have then?"

"Mel, I talked to Ratty yesterday, when he told me about this move to Hugh's new office. He talked a lot about you."

"Really, what did he say?"

"He made it very clear that he's got it bad for you. He said he'd never harm a hair on your head and all that stuff. He meant it Mel. I could tell. His permanent smile disappeared while he was telling me how much you meant to him. If you mean to get back on terms with Tim you've got to deal with Ratty. He's not going to fade from your life on his own."

"I don't want him to fade, that's the trouble, Neen. I want my marriage, mainly because of the kids, but I want what I could have with Ratty as well. I wish I could spend some quality time with him. We have so much in common, we even think alike. What have I got in common with Tim apart from this house and the brats?"

"And we both know that the children will determine our way of life for a few years yet, don't we?"

"But that's the point, Neen. Ratty would be happy to take me and the kids. He told me so, and he'd be brilliant with them. Maybe I'm not too old to have another, who knows?"

"Why don't you run this past Tim and see what he thinks?" Nina laughed at her suggestion and Melanie joined in.

"Good idea Neen, who needs men anyway?"

CHAPTER FOURTEEN

Life in Willow Brook, in the village of Elmthorpe, wasn't exactly dull. It provided a haven of comparative tranquility for those who worked in the busy offices in town. A week had passed since Melanie's return and life had got back to what passed for normal.

She got up early and drove to the bank, where she worked flat out until five or sometimes six in the evening. She drove home in time to snatch some food with the kids and spend a couple of hours with them before they went to bed. Trudy was now an essential part of this routine and they usually had an hour together after the children went up before they followed them.

Tim also left early and sometimes stayed away overnight but even when he wasn't away he seldom got home before six thirty. He had usually eaten during the day and wasted little time in heading for the Globe.

Whether it was an improvement in their relationship or simply a lack of opportunity Mel wasn't sure, but they hadn't had another row since that night in the Walnut Tree. They'd made several more attempts to find physical satisfaction together but each time it had been a failure.

Tim apologised to Melanie, but she blamed herself for not being ready for him yet. He didn't understand that but then he never understood women, so it was nothing new to him.

As he left for the Globe each evening, Nina was in her front garden where she could catch a few words with him. As tonight was Friday there would be a pool match. He was in the team and couldn't wait to get there. He saw Nina hovering with secateurs near a climbing rose. To anyone else she would have appeared to be busy deadheading but to Tim she looked like a cat waiting to pounce on an unsuspecting bird.

"Tim, that's lucky, I was hoping to get a word with you before the weekend."

"Why, Neen, are you off somewhere?"

"No such luck. No, I wondered how things are between you two... Mel hinted to me that you aren't having much success in the bedroom."

"Bloody Hell, Neen. Why's she telling you that?"

"Because she obviously sees it as a problem, one she wants to share with a friend. Tim I need to talk to you. I'm missing you like anything, I know we said it would have to end once she got back, but be honest Tim, it isn't working for you or her is it, not like it did for you and me."

"Neen, we shouldn't be having this conversation. That's past and we both knew that when we did it. There's no way I could see you, not with her next door, you must be mad to suggest it."

"I wasn't suggesting we did it here, we could meet somewhere else. You must get times when your boss doesn't need you to drive him anywhere. With my new job I can take a few hours out any time I like. We could meet in town, you could pick me up in that car you're always going on about.

Does it have tinted windows or a bed in the back?" She smiled to put him at ease.

"Nina, be sensible. I know what you mean about us ... and yes ... it was better with us than with me and Mel, but it's too risky."

"So you'd like to if it wasn't so risky, is that what you're saying?"

"I suppose so, yes, but it is and just think how hard the shit would hit the fan if we got found out."

"We won't get found out, I promise. Tim you've got my mobile number, let's meet tomorrow, you can easily get away on a Saturday for a while. Ring me when you've got a couple of hours free."

"I'll see, Neen, I'm not promising."

"If I don't see you tomorrow, I'll see you next week, Tim, I'm looking forward to it."

Tim was surprised to find Ben waiting for him in the Globe.

"What are you doing here? You're a stranger here these days. How's Beckie?"

"Beckie's fine, we're fine, she's out with Sophie tonight so I'm here to catch up on the news from my old digs; you know, loud lady with an attitude problem, lives next door to you?"

"Nina's sound, you aren't fair to her. She's just got a promotion, did you know?"

"No, funny enough she must have forgotten to phone me up and tell me that. Tim, I haven't spoken to Nina for weeks and I'm not likely to. If I need to send her messages I'll tell you, OK?"

"Yes, OK Ben, you might as well, I see her every day pretty much."

"Unlucky you, you could always move I suppose. How's your job working out?"

"Very nicely, I'm driving Simon's sister around at the moment; she's over from Australia for a short break. Makes a change from driving him about."

"How are you and Mel now?"

"Pretty good... I think... that four weeks away was a bad time for me, gave me a lot of problems."

"Like what?"

"Oh, it doesn't matter, just silly problems, in my head mostly, but I still have to deal with some of them now she's back."

"Well if you want to talk about them you can... that's what mates are for, Tim."

"Thanks, Ben. I will if it gets to be a real problem." He shuddered at the prospect of telling Ben that his biggest problem was that he was having an affair with his ex-wife, no, correction, his wife. Although Ben made a big thing of slating Nina at every opportunity there was bound to be something still between them, surely after so many years and three children together? Would Ben laugh at the idea or would he see it as a betrayal by his best friend?

What about tomorrow? Could he really meet up with her behind Mel's back? His moral instinct said no but his basic instinct said yes. The battle within his brain might decide his entire future. Get this wrong and he might not have a future.

Saturday dawned with the rain clouds gone and the sun back as bright as before. Tim would go to the Manor and offer to drive Veronica out for the day. That would make it impossible for him to do something he shouldn't. He found

Veronica strolling in the rose gardens and joined her. "I thought we might take a drive out today, perhaps to the coast or anywhere that takes your fancy," he said.

"Oh Tim, that's so kind of you, but I've managed to track down an old school friend, someone I haven't seen since I left for Brisbane all those years ago. She's coming over for lunch and I expect we'll sit out here and have tea as well, but it was lovely of you to think of me like that."

"I enjoy driving you places, and to be honest when we go off it's like a holiday compared to driving Simon, where it's always business. I've enjoyed having you here. I shall miss you when you go back."

"That's nice Tim, but don't worry, I'm not planning to go back just yet. I think Simon may have to get used to living in the same house as me for a while, whether he likes it or not."

"Good for you. Can I bring the family over on Wednesday for the meal?"

"Of course. I'll tell cook to lay on something special. I'm so looking forward to meeting your family. Now as it's Saturday you must go home and look after them, I'll be fine, I'm quite certain they need you more today than I do, so run along and I'll see you on Monday. I want you take me to Stratford upon Avon, and maybe we could head across into North Wales, that's if your wife won't mind you being away overnight?"

"No problem, leave everything to me, I'll see you on Monday."

Tim decided to drive the Maybach home. Simon had said he could use it and the thought of having it for a whole weekend where he could do what he wanted, go where he wanted was too good to miss. Less than a mile from the manor his mobile rang. He had it on hands free and guessed it was probably Veronica changing her mind and wanting him to drive her and her friend out for the day.

"Tim, what are you doing, where are you?" It was Nina's voice that was asking.

"Oh, hi Neen, I'm on my way home from the Manor, is there a problem?"

"Yes and no. I'm missing you like anything and if I don't have you soon, today even, there will be a problem, but if we can meet up for a couple of hours I'll be fine. I could head out and meet you, say on Kingshay Common in half an hour?'

This was as near to a threat as made no difference. However you looked at it, Nina held all the cards, her marriage was already in tatters, she had nowhere near as much to lose if this all blew up as Tim did. He stood to lose everything and if all she wanted was a couple of hours of his time why risk everything by denying her? After all, he'd sworn to be her friend, always to be there for her, he could hardly go back on that. All she wanted was a shoulder to cry on, someone to tell her things would soon get better, even Mel would expect him to do that much for her.

He found a well hidden place to park among some trees on the common, well away from the busy side near the main road. He rang her back and gave her directions to find the track that would lead to where he was parked.

"My God, Tim, I thought I was on safari, are you worried we might be seen or something?"

"Of course I am. We'd have a lot of explaining to do if we were seen talking together out here, don't you think?"

"Well even the sheep looked surprised as I drove the last half mile, so it's not a problem is it? Perhaps you found this isolated spot in the hope that we would do more than just talk, is that it?"

"Of course not. I was protecting your good reputation."

"Rubbish Can we sit in the back Tim, it would be a bit more sociable?"

"Better still let's get out and mooch about, it's a fabulous spot."

They walked slowly under the trees, each waiting for the other to make conversation. After a minute Nina stopped. Tim turned to see why and she looked him in the eyes and reached out to pull him towards her. He didn't resist, even when she ran her hands up his back inside his shirt.

His determination to keep this meeting plutonic was evaporating rapidly. All the urges he'd experienced when Melanie was in Poland were surging back though his veins. What was it about this woman that could turn him on in seconds, electrify him with her touch? Already he wanted her, he knew that if she decided to have him he would agree willingly.

They stood under the trees groping at each other for a while; it was a beautiful way to reach the crescendo of emotion that would shortly explode into an all out desire to pull each other's clothes off in a deeply passionate session of sex.

They'd already started removing clothes by the time they made it back to the car, where they took everything from each other in turn, wrapping themselves tightly together in a huddle of lovemaking.

When they'd satisfied their needs they slowly dressed,

talking about their plans for the weekend as if they'd just shared a coffee instead of each other.

Nina explained, "I'll probably take the kids out tomorrow for the day, what about you?"

"I'll do the same if that's what Mel wants. Trouble is she's hard to talk to since she got back. All I ever get for a reply is, 'I don't mind, it's up to you,' and I'm left wondering what she wants. She used to be quite definite about what we were doing but now it's like she doesn't care."

"Tim, why don't you face it, it's not working with you two is it?"

"How can you say that? She's been away, we've had a lot to contend with ... and, let's be honest, I've got a lot to deal with in my head, thanks to you."

"Is that an attack on me? I didn't hear you saying no just a minute ago?"

"I'm not attacking anyone, but surely you can accept that my head's in a mess, can't you?"

"Only because you're too blinkered to see the obvious, to see what's staring you in the face."

"I don't follow you, what is it that I'm not seeing?"

"Tim, wake up, Mel's been away for a month, she's come back and instead of being all over you like a rash she's luke warm to you. Doesn't that tell you something?"

"If you're hinting at her having been with someone while she was away, forget it. I know Mel too well for that, she isn't that kind of woman."

"You mean I am that kind of woman, is that it? After all, I'm still married."

"Yes, I suppose so. You are very different to Mel, you know that, she's more shy than you are, you've always been more..."

"Brassy. Is that what I am Tim? Brassy?"

"No, stupid, you're worldlier."

"Maybe travel and independence, being away for so long on her own has made her more … worldly?"

"She wasn't on her own was she?"

"No, Tim, she wasn't. Isn't that the whole point?"

"Don't even suggest that, Neen, I thought about that while she was out there, you know I did, but once she got back I realised how daft I'd been to even think about it. I'd know if Mel had ever been unfaithful to me."

"Would you, Tim? How would you know?"

"I just would, she'd feel different, she wouldn't be the same as she's always been."

"I thought that's exactly what you said not five minutes ago… she was different."

"Not in that way though. Why do you want me to think she's been unfaithful … so that I leave her for you?"

"Don't flatter yourself, Tim. I'd only have you on my terms, not because Mel had finished with you."

"I've had enough of this, let's get back. I've got things to do, better things than sitting here tearing my marriage apart."

"Wasn't that what you were doing when we made love just now? You seemed very willing to 'tear your marriage apart then' … or was it only to get what you wanted?"

"Why are you doing this, Neen? You're twisting my head inside out? It was you that wanted us to meet here. I agreed to please you. OK, I enjoyed it, of course I did, I've told you before you're a beautiful woman and we are great together, but why do you have to say things that you know will hurt me? Why?'

"I don't know, Tim, I'm sorry. Maybe it's because I'm a woman, women do that to men, I read it in a magazine. Eighty per cent of men say their women abuse them verbally. I suppose it's a bit like men abusing women physically."

"But I've never abused you in any way, and I never would... I thought we agreed to be friends, to be there for each other?"

"We did and I'm sorry. I'm jealous Tim, I'm jealous that you are going home to spend a weekend with Mel while I spend mine next door without you."

"Tim pondered what to say that wouldn't send her away angry and upset. Jealousy was a powerful emotion; it could run wild, go out of control. Sending her home in this state was not a wise move."

"Come here ... he took hold of her and cuddled her into him and she instantly responded with her arms and her lips. It was a while before they spoke again."

"Neen, what we have is a kind of arrangement isn't it?"

"How do you mean? That sounds business like, legally binding, not at all romantic..."

"I don't mean it like that, but I'm seeing you while carrying on my marriage to Mel. It's like we're having the best of both world's isn't it?"

"For you maybe, Tim, I'm sure lots of men would find your position in this 'arrangement' enviable. I'm certainly not getting the best of both worlds, that's for sure."

"But you've got your freedom. You said yourself you enjoyed not having Ben around you all the time, you said you didn't miss his company, and when you want... well, you know, what you wanted this morning, you just ring me. Isn't that a good situation for you?"

"Tim, I said I didn't miss Ben because he is a thick, stupid waste of space. That doesn't mean I want to spend the rest of my life on my own, ringing you for the occasional sexual encounter. I want to be loved, respected and wanted. That's what every woman wants."

"So how do we go on from here?"

"You have to decide that, Tim, you have to work it out for yourself, whether Mel wants you or not. When you know the answer to that you might know whether you want me, the way I want you. Until then we go on with our clandestine meetings, OK?"

"If you say so, Neen."

On the drive home Tim shuddered at his ability to deceive Mel, to behave as if everything was normal, and yet he couldn't say he hadn't enjoyed the time spent with Neen. He had. That must mean something, because if his love for Mel was as it should be, what had happened on the common would have been impossible.

Mel greeted him warmly as he walked in the kitchen, "You're back sooner than I thought, didn't her highness want your services today?"

"What do you mean... ? Oh sorry, Veronica, no she's meeting a friend."

"Well who did you think I meant, The Queen of bloody Sheba? What's the matter with you? Ever since I've been back it's like you're in another world. Is there something you're not telling me? If you've got a problem share it with me, please, that's what we've always done isn't it? You're not ill are you; if you are get yourself booked for a check up, OK?"

"OK Mel, but I'm fine, honestly, just a bit tired that's all."

"Well perhaps if you got back earlier from the Globe you could get to bed earlier and that might help us. You know what I mean, it might help us to sort out the other problem."

"You're right, I will."

"Tim, the kids are all out, Trudy's with Amy, Henry's playing football and James is at music all day. He's gone with a friend whose mother is driving them... that means we've got the house to ourselves." She looked at Tim in a knowing way, as if she was making him a present, a present of herself. Three hours ago he would have been over the moon at her suggestion, he'd have had her halfway up the stairs by now, but this was awkward. He wouldn't be much good as a lover right now. His head was still recovering from another experience, as was his body.

"Well don't look so enthusiastic, Tim, Christ. I'm offering it to you on a plate and you need time to think about it! Don't bloody bother, I'll do some work on the laptop, better still I could go into the office and work for the rest of the day, then you wouldn't have to even look at me."

"Sorry, Mel, I wasn't hesitating, I was... just thinking about your proposition. It's a great idea, of course I want to, come on." He took her reluctant hand in his and put his mind into damage limitation mode. Hopefully he could fully recover the situation before she changed her mind and went into a sulk; if she did it would last for days.

Once upstairs he tried to turn on his desires, he tried to induce in her the feeling of being wanted, wanted so strongly that nothing else mattered, but his efforts were limp. He wasn't convincing himself, let alone Mel. She tried as well, but after five minutes she got off the bed and started to dress.

"I don't know what's wrong, Tim, but I think you probably do? You'd better see a doctor or get this sorted out. We can't carry on like this."

She left the room and he laid there thinking how he had managed to mess up yet again.

He dressed and went downstairs. Maybe he'd go out and buy her flowers, suggest a meal together tonight, not at the Walnut Tree. He saw her putting her shoes on.

"Where are you going, Mel?"

"I'm going round to see if Neen fancies going shopping with me. If she does I'll be out until five or later. Get yourself something, see you later," and with that she was gone.

Shit, not now, please. This was the worst possible moment for her to land on Nina's doorstep. She'd spend the next five hours telling Nina what a lousy state the marriage was in and Nina would repeat it all to him on their next meeting. Yes, there would be a next meeting; for one thing it was the only time he could find satisfaction. He needed those stolen moments with Neen as much as she needed him, but for different reasons. Without her he would begin to think he was unable to function in that department. A failure in bed – wasn't it what every man feared most? But he knew that with Nina he could do everything asked of him. It was only with his wife, where it mattered most, that he was a total failure.

Chapter Fifteen

Nina was readying herself for a Friday evening out with Hugh, her new boss. He'd told her this morning that he had two tickets for a West End show this evening, but the lady friend who had been going with him had cancelled at short notice to fly out to Hong Kong for a business meeting.

"We've been friends for years," he'd explained. "Twice a year we have a night at the ballet or a show and dinner in town, so Nina, I was wondering if you'd do me the honour of being my companion for the evening?" The offer was as much to do him a favour as her but given that her only other option was to spend another night alone in front of the TV it didn't take her long to accept. She'd pretended to phone a friend to cancel a previous dinner date, in an effort to play hard to get, but Hugh probably saw through that, understanding that she had to feign reluctance before gladly accepting his offer.

He duly thanked her and arranged for a car to pick her up from home and take her to the centre of town where they were to meet. As she looked out from behind her curtain for the taxi she congratulated herself on her new found status. She was keeping pace with Mel with her promotion and even an upgrade in her social life, although annoyingly she had to admit that her good fortune had more to do with

Mel's friendship with Ratty than anything she had done to impress Hugh.

The show was brilliant and they left with that larger than life feeling that follows a truly great stage performance. When Hugh offered her a nightcap at his flat in town she never even considered turning it down. She was well aware that once they said goodnight she would once again be alone in a taxi on her way to an empty house in Willow Brook. Far better to make the evening last as long as possible, and Hugh was the most charming man she'd spent an evening with in half a lifetime.

His flat left her speechless. High up on the sixth floor of a beautifully restored building overlooking the river, it was intoxicating. Classic furniture spread out across rooms that were bigger than her entire house and deep pile carpets that required serious effort to walk across.

This was living; really living. Not existing which is what she did in Elmthorpe. Hugh sat beside her on the antique leather settee and poured her another cognac. They chatted and laughed as if they'd known each other forever and before long the gap that separated them had vanished into thin air. Once their bodies made contact the mood was unstoppable and an hour later they climbed into Hugh's four poster bed.

Monday morning was never a favourite with Nina and the sudden change to wet weather matched her mood as she made her way to the office. If Hugh was expecting more of the good mood she was in when she'd left his place on Saturday morning he was to be disappointed.

His ever present smile did nothing to raise her spirits. She ignored his welcome, preferring to dump herself at her desk and launch into her work. She'd spent most of the weekend reflecting on her assignation with Hugh and the intimate outcome.

She was certain now that she had been steamrollered into that sexual encounter with him, one that she had not been prepared for and never wanted. Each time she'd spotted Tim at the weekend she'd felt remorse for having cheated on him, even though he kept protesting that their relationship was at an end. She knew he couldn't mean it, not after the fulfillment they'd found together while Melanie was away, and even since she returned.

She turned things over in her mind again and again well into the night, which was partly to blame for her present mood. Sleep deprivation wasn't something she could cope with at the best of times, and these were definitely not the best of times. Her initial pleasure at being wanted by two men had quickly evaporated into a feeling of being used.

She reserved the bulk of her anger for herself, for being so willing to jump into bed with a man she hardly knew, for cheapening herself so readily. She decided that his smile was less a measure of his respect for her, simply an indication of his joyful anticipation of their next rendevous in his luxury pad overlooking the river.

Well, he could forget that, just as he could forget any thoughts of her being friendly to him today. He had used her and she would punish him. He would see the effects of messing with her; this office would be a tinder pile today, liable to ignite with one badly chosen word.

"Nina, you don't look too happy, is anything wrong?"

"What do you think?"

"I don't know, what am I supposed to think?"

"I thought you were the clever one around here!"

"Nina, I'm getting the distinct impression that your discontent is directed at me ... I thought we'd become friends, I thought we'd found something quite special together."

"You thought, you thought ... all you thought of was getting me into your expensive bed in your lavish flat. Put another tick on your chart have you? Do men still carve notches on the bedpost? It would be a shame to vandalise such an expensive asset I suppose, no doubt someone as sophisticated as you will add my name to an excel spreadsheet instead."

"Nina, you're upset, let's nip out for a coffee and you can explain to me what you think I did wrong."

"Hugh, we are not nipping out for anything, you know what you did wrong and why I'm upset."

"When you left my house on Saturday you were content ... what's changed?"

"I've had time to think, that's what."

"You think I took advantage of you ... is that it?"

"Well didn't you?"

"No Nina, I took *you* as willingly as you took *me*."

"But I wasn't *yours* to take Hugh. I should have told you then, there's someone else. I betrayed that someone on an impulse. Because you are so full of charm I forgot where I was, who I was with, you knew I was going through a difficult time and you took advantage of that to woo me into your arms and then into your..."

"Into my bed. I know what we did Nina; I just don't buy this story that you weren't as willing as I was."

"I'm lying? Is that it?"

"I'm saying you're upset, you need me to reassure you

that the things I said were true. I meant every word, I want us to be long term friends ... and more if you want it."

"I think I know what 'reassure' means Hugh, it means we go back to your place for more of the same, right?'

'Wrong, Nina, it means we sit and talk this thing through until you understand that I have some real feelings for you, not just sexual ones but caring ones."

"Hugh, the other day was a mistake on my part. From now on we just work together and that's it, OK? I don't want to mention what happened again."

"I'm very sorry you feel this way, Nina, but I'll try to respect your wishes. Let me just tell you, it will be hard, very hard."

"Is that because I'm the first woman who failed to be mesmerised by your charms, Hugh?"

"Like I said, Nina, I'm very sorry."

Hugh returned to his office, aware that in her present state of mind reasoning was out of the question. He hoped she would see things differently in a day or two, but right now he wouldn't have put money on it.

As soon as the kids had finished tea they shot off as usual, leaving Nina to clear up before sitting down to another evening on her own. 'Quality time' she called it when she didn't want to face the fact that she was set to spend every evening alone from now on.

As she sipped her wine a plan came into her head, one that might allow her to spend some 'quality time' with Tim, but it would require careful handling.

She started by calling Ben's mobile.

"Hello ... This is Ben ..."

"Ben, it's Nina ... how are you?"

"Neen, is it really you? I didn't expect you to phone me... what's wrong, is it the kids?"

"Yes, can I explain?"

"Of course, Beckie's out for an hour so take your time and tell me what's wrong."

"The kids are missing you a lot."

"Oh, I suppose that's normal. Not much we can do about it though, is there?"

"I think there is, Ben. I've been thinking, why don't you take them away for a week?"

"But they're back at school now, it's too late for this year."

"I could get permission to take them out of school."

"Do you really think it's worth it? I mean, is it that important?"

"I do, think so Ben, in fact I'm quite positive it is."

"Nina, I can't afford hotel bills to take Beckie away, let alone five of us, you realise I'd only go if Beckie went as well? This isn't an attempt to split me and her up is it?"

"No, Ben, it's not, and why would I have any interest in doing that? I don't want you back, not now, not ever, but you can't abandon the kids quite so easily."

Ben tried to absorb all of this, but it was sudden and he had never been a quick thinker. He struggled for the right answer. "I might be able to take them camping, but even then I'd be struggling for money."

"Ben, If you get it sorted to take them away for a week I'll help with the cost, but on one condition. You don't tell anyone I helped pay for the trip, not even Beckie, is it a deal?"

"OK, I'll talk to Beckie tonight and check out with work tomorrow. I'll call you tomorrow night and let you know, OK?"

"I'll tell the school tomorrow that they'll be off from Monday for a week, you make sure you fix your end of it. Goodbye Ben."

Beckie was puzzled at Nina's sudden desire to have Ben assume his role as father. She was suspicious that the trip was concealing an attempt to get Ben back by using the kids as bait. She knew it was unwise to try and sabotage the trip, better to join in and have as much fun as possible with the kids. This way they'd enjoy coming to stay with them and Nina's plot would fail miserably.

"I think Nina's right Ben, we should take the kids away. What about the Lake District?"

"Where's that?"

"Ben, are you serious? Everyone knows the Lake District, well everyone except you."

"I wasn't thinking of going abroad Beckie, anyway we couldn't afford it. Nina said she'd help with the cost on condition I didn't tell you she was chipping in. Bloody cheek. We don't have secrets, but I didn't tell her that. I said, "yes OK Neen, whatever you say," She's got far more money than I have, she earns more than us two put together, why shouldn't she pay?"

"Ben, I'm talking about the English Lakes not the bloody Swiss ones. I'll tell work tomorrow, then I'll go and see about hiring a tent for a week. We'll need a trailer as well."

"That could be tricky, I haven't got a tow hitch."

"But you visit dozens of garages everyday in your job, Ben. Ask around tomorrow and find someone who'll fit it cheaply. I'm beginning to look forward to this holiday already. I haven't been camping since I was a kid. It's going to be great. Funny though, why Nina suggested it, don't you think?"

"I told you she's mad?"

"Well if we get a nice holiday out of it, who cares?"

When Ben phoned Nina the next night to confirm that he would take the kids off on Saturday she was delighted. "Come over about ten, Ben, and I'll have everything packed for them. Where have you decided to go?"

"We're going to the Lake District. It's up North, according to Beckie."

"Ben, I know where the Lake District is, thank you. I just hope you can find it. Anyway the kids can read a map, probably best if you let them navigate, and while you're at it let them put the tent up. If you do it it'll blow away the first night there's a breeze."

"Nina, I thought you wanted me to take *them* camping, not the other way round."

"Yes, but I trust them implicitly, whereas I don't trust you to do anything properly. Just take care of them and make sure they have a good time. I'll see you on Saturday."

When Melanie saw Ben arrive with his girlfriend on Saturday morning she suspected trouble. "Tim, I think Nina's got some problem with Ben and that girl. He's just pulled up with a trailer. He's probably trying to take half her furniture or something."

"Well, he won't get it on that piddling little thing, so stop worrying."

"Tim, go round there and stop him; find out what he's up to, please."

"Mel, he's still married to her, if he wants to visit he can. If she wants our help she'll ask, otherwise I'm not interfering."

"Do you know, Tim, you've always had it in for Nina, I

know Ben's your so called mate, but you've always resented helping her. You might like to remember that she is my friend and she still lives next door, that makes us neighbours, unlike that prat who lives somewhere else with someone else, OK?"

"Mel, I'm not taking sides, it's just that I don't think I should interfere unless I'm asked. Anyway, you know I hardly ever see Ben now that he's with her. I don't even know what he gets up to nowadays. He doesn't play pool at the Globe any more and he's so wrapped up with Beckie that he never phones me. The only time we speak is if I phone him. Fine, if that's how it suits him, but we were best pals for three years and he's dropped me since he met her."

"Oh dear, is poor Tim missing his little pal? Only trouble is he isn't little is he."

"Mel, you've never had a good word to say about Ben. OK, he's not the brightest in the class but he's a good sort at heart. You need to give him a chance, like you keep asking me to do for Nina."

"OK, Tim, but if he hurts her I hope you'll remember those words."

"He isn't going to hurt her, that's one thing about Ben. He's big, but he's as meek as a mouse inside, and let's be honest, Nina can certainly stick up for herself. The Russian bloody army wouldn't frighten her."

"I thought we were going to be fair to both of them. Is that your idea of fair? You can't stand Nina, I know that, you've made it obvious often enough. You'd better be right about him, Tim."

Melanie watched from behind the upstairs curtain, making sure to keep out of sight.

"Tim, he's taking the kids away from Nina. You've got to go round there, now!"

Tim came up to the window. "So if he's taking them by force, why is she waving them goodbye? Why isn't she in floods of tears? He must be having them for the weekend, though how the hell he's going to get three kids in that flat I don't know."

If Melanie thought her covert observation had gone unnoticed she soon realised it hadn't when Ben cheekily looked up at the window and waved as he pulled away. Melanie lip read his words, clearly directed in her direction. "I think he just called me a nosey cow," she said.

She looked round for support but Tim had gone downstairs, fed up with the goings on next door, which would inevitably result in Mel spending more time round there on a fact finding mission. She waited a respectable five minutes before going round to check on her best friend.

"Neen, is everything all right? I saw Ben take the children off."

"Yes, it was a bit of a shock. He rang up a couple of nights ago insisting on taking them camping in the Lake District for a few days. It's a complete turn around for him, but I can't refuse him, they're still his kids after all. Well, in law at least."

"Neen, are you OK?"

"Yes, I'm fine, he's a crap husband and he'd never win a 'Father of the Year' award but he wouldn't hurt them. I'm sure he loves them, in his simple way."

"That's roughly what Tim said, he wouldn't hurt anyone."

"Except me Mel, he's hurt me enough."

"Do you still miss him, Neen?"

"Like a ticking clock I suppose, it annoys the hell out of you when it's there but you miss it when it's gone. I haven't loved him for ages, so if I miss him it's just the getting used to being on my own, not the loss of his deep love and affection for Christ's sake."

"I've been so busy I haven't seen you all week, Neen. How's the job working out?"

"It's much as I expected, pretty routine, nothing out of the ordinary."

"And Hugh Ballantyne, how is he working out?"

"I see him around the office, but he's busy and so am I, so we don't talk much. To be honest I don't think he notices me there most of the time. What about you? You went to dinner with Tim's boss at the Manor on Wednesday didn't you?"

"Neen, you should see how the other half live. Veronica, that's his boss's sister, showed us around the Manor House. It's beautiful. They still employ staff, can you imagine that? A cook and a chauffer and a security man and a housekeeper ... it's like something from the eighteen hundreds."

"Mel, are you forgetting, you also employ staff, you have a Nanny ... remember? a-ha!"

"I hadn't forgotten Trudy, Neen, but that hardly stands comparison with the Manor. So you've got a couple of days all to yourself... got any plans?"

"No, I'm just going to laze around and take it easy."

No sooner had Melanie got back to her house than Tim was questioning her about what Nina had told her. Although he hadn't wanted to go round and get involved – that was far too risky given all that was going on – he was as anxious to know what was happening.

"Neen didn't seem too concerned. It seems Ben just phoned her up and offered to take the kids camping in the Lake District for a few days. She said the same as you – that he wouldn't hurt them – but I think she's a bit concerned that he's not very sensible, and you can't argue with that."

"That's for sure but Beckie probably has enough brains to keep them out of trouble. You can't come to much harm camping can you? Especially in the Lake District."

"Famous last words Tim?"

"No, they'll be fine, and now that we've sorted out what's happening next door could we think about our plans for today?"

"I don't have any plans beyond taking James to his music lessons. He's arranged a lift back. Are you going to watch Henry at football?"

"Of course, but then I thought tonight we might go out to that Indian restaurant by the station – everyone's raving about it – and then home for a night of pure passion... what d'you say?"

"I could be persuaded... perhaps."

"Do you fancy giving me a few hints on the best way to persuade you?"

"No, find out for yourself. You should know me well enough to know what I like."

"Whatever it is, you've got it, I'll book the table for seven thirty, OK?"

"I shall look forward to it, and whatever you have planned for afterwards."

Tim was pleased that Melanie was trying hard to get their relationship back to normal despite the problems they'd encountered since her return. They'd stopped blaming each other, but it still wasn't as good as it should be. Tonight he'd get it absolutely spot on starting with a single red rose, which he'd buy this afternoon and give her before they left the house.

He'd pay special attention to her throughout the meal and then hold her tight in the taxi home. He would prove to her that he was still the perfect partner, even after twenty years.

Melanie came out of the shower and walked naked into the bedroom where Tim was waiting with his rose. She took it and gave him a kiss which sent shivers down his spine. He was fully dressed and ready to go and she was completely naked and as beautiful as he had ever seen her. This would be a fabulous evening with a fairy tale ending.

The meal was good. The restaurant was buoyant, happy, noisy. It was impossible not to become infused with the enjoyment around groups of diners and the sincerity of the waiters who gave each table seemingly special attention.

They held hands as they waited for the taxi.

Melanie pulled Tim to her and kissed him enthusiastically, "Thank you, Tim, for a lovely evening."

"It's not over yet Mel," he replied, his thoughts occupied by the promise in that kiss.

They cuddled like teenagers in the back of the taxi and then ran indoors as they hurried to get upstairs. Trudy and the kids had gone to bed, so Melanie took her shoes off at the bottom of the stairs signalling to Tim to go quietly. They sneaked up the stairs as if they were in an illicit relationship, but that only heightened their excitement.

Once behind the closed door they wasted no time in undressing each other and tumbling into bed. As they cuddled Tim sought to seduce her, but his mind wandered to the last few occasions when it had all gone horribly wrong. Somehow Melanie sensed that he was uncomfortable, but as soon as she asked him what was wrong he fell to pieces.

"I don't know, I'll be fine in a minute, don't worry."

But she did worry, she tensed up as she sensed his lack of confidence and within seconds they had lost the magic that promised to make this moment special.

Tim rolled onto his back and sighed. Melanie silently turned and waited for him to say what was on his mind. All he could think about was his failure, failure to make love to his wife! He doubted if there was any failure worse than this in a man, it was the ultimate shame, to have to admit that he couldn't satisfy his wife when she was ready and willing to make it happen.

As he laid there in the darkened room his eyes filled with tears. He put his hand down at his side and found her hand. She clamped his hand in hers in an attempt to reassure him that it wasn't a big problem.

"Tim, it's no big deal. Maybe you had too much to drink?"

"Mel, I've had hardly anything to drink and you know it. It's me, I'm the problem. It was never like this before you went away, what's changed?"

"Nothing's changed, Tim. You're worrying about it and that's the problem. You have to relax and believe that it's going to be all right and then it will be. We'll try again tomorrow. I bet it'll be perfect.'

When they tried again on Sunday evening Tim was in trouble even before they got started. He was so afraid of another failure that he made it a certainty. Nothing Melanie could say would help. He was angry with his own inability to function normally, yet there was a deeper issue, one that he couldn't share with her, the fact that each time he made love to Nina it was easy, there was no problem. Why then was it impossible with the woman he wanted so much?

Had he imagined it to be perfect with Nina? Was his memory playing tricks with him? Only a week ago he had met her on the common and they had found it easy to satisfy each other without a hint of anxiety.

Perhaps the answer to his problem lay with Nina; maybe if he could make love to her one more time he could prove to himself that he was imaging the problem. He could hardly ask her to partake in an act of intimacy purely to assist him in his need to overcome his lack of confidence, a problem that only manifested itself when he tried to make love to his wife.

The only way he could take Nina was by pretending to want her. She'd be keen enough to cooperate in the belief that he was showing his true affection for her. What he was proposing was highly dangerous, but there was no other way to restore his belief in himself.

She had told him to ring her during the day, but that was a bold move which would strike of desperation on his part. She'd be suspicious if he rang out of the blue and suggested an illicit meeting, so tomorrow he would be dignified in his request.

On his arrival at the Manor he was greeted with the news that Simon was returning on Wednesday. Apparently he'd got the message that Veronica wasn't in a hurry to go and he couldn't stay away any longer. This could get interesting! A note gave him the ETA at Heathrow.

Veronica called him over to say she wanted the car tomorrow as she thought it unlikely she'd have it once Simon was back. This meant that if he was to put his plan into operation it had to be today. He walked off to a quiet part of the garden and called Nina's mobile.

"Tim... how nice to get a call from you so early on Monday morning, what a good way to start the week. What can I do for you?"

He wished she hadn't asked that question, it made it kind of awkward, when what he wanted to say was, "Can you let me make love to you to prove to myself I can do it and can you make it today as I've got a lot to get through this week."

"Neen, it's a nice day and my boss, Simon gets back the day after tomorrow, I was wondering if you fancied a spin out somewhere for an hour or two, but if you're busy I understand ... it was probably daft me ringing you and expecting you to be able to make time just like that ... sorry Neen ..."

"Tim, if you stop talking for a moment you'll be able to hear me ... that's better ... I'll see you in an hour, on the common where we met last Saturday, OK?"

'That would be nice, really nice, I'll see you in an hour.'

He ended the call and then thought about what he was doing. Nina had sounded so keen. She'd understood perfectly what he wanted, she was wasting no time.

He made his excuses and headed off for the Common, where he waited in the same spot as before. Twenty minutes later she arrived, parked next to him and got into the back of the Maybach. He was still seated in the front.

"Well ... what are you waiting for Tim?"

Nervously, he tried playing it cool. He knew he was unconvincing.

"I thought you might want a ride."

"I do, so get yourself in the back before I run out of time. I told them in the office I had to go to the Town Hall to check out some searches. I can't be too long, so let's not waste what time I've got."

Tim scrabbled into the back as if obeying orders. This episode was in danger of losing any semblance of romance.

She pulled at his clothes with an eagerness that was born of lust more than love. What followed was sex, not lovemaking, and although he proved well capable of meeting her demands he found himself feeling shabby straight after, not at all what he had expected. Nina seemed unperturbed by the lack of grace with which the session had been conducted and, after thanking, him made her excuses and drove off back to work.

Tim sat there for a while wondering what the last half hour had proved. One thing for sure was that some parts of his body were in full working order, but in his head he had an issue and he doubted whether this would be better because of what had just taken place.

He looked out across the common and watched a couple of blackbirds busily feeding from the grass. They were so obviously a couple, united in their struggle to find food, but keeping watch over each other like two lovebirds.

That was what was wrong at home. It had started when Mel was in Poland. He'd been convinced for a while that she was having an affair with this Rattani fellow, the one who'd insisted on her going on the trip. It was so obvious, she'd hardly had two words to say to him on the phone from her hotel, which could only have meant one thing... she was entangled with this man.

He was still bearing the scar of resentment for her going off like that, for her making herself available to him, for leaving him, her husband, to spend a month alone, without the love of his wife. She shouldn't have done that, he was still upset about it and every time they made love the anger, the revulsion of her spending all that time away from him ate him up.

He would have to have it out with her ... he had to know, once and for all, what went on. He'd ask her tonight, surely she'd understand his fears, it was quite natural that he should want to know.

He started the engine and made his way back to the manor, but the only thing inside his head was the answer she would give. What if she said, 'Yes I was unfaithful to you, Tim.' What then?

That evening he waited for the right moment. What had seemed so simple as he sat in the sunshine on the Common now seemed impossible.

"Whatever it is, Tim, it must be very serious to make you look so unhappy. Do you want to tell me about it?"

This was it, decision time, either ask her now or forget the whole idea.

"I was just wondering about your trip to Poland. I want to know if it was what you'd expected or if there were any surprises, maybe unpleasant ones, that you didn't enjoy." He was skirting around the question, he knew that, but he'd lost his nerve, he'd never ask the question now and he'd never know the answer.

"You're funny Tim, I already told you. I loved Poland, I

loved Poznan and I loved the hotel and the lake. Next year I want to take you there, I want to show you just how lovely it is, and no, there were no unpleasant moments, all my memories of the trip are good ones." She instinctively thought back to some of her better moments, the nights spent walking around the lake with Ratty, and one special night. She was quite certain; all her memories were good ones.

She'd pushed Ratty right out of her mind now, but Tim had forced her back to the lakeside and to some of the most romantic interludes of her life. Yes, you are supposed to do all that before you marry, that's quite in order, but it can't always be like that. Sometimes you meet someone special, but you don't meet them until long after you're married. Was it wrong to take those precious moments and to enjoy them briefly, would it make sense to deny yourself of the chance to have happiness on tap for a few days or nights?

Could you honestly look back later in life and say, 'I'm glad I threw away the opportunity to have a few brief moments of loving with someone who loved me, who wanted me, who would have given up everything he owned to be with me?' No, I regret nothing. She knew in that moment what Edith Piaf had meant in her immortal song, and like the sparrow she was adamant, she regretted nothing.

Tim seemed satisfied with her answer, although he'd unwittingly unleashed the memory of the very acts that he'd feared. His questions had an outcome tainted with the irony of a situation outside of his knowledge or indeed his control.

When he made love to Melanie that night he performed faultlessly, but their ecstasy wasn't to be, as Melanie was unable to give herself willingly with her head full of thoughts of Poznan and of Ratty. It was she who found herself saying sorry now to an ever increasingly frustrated Tim, who felt that powerful forces were conspiring to prevent him returning to a normal life with Melanie.

Veronica sensed his misery as he drove her to the beach. She made him stop at a thatched cottage tea room in a small village near the sea and insisted he join her in a cream tea.

"What's wrong, Tim. You can tell me anything and everything. After all, I'll soon be leaving these shores, so your secrets are safe with me. And anyway, we were brought up to guard secrets to the grave, family honour and all that stuff, and you know I'd never tell Simon."

He considered her point. She was right, and there was no one else to whom he could turn with his problems that wasn't involved in some way or another. Not Ben, Nina or, of course Mel. He desperately needed to unburden himself and again she was right, in a few days she'd be off, back to Australia, which made her the perfect person to help him, and he found her easy to talk to and understanding. His mind was made up.

"It might take a while and you might find you don't like me very much once you know me, properly I mean, once you know what I'm capable of."

"Tim, don't dramatise things, do you think I haven't left a few skellies in my closet back there in Brisbane? If you've done something you're ashamed of get it off your chest. You'll feel a whole lot better and I promise you I won't sit in judgment. If I can't say anything helpful then I won't say anything at all."

Tim related the whole story, from the original row with Melanie, her trip to Poland and his adulterous affair with

Nina. He left nothing out, even telling her how he'd used the car twice as a love nest when meeting Nina. When he'd finished his story she looked at him and said nothing for a while. He was afraid, afraid that he had gone too far, shocked her with his antics such that she could not countenance further conversation with him.

She looked at him and smiled, "Tim, you're a fool ... welcome to the human race."

"You must think I'm pretty low to have done what I've done?"

"Yea, sure, you're lower than a snake's belly, but so what? I told you, it isn't for me to sit in judgment, and anyway I've done things every bit as bad in my lifetime. What we have to do is sort out where you go from here, right?"

"Right. Do you really think you can help me sort this mess out?"

"I'm sure I can. First, go and order more tea, this might take a little while."

Over another pot of tea she gave Tim instructions, which she said he could either follow or ignore, but in the end he had to come to terms with what he wanted. Only when he knew that, could he find happiness.

Eventually he drove her back to the manor and prepared for his trip to Heathrow the next day to collect Simon and his wife. "I hope this won't mean that we never get to talk again Veronica," he said, "I've got used to you. I'll miss you when you go."

"Don't worry, Tim, we'll find plenty to talk about and even Simon can't stop us talking." She laughed at the thought of her brother trying to stop her from doing anything. After all her years in Brisbane, Simon held no fears for her, only a sadness born of many wasted years of their sibling non-contact.

That evening, as he walked into the kitchen his mind was a long way off, so when Melanie spoke he jumped.

"Nina's in a right state, we've got to do something."

"What's she in a state about? His guilt fuelled his anxiety."

"She thinks Ben's run off with the kids. She's been trying all day to phone him but no answer. She's tried the kids phones but their not answering either. She thinks Ben's taken their phones off them and is deliberately not answering. She wants you to try ringing him. She thinks he might answer you."

Tim took out his phone and called the number, but it went straight to answering mode. "Maybe he's turned it off. After all they are on holiday, or maybe his battery is flat. There is no way he would run off with the kids. I was surprised he even wanted to take them away for a couple of days."

"But that's what's worrying Nina. It's so unlike him to want to take them she thinks it's part of a plan."

"What plan? Ben's not bright enough to have a plan."

"I almost told her that but I stopped myself just in time."

"You have to admit it is strange that he suddenly wanted to take them away."

"Why? They're his kids. Maybe he wanted to prove to Beckie that he can be a good father."

"Or maybe, Tim, maybe he wants to blackmail Nina into dropping her claim on him with the CPA. Nina could

411

take him for every penny. If she did he'd never be able to marry Beckie or afford to buy a square meal for them."

"I can see that Nina could mess his life up with her claim, but I still can't see how taking them away would change that."

"What if he's taken them out of the country?"

"Did he take their passports?"

"No, but he could have got them out on illegal ones, or maybe he just took a chance and smuggled them out in the back of his van. They hardly ever check people leaving the country. It would be quite easy."

"But this is Ben we're talking about. He'd never find his way to Dover, let alone to Spain or wherever. No he's probably lost on the M6. Maybe he missed the turning for the Lakes and now he's in the Scottish Highlands. Let's have our meal and then we'll go round and calm her down."

They had barely finished the meal when Nina arrived.

"I'm distraught Mel, what am I going to do?"

"If you really think he's taken them for good then you need to ring the police."

"They won't do anything, Mel, They'll say he's got a perfect right to take them. They'll say I have to go through the court to try and get them back, but that could take years."

Tim tried to be helpful. "Why don't you give it a couple more days? He might get in touch tomorrow?"

"Tim, I can't sleep for worrying about them. I'm going up there to try and find them"

Melanie was horrified at the thought of her heading off to search for them on her own and she said so. "Neen, that's crazy, you can't go off on your own searching hundreds of square miles looking for five people and a tent, anything could happen to you."

"I can't stay here another minute, I'm going crazy with worry."

"But do you have any idea where to start looking? Like the name of the camp site or anything?"

"No, but if I go to every campsite in the Lake District I'll find them, if that's where they are."

"But what if he has taken them abroad, they won't be there to find." Tim was simply applying logic to the situation.

"You do think he's taken them out of the country, don't you?"

"No, but if he has, there's not much point in searching up North is there?"

"I think he would have gone there first while he made his plans to get them out of the country. That way they wouldn't suspect anything until it was too late."

Melanie decided to take control of the situation. "Nina if you insist on going on this search then Tim will have to go with you. After all it's his best mate that's caused all this worry."

"Mel, I can't go off just like that. I've got to be at Heathrow in the morning to pick Simon and his wife up."

"OK, you can do that, then tell him you need a couple of days off to help a friend find her lost children. If you explain how they might have been stolen I'm sure he'll understand."

"He'll more likely think I'm mad."

"Is that what you think I am, Tim? Mad? For wanting to know where my children are?"

"No, Neen, of course not, but I just think we're jumping to conclusions without reason."

"Tim, I'm a mother, ask Mel, she understands what I'm going through."

"That's right, Tim, you fathers have no idea what goes on in a woman's body when she has children, or inside her head. If I was in Neen's shoes I would be setting off to find them just like her."

"I'll do my best, but if he says I can't have the time off, what then?"

"Then I'll speak to him Tim, I'm sure he'd listen to your wife."

"I'll do what I can," he said resignedly.

Melanie continued to console Nina while Tim made himself scarce.

The plane was on time at Heathrow and by nine o'clock they were heading back down the M3 Motorway. Simon was keen to know what had taken place while he'd been away.

Tim had a lot he wanted to say, as well as needing to ask him for time off. 'Everything's been fine while you've been gone. I've driven Veronica around quite a bit, I've become quite used to her. She's not a bit like you described her.'

"That's because you don't know her, Tim."

"Simon, I know I'm speaking out of turn here, but I think you're wrong about your sister. I think it's you who doesn't know her, how can you? You haven't spoken ten words to her in ten years, well not at a personal level anyway."

"She told you that?"

"She told me about your father's will and her ousting to Australia. She's missed you, she's wanted to have proper contact with you for years but you have made it nigh on impossible for her."

"Tim, it's not like you to speak to me like this. You're pretty upset over this aren't you?"

"Simon, I'm sorry, but please, say you'll talk to her when you get home and give her a chance? You two are family, it's crazy that you go on shutting her out of your life. She's not after your money, Simon, if that's what you think. She's done incredibly well in Brisbane, do you know how well?"

"No, I've never taken any interest in what she's up to."

Simon's wife had sat silently through this exchange but she'd heard enough. "Simon, sometimes you are a pigheaded old fool. Tim's right, she's your only sister and you should have listened to her years ago when she tried to make contact with us, instead of running away from her. Listen to him, and better still listen to her. Hear what she's got to say before you make your mind up about her intentions."

Simon rarely received a dressing down from his wife, and never outside the privacy of their own home. He was shocked, doubly shocked that two people who he was close to had expressed such strong views. He was a reasonable man, he thought, so perhaps it would be best if he followed their advice before saying any more on the subject.

"As you are both so clearly in agreement on this I shall do as you ask."

Tim was aware that he had pushed his position to the limit in his defence of Veronica. "Thank you, Simon, I really appreciate you taking account of my feelings on this one."

"It's kind of you to concern yourself with my family problems Tim, so think no more about it."

"Simon, on the subject of family problems, my neighbour thinks her ex-husband has run off with her three children.

Melanie wants me to go with her to try and find them, although personally I don't believe he's done it."

"Tim, she's right, you must help the woman, when does she want to go?"

"As soon as she can. She's out of her mind with worry at the moment."

"Of course, well as soon as you've dropped us off at the Manor go and help her. I need a couple of days to recover from my trip, so that's fine with me. Take the rest of the week off and ring me on Friday to let me know if you'll be back on Monday."

"Thanks, Simon. I'll be back next Monday, whatever happens."

By lunchtime he was ready to set off in the hunt for Ben and the others. Melanie had packed enough stuff for a few days and it was all stacked in Nina's car, along with her two suitcases.

When Tim saw her luggage, he recoiled. "Nina, we're going to the Lake District, not Spain."

"I know that, Tim, but I always take more clothes than I need, Ben always used to complain at carrying my cases, not that we often went anywhere."

Melanie took Tim by his lapels and pulled him to her face where she kissed him. 'It's really good of you to do this for her, I really appreciate it.'

"OK, but I still don't believe he's done anything. I'll be back as soon as we've found him."

Within two hours they were north of Birmingham and making good time.

"Nina, do you have any clue as to where we should start looking? Didn't he say anything that would help us find him?"

416

"Nothing more than I've already told you, Tim."

"Shall I try ringing his mobile again?"

"No Tim, don't do that. If he realises we're on to him he'll move somewhere away from the Lakes and then we'll never find him. Our best chance of finding him quickly, before he takes off abroad is to surprise him."

"We'll do it your way Neen. After all, the quicker we find him the quicker we can get back. What is your plan exactly when we do drop in on him? Do we grab the kids and run?"

"I suppose so, once I've made it clear that I know what he's up to, he'll have no choice but to forget the idea. After all, the kids won't stay with him once they see me and I explain what's behind this trip."

"We should be there by six. It gets dark at around eight, so we can't do much searching tonight can we? Where are we going to stay?"

"We'll book into a hotel in Windermere or somewhere. After all now the school holidays are over it shouldn't be that busy. Tim, you know I appreciate you doing this for me."

"I didn't have much choice, Neen, with Mel giving me orders to help you find them."

'I still think it's nice of you to help me like this. A couple of weeks ago when you talked about us being friends, do you remember? ... You said you'd always do anything to help me, I've thought about that a lot since then, and now you've proved it to me.'

The last thing he wanted right now was to be reminded of things he had said when Melanie was away and he was sharing Nina's bed. He'd meant every word of it, of course he had; after what they'd done together it was natural that they would be friends, but he hadn't thought then that he'd be called upon to be part of a two person search party in the Lake District.

The car went quiet for a while. Each of them had things to think about. Tim was still trying to come to terms with his sudden trip north alone with the woman he was trying to end an affair with.

The plan Nina had devised to get Tim away was working. She congratulated herself on having executed it so skilfully. She knew Ben and Beckie had no credit on their phones because they told her so when they were leaving. They wouldn't be able to phone back even if they wanted to. It was a fair bet that once they'd arrived in the Lake District the signal would be poor. When she'd rushed round to next door and Tim had tried to phone he'd got the same problem.

She had plotted this down to the last detail. She knew that Melanie would never let her go off alone, she was sure that Mel would enlist Tim to help her find her missing husband. So far her plan had worked perfectly and she had several alternatives in her head in case they found them too quickly. She had even considered telling Mel that they had gone to Cornwall; that way she could have enjoyed a few days there with Tim, certain in the knowledge that they wouldn't find the missing party.

That was too risky, she decided, and with any luck they could take days to search the Lake District. Nina planned to do the actual investigation at each campsite, so that if she spotted their name on a list she could divert Tim away before they made contact. It would only be if they actually bumped into them at a campsite that the game would be over.

Nina was certain that once Tim relaxed with her at the hotel he would start enjoying the trip as much as she was. She might even persuade him that the search could wait for a day or two while they worked out if they had a future together. Sitting here in the car, with Tim driving her, she felt a warm glow from the satisfaction of having got what she wanted.

The next few days could shape her entire future. She was playing a cruel game where Melanie was concerned, but that was a price she could live with to win the prize of a lifetime with Tim.

As they caught their first sight of Lake Windermere the sun was already casting long shadows, and once at the water's edge and out of the car they needed their coats.

This was like looking for the proverbial needle in a haystack, Tim decided, but best to go along with Nina's crazy plan. At least that way their failure wouldn't be his fault. He was hungry and tired. He'd been up at four this morning for his journey to Heathrow. Now, fifteen hours and more than six hundred miles later he was in no mood to start searching for campsites.

Aware of his state, Nina booked them into the first decent looking hotel they came across. Tim struggled up two flights of stairs with Nina's cases before lugging his travel bag up to the room next door. He looked out of his window hoping to see the water, but his only reward was a view of the hotel's car park. Nina had told him to get showered and ready for dinner and to meet her downstairs in half an hour. She was taking charge of this project to find her missing offspring as firmly as he'd supposed she would.

Nina would decide when they ate and probably what

they'd eat, and then tomorrow she'd take charge as they went in search of her brood. With any luck they'd find them quickly and get home tomorrow night.

Meanwhile, Nina's head was filled with different thoughts. If she was to entice him away from a marriage that, by his own admission, was far from happy, then she had to work fast and use every ounce of her charm. There was no way she could live next door to Tim after what they'd shared together; no way she could lay there at night knowing he was only a few yards away from her, cuddled up to another woman. OK, so that woman was his wife, but what of it? Did his wife care about him when she'd buggered off to Poland, leaving her to keep Tim happy, or when she'd had her 'fling' with her boss, who was obviously infatuated with her? No, Melanie had had what she wanted and now it was time to harvest what she was owed.

Once she had Tim to herself for good she could make him happy, content with his lot. She was better in bed than Mel, he'd told her that more than once. The culmination of this carefully structured plan was bound to work out, but the next couple of days were crucial. She needed more time with him, time to let him see what life with her could be like.

When Tim strolled up to the bar, he was stunned by the sight of Nina. Gone was the worried woman, intent only on finding her lost flock, and in her place was an elegant picture of poise and beauty standing before him with a smile on her face and a glass in each hand. She had packed enough clothes in her two cases to have a choice to suit every occasion. Tonight she had chosen a taupe dress in a silky fabric that clung to her seductively, showing her figure to perfection. The low neckline promised delight, making no effort to conceal her ample cleavage. Her brown hair was tied up so that it fell enticingly to one side of her head, leaving the other side bare and inviting.

To a tired and hungry man, Nina was an oasis of hospitality. She wore her smile perfectly and only ever directed it at him, which added to his feeling of security and delight.

"Here you are Tim, a pint of Stella, that was right wasn't it?"

"Perfect Neen, just what I need"

"Well, take your time over it. I've booked us a table, but they can't seat us until eight thirty, so you've got time for another if you want while we choose something from the menu."

They sat down on a red velour sofa, softly lit from behind by a gold standard lamp. The hotel was nothing if not opulent, catering for those who could afford the best, the kind of place, thought Tim, where Nina is totally at home. This is so her, she looks at one with the carefully crafted furniture, like a piece of delicate porcelain sitting provocatively on the edge of the sofa, legs crossed to reveal her thigh in a pose that is truly aristocratic.

"How are you feeling now?" she enquired. "are you very tired?"

It would have been boring to admit to her how tired he was, and given the effort she had taken to make herself look nice, the least he could do was give her some attention.

"No, I feel a lot better for a shower. I'm looking forward to tucking into a good steak."

"That's exactly what I was thinking Tim, look, third line down on the second page, Fillet Steak with a pepper sauce, dauphinoise potato and sun dried tomatoes, how does that sound?"

"I was hoping for chips, but I can make do with whatever-it-was potatoes."

"Get some red meat into you, Tim, and you'll be fit for later."

"Later? Why, what's happening later? I thought we'd eat this and then get to bed ready for an early start tomorrow."

"Tim, just imagine how Lake Windermere will look in the dark, with the lights reflecting off it. We can't miss that, can we? We'll take a short stroll along the road by the lakeside, get some fresh air and then settle down for the night."

It was an instruction, Tim decided, not an offer, but if that's what she wanted, that was OK by him. After all, what difference could a few minutes spent strolling around outside make?

The waiter brought the red wine she'd ordered and poured a glass for each of them.

"Nina, I don't think I should drink wine. I've had a couple of lagers and I'm tired already. I've got to drive again first thing in the morning."

"Nonsense, Tim, you can't enjoy a fillet steak without red wine to wash it down. Drink it and don't worry about tomorrow until tomorrow."

He was too tired to argue, so he emptied the glass there and then, and again each time she refilled it. He didn't notice the waiter bring a second bottle. His mind turned to the meals he'd tried to enjoy with Melanie at the Walnut Tree and he couldn't help but compare the tranquility of this with the open hostility he'd suffered in the company of his wife. Why couldn't she be like Nina; relaxed and caring?

As the wine took effect, his inhibitions deserted him. He leant across the table towards her, "...Nina, you're beautiful, I told you that before, if you remember?"

"Of course I remember, I remember everything you've ever said to me, Tim, like how we would always be friends, I even remember you telling me you loved me once."

"It would be very easy to love you, Nina."

"Then feel free to do so, Tim. My only wish is to make you happy."

"Oh, you do make me happy, Neen, you make me very happy. You are a special lady, do you know that?" The slight drawl in his voice warned Nina not to ply him with more drink. Too much could be as bad as too little.

"Tim, let's go for our little walk now and then when we come back I'll make us some coffee in my room before you turn in for the night, OK?"

"Sounds good to me, Neen." It was only when he stood up that he realised the effect the drink and his tiredness was having on him. Never mind, a walk outside in the cool air would soon have him right.

They walked a little way from the hotel towards the water before Nina noticeably shivered. Tim's instinct was to be gallant and he offered her his coat, which he put around them both as she cuddled tight to his waist in an effort to warm herself.

Like this they reached the water's edge and stood staring at the bouncing colours of the lights on the water, until even being huddled together was not enough to keep them warm. Nina was shivering for real now and Tim readily let her lead him back towards the hotel and straight up to her room.

She laced his coffee with a generous helping of brandy and then stretched herself out seductively on the floor at his feet. As she eased her body to the floor, her silk dress slid up to her waist, revealing her legs. He was enchanted by her. He knew from past experience how irresistible she was and his thoughts were already out of control.

His pulse raced at the sight of her body, the excitement mounted inside him until it had erased any thought of him going back to his room to spend the night alone. Instead, he slid down onto the floor alongside her and searched her body with his hands until he was holding her tight. She moved only to unzip her dress and slide out of it, before undressing him.

A knock on the door was followed by the retreating cry of 'breakfast is served,' suggesting to Nina that they were fast approaching the time when breakfast would end. That meant it had to be nearly ten o'clock. Tim would need a full English breakfast before she got him out in those hills, ostensibly searching for campsites.

"Tim, we have to get up or we are going to miss our breakfast." She slid herself out from his grip and took to the bathroom. Ten minutes later she emerged in her underwear as Tim was just getting out of bed. He looked at her in her white bra and pants and felt all the pangs of lust return.

Reading his mind she put her finger to her lips and whispered, "No, get showered and then downstairs. You can look at this later, but right now I'm going for breakfast."

They sat at a small table overlooking the lake. Tim tucked into a cooked breakfast while Nina sipped coffee and pulled a croissant apart.

"Did you sleep well, Tim?"

"I don't know, Neen. I suppose I did judging by the time we woke up."

"We didn't get to sleep until gone two, and you know why."

"Sorry, Neen, I never intended to do that, but you did look lovely and I lost control, not for the first time. You must be fed up with me using you like this, knowing each time that I always have to go back to Mel."

"Do you, Tim, do you have to go back to Mel? What if I kept you ... forever. Would it be so bad?"

"It would probably be fantastic, probably better than it will ever be with Mel ... but that's not the point is it?"

"What is the point Tim?"

"It's simple. I'm married to her. We have three children and that's it."

"So even if you're not happy with her, you can't make love properly to her and you know you would be happier with me, you still have to go back to her, is that it?"

"I don't know. I couldn't just walk out on her, it's not me, you know that."

"It doesn't make any sense, Tim."

"Neen, you're lovely. I'm happy when I'm with you ... and yes it's true, we are fantastic together in bed, and Mel and I can't get it together at all, but ... she's my wife, she doesn't deserve to be dumped the way Ben dumped you. She is the innocent party in all of this."

"She's not as innocent as you think, Tim!' Nina knew she shouldn't have said that.

"What do you mean, Neen, she's not so innocent? Do you know something? Has she told you something that I ought to know?"

"No, of course not. I'm sorry I didn't mean it to sound like that, but you put her on a pedestal, as if butter wouldn't melt in her mouth. No one is that good, that pure. Wake up Tim, before you get hurt."

"I don't want to listen to this, Neen. I'm going up to pack. I want to be out of here and finding the kids before this day is out."

"Stop, Tim, listen, I'm really sorry. I was just letting my jealousy run away with me. You know how I feel about you. Look, we might as well base ourselves here. That way if we don't find them today we've got a room booked for tonight."

"No, Nina, I am not spending another night in this hotel, I'm sorry. We have to find them and then head for home. Do you have some sort of a plan, where we should look first?"

"Tim, maybe I was a bit hasty in accusing Ben. It's nice here, we could have a look around, get lunch somewhere, go to the tourist office and get a list of all the campsites so that tomorrow it won't take us long to locate them. When are we going to get another chance to be on our own, doing what we want to do, without having to sneak away for an hour in the daytime, afraid Melanie will find out? Think about what we've got here Tim ... paradise, that's what this is. What difference is one day going to make, tell me?"

"Nina, back home you were frantic, out of your mind with worry, now suddenly you want to take a holiday? I'm asking myself if you didn't set this whole thing up just so we could be together, honestly."

"What if I did, Tim? Would it be a problem?"

"Are you serious, Neen? Are you telling me that this was all a hoax? A scheme, dreamed up so that we could get away together?"

"Please don't be angry with me, Tim, can't you see how much it proves my love for you?"

"So what do we tell Mel when we get back empty handed and happy as Larry?"

"We tell her we couldn't find them, and then at the end of next week Ben will come back and everyone will forget all about it. We haven't done anything wrong, Tim. I want you, I want you to leave Mel and make a life with me. I can give you all the things she is incapable of giving you. I wouldn't go off for a month and leave you, for one thing."

"Nina, you've lost touch with reality. You've slipped a cog. You're mad. I can't believe you've dragged me all this way for nothing. Did you seriously think you could shag me into submission?"

"That's horrible! You wanted me badly enough when Mel was away. Now she's back you can't wait to dump me. Well I'm a person, Tim, not a rubber doll. You wanted me, now you've got me, and unless you want me to ring Mel up and tell her everything, you had better start treating me like a human being. Do you understand?'

"I'd have to be pretty bloody stupid not to, wouldn't I? Look, I'm sorry, I never meant to use you and you know that. We got carried away, you have that effect on me, for God's sake, but you always knew I was married. We both knew this passion was satisfying our basic needs. It was never going to be forever. I can't leave Mel, I love her."

"And what about me? I seem to remember you whispering those exact words in my ear last night just as your fire extinguisher went off. You say those words but they don't mean a bloody thing to you. Sod you, let's ring Mel and explain to her how you came to tell me you loved me, why I mistakenly thought that your relationship with her was over, why I thought you wanted me more than her ...shall we?"

"Neen, don't do that ... please. If you do you will destroy everything, even us. Let's talk this thing through. We can find a way of keeping our relationship, but without me leaving Mel... please?"

"If I go along with this can we stay here today? Go home tomorrow? After all it will look strange if we go home so soon without finding them."

"If I go along with this, Neen, you must promise me that you'll never, ever tell Mel what has gone on between us."

"Like you promised that we would always be friends? Like you promised you would take care of me? No Tim, if you're going to dump me the minute we get back, you might as well do it now. Let's get the painful bit over with. I'm not looking forward to telling Mel anymore than you are, but what else can I do? I'm in love with you, Tim, you've had me every way you wanted, now you think it's time to say thank you but no thank you? I'm telling you this will hurt me as much as it hurts you but, make no mistake I will do it if you leave me."

"That works both ways, Neen. If you tell Mel, I lose her, OK, but you lose me too because if you deliberately set out to destroy my marriage I won't be able to forgive you. The only way that this can work is the middle road ... you can have me when you want me, yes; you get my body, but not my heart, that stays right there with Mel."

"We don't have much option but to trust each other then, do we?"

"We have one other option ... we can destroy each other! Is that what you really want?"

"Of course not. I told you, I love you. I never want to hurt you, but I can't live without at least a part of you. If all I can have is you now and again I'll live with that. Just don't ever tell me again that it's over, that I'm not going to have you ever again. I couldn't handle that, Tim. I don't mean it to sound like a threat. I'm trying to be honest with you."

"I know ... I may be pretty stupid but I can see that you wouldn't have gone to these lengths, to drag us both up here if you weren't serious. Try to understand, Neen, I do love you in a way, and I meant it when I said we'd always be friends ... but in front of all that is my marriage, that's just the way it is."

"So are we agreed Tim?"

"Yes, like you said, I have no choice if I don't want to start a war I can't win."

"And we stay here tonight?"

"We'll have dinner in the restaurant then you can come round to my place – you know, the room next to yours – and we'll make last night look like we were just practicing, OK?"

She saw from his smile that he meant it. It wasn't as much as she would have liked but there was always another day. For now at least she had a promise that he would make love to her whenever she asked, and more than that she knew it was a promise he would have to keep.

Chapter Sixteen

Melanie's office was a depressing place on Tuesday morning. Rachel, her secretary brought two cups of coffee in at ten and, after closing the door, sat down in front of her.

"Are you going to tell me what it's all about?"

"What what's all about?"

"Mel, I've only worked with you for a short while but I know you well enough to know that you've got a lot on your mind, and I'd say it was outside of work ... right?"

"You're right Rachel."

"My job is to support you at every level and I can't do that unless you tell me what's going on."

"And supposing you don't believe me when I tell you?"

"Try me, Mel. It's got to better than sitting there looking like a duck in a desert."

"Do I really look that bad?"

"You should see your lips, you could pout for England."

"Rachel, my husband is spending a few days in the Lake District with Nina, looking for her husband and kids, oh and her husband's lover. I told you it would be hard to believe, didn't I? It was me who insisted he went with her, after all she's my best friend. And Ben, that's Nina's husband is Tim's best mate, and they are our next door neighbours, well were, until Ben buggered off with this girl he met in a disco."

Rachel burst out laughing, "Mel, can I come over to your place one Weekend for some laughs? Where I live people just cut their grass and wash their cars."

"It's bloody well not funny."

"OK but you have to admit it's a touch on the weird side."

"Oh, don't worry, there's more, quite a bit more, but I'll save that until you write my biography."

"Come on, out with the rest of it. Tell me the full story and then I'll give you the benefit of my advice."

"I'm not sure I want your advice Rachel, all I want is for things to get back to normal."

At that moment Mel's mobile rang and when she answered it she became coy. It was obvious this was a private call and one she didn't want to share, but she hadn't called him Tim. Who, then, Rachel wondered, was Ratty?

Mel, took the phone from her ear just long enough to signal for her to leave. Once alone she couldn't wait to find out why Ratty had chosen this moment to call her.

"I didn't expect to hear from you, I was beginning to think you had forgotten me."

"That's funny, I'm sure you told me in Poland that I was not to phone you."

"Did I? Well you didn't, so that's OK, and now you did, and that's OK too."

"Good, you're making perfect sense as always Mel, so let me tell you why I risked calling you. If you must know I'm missing you terribly and I thought it would be nice if we could meet up for lunch, take a walk along the quay and talk about ... you know, about Poland and us and things."

"OK, what time?"

"Did I hear you right?' I expected you to say no, to tell me I wasn't to speak to you. You never fail to surprise me, Mel. Can we meet at the Fiesta bar, on the quay at twelve?"

"I'll see you there, oh … and thanks for ringing, you don't know how fed up I was before you rang."

"And now...?"

'Never mind, you can find out at twelve.' She clicked the red button and put the phone down as Rachel walked back in.

"You were listening, weren't you?"

"Not on purpose, Mel. You look a lot happier now than you did five minutes ago, so whoever it was he certainly pressed all the right buttons."

"Yes, he's very good at doing that!"

"Don't knock it, Mel, some women spend their whole lives with a man who can't do that."

"I know. That's what I was about to tell you when my phone rang." She laughed so that Rachel wasn't sure if she meant it or not.

Somehow, Rachel thought, I detect smoke, and they say there's no smoke without fire. I wonder who's providing the heat?

At a quarter to twelve Melanie left the office and made her way down to the quayside. It was so warm still that she didn't bother with a coat, her black trousers and pink short sleeved top providing all the cover she needed for a glorious day like today. The Fiesta bar was a fairly new addition to the quayside. Part of a chain of bistro style wine bars, it was a trendy meeting place for people who were happy to pay way over the odds for food and drink in return for the kudos it offered. Melanie made her way through the throng of drinkers, who stood mostly in groups talking loudly against the background music. She spotted Ratty at the bar just as he saw her.

"Dry white, Mel?"

"Thanks ... just what I need"

"Shall I order us a couple of prawn sandwiches?"

"Sounds good to me."

He carried the drinks to a table in a corner away from the crowd. "It's been weeks, Mel, since Poland. How are things at home?"

"Good, yes absolutely fine, and with you?"

"Same. Amazing in fact. I suppose Nina has told you all about her move into Stellar Haufman's office?"

"Yes, did you arrange that with Hugh while we were working out there?"

"Sort of yes. It's a good move for her, so don't worry, I haven't done her career any harm by pushing her into it. I hear on the grapevine that you've gone up to the top floor in the bank; own office, own secretary, you must be doing something right."

A young woman brought the food to the table. 'Can I get you more drinks?'

"Thanks, two more dry white please, large ones."

"Ratty, you know very well why I got promotion. As soon as I got back from our trip John Higgs had me in and told me about the glowing testimonials from you and Hugh and told me I was moving upstairs. I've got you to thank for my success and I really am grateful, honest. Do you remember when we first met, at Nina's house party? I was going through a crisis right then, convinced I was losing my mind and my job. Since that night when we sat and talked and you invited me to your seminar my life has changed completely."

"Has it changed for the better though?"

"I'm a lot happier at work... and I've got all my old confidence back. My career has always meant a lot to me, so after ten years back at the bank it's rewarding to have reached the top."

"You're happier at work ... does that mean you're not happier at home?"

"Things are a mess at home, Ratty. Why is it I can be so successful at work yet I can't manage three kids and a husband?"

"Our private lives aren't structured like our work, Mel. At home no one has to do as you tell them. It's much harder to make a success out of a marriage than out of a career, believe me, I found that out when I tried it."

"But my marriage has always been sacred to me. I've never even looked at another man – well not until I met you, but we don't seem to have much to say to each other these days, well not anything worth saying that is, and in bed it's a disaster. But I'm sure that's my fault. I'm feeling guilty over what happened in Poznan."

"Do you think that's fair ... on yourself I mean?"

"Of course it is. I should have said no to you."

"Mel, what happened that night was bound to happen. We were both bursting with feelings for each other. It's no use you denying that. I could feel the passion between us from twenty feet. What we had there is too special to be swept away in a tide of guilt."

"I'm not denying it, I did feel deeply for you, but it was wrong ... I shouldn't have let myself have those feelings in the first place."

"If your marriage was working well you wouldn't have had those feelings, Mel. Maybe it's the marriage that's wrong, not us?"

"Ratty, d'you think I haven't thought about that, but we've got three children. I don't want them suffering all the problems of a broken marriage."

"Are you saying that if you didn't have children you would end the marriage and let me take care of you?"

"Probably, yes ... but I do have children, so it can't happen."

"Is it really better for them to grow up in an unhappy marriage than in a good relationship? After all, if we were together they would still see their father whenever they wanted."

"That's not the same as seeing him everyday though, is it?"

"It might be *better* than seeing him every day. At the moment he takes them for granted, the same as he takes you for granted. If he saw them two or three days a week he'd appreciate that time with them and work much harder at being kind and caring. It's natural. Any father would value his time with his children more if he didn't have them around him every day."

"It would hurt him terribly. I could never do that to him."

"So you're willing to give up the chance of the happiness we could have together to save hurting him?"

"Yes, that's about it. Sorry, Ratty, I told you before, it wouldn't work between us."

"Yes you did, but you never told me why."

They finished their drinks and Ratty paid the bill. "We're

wasting this lovely day in here, let's walk along the quay."

They walked until they were out of the busy waterside, past what used to be boat yards but now satisfied the ever increasing demand for car parking within walking distance of the centre. Small trees and shrubs formed the boundary from here on, until the waterside went into more rural territory. They stopped at a seat, neatly surrounded by bushes except to its front side, which faced the river.

Ratty sat close to her, his arm round her waist, his hand slipping easily inside of her pink top so that his hand cupped her waist. "I am so happy, Mel, when I'm with you. I'd give everything I have to be with you properly."

"You'd soon get fed up with me. I'm not nearly as nice as you think. Don't forget you only see me when I'm in a good mood."

"I'd make sure you were always in a good mood."

"Impossible ... you see me through rose tinted glasses, you might not like me if we had to spend every day together."

"Let's try it. Give me a chance to prove how happy I can make you. Does sitting here by this river remind you of our walks around the lake?"

"Yes it does, and yes they were fantastic times, but it wasn't real, Ratty. They were moments we stole to spend together while we were a long way from home and I was a long way from Tim. This is real life, and I've got to go home to him, whether I want to or not."

As Ratty pulled her closer she made no attempt to stop him. In fact she co-operated as he moved his hands to cup her breasts under her top.

"Can I slip you're bra up and hold you properly Mel?"

She sighed but lifted her arms to make it easier for him.

They didn't speak as they sat in a state of intimacy staring out over the river. A kingfisher swooped down to the water and then disappeared into the trees opposite. This was a peaceful spot and the buzzing of a huge dragonfly was louder than the background hum of traffic somewhere behind them.

No words were needed as they sat clamped together, each of them enjoying their thoughts of the other. Suddenly footsteps disturbed their privacy as a couple came into view further along the path, heading straight for them.

Melanie gently pulled Ratty's hand down and replaced her bra. He still held her but outside her clothes. The couple passed, merely nodding in acknowledgement. Ratty knew he couldn't have her again, but nothing could take from him the happiness she had just bestowed by allowing him that moment of possession.

They started walking back towards the centre, comfortable in each other's company, released temporarily from the bands of conformity, free to be at ease with each other for a an hour or so, knowing that the clock was ticking until they must let each other go and return to their other lives.

It was harder for Ratty than for Melanie. She would go home to Tim and, even though she'd admitted it wasn't perfect, she would go through the routine of eating, talking and sleeping with him. Ratty would go back to his place alone. He had friends with whom he could spend his evenings; some of them women, attractive women, but there was only one woman that he wanted to be with and for a few more minutes he had her all to himself. He remembered the words of the song, 'Only One Woman.' He thought how it could have been written for him, or maybe the singer had suffered the same pain as him each time he'd left the woman he loved.

They were nearing the busy stretch of the path and soon he would have to release her altogether and walk by her side just like all the other people out walking 'together'.

"I love you, Mel. Truly I know you don't love me because your head is filled with loyalty for Tim, and you won't let yourself think about how it could be ... for us ... together, but know this, Mel, I will always love you, always. If I never get to have you, to keep you, then I will have lost the best thing that could ever have happened to me, and I think you will have lost something too. I would give everything I own, every penny, every minute of every day to make you mine, to make you happy. I would willingly take you with your children, and try to make a good life for them as well. I wouldn't put conditions on you and I wouldn't try to tie you down. You're a butterfly, a beautiful butterfly, and I want to be the branch on which you settle when you're tired at the end of every day. I will love you forever Mel."

She knew he meant it but she was resolute in her belief that her duty was to her marriage. She was sacrificing a great deal to stay with Tim, but she owed him that. They'd vowed to look after each other, 'until death us do part,' and she would honour her vows.

"I'm sorry Ratty. I know how you feel about me but you must find someone who is free to love you back. You've got a lot to give and there is a woman out there somewhere for you, you just have to find her."

"I've already found her, Mel. I found her too late, that's the problem."

They were back in the town and it was time to say goodbye again and head back to their offices. They stood for a moment looking at each other. Ratty wanted desperately to kiss her goodbye but he knew she wouldn't let him, and he hated the thought of her rejecting him, especially after she had just shared herself with him. He couldn't risk spoiling the beauty of what she'd gifted to him this lunch time, so he could only hope that they'd do it again soon.

"Mel, can we meet again soon, like today?"

"Maybe, Ratty. I've really enjoyed our walk together, thank you."

He turned and walked away looking back just to raise his hand. Her face showed just a touch of sadness as they went off in opposite directions to their offices, to carry on as if nothing had happened.

"How was your meeting, Mel. You have a healthy glow, so I'm guessing it was good."

"It *was* good ... very good in fact."

"So, do you want me to keep some lunchtimes free in your diary?"

"No, Rachel, no that won't be necessary."

"Mel, one of your pals from downstairs called in to see you while you were out, a guy called Roddy, he said he thought you'd forgotten them since you moved up here."

"Of course I haven't, it's just that there's been no time ... I'll make some time, in fact even better, I'll have a party for all of them ... you can come too of course. It's about time we had a party to brighten up our dull little lives."

The drive home was Mel's thinking time, her half hour, when she could let her mind flow from the problems at work to those awaiting her at home; her winding down period, but tonight it was taken up with planning the party.

If only Nina was at home so she could share the news with her. Neen loved parties. Never mind. She'd go on and organise it and let it be a surprise for them when they returned, which reminded her she'd better try to ring Tim and see what progress they'd made with finding Ben and the missing children. He answered at once but seemed disturbed at the sound of Mel's voice, as if he wasn't expecting her to ring.

"What's wrong, Tim, have you found them?"

"No, we've decided to call off the search. We're coming home tomorrow."

"But I thought Neen was intent on finding them. What's changed?"

"I don't know ... I mean, nothing's changed, it's just that we can't find them."

"Well, surely you need to keep looking?"

"No, we've made our minds up. We'll be back tomorrow."

"OK, but I don't understand why she's giving up so easily. I wouldn't if you tried to run off with my children."

"Don't you mean 'our children'?"

"Whatever ... Tim, I've had this brilliant idea. I'm arranging a party for some of my friends from work, you know the one's I used to work with, Tell Neen, she loves a good party."

"Yes, I remember the last one, you sent me out for the night with Ben, some excuse to get rid of us if you recall."

"Yes, well you won't need to this time will you? Ben's not a problem; at least he's not going to show up at my party. I'll see you tomorrow then. Give my love to Neen."

The first thing she had to do was make a list of everyone she would invite. The people she'd worked with for years downstairs of course; Neen, who might want to bring her new friends from her office; Hugh and whatever the secretary was called. Her mind flashed back to Neen's party next door where she had first met Ratty. He would be devastated to know she was having a party and not inviting him, but it was out of the question, or was it?

Given how touchy Tim still was about her trip to Poland and Ratty's involvement, he'd never welcome him at their house for a party. But as it was him who had been the catalyst for her promotion, which, after all, was the reason for the party in the first place, how could she not invite him? It would be unbearable if Tim was rude to him and she couldn't get rid of Tim for the night, the way Neen had got rid of Ben. Bugger him, Ratty had helped her to find herself when she was close to despair, he'd rescued her from a breakdown, brought her back from the abyss to do better than she had ever done and he had single handedly given her a future. He had to be invited, sod it if Tim wanted to get the needle. She'd helped him to get a job he loved and what thanks had she got?

She sat with her glass of white and listened to Trudy who was upstairs getting the kids calmed down and ready for bed. She was a gem, that girl. How lucky she'd been to find her. Poland would never have been possible without her. She owed her so much. Melanie waited for her to get the kids quiet and return downstairs. She sat her down and pushed a glass of Chardonnay into her hand.

"Listen, Trudy, I'm going to put a party on, a week next Saturday, and you are going to be at my side enjoying every minute of it. You've been such a help to me, I don't know how I'd have managed without you."

"What about those three?" Trudy pointed to the ceiling.

"They'll be fine, they can have a few soft drinks, then go upstairs and watch TV like they usually do. So, let's start planning; we need balloons, gas, food, drink, lots of it, those guys from work like a drink or two. I'm getting excited at the thought. I love a party."

It was gone eleven when they finally had all their plans written down.

The next day at work, Melanie was buzzing with excitement. The list grew steadily longer as she invited first one and then another, never giving a thought to how many people she could fit in at Chez Fisher.

She'd saved the most important invite till last, but at eleven thirty she rang Ratty. His hopes were at once raised that she was about to suggest another walk along the quayside.

"Mel, I've got an idea. I want to talk to you about, another of those legal seminars. Can we do lunch and a walk like we did yesterday?"

"No, Ratty, and you don't really want my advice on a seminar, you just want to touch me again, that's the truth isn't it?"

"Whatever you say, Mel." His voice sounded dejected. He waited for her to speak. It was her who rang him after all.

"Ratty, I'm having a party at my place next Saturday. Would you like to come?"

'Of course I would, Mel. What time and what shall I bring?'

"Seven onwards and ... let me think, why don't you bring a nice girl from your office. You know there are plenty there you could invite and it might just stop Tim from getting jealous. You know he still blames you for taking me off to Poland."

"So he should. Yes, I made you go, but I don't care Mel, let him be jealous if he wants."

"Thanks, Ratty, and where does that leave me? In the middle... I'm worried he might be rude to you, especially once he's had a few beers."

"It's going to be hard for me, Mel, being there at your party, so close to you and yet unable to talk to you."

"Of course you can talk to me."

"You know what I mean ... I'm sure Tim will be jealous if I hold you tightly and tell you how much I love you."

"Yes, that would probably confirm his suspicions about you. Even he isn't backward enough to miss a clue like that."

"When we celebrate our getting together I'm going to give you the biggest party you've ever seen; we'll hire the Hilton and we'll invite everyone, and I mean everyone."

"Ratty, I've told you... it wouldn't work, behave yourself. I'll see you at my place... bye until then."

The next day, Rachel put the post on her desk as usual but on top was an envelope, not opened, addressed to Melanie Fisher and marked Private and Confidential.

"It looks like a greetings card so I decided you'd better open it yourself ."

Melanie tore the envelope open to reveal a card. The cover had a picture of a lake and alongside it stood two people, arms around each other, obviously in love.

She opened it and read the words inside:

The senses it's said, are just five,
Seeing you is being alive,
To be with you is all I strive,
Needed most, it must be right,
or life would not be worth the fight.
To touch you is my greatest pleasure,
I hold you tight, and long once more,
For the thing I hold most dear in life,
to be your husband, and you my wife.

We share good food, and never in haste,
Wine from ships, syrup from hips,
but the finest treasure I've yet to taste,
the thing I long for, to taste your lips.
What use at all is a sense of smell,
if I can't let your perfume dwell,
We walk in woods where wild garlic grows,
I'm lost without you, God only knows.
I need my touch, I need my ears,
I need to taste, to smell, all the things above,
I want so much to stop your tears,
With my gentle touch and with my love.
But those who claim there are senses five,
are missing out; trying hard to stay alive
I have another sense, with you to share,
The sense of love, any when and anywhere.

Melanie wiped away a tear and closed the card. She put it safely in her desk, where she could reach it later. Theirs was a very special friendship, did she deserve his love when she could give him so little in return?

Ratty had told her he wanted to share the rest of his life with her. He wanted to take care of her and in that he was including her children, but had he accepted that she couldn't end her marriage simply because it wasn't working? Could he find happiness in the few stolen hours they shared together?

In truth, she knew that Ratty enjoyed an hour of having her in his arms so much that he refused to contemplate a relationship with another woman, even though there were plenty willing to offer themselves.

His love for her was the most powerful display of affection she had ever experienced. When she was with him she was injected with moments of sheer ecstasy, feeling her entire body and mind fuse as one with his. They shared thoughts, desires and pleasures through simply holding one another close.

She would never reach this state of excitement, of longing, indeed of loving, with Tim. What then was to be her future? Was it fair to deny Ratty her body and in so doing deny herself moments of perfect inner peace? Could she survive her less than perfect marriage if she was denied these moments of escape with her friend and lover?

She looked again at the card and felt a small pain, a feeling of loss for something that she could only enjoy briefly in moments hidden from the view of her other friends, a dark secret she was unable to share with anyone. She uttered the word to herself, 'lover'. Was it so very bad to have a lover, to *be* a lover?

She was trapped in a marriage love had left long ago, so was it right to abstain from letting Ratty touch her, releasing the pent up emotion that she wanted to share but had been brought up to believe was wrong. How could it be wrong to love someone who loved you more than anything in the world simply because you were tied into an agreement made long ago?

Ratty was a part of her life, she had confirmed that when she let him enter her body in Poland. He would forever be her lover, the only question remaining was should his love be in the past or in the future?

Tim's phone call yesterday evening had made it clear that they would be home today come what may. 'You should stay and try to find them,' she'd said, but he'd sounded despondent and resigned to giving up on the search. No doubt she would hear the full story tonight when she got home.

She walked in the door to the sound of Amy talking above her brothers in a futile attempt to gain the exclusive attention of her father. She took her shoes off and went in, almost unnoticed, to the mêlée that was her lounge.

Mum, Dad's back and he's brought us a huge jar of sweets. There was no point in trying to ask him now about their failed search and so she returned to the kitchen, where Trudy was preparing the evening meal.

"How long has he been back?"

"Only ten minutes before you arrived. The kids leapt on him as soon as he came in. Nina has gone straight to her house, but Tim said she'd be round soon. I offered to cook extra for her, is that OK?"

"Of course, it'll be good to hear all about their little adventure in the Lake District."

With that, Nina opened the door carrying a huge bunch of flowers, which she thrust into Melanie's hands. "These are to say thank you, for his helping me these past couple of days."

"But he wasn't much help, Neen, was he? He couldn't find his best mate or your children."

"But he tried, he was a great help to me. In the end, Mel, we had to give up. It was like looking for a needle in a haystack and once I was there I began to wonder if I had imagined that Ben could really run off with them. I think I was confused, frightened perhaps, not thinking straight. Tim helped me to put things into perspective. He helped me get a grip on reality and then I found myself thinking we should come home and wait for Ben to bring them back. I really think now that he will.'

"Good ... I'm pleased that Tim was so helpful, he obviously has hidden depths of persuasive power. Power that I haven't seen in a long time." She tried not to let her anger show in her voice.

'It was beginning to sound as if they'd gone all that way to have a cosy little chat, one which had, after two whole days, brought her round to thinking there was actually no reason to be concerned in the first place.'

Trudy's Lasagne was a feast and once she served it up conversation dwindled to a halt until every last morsel had been dispatched.

True to form, the kids disappeared upstairs as soon as they had given Trudy the required help in the kitchen. Melanie intended the four adults to relax over a glass of Chardonnay, giving her the opportunity to prise more information from her husband and her best friend on their trip north.

"So, tell me all about the trip, was the weather as good as here?"

Nina needed no encouragement to talk about the

excursion, which had Tim worried. One mistake and their secret would be out; the whole charade would be exposed, the balloon would go up and the shit would hit the fan. He silently prayed that she would not leave questions in Mel's mind for later, questions he would have to answer when she had him alone. Mel would mentally record every detail and if his version differed slightly she would push him to explain until he broke down.

If he tried to change the subject it would be obvious, so he had to go along with Nina's version of events and try to remember every detail for later. This was something he wasn't good at.

Nina was at her best when relating a story to an attentive audience. She wallowed in being the centre of attention, so much so that she left no detail from her account of their trip uncovered, or so it seemed. There was nothing more, it seemed to Tim, that Mel could possibly need to know.

When the second bottle was drained, Trudy announced that she was off to bed and Nina made her excuses. Hugh had been great, letting her take time off, but she wasn't about to take advantage by getting in late.

Tim hastily cleared the glasses and made his escape to the bathroom, leaving Melanie to see Nina out with a final few words on the way.

He dreaded her coming upstairs, but he couldn't feign sleep. That would be like screaming 'guilty' at the top of his voice to her. In his effort to play it cool, he brushed his teeth and messed about in the bathroom, waiting to hear her come up. At last the bedroom door closed and he came out, suitably ready for bed and yawning to emphasis his unwillingness to enter into more conversation.

Melanie was in the bathroom for an age, which meant that he was in a state of near genuine sleep when she climbed in alongside of him and settled herself down. She switched off the light and it was peaceful at last.

Three minutes passed before she spoke, "So why *did* you give up on finding Ben so easily?"

Tim felt his throat go dry and his brain go numb. He had roughly five seconds before she would shake him from his supposed sleep to answer her.

"Like Nina said, we looked around but there are just too many places that he could have been, it was hopeless."

"Tim, while you two were busy searching, I typed, 'Camping in the Lake District' into my search engine ... do you know how many campsites I was able to find?"

"Hundreds I expect."

"I found forty two and that included some outside of the immediate area. You could have got to at least twenty each day and you would have found them."

"But we didn't have access to the internet."

"Tim, how many campsites *did* you visit?"

"I can't remember, probably twenty or thirty."

"Tell me the names of some of the ones you called at."

"I don't know, Mel, I just drove. Nina took care of the names and talking to the campsite people."

"Well, I visited a few campsites myself. I sent a simple E-mail saying I was trying to find my friend and his girlfriend and children because I wanted to meet up with them. Do you know how many sites I visited?"

"No, of course I don't."

"Five, Tim, and I found out which site he was on in under an hour. Then I called the site and asked them to get a message to him. I asked if he could call me back, which he did in less than ten minutes."

"You've spoken to Ben?"

"Yes, Tim, I asked him how he was doing and how the kids were. I made some excuse about Nina being worried about the kids not putting their sun cream on. I told him she had asked me to phone because she didn't want to speak to him. He was absolutely fine. Obviously he hadn't seen you or he would have said, and I didn't let on that he was about to get a visit from you, but then he wasn't, was he?"

"So why didn't you say all this before we went? You could have saved me a long drive and from having to listen to Nina going on about Ben for two days.'

"Are you sure you would have wanted me to save you the journey Tim?"

"Just what is that supposed to mean?"

"Nothing, Tim, absolutely nothing. I'm just tired, fed up and confused. I'm sorry. Goodnight, Tim, and thanks for coming back."

"Of course I was coming back. I couldn't wait to get back, and that's honest."

He put his arm around her and met with no resistance. The matter was closed. He knew she wouldn't mention it again. He could relax ... for now.

Nina had to explain to Hugh Ballantyne the background to her sudden expedition in search of her children. She'd sent him a text to say she needed a few days off urgently but he really had no idea what he had agreed to.

"Are you sure that he'd run off, abroad even, with three children? You told me before that he wasn't that good a father, seems a bit unlikely to me."

"Hugh, let's just say it was a mother's instinct, but then once I got up to the Lake District I got a different feeling, one that told me I was barking up the wrong tree, so after a brief search we high-tailed it back home."

"We... who went with you?"

"Oh, Tim, Mel's husband. He drove."

"You went away for two nights with your friend's husband? She must be a very understanding friend."

"She is, Hugh, she knows she can trust me ... and anyway I'm sure she trusts her husband. After all why wouldn't she?"

"Because... maybe because of what she did in Poland. She became very close to Rattani you know."

"I know ... she told me, but she didn't tell me that you knew what had happened."

"I didn't until now... although of course I knew what his intentions were. He made it clear he was out to win her, and it seems he succeeded."

"Hugh, don't you dare tell anyone else. You tricked me into that but it goes no further, OK?"

"Of course Nina. Anyway, it's not his wife's affair that bothers me. It's his affair with you in the Lake District that I don't like."

"Hugh, I may have fallen for your little trick once but I'm not about to do so again."

"So you did have an affair?"

"Hugh, I didn't have an affair and you are going where you have no right to so leave it ...please?"

"Nina, my concern is based purely on the oldest motive for crime on our planet ... jealousy. You know how I feel about you. I want you again, in fact I want you full stop."

"It was a mistake, Hugh. I already told you ... there's someone else."

"But that someone is married to your best friend, Nina. You are messing with dynamite and when your little secret comes out, as it will, then you'd better be prepared for the fall out."

"Hugh, is there anything I can say that will make you butt out?"

"You could say you'll have dinner with me tonight ... and stay over."

"Dinner yes, stay over, no. I'll ring my mother and check she'll have the kids tonight, but I'll be sleeping in my own bed... OK?"

"Very reasonable. I'll pick you up from your place at eight."

"Actually, Hugh, It's just what I needed, a night out to cheer me up and make me forget all my problems."

"You can tell me all your problems tonight."

"I don't think so, Hugh, but thanks anyway."

Hugh was a regular in several of the best restaurants in town. He could get a table with one phone call even when the place had been fully booked for weeks. The Lobster Pot was a favorite of his, one he knew she would appreciate. She'd already told him of her love for all things fish.

The head waiter showed them to their table in the marbled palace that was a shrine to good food. A glass chandelier lit the room, while at the table a white candle lit their faces. In a cut glass vase, a single Ena Harkness red rose exuded its fabulous perfume. The setting was perfect, as was the service. The food was divine.

"Hugh, you're hoping this meal will be an aphrodisiac... right?"

"Nina, I've already proved I don't need any stimulant to win your affection, have I not?"

"You caught me in a moment of extreme weakness, Hugh, don't assume that I'm an easy lay just because you got lucky last time, OK?"

"I employ you to give me good advice, Nina. Is that the best you can do?"

"For the moment, yes."

"Good, then I'll ask you again in a couple of hours."

"My advice will be the same, Hugh, sorry, but if it wasn't, you'd say I was inconsistent."

He smiled easily and let her have her way. He'd found her weakness, her continual desire to be in control, to show her power. He'd let her have her way ... for now.

By the time the coffee and mints were served they'd both drunk far too much to drive. Hugh called a taxi and they rested on each other as they headed towards Elmthorpe. Nina didn't question his decision to pay off the taxi and help her inside.

"Nina, do you think we could have a drop of something to go with the coffee?"

"How about a Cointreau?"

"Perfect."

She poured the drinks and then slumped ungraciously next to him. "Cheers."

He raised his glass, "Cheers, Nina, thank you for a wonderful evening."

They clinked glasses and stared at each other. Hugh took her free hand and kissed it before moving in to kiss her lips. She responded willingly and they put their empty glasses on the floor to give themselves two free hands.

Nina warmed to Hugh's advance. She hated spending her nights here alone and he was not only handsome and worldly, he was unattached.

The clock radio burst into life as usual at six thirty. Nina rubbed her eyes and gently sat up. At first her recollections of last night were hazy, distant ... but when she saw the sleeping torso of her boss beside her it all came flooding back with startling harshness. The reality of morning.

No point in complaining now, better get up, shower and bring him breakfast.

As she drove him into town to pick up his car, they talked about the day ahead as if nothing had happened. She dropped him off at the multi-story, then carried on to the office where they would soon meet up again for work.

When she checked her e-mails just before lunch she found a short message.

"I promised you would sleep in your own bed last night, and I kept my promise. Until next time ... Love Hugh xx"

An exchange of mails followed.

"You were a perfect gentleman just as I expected. I wasn't disappointed. Nina xxx"

He replied within seconds. "I'm serious, Neen, I want you 24 x 7 x 365."

"Is that a proposal Hugh? ...If so it lacks the romance I would have expected from you."

"It wasn't a proposal ... that comes later, over dinner tonight ...?"

"I accept the invitation. Will sir be requiring a room?"

"Sir would be pleased to accept your kind offer."

She heard him laughing from behind the partition which

separated their offices. She smiled to herself. Life was better than it had been in years ... Ben had done her a huge favour when he moved himself into Beckie's little hovel.

CHAPTER SEVENTEEN

Planning a party would have to involve Nina, even if Mel was a bit sore with her over the seemingly pointless trip in search of Ben and the children. Anyway she wasn't one to stay moody for long. When Nina said she wanted to share a bottle of white and bring Melanie up to date on things at work, she saw it as an opportunity to involve Nina in the plans for the party.

They sank back onto Nina's cream leather sofa in preparation for an evening of tittle tattle, to be washed down with a Pinot Grigio that she had picked up at lunch time. As we don't have the luxury of a nice Italian man to spend the evening with I thought this would be next best, she said.

"Fancying a Latin lover, are you?"

"I'm not sure if I'd have any time spare for one right now," Nina replied.

"Really... does that mean that there's romance in the air, Neen?"

"Could be. I think it's up to me ... Hugh is coming on strong."

"Wow, you could do a lot worse. I watched him when we were in Poland, he's sophisticated, he's exactly what a lot of women yearn for, me included."

"I know, what a difference to Ben. I look back now and wonder how I put up with him for all those years."

"Ben's a slob, Neen, but even slobs can be attractive sometimes."

"Well, I'm done with slobs. From now on I want my men to be successful, well heeled and passionately attentive to my every need."

"Men... how many are you planning to have?"

"I don't know ... how many do you think I should have?"

"Well, you know what they say, Neen, if two isn't enough, ten isn't too many."

"Actually, Mel, I think it's... 'if one isn't enough'..."

"Oh who cares ... what's one man more or less between friends?"

"Exactly, but the advantage of Hugh is that he's unattached, which means that if he's serious ... well who knows? He's got distinct possibilities!"

"Is that what you want, Neen, a partner? Another long-term one-on-one relationship?"

"Isn't that what we all want, deep down, Mel?"

"Yes, I suppose so, but only if it's with someone who lights you up inside, someone who can touch that soft spot, make you feel special when you're feeling like shit."

"Doesn't Tim do that for you?"

"Not any more, Neen. In fact if I'm honest, he hasn't done so for years. Sure, I love him because we've been together a long time. We've got three kids, we rub along together, discuss problems when we have to, get through life's ups and downs together, but I can't put my hand on my heart and say I long to spend time alone with him."

"What you're really saying Mel is you love him, but you're not *In Love* with him."

"That is exactly the way it is ... we make love but we're not lovers."

"Tell me honestly, Mel, is he you're best friend?"

"Honestly... no. I can talk more easily to Ratty about my period pains or my varicose veins or about anything than I can to Tim.'

"That rhymed, Mel; that was quite good for a spontaneous quote."

'Spontaneous, that's how I am when I'm with him. I do things I wouldn't dream of doing ordinarily. I behave differently because he makes me feel different.'

"So would you say Ratty was your best friend?"

"I suppose he is, well apart from you, of course but if you mean 'man' then definitely. After all he knows lots more about me than Tim knows. He knows about my affair with him for a start."

"Could you ever see yourself leaving Tim for Ratty?"

"It's impossible Neen. I've got three children, they're Tim's children too. No we're committed to each other, for better or worse."

"Which is it?"

"Some days I'd say it's for the worse, but he can be kind and thoughtful occasionally. He's never going to understand me, or be passionate the way Ratty would be. He's never going to share the same pleasures as I do in life but I have to accept that."

"Why do you think Tim can't be passionate with you Mel?"

"Hey, why all the questions? I don't know why, he's just not a passionate bloke Neen. He doesn't have a clue when it comes to that sort of thing. He's like so many men. Believe me, Neen, If you knew him in bed you'd know he's never going to win any prizes in that department."

Nina swallowed hard as she tried desperately not to think about him in bed. Mel's description of Tim was a thousand miles from what she knew. Why was it that Tim couldn't arouse Mel the way he did her? And why was it that Ratty could? Obviously there was nothing wrong with Mel and she knew only too well that there was nothing wrong with Tim. Nina had to change the subject.

"Who are you going to invite to your party?"

"Well, everyone from the bank, especially all those downstairs. I miss them, our daily banter was part of keeping in touch. Now I'm upstairs I have to contrive a reason to go downstairs and when I do it isn't the same any more. There all talking about this or that and when I walk in I feel like an intruder."

"But you wouldn't swap your new job to go back down there?"

"No, I love my new job and Rachel is a great help. She's good to work with and I'll invite her of course."

"What about Ratty?"

"I know... I've spent hours trying to work out what I should do. He'd have been really unhappy if I hadn't invited him but I'm not sure how I'll feel having him and Tim in the room together. And what about when I have to introduce the two of them? Don't forget Tim still hates Ratty for taking me to Poland."

"Won't it look a bit odd if you don't invite him?"

"I hadn't thought about that. Do you think I should ask Tim if he minds Ratty coming?"

"Isn't that a bit like admitting there's a reason why he should mind?"

"Perhaps, but he's the one who got nasty about my trip to Poland ... I don't know if he's going to be rude to him, or maybe he'll just blank him, either way it'll be embarrassing."

"Supposing we did the same as we did for my party ... get rid of Tim for the night? Ask Ben to take him out drinking."

"Oh yes, he'd love that ... 'Tim I'm inviting Ratty round to my party at our house, do you mind buggering off for the night?"

They burst into laughter at the thought of Tim's reaction.

"Neen, we've got a more immediate problem, this bottle is empty!"

"Don't worry, Mel, there's a Blossom Hill in the fridge."

Suitably replenished, Mel sat down again.

"Mel, why don't you let Ratty jump out of a cake at Midnight? That would be a bit different, and I'd pay to see the look on Tim's face!"

"You might have to pay for my divorce as well if you did that."

"No problem, I'll do you a free one. Call it an early Christmas present."

"It was your bloody fault all this started ... if I hadn't met Ratty at your damned party I would have gone on happily with Tim never knowing what I was missing."

"So I did you a favour?"

"Yes, you did... I'd have hated to miss those precious moments with Ratty ... but make no mistake, it's over. I've told him it wouldn't work. We can still be friends, even best friends, but I can't give myself to him the way he wants."

"You're being too hard on yourself Mel, and for what? Let's be honest ... you've put a lot more effort into your marriage than he ever has and yet you get very little out of it. You wash his clothes, you bring up his children, you cook his food and you supply his pleasure whenever he demands it. What do you get out of it ... what's in it for you?"

"Not much."

"Precisely. And in a stolen hour or two with Ratty you find love and passion from a man who wants you for yourself, not as someone to service his lifestyle. You'd be a fool to throw away a once-in-a lifetime chance of happiness with him, and he's told you, hasn't he, that he wants you forever... what more can you ask?"

"I know... I'm being stupid... but it just seems wrong."

"What you do for Tim and what you get in return seems wrong to me." This is your life, Mel, your only life. When this one's gone you don't get another. Enjoy happiness when you can... it may not come your way again."

"What about you Neen? Where do you find the most happiness? With Hugh? Or could someone else make you happier?"

"I can't answer that, Mel. Not at the moment, but one day... when I know the answer I will have to tell you."

They sat silent for a moment, until Nina broke the peace.

"Are we doing the food or are you getting caterers?"

"What do you think I should do?"

"Oh bugger it, Mel, you're celebrating your new job, your new salary scale. To hell with it. Get someone in to do the food, and while your at it get them to decorate the place up a bit, you know balloons and streamers and stuff."

"What about Chris Rea? Should I book him to sing 'Woman in Red' to me?"

"Scarlet Woman maybe... definitely more appropriate."

"Stop it... I'm not that bad ... am I?"

"I don't know, Mel, I'll have to ask Ratty."

Saturday mornings were always manic in the Fisher household, but this one was more so. Trudy was taking care of James's music lesson and Amy was going with Melanie to the hair salon. Tim was being his usual self and complaining bitterly about the disruption the party was causing.

At two o'clock the party people arrived to start decorating the house, turning it into a mini wonderland for the night. Tim made himself useful by filling balloons from the Helium cylinder and leaving Henry to get them off the ceiling. Outside, coloured lights were being strung across both gardens. Willow Brook had never seen a party like this before.

Melanie had felt bound to invite a couple of neighbours. They were going to be sharing the noise so she figured it was best to invite them. When three women from the caterer took over her kitchen, she began to wonder if it had all been a huge mistake.

"Neen, what the hell have I done? Our house isn't big enough for sixty people. Why didn't you make me do this at the village hall or somewhere?"

"Because, Mel, nothing beats a house party. Village Hall parties never work, you know that. No atmosphere. Not the same as inviting all your friends into your home. It'll be fine, you'll see. Less space means it's more intimate. It'll be great"

The bank's contingent arrived en-masse – whether by coincidence or by mini-bus Melanie wasn't sure. Sam, the effervescent Office Manager was arm in arm with her husband Nigel, who looked as if he had been dragged along unwillingly; Roddy was wearing one of his outrageous bow ties and had a gorgeous lady friend in tow; Joe the Business Manager and Cindy his wife were carrying a bottle and flowers and each hugged Melanie in turn. Joe was ecstatic in his admiration of the lights and decorations. The party had started.

In a move to placate Tim over Ratty's inclusion, Melanie had suggested that Tim invite a few of his friends, although she couldn't quite see why they would want to celebrate her promotion ... maybe they wouldn't come? She hadn't realised that Tim's friends would enjoy a party regardless of the reason, or indeed even without a reason. They were just happy to consume the free drinks.

Jim, Landlord of the Globe led a small procession into the kitchen. Andy, one of Tim's pub mates was closely followed by Dave, the pub's resident loud mouth. He was already in a raucous mood, gesticulating as he described to Andy how he would have better managed a pub football match.

Jenny, Melanie's friend from the bank who had been sacked last year was standing alone in the kitchen clutching a potted plant which was intended to be a present for Melanie. Her small frame was obscured by Dave, who was busy waving his arms around to emphasise his point. The pub crowd would have to be moved out of the kitchen; it had already been agreed with the caterers that they would have unrestricted and exclusive access to the kitchen until after the food was served.

While Melanie was placating the mob and trying to herd

them into her lounge, she caught sight of Jenny tucked away in the corner, looking like a china doll.

She went to her and hugged her, her feelings of guilt returning as she remembered how she had promised to help Jenny and how she had done nothing. Now she was one of the Bank's Senior Managers and yet Jenny was here, bearing a present for her, in spite of what had been meted out to her at the bank. Melanie held Jenny for several minutes, listening to her and trying to think of a way to help her. Jenny explained that she did cleaning jobs for a few hours as well as delivering papers two mornings each week. She smiled as she told Mel this, showing no bitterness for her plight, seemingly accepting what life (and the bank) had handed out to her.

By eight thirty the house was bursting at the seams. There was no corner in which people weren't huddled, holding drinks above them in an effort to avoid tipping them as others tried to pass through. The call to food simply exacerbated the problem, as a stream of hungry guests tried to get to the kitchen. A few smart ones went out of the front door and round the side to the kitchen door, but even the garden was crowded.

Once the pub mob had been fed they saw no further point in staying. It took longer to get a drink than it did to drink it and Dave announced that they would all be better heading back to the Globe. Like lemmings to a cliff they followed him and Tim was left to decide where he wanted to spend the evening. He was unhappy at the prospect of meeting the famous Ratty, the man who had taken his wife away for a month, and without his pub friends no one would talk to him anyway. He had very little in common with this lot, but he was determined not to be forced out of his own house. He decided he'd stick around for a while and then when he could take no more he'd head off to the Globe.

When Ratty finally arrived, alone, it did nothing to make Tim feel better. His very presence seemed to draw people around him and the warmth of the welcome he was getting just annoyed Tim even more.

At nine o'clock Trudy decided it was time for Amy to go to bed, but Amy was equally determined to stay there, in the crowded room with bags of attention, which suited her just fine. Trudy tried the argument that at Amy's age she needed lots of sleep, but that provoked Amy to ask Trudy how old she was, to which she replied, 'That's a secret Amy. You'll discover one day that ladies never admit their age in public."

In her coquettish desire to remain the centre of attention Amy replied nonchalantly,

"Well, I've got a secret as well."

"Oh yes, and what might that be," Trudy said.

Amy swelled with importance as she loudly announced that Dad had spent most of the nights when Mum was away next door and hadn't come home until breakfast time. Not only was her secret no longer a secret but Melanie had been close enough to hear every word.

Her face went crimson as she stared at Tim, who had turned pale and ghostly looking.

At that moment Nina returned from the kitchen, blissfully unaware of this revelation.

'I bloody knew it, you cow... you bloody two-faced bitch. And I thought we were friends!'

Nina was astonished at Mel's sudden outburst. They'd both had a few drinks, but this was well out of order.

"What? What was that for Mel?"

"How dare you? You thought I'd never find out, you slept with my husband, that's what! Or was it so bloody rubbish that you've forgotten it already? You slut... you bloody slut.'

By now the room had descended into silence and both Hugh and Ratty stood motionless as the two women angrily faced each other.

Nina opted for the only strategy she could. Attack was the finest form of defence.

"Hang on a minute, Mel, before you brand me a slut in front of all our friends, you might like to tell Tim what you got up to while you were in Poland."

This was low. Mel looked stunned as she turned to see Tim's face crease with anger.

"So I was right all along! You went there to be with that low life, what is it exactly that she forgot to tell me, Nina?"

Nina had been pitched headlong into this and there was no way of going back now.

'I think she'd better tell you that don't you?" she said, pointing an accusing finger at Melanie.

"Well, Mel... would you like to tell me what that bastard already knows?" Tim stabbed his finger in Ratty's direction.

"Ok, what I did was bad, but I've regretted it every night since, not like you. It sounds as if you slept with her every night I was away and then you two invented that little story so you could spend a few more nights together in the Lake District. You clearly can't get enough of Nina, so fine, bloody fine. She's all yours because you'll never touch me again."

Ratty should have enjoyed hearing those words, but this

wasn't how he'd wanted it to be. He'd wanted a romantic affair and a gentle break from her marriage into a new and better life with him. This was messy and could upset her to the point where she wanted neither of them.

He exchanged glances with Hugh and then said in a loud voice, 'OK guys, I think the party's over. There are things to be said that are best said in private and I know we can rely on all of you not to let this out in the office on Monday.' It was a warning couched as a request, but everyone knew it would be very unwise to broadcast this to the office network next week. One by one everyone filed out, thanking Mel as they went until only five of them remained.

Hugh looked at Tim, partly with disgust but also with pity. He was looking at a broken man, even if he was now a direct challenge in the competition for Nina's affection. Nothing would be decided tonight, that was clear. With everyone gone the little group stood in silence.

Eventually Ratty decided to deal with the issue head on: "Tim, I don't blame you for hating me, but the truth is I love Mel and I'd walk twice around the world, barefoot if necessary, to have her."

"You've destroyed my marriage and you think I care what you want?"

Mel raised her voice angrily. "Tim, get this into your head; you destroyed our marriage, not Ratty. Yes, I had a one night stand with Ratty in Poznan, but that was it. I'd told him it was over, I was married to you and I intended to stay married to you, for better or for worse. Worse in my case, but that was my decision, until tonight. Now we're finished Tim, and I'm not spending another night under the same roof as you, so go, get out!"

Tim was wounded by her verbal onslaught. He stood there wondering what to do next.

Nina took one last look around the group and then made for the door. She slammed it defiantly in a last ditch attempt at retaining some dignity.

Tim waited a few seconds and then followed her. Once outside the house he made for next door but to his surprise the back door was locked. He tapped quietly at first but then louder until finally Nina opened the door.

"Yes Tim, what do you want?"

"I want to come in, of course. You heard what Mel said, we're free at last to spend our time together, just like you've wanted."

"Yes, Tim… wanted! Past tense. You've been thrown out of your happy married bliss and now you want me. How many times in the last few weeks have you told me I had to learn to live without you? Well, I did, I've learnt to live without you Tim. I'm sorry but I'm rather upset at the moment and I'd like you to leave. Good night Tim."

Shocked and puzzled he stood outside the two homes that had been his life until tonight. Now suddenly, he wasn't welcome in either of them. How did he get into this mess, he asked himself over and over? He knew he could stay at the manor, but he'd had far too much to drink to risk driving so the only option was the Globe and later a taxi maybe, or maybe not. No, damn it, this was still his house, why should he leave? He'd come back here when he left the pub.

Back inside, Hugh made an effort to console Mel but he was glad when his taxi arrived. He wished them both good night and left.

Mel looked at Ratty and said, "Ratty, please can I stay at

yours tonight. I don't want to talk about it but I have to escape from this house. I'm too upset to sleep here tonight."

He called a taxi while Mel grabbed a few things for an overnight bag. He had to be supportive but give her space, she needed time to recover from the party that never was.

When she returned downstairs with Trudy she was clutching her bag and sobbing.

Trudy gave her a big hug. "Well, none of us ever expected a party like that… that's for sure. Come on, Mel, you've still got the kids and me and the job you love so much. Look at the positives and maybe tomorrow it won't seem so bad."

Chapter Eighteen

Trudy went downstairs as she always did at a quarter to seven, to prepare breakfast for the children. The dozens of empty bottles and glasses strewn across the kitchen tops were a stark reminder that it was Sunday, the day after the party that had ended so badly. She pushed open the lounge door to see Tim sprawled in a chair, asleep and disheveled. He sat up and tried to focus on her through bloodshot eyes.

"Tim, you look awful." There was no point in her hiding the truth.

"I look better than I feel."

"Did you go drinking after Mel left last night?"

"I had one or two. I needed to think."

"And did it help you to think?"

"No, but eventually it helped close my eyes, the nearest I could get to sleep."

Trudy sat down facing him. He was in a terrible state – all of his own making she thought, but still she felt sorry for him.

"What are you going to do about it, Tim?"

"What can I do, Trudy? ... I've lost her haven't I? She meant it... she never wants to see me again."

His eyes were red from crying.

"Tim, I took the children up to bed when the row started.

I don't know what she said but I already knew about you and Nina. You must have known that I could see what was going on."

"But *you* didn't tell her did you? She didn't know anything until Amy blabbed it out."

"It wasn't my place to tell her... my job is to look after the children and that's what I do, but Amy's a child. I hope you don't intend to get cross with her over this, because if you say one word to her, Tim, you'll have me to deal with. I'm sorry to see you looking like this, and I'm sorry for Mel, but before you ask, let me tell you whose side I'm on ... I'm on the children's side. You two are supposed to be grown ups, yet from what I can see you've both been pretty silly. Whatever you decide to do, you'll have to talk to each other. Just make sure that those three upstairs don't see you hurting her more than you already have."

Tim listened intently. At least *she* was talking to him. After Mel had left he'd felt terribly alone. His friendship with Nina was apparently now history. Trudy was the only person still speaking to him. He'd take her advice, it might help.

"Trudy, what should I do now... what can I do?"

"You can go upstairs and take a shower, you look a mess, and I don't want them seeing you like that, then get down here and be ready to explain things to them. I'll get their breakfast, but don't kid yourself, they know things are serious. They're young, Tim, but they're not stupid. You've a lot of explaining to do."

She was right, but first he had to explain to *himself* how he'd managed to mess up his marriage. He would tell the children what was happening, once he'd worked it out.

Melanie would be the one who would eventually decide what was happening, she had always made the decisions... had she really decided it was all over?

The shower helped him recover so he looked a lot better. The children stopped their chatter as he walked into the kitchen. He faced three pairs of staring eyes, all waiting for reassurance that everything was normal.

"You know, Mum and I had a bit of a row last night, don't you."

Amy was first to reply. "Yes, Mummy was cross because you lived at Nina's house while she was away."

"That's right, Amy, I did ... I was lonely and missing your Mum, and Nina was lonely without Ben so we sat up late and talked each night. I didn't want to wake you by coming in late so I stayed at her house." He heard himself lying, but it was the best he could do.

Henry had said nothing until now. He'd been the closest of the three to his father, mainly because of their love of football. Tim had no ear for music and had never been able to share in James's talent, any more than he could relate to Amy's numerous activities. Henry's admonishment would hurt more than any, except that of Mel.

"Dad, we're not six year olds, we know about sex and stuff, and we know what you and Nina did. We heard you both shouting last night. You've cheated on Mum with her next door, and because of you Mum's had to leave."

James still said nothing, but Amy was determined to have her say, oblivious to the fact that it was her revelation that had brought the furor into the open.

"I hate you... you're the one that should go... then Mum would come back and everything would be all right again."

472

Tim hadn't expected the children to make their opinions so clear. So far he'd had Mel and Nina tell him what a shit he was, but hearing it from his children was something else. What really hurt was the certain knowledge that the kids would always support Melanie. He'd never made a huge effort to be close to them as they were growing up. He'd held their hands when they were younger and he'd taken Henry to matches most weeks, but he'd always been too busy to get involved in their work at school and the things they did at weekends. Now it was pay back time.

"I'm sorry for what's happened and I promise you Mum will come back. I'll call her. I'll tell her that I'm willing to do whatever's best for you three. If I have to go I will."

"Where will you go, Dad?" Henry asked.

"Not sure yet Henry. Probably stay with a friend for while."

"Will you stay with Ben?" Amy asked.

Despite everything Tim smiled at the thought of staying with Ben and Beckie in their tiny flat.

"No, I don't think so, Amy, but don't worry, I'll think of something."

"We're not worried about you. We want Mum to come back and she won't as long as you're here." Amy wasn't mincing her words.

The rest of the morning passed slowly. No one seemed sure what they were meant to do. It was painfully clear that without Melanie they were rudderless. Tim drove up to the manor, he had to talk to someone. Maybe Simon could help him, tell him what to do next. While he was looking for Simon, he saw Veronica.

"Tim, I didn't know you were in today ... you do know

it's Sunday?" She said it with a chuckle, but then she noticed that Tim wasn't sharing her mood.

"Tim, is something wrong?"

"I'm afraid it is ... I was hoping to talk to your brother, I need his help."

"They went off with some friends last night. They're staying over, probably won't be back until late. Can I help?"

"I doubt if anyone can help, Veronica. I've been very stupid."

"Oh dear, it looks as if we need a strong cup of tea and a long talk, come on."

She took him inside to the drawing room and arranged for a pot of tea to be brought in.

In the guest room at Ratty's apartment, Melanie had got up at eight o'clock, showered and then sat brooding over the mess that was her life. Ratty would be a tower of strength, but it was going to be a tough few days and nothing could change that. Mid-morning she phoned Rachel, her PA, at home and explained briefly that domestic problems would mean she was taking a few days off. Rachel agreed to call her about anything important and otherwise hold the fort until she returned to work.

Ratty made coffee and they sat looking out over the quay from his alcove window. Wise words were helpful, but some painful decisions would have to be faced soon.

"Mel... you know exactly how I feel about you... I love you with all of my heart and I'll take care of you forever, but I know that right now you're thinking about the children... right?"

"Of course... I'm thinking where does this leave them?"

"Mel, Tim is still their father and he always will be.

474

Please don't ever subject him to the degrading spectacle of having to beg to spend time with them the way we've seen some fathers doing. He's made mistakes, but I'm sure he loves them in his way as much as you do in yours. If you do me the honour of saying you'll live with me I promise that I'll do everything I can for them, but I'll never try to take over his role as father. You'll need to teach them to respect him as if you were still together."

"Thanks, Ratty. I'll have the children most of the time simply because Tim couldn't cope with their needs, and anyway, his work would mean he couldn't look after them properly."

"I know I'll have to get in the queue for your affection, but you have enough love for all of us."

"We couldn't all live in this flat, Ratty. Are you willing to leave all this and live in a mad house full of screaming children?"

"Mel, I'd be happy living on the moon if it was with you. Please put me out of my misery and tell me you're going to spend the rest of your life with me."

"I can tell you that I'm not going back to Tim. Things weren't very good before this, but I was willing to keep trying. Last night I knew it was finally over. It's too soon for me to decide my future, but there's no one else in my life except the children. Please... give me some time."

"I won't push you.' He smiled wickedly... 'how much time?"

She knew he was teasing so she played him at his own game: "What do you think... about two years?"

"No, I think we need to make a trip to London as soon as we can."

"Why?"

"I want you to meet my parent's. They'll love you and the children."

"Won't they be upset that you're getting involved with a married woman with three children?"

"My father was disappointed when I chose not to be a bus driver; I think he'll handle this a lot better."

"But they must be hoping you'll give them a grandchild."

"Who says we won't have one of our own... maybe?" His smile was as infectious as ever.

She returned the smile. "Nature might say we can't... Ratty I'm forty years old."

"No problem, and on the matter of your being a married woman, I hope you'll do what has to be done, Mel. I'd like to marry you, properly... in time."

"We'll see ... but yes I'll have to deal with the business of divorce. You're a solicitor, what do I do first?"

"Do you remember the night we met? You tipped wine over Miss Margaret Highnam, that rather stern looking lady from my firm... do you also remember I told you she is the best divorce solicitor in the town ...you're going to have to hope she's forgotten that little incident. I'll talk to her tomorrow if you like."

"Yes, I'd like your help with the legal stuff. God knows it's going to be painful enough dealing with Tim."

"Mel, I know it's too soon to be making plans, but it might take your mind off things if I tell you where we're going on our honeymoon ..."

"You're crazy, you know that? ... OK go on, let me have it."

"We're going to do the Orient Express."

"Oh, I know a girl in work who did that with her parents, from London Victoria to Dover and back, yes?"

"No darling... I mean the real Orient Express... from Venice to Istanbul. But first we'll go to Paris. We'll start the trip properly from there, and then later we'll spend a few nights by the Bhosprorous, before retracing our steps through Italy, where we'll stay in the beautiful city of Florence and then finish up in Switzerland – Lucerne maybe. It'll be a trip to remember forever."

"We'll it depends..."

"On what?"

"On whether I get a better offer of course."

"How stupid of me to imagine that such a beautiful woman, newly nearly divorced would not have dozens of suitors. I shall bombard you with flowers until you have hayfever and I shall send you Belgian chocolates until you are too fat to attract another. This way I will eradicate the opposition and have you all to myself."

"You really are the craziest man I've ever met."

"So is it a pleasure?"

"Of course ... if I weren't with you right now I'd be in a hotel room somewhere crying my eyes out. Last night was the most difficult moment of my life. I walked out on my husband knowing that it was for good. Thanks for helping me to get through it. I know you mean every word but you must understand, I can't make any promises ...not yet."

"Of course I do ... and you must understand that however long it takes you... I'll be here waiting... OK?"

"Thanks, Ratty. Now comes the hardest bit, I've got to go back to the house and sort out what we do next."

"Do you want me to come with you?"

"No, that would just make Tim more angry... and it would hurt him to know that I'd run straight into your arms last night. It's better he doesn't know where I was. I may tell a white lie to save him any more pain."

She put on her coat and readied to leave. They embraced, knowing the next few hours would be difficult.

"Good luck darling, call me as soon as you can."

He watched her leave, he hated the idea of her facing Tim alone, yet he knew she was right to do it that way. He'd sit here wondering what was being said, what was happening. What if Tim became angry and hit her ... what if she felt so sorry for him that she took him back?

Amy saw her pull up outside the house. She ran downstairs screaming at the top of her voice.

"Mum's back ... she's back."

Tim felt a lump in his throat. What was she going to say? Was there a chance that she might be about to forgive him?

Amy looked at him angrily as she spoke. 'Don't you dare make her go away again.'

What could he say? He didn't want her to go either, but it wasn't up to him.

By the time she reached the kitchen door the entire household had assembled to meet her. She looked surprised to see them all there, like a reception committee, waiting for her to speak.

"Hello kids, were you OK while I was out?"

Amy ran up to her and hugged her. 'Mum, you won't go away and leave us will you?'

"Of course not Amy ... I was never going to do that. We'll sort this out."

She looked across to Tim. He had a sheepish look. He

was ready to acquiesce to her demands although he was praying that her plans might include him.

"Tim, we need to talk ... alone, is that OK with you?"

"Of course ... do you want to go somewhere? Could we talk over lunch perhaps?"

"I don't think so, Tim. What we have to talk about is not likely to give either of us any appetite."

She saw his eyes fill with tears. He was trying to come to terms with the words he had dreaded hearing. He knew now what she was going to say but how could he get through it?

He turned and left the room. Upstairs in the bathroom his mind accelerated through a dozen thoughts at once. He would end his life, there was no point in living now, and if he did it quickly he would never have to hear the words he feared the most. This way he could die still married to her. If it could be an accident everyone would feel sorry for him, no one would need to know that he had cheated on her and driven her away. But unless he did it right now, here in this room, he would have to listen to her telling him it was over. He looked around for a razor. That was the quickest way, wasn't it?

He was so frightened, he couldn't think clearly. The kids, what about them? Was it fair to take his life here almost in front of the kids? No ... the car, that would be better, he'd use the car ... a pipe from the exhaust, he could go to sleep and never wake up again. And when he went to sleep he would still be her husband, there would be no divorce, no end to their love or their marriage ... she would be a widow. She could wear black for a few weeks, just long enough for people to get used to the idea and then... and then she would throw off her dark clothes and wear bright colours again as she prepared to spend the rest of her life with *him*.

I can't bear the thought of her giving herself to him, I love her. She can't do this to me. I'm sorry about what happened. I hate myself for every minute I spent with Nina, they meant nothing to me, nothing. Please, Mel... please...' He sank down onto his knees, his head resting on the edge of the bath. He cried for everything he had lost, but in truth he knew he hadn't lost it, he had thrown it all away. If only he could turn the clock back, if only he could be given another chance. "Please Mel... let's start again... please..."

Melanie stood outside the bathroom for several minutes before she knocked on the door.

"Tim are you OK... can we talk now?"

No he didn't want to talk ... not if she was going to say, 'it's over', and there was no doubt in his mind about that. He slowly stood up and opened the wall cabinet. There was a full packet of pain killers, would that be enough? He doubted if one packet would be sufficient to take him out of this misery for good, but if he swallowed them before she got to him at least she would have to wait until he recovered before she could utter those fateful words. She might even take pity on him when she saw how much he was hurting. He tore open the packet and popped the tablets into his shaking hands one by one. He pushed a few into his mouth then took a swig of water from the glass on the shelf.

Outside Melanie heard him choke on the water and guessed what he was doing. She was in no mood to take any more from him. He'd caused her all the pain she could take already.

"Tim, if you're thinking of taking tablets, don't. That

would be a cowardly way to end our marriage and would make a mockery of everything we ever did together. I trust you are only taking enough to clear your head … right?"

Her voice sobered him instantly. He wasn't strong enough to defy her.

"Yes Mel, I'm taking them to clear my head, don't worry."

"I'm not worried Tim, I'm angry, and the sooner we say what has to be said, the better."

"Mel … I don't want to hear you say it. I can't come out if you're going to tell me it's over."

"Would you rather I took Trudy and the kids away from here, now, and had my solicitor write to you… the words would be the same, it would be less personal… perhaps that's what you'd prefer?"

"Mel, what I prefer is that you give me another chance… please Mel?"

"That's not possible, Tim. Our marriage is over, OK? There you are, I've said it. Now deal with it… just like I have to. I'm as much to blame as you for what's happened. If it makes it any easier for you, I'm not ending it just because of your affair with Nina. I'm not even the one who's ending it, it ended itself. It was over months ago Tim, we both know that but we felt like we had to try and fix it. We spent those nights having meals together, trying to pretend that we could remake the magic… but the magic went a long time ago. It's time for us both to move on, Tim."

He opened the door and stood staring at the woman who had guided him safely through the last twenty years of his life. How would he get through the next twenty without her? His head was so painful it obliterated the worst thoughts from his mind. He was sinking in and out of consciousness thanks to copious quantities of alcohol and paracetamol. He was finding it hard to focus properly and his vision was blurred.

Melanie knew he needed help. Did he need to go to hospital or just lay down and sleep it off? She saw the packet on the floor. Eight tablets were missing from it.

"Did you take all of those?"

He nodded in agreement.

"You'd better lay down before you fall down, but Tim, don't think this changes anything."

She led him to their bedroom, where he collapsed onto the bed. In seconds he was snoring loudly. He looked disgusting, sprawled across the covers in a drink-induced state topped up with tablets. Was this the man she had looked up to for so many years? She stood there for a while. She needed to look at him, to see him like this, reduced to a scrambled mess. He'd never been strong-minded, she'd always had to show him the way, to lead him along, but it had seemed quite natural for all those years.

That was just the way he was. She had planned and booked holidays, seen to the kids' schooling, dealt with their finances, in fact she tried to think of what Tim had dealt with in their twenty years together. He'd got himself to work each day and got himself home each night. That was it, she'd done the rest. Now it would be different. She was free from him, no longer his keeper. From today he would have to fend for himself. She looked down at his helpless body and sighed. Could he ever look after himself?

He'd better learn to, and learn quickly because she had made the last decision for him as his wife... from here on she would make the decisions that had to be made for her and for the children. He could make his own way from now.

Trudy was clearing the last remnants of the party away. The celebration had turned into a wake. Now it was best forgotten, as quickly as possible. Melanie was in the lounge searching the web from her laptop. She typed the words ... 'Hotels, Short Breaks' and within minutes she had found what she was looking for. She phoned the hotel and confirmed the details.

Trudy came in from the kitchen looking pleased with herself. "I've done it. I've finally cleared up every last thing from the party."

"Trudy, I want you to go upstairs and pack as much as you need for a week and do the same for the kids. Get them to help you. The bags and cases are in the loft, send Henry up for them. I'll get my own bag sorted and I'll take care of packing the car. It's going to be a tight fit but we'll manage."

"Where are we going, Mel?"

"Devon. I've booked us on a family package deal at a hotel in Dartmouth. We can do some sailing, the boys can do some fishing, we can walk along the cliffs, we can find plenty to keep us busy, and when we come back things will have started to sort themselves out."

"What time in the morning are we setting off?"

"Not tomorrow... we need to leave here in an hour. I've booked us in tonight and it's a three hour drive."

The sudden announcement drove all the bad memories of last night from their minds. In minutes they were in holiday mood. Melanie wrote a note to Tim. She would place it for him to read when he woke up.

"Dear Tim,

*Thank you for everything we shared together. Like all good things it had to come to an end. I'm looking forward to making a new life for myself and I hope you find happiness with someone else. I'd like it if we can remain friends for the kids... remember Tim, they are **our** kids, and they will always be our kids. I don't ever want to shut you out from their lives and I hope that when you find a new partner she'll want you to share some time with them so that you stay close to them as they grow up and always.*

Yours sincerely, Mel

She wiped away a tear as she placed it on the bedside table next to him. He was still asleep and probably would be for hours yet. She checked he was breathing normally and then quietly closed the door on a chapter of her life.

The drive to Devon gave them the chance to talk. For the next six days she and the kids would spend all of their time together, and the events of this weekend would be consigned to history. She would make sure that everything they did would help them look forward, not back.

Their rooms overlooked the river and as soon as they had unpacked they set off on a walk around the town. It was half past seven and they were all starving. Melanie pointed out a few places that they could eat, some overlooking the river and others in the quaint side streets which made up most of the town centre. They completed a circuit, arriving back at the Boat Float, a small protected tidal basin housing lots of small boats. Some seagulls were standing nearby, inviting them to throw scraps for them.

"Well, what's it to be...?"

Before she could finish the kids chorused their choice, "Fish and Chips!"

"You OK with that Trudy?"

"I'm OK with anything as long as it's food. I'm ravenous."

With a good meal inside them they sat on a bench overlooking the river. There was a constant stream of activity; ferry boats plying backwards and forwards to and from Kingswear and other river traffic heading up towards Totnes, or down river towards the open sea. They made a list of the things they wanted to do before the week was out. None of them mentioned the crisis they'd left behind a few hours ago. Was it forgotten already?

The holiday was a great success, helped by fabulous weather. One night they ate in a pub that specialised in fish and another night they cooked burgers on a throw away bar-b-que on a beach. They hired a small boat, which Henry took charge of as they cruised gently up river to Dittisham and back. They took picnics with them for the long all-day walks along the cliff paths from Start Bay Lighthouse to East Portlemouth, and then the ferry to Salcombe, before catching a bus back. By the end of the week they were tired but happy.

Friday was their last full day and they went on a boat trip out to sea. That evening they ate in the hotel dining room, too tired to walk anywhere else. While Trudy and the kids watched TV in the lounge bar, Melanie slipped off to her room. She had an internet connection and she plugged her laptop in. She e-mailed Ratty for the second time this week. In her first note she had simply explained what they were doing. This time she sent him a simple poem.

You've told me how much you love me,
All you want is to take me away,
I'm thinking that now is the right time,
I'm too tired to wait for the day.
If you love me enough and you want to share,
The rest of my life, here, there, anywhere,
Me, my kids and Tabby the cat,
Then call me please, I'm hoping for that.
Ratty, I'm sorry, my poetry's no good,
But which would you rather recover,
I might have tried harder and I know that I should,
I can't be your poet but I will be your lover xx.

She closed the laptop and went downstairs to join the others.

Saturday meant a long drive home and when they pulled up on the drive everything looked peaceful.

Outside there was no sign of Tim's car and inside it was as tidy as they'd left it. Melanie searched for clues of his presence, but found none. It was clear that he'd left soon after he awoke and hadn't been back. The note she'd left him lay crumpled on the floor beside the bed. He hadn't left her a reply, but then she never expected that he would. She fetched her things in from the car and dumped them unceremoniously in her room. She opened her laptop case and booted it up to check her e-mails. There was only one that mattered. She opened it and read the words aloud :-

Dear Mel,
Your sonnets are awful, as rightly you say,
but don't worry about that, we're on our way.
Ratty xx

She sent him a quick reply.

Ratty,

I'm home again, got your message. Love you. xx

Around the house, the children were noisily doing the things they always did, while Trudy set about making them a glorious evening meal, which she told Melanie was her thank you for a fabulous week away.

First things first, she thought, I'll empty the mail box. They were probably all bills but if they were moving to somewhere new with Ratty then maybe these would be the last bills she'd have to pay. As she walked outside again to get the mail, the thought hit her that maybe the kids would have their own ideas on where they lived and who with. Supposing Henry said, "No, Mum, I'm going to live with Dad. I don't want to live in the same house as your new lover". What if the other two said we're going with Henry? She turned the key and pulled the flap down to reveal a dozen or so envelopes.

The top one was hand written and she recognized the writing at once. It was Nina's. As she walked back to the house she tore it open and started to read it:

Mel,

None of this should ever have happened, I can only beg your forgiveness and pray that one day we'll be friends again. I know you won't feel the same now. I wouldn't if I were in your shoes, but that won't stop me hoping against hope that we'll share some evenings together again and put the world to rights.

I saw you all leave together on Sunday and I'm guessing you just needed to get away for a bit. By the time you get back I'll be gone too, for good. Hugh has asked me to move in with him and I think I probably love him enough to make it work. At least you won't have to worry about seeing me in the garden and having to look the other way. If you find it in you to forgive me, I'd love you to give me a call.

I'm hurting too, Mel, but that doesn't justify me putting you through all this pain.

Sorry xx

Nina

Despite the anger Melanie had felt just a week ago, she felt a lump in her throat and a tear in her eye as she looked at Nina's empty house. All those evenings spent together were in the past. Could she ever see Nina as a friend again? It was like a missile had landed in Elmthorpe this summer, not Cupid's arrow. It had destroyed everything that she had taken for granted just months ago.

Ben had left Nina and was now expecting a baby with a girl called Beckie, and her own marriage was over and she was planning a new life with Ratty; that would have been too far fetched to contemplate before that fateful trip to Poland. And now Nina had left to live with Hugh. Soon there'd be very little here to show where all the happy days they had had once existed. She looked at the house where she and Tim had once been so happy. Maybe Tim would live here with someone new. It was half his after all, and she wouldn't need it once Ratty found them a new home across town. She made a decision in that moment. I'll give Tim my half of the house, it'll help him to cope with what's happened. He'll still have his mates at the pub and I'll even show him how to use the web to find new friends, hopefully one special friend. Deep down, Mel knew that her happiness would come easier if Tim was settled. Seeing him lonely and broken would not help her or the kids to get a foothold in their new surroundings.

She went back inside feeling a lot better about the future, and now that she had arranged some kind of a life for Tim she could think about her own. She flicked through several brown envelopes and then stopped short at the cream one with her name in large, printed handwritten letters... Tim's witing. Standing in the middle of the kitchen she tore it open and wrenched out the note inside.

Mel,

I've been a fool, a selfish, stupid fool and I've paid the price. I so want to blame you or your work but I know I lost you a long time ago. I can't live where I would have to see you with someone else and 'borrow' my children for the weekends, that would be worse than never seeing them again. By the time you read this...

Mel clenched her fist and took a deep breath, He's done it, hasn't he? He's killed himself and any chance I might have had of happiness. How can I start a new life with Ratty now? How can the kids watch me trying to be happy when their father has taken his life, rather than see it all happening? You selfish bastard Tim! You've not only taken your life but you've taken mine as well. You finally got your own way. She glanced at the next line of the letter.

...I'll be gone. I'll be out of your life forever. I'm flying out to Brisbane with Simon's sister, Veronica, tomorrow. It'll make things easier with no goodbyes to say. I'll cry when I leave

because, for all I know, I'll never come back, but at least you'll have a better chance at a new beginning.

Loving you forever,
Yours unfaithfully,

Tim xx